Love and Best Wishes
to Russ from Jack and Eli
December 25th 1941

A GOOD ROOSTER *Crows Everywhere*

GEORGE PATTULLO
Illustrated by George R. Depew

Acknowledgments are due to The
Saturday Evening Post for permission
to republish all except two of these
stories. The first and last are new.

To
PAUL ELDRIDGE

Dear Paul:

You have won against my indifference—and here in book form is that selection of my southwestern stories for which you have been hounding me many years. Another of several good reasons for dedicating it to you is that I know no man with a wider knowledge of our western country or as great affection for it.

In selecting the yarns for inclusion here, I have endeavored to show in fiction form something of the development of the southwestern country during the past thirty years and the radical changes that have taken place in the modes of life. A new empire is rising there.

Readers unfamiliar with that vast territory comprising the states of Arkansas, Texas, New Mexico and Arizona may be puzzled by pronounced dissimilarities. To such, the West is the West and all of one pattern. Whereas, except for a common language which also varies in its colloquialisms, these states differ one from the other quite as much as European countries. East Texas is absolutely unlike West Texas; both differ from Arkansas and New Mexico. And Arizona is different from all three. Time was when a close observer could place a citizen of any of these states on sight.

Several of these stories were written with lead pencil on lard buckets in cow-camps. All are fiction—but they give a true picture of the life as I saw it.

G. P.

Dallas, May 1st, 1939.

Contents

BAD MAN

Arizona

Don Redden

I jumped in my saddle
An' I give a li'l' yell
An' the swing cattle broke
An' the leaders went to hell.
Tum-a-ti-yi, yippi, yippi, yea, yea, yea.
Tum-a-ti-yi, yippi, yippi, yea, yea, yea.

Bad Man

Red Fox said to me, "Go git your warbag."

"Where you bound?"

"Clint's bought some stuff from Ol' Man Salazar and I gotta go bring 'em up. Ol' Man Salazar is closin' out. No grass."

"What else'll I fetch?"

"Nothin' but your warbag and beddin'. I'll rustle the chuck."

We started with eight horses each. Red's idea of chuck was six bottles of mezcal and some coffee and flour and frijoles and a sack of chewing tobacco.

We crossed the Border and rode southwest one hundred and twenty miles. Old Man Salazar was dying when we got there but his sons and sons-in-law and a horde of poor relations, such as always live off the rich member of the family in Mexico, received us with courtesy. They served us tequila in tiny copper cups in the patio of ranch headquarters and Red drank first, then I drank, then the host and so on down the line to the last vaquero.

The old man lay in the room next to mine and his moans and strangling breaths kept me awake all night long. Early in the morning we began cutting the herd and next day headed back on the long trail to the Border. The Salazars sent a bunch of vaqueros with us, that being part of the contract.

It was slow, tough work. They were cows and calves and looked a sorry bunch to me. Being a green hand, I was with the drag and consequently got all the dust and misery. Some of the cows were heavy with calf, so moved slowly. Quite a few gave birth on the trail and it was up to me to wait until they got enough strength back to follow. Our calf-wagon was soon full. Once I had to use my arm to help a bull-calf come into the world, but he arrived as strong as horseradish. The mother tried to hook me later. That's the female of the species.

Everything went smoothly enough because Red did not push them, but we surely did go short of sleep. Red didn't trust the vaqueros much and he and I stood more than our share of nightguard. The cows would sink to their knees on the bedground and stay that way a moment—perhaps that's why they say a cow says her prayers—then lie down, heave a few windy sighs and settle to rest. However, any unusual noise or smell can bring them alive in a flash and away they'll go hell-bent-for-election, so we took extra precautions.

Nightguard is all right for those who like it, but riding around a herd for hours in the dark, crooning to them so they won't take alarm, palls on a fellow mighty fast. We were both worn out when we penned them in the Big Corrals just below the Border and Red said, "Jesus Christ, I'm glad that's over. Got anything to drink? Hell, kid, we'll both die if we don't git some. Let's ride into Naco and see ol' Lee."

We rode into Naco and had a few drinks with Lee Hall, and Lee gave us a bottle to hearten us on our way. And while we slept in a sizzling adobe hut that night not half a mile from the Big Corrals, the cattle stampeded. There was a crash, bellowings and bawlings, and they went through and over the stout post-fence as though it were matchwood. A lot of them were killed in the crush against the fence and it took a day of sweating work to gather the herd. What caused the stampede we never found out. Big John said it was a lobo wolf on the prowl.

We finally put them across the Line and that job was over.

"Now" said Red, "I say we have a li'l' fun. It sure is comin' to us, ain't it?"

Five outfits were rounding up along the Border with one hundred and twenty six cowboys. The combined camps lay in the foothills of the Huachucas and we hied us thither at a lope. It was nearly sundown when we reached our own outfit and Clint Caldwell kept Red busy until supper with questions about the cattle and the condition they were in and why the hell he'd let 'em stampede. I fooled around camp, talking to Mitt, the chuckwagon cook, and then a big thin man rode up on a roan horse.

"That's the buyer" Mitt said. "Comes from Kansas City. Name's Suggs."

The buyer gave a tired sigh as he turned his horse loose and he remarked to me, "This is a hell of a life, boy."

"Suits me."

"Well, you're young."

He came over and sat down on a lard bucket beside me. Some cowboys, through for the day, were walking up the slope a few hundred yards from camp, bound for Riley's. Riley's was a saloon and dance hall, with a few girls attached, run principally for the soldier trade from Fort Huachuca. It was the only building within miles.

"Look at 'em" said the buyer with a laugh part amusement but mostly contempt. "The poor ignorant bastards'll go up there and get drunk and spend every cent they've got coming to them for months of work. They always have and they

4

always will. That's why they don't get nowheres. How come you ain't dragging your ass up there with 'em, boy?"

"I don't go in for that sort of thing."

"Now you're talkin'. Me and you both. It's all right to take a drink now and again, but the man who drinks when he's got work to do is just a plain damn-fool no-account. Yes, sir. You never catch me drinkin' on the job."

Clint called to him then. The buyer must have told him of our talk because Clint said to me next morning during a pause in the work, "Suggs thinks you've got a lot of sense. What gave him that idea? Huh?"

There was a ball at Riley's that night. In camp we could hear the slot-piano going full blast and the place blazed with lights. Every cowboy in the five outfits who could get off, went up there. The stamp of their feet on the floor often drowned out the piano.

When I came back off early nightguard there wasn't a soul around except the cook and one horse wrangler—and he was a Mexican and busy fixing a hair rope. The cook was plastered—drunk as a lord. He tilted his nose to the sky and began to bay the moon like a hound pup.

"What the Sam Hill're you doing, Mitt?"

"Singin', of course. Are you deef?"

"Sounds to me more like a coyote."

"Aw, gwan and leave me be," Mitt said peevishly. "I'm thinkin' big thoughts."

I spread my tarp and pulled off my boots and pants. It surely was lonely there in camp. Riley's blazed like a Christmas tree and every so often one of the boys would raise a yell. They were having one hell of a good time.

"Shucks, a man's a fool to punish himself. I'll just go take a peek."

So I climbed aboard my nighthorse and ambled up to Riley's. The bar and dance-hall were jammed. There were ten men for every girl, so the boys danced with one another until they got a chance to grab a girl. The dust rose in welling clouds, a stinging odor of sweat smacked me as I made for the bar, and everybody was whooping and shouting.

What was my surprise to see the buyer installed there like a permanent fixture, with Clint and Red Fox and Pink Murray, our wagon boss. He said, "Hello, kid. Come and have a drink. We ain't workin' now."

We had several drinks and then Caldwell asked me why I didn't dance.

"No partner."

"I'll get you one."

He came back with Dutch Annie. Dutch had a black eye her soldier sweetheart give her, but she swung a wicked foot. Every few minutes the buyer would come weaving to wherever I might be, with an urgent recommendation that we shouldn't let the fire go out. And if in the press of business he forgot me for a while, I would hunt him down and we'd buy more fuel.

How I got back to camp that night only my horse ever knew. I dimly recall trying to unsaddle him and feeling baffled and full of wonder because the cinches seemed to stick; but I couldn't get the saddle off even though I crawled under his belly once to get to the other side, instead of walking around. He was known as a mean horse, but he stood perfectly still. It's curious how often horses take care of men when they're helpless. However, I was cold sober compared with the

buyer. They carried him down the hill.

Just what the price of cotton was that year escapes me, but at eight cents a pound I could have made a fortune off my tongue in the morning. Pink Murray came to my tarp, shoved the neck of a bottle in my mouth and said "Here, take a snort of this. And maybe this'll learn you to leave liquor alone, kid." It was rotgut, but it took hold after a while and when Pink broiled a thick slice of steak for me on a shovel over the fire, I could tell I was going to live.

As I was wolfing the steak and gulping black coffee for a chaser the buyer stuck his head up like a turtle, surveyed our surroundings in mild wonder and then crawled out of his tarp. He hacked and spit and cussed a little, and once he stumbled and fell when drawing on his pants. Then he came zigzagging toward the chuckwagon.

"So" he said, "It's you, huh?"

"What's left."

Suddenly a memory hit him and he slapped his leg and broke into a laugh cut short in the middle.

"Gawdamighty, my head! What is that stuff they sell up there? Kerosene? Say, kid—remember how we were tootin our horn yesterday evening?"

"That was years ago. Forget it."

He stared at me glumly a while and then: "Do you know what I think, kid? I think Caldwell and those other fellers and you ganged up on me last night. Yessir, that's what I think."

"What'd we do that for?"

"You're either green or you think you're mighty smart, boy. If you or

6

Caldwell or Pink or anybody else figures he can run any culls past Ol' Man Suggs just because he's had a few drinks, you've got a surprise comin' to you. To hell with Caldwell and you and Pink. I know cattle. You ask anybody in the business whether Ol' Man Suggs don't. It'll be a cold day—"

The sight of Pink Murray inspecting the fluid line of a bottle against the light diverted him and he moved away. He and Pink talked a moment and I heard Suggs say, "Well, just one then. Maybe the hair of the dog that bit you—"

He did well for a few hours while we were working the herd—Suggs was a sure-enough cattleman—but Clint and Pink kept plying him with drinks and toward the end of the day he grew very sleepy and they ran a lot of coldbloods by him. It just goes to show.

"Well, that's over" said Red Fox. "I gotta go to headquarters. Wanta come along? You don't wanta git all stove up loadin' them cattle."

This was straight thinking and we pulled out early in the morning with our string of horses, but we had ridden barely ten miles when a rider overtook us with an order from Clint for me to go over to the Lazy L across the Line and report to Tud Tarwater.

"What the Sam Hill does he want me to do now? I'm no use over there."

"It's like Tud just wants comp'ny, same as I did, and asked Clint for you. They'll be roundin' up on the Lazy L soon. Tud's got some work to do first." He leered at me under his longhorn moustache and I wondered why. "Clint done sent him over three days ago. Him and Otero've split and they're dividin' up the cattle. They never did git along as partners. Always tryin' to screw each other."

Red rode with me as far as Naco to have a few drinks with Lee Hall and I made Lazy L headquarters about midnight. Tud was paring a corn with a clasp-knife and seemed glad to see me. He had three cowboys with him in the shack, but I knew none of them and he told me confidentially they were scrubs and no damned good.

We spent a week rounding up young bulls and heifers and the pick of the steers in the valleys and lower foothills. These we drove away up into the mountains and beyond, where Archie Campbell took over with a couple of other boys. Then we rode back to headquarters and found that Otero's outfit had arrived. For the next three weeks we were rounding up on the four hundred thousand acres of the Lazy L and it was bitter work in the heat. Sometimes the temperature touched 110 in the shade.

At last the division of cattle was complete. Otero's outfit drove off his herds, and Tud and I went back across the Line to company headquarters. These consisted of ranchhouse, corrals, barns and silos, two bunkhouses, eatinghouse, and a combination store and saloon. We put our horses in one of the corrals and hit for the saloon. There was nobody there except the barkeep, who also clerked when his services were required.

"Whiskey for me. The kid says he wants beer."

"If it's cold."

"Sure it's cold. Fresh from the spring-house."

Something about the barkeep prompted me to ask, "Aren't you from Texas?" We used to be able to tell a Texan as far as we could see him.

"Sure I'm a Texan. But what made you go and bring that up?" he replied, as sore as a pup, "And my name is Short and that's my real name, too. Just because I was born in Texas—hell's bells, I been long enough away from there to live that down."

"He didn't mean no offence" Tud put in. "Come on and have a drink with us, Jeff."

The barkeep cooled off quickly and when a Line Rider came clanking in, we had another round. The Line Rider's job was to patrol the border to prevent Chinamen and such from sneaking across.

"Say, Tud" said the Line Rider as the barkeep set them up again, "Don Padden was around here lookin' for you this mornin'. I run into him down by the river."

"Don Padden? What'd he want?"

"How should I know? I just thought you might like to know."

"He didn't say anything? What he wanted?"

"Uh-uh. Just asked where he could find you."

It seemed to me that the Line Rider winked at the barkeep, but I could not be sure. Tud said "Huh" very thoughtfully, tossed off his drink and then announced, "Well, I gotta drift. See you-all later."

"Where you headin', Tud?"

"I gotta go over to San Pedro to see Big John."

"Well, adios. You're liable to meet Don if you take the river road. Just thought I'd mention it."

I followed Tarwater out onto the porch of the store.

"What's the matter? Who's this Don Padden?"

"Nothing's the matter. I gotta see Big John, that's all."

"Who's this Don Padden?"

"Oh, just a big windbag. Thinks he's a bad hombre, but he ain't. Mean as a rattlesnake though. He's Otero's gunfighter."

"Oh."

8

Tud got on his horse and rode off. I watched him until he was out of sight. He did not take the river road.

"Tud's got sense" remarked the Line Rider when I returned.

We had another drink and talked idly a while about this and that. The Line Rider was interested in the ball at Riley's and crowed over what had happened to Suggs. After a while I left the bar to make some purchases at the store counter and the barkeep came over to wait on me. While I was looking at some cotton shirts, a horseman dismounted at the door and strode inside with a brave jingling of spurs.

"Hello, Curly."

"Hello, Don."

"Ain't seen Tud Tarwater anywheres around, have you?"

"Just rode off a few minutes back. It's a wonder you didn't meet him."

"You mean it'd be a wonder if I did."

Then he saw me and said, "Well, well. Come 'ere, kid. I wanta talk to you."

"What do you want?"

"You think you're a pretty smart kid, don't you?"

He said it with slow deliberation, in a flat, rasping voice. I stared at him in surprise because I had never seen him before. A solid man, with gray-green eyes set too close together and yellow flecks in them. He wore his hair long and the sun had bleached it.

"Well, what've you got to say? You heard me."

The Line Rider listened, smiling expectantly.

"I don't know what you're driving at."

"It's a pity you don't. Who drove off all them young bulls and heifers over on the Lazy L, huh? I reckon you and Tarwater figured we'd never find that out, didn't you? I reckon him and you figured you could slough off all them culls on us and get away with it. Well, I'm out to square accounts and—"

"I was there, but I didn't know anything about what was going on—"

"Don't try to lie to me, kid. You and that son-of-a-bitch Tarwater—"

"Listen—please. You're trying to pick a fight, and I don't know what it's all about. I haven't got a gun and couldn't use it if I had one. And in a fist fight you wouldn't stand a chance."

He had drawn out a big claspknife to cut off a chew of tobacco—it had a blade like a young sword. His eyes popped when he heard this.

"It's a damned pity I wouldn't" he snorted, snapping the blade up and down with his thumb. "Let's fly at it. That's music to me, kid."

The Line Rider stopped smiling and said, "Shucks, quit pickin' on the kid,

9

Don. He don't know any more about what they put over on you-all than I do."

"Who asked you to horn in, Curly? You keep outa this."

"Nobody tells me what I gotta do, Padden. Not ever" said the Line Rider.

"And how d'you want me to take that?"

They eyed each other a moment and then came a diversion. A Mexican slunk into the saloon and took up a position at the far end of the bar. Smith went to serve him. The Mexican took beer.

"Gawdamighty, Jeff, you aim to let a yellow-belly drink in here with us?"

"They never bother nobody. And they go out quick."

"You're damn whistlin' they go out quick. I'm a white man, and I don't drink at the same bar with no yellow-bellies this side of the Line. This hombre is goin' out almighty quick, like you say. Here, you! Drag it."

The Mexican looked at him questioningly, but before he could grasp the idea, Padden had him by the scruff of the neck and seat of the pants. He rushed him onto the porch and booted him off into the dust. The Mexican got up and dusted his shirt and his knees, then walked away; but he walked slowly and with many a backward glance. The gunfighter came back to the bar.

"All right, kid. Maybe I was wrong. Let's all have a drink. Name your poison, Curly."

There was relief in his voice and there was relief in the alacrity with which the Line Rider accepted the invitation. All three of us were rapidly getting to be bosom friends when the arrival of a couple of horsemen at the store porch stiffened Jeff and he said, "Jesus, here's Tarwater and Cash Hardin!" I happened to be looking at Padden. A subtle change came over his face.

The newcomers dismounted slowly. They entered with the same deliberation. The man with Tud was very dark, thin to the point of emaciation; but what he had on his bones must have been all sinew and muscle because his step was catlike, an effect heightened by the fact that he did not move his arms as he walked. He carried them slightly forward, hands ahead of his thighs. A pearl-handled six-shooter was in a holster at his groin.

"Gentlemen."

"Howdy, Cash" the Line Rider answered.

Padden said "Hello" and gulped his drink. Hardin stepped to the bar, where he seemed to ponder for a moment on what he would order, but Tud edged along to me and whispered out of the side of his mouth, "Drag it outa here, kid. There's goin' to be trouble. Plenty of trouble."

"Who is that man?"

"Comp'ny gunfighter. He's a killer. You drag it outa here pronto."

10

There was no time for that. Evidently Hardin could not decide on a drink. He walked slowly up to Padden and leaned his left elbow on the bar. Then he looked at Padden without saying a word for half a minute—not a flicker of an eyelash, not the slightest nervous movement. There was an overpowering sureness of self in the man.

He said in soft, measured tones: "I heard you had some accounts to settle with me, Don?"

"Hell, no. Who told you that? What've we got to quarrel about?"

"Maybe it was Tarwater then. Maybe you've got some accounts to square with him."

"I reckon Tarwater and I can handle things ourselves."

"I'll be there when you do." Ice tinkled in every syllable now. "Tud's a friend of mine."

Padden kept quiet.

"You understand what I mean—Padden?"

They stared into each other's eyes and stared and stared. And Death was in that room. I could feel it. The barkeep was gaping at them: sweat stood in beads on his nose. Nobody moved.

Then Padden's eyelid twitched uncontrollably and he half turned and said, "Shucks, what's the sense of you and me quarrelin' over nothin', Cash? Let's have a drink and forget it."

Hardin stared at him a moment longer.

"You satisfied, then?"

"Sure. Why wouldn't I be? There's no reason why me and you and Tud should tangle. That business is done now and nobody can't do nothing about it."

"Give me straight whiskey, Jeff" Hardin said.

"This is on me, Cash," said Padden.

He set them up for everybody, including the barkeep, and then Hardin wiped his lips and said: "Well, we gotta be drifting. Tud and I've got a long ride. Adios, Don. Regards to Otero."

They went out and I went at their heels. Otero's gunfighter wasn't going to catch me there alone and work out his humiliation. I went down to the corral to saddle a fresh horse, being minded to spend the night at San Pedro with Big John.

Padden probably took on more drinks with the Line Rider. When he came out he wasn't steady on his feet and walked carefully. Then his feet would get away with him and he would lurch into a shambling run for a few steps. His eyes were glaring and he dribbled at the mouth. I gave him a wide berth when we passed each

12

other near the corral and he did not see me.

The Mexican he had kicked out of the saloon happened to be coming out of the gate, leading one of the company's mules, when the gunman reached the corral. Padden yelled a name at him and slashed with his quirt. The Mexican cowered away and Padden slashed again, raising a welt across his face. The Mexican let go of the mule's rope and sprang, and drove a knife to the hilt in the gunman's heart.

Of course they hanged the Mexican, just to learn those yellow-bellies.

MANKILLER

Arizona

Tommy with Apache

Mankiller

ARIZONA

ALL this happened in the Bad Year. The outfit issued daily from their camps—riding bog, skinning cattle and driving in the helpless to the home pastures to be fed on oil-cake and alfalfa. The cows were walking skeletons, wild of eye, ready to wheel in impotent anger on their rescuers, or sinking weakly to the ground at the least urging, never to rise again. Every creek was dry. Springs that were held eternal became slimy mudholes and a trap. A man could easily step across the San Pedro, oozing sluggishly past mauled carcasses.

Wherever one rode he found bones of hapless creatures, or starved cows stretched flat on their sides waiting for death to end their sufferings. And the flies settled in sickening, heaving clusters. Each mire held its victim. Wobbly-legged calves wandered over the range, crying for mothers that could never come. And the sun blazed down out of a pale sky.

Even the saving mesquite in the draws and on the ridges was failing as sustenance; of grass there was none. The country lay bleak and gasping from Tombstone to the border. Not even a desert cow, accustomed to slake her thirst by chewing cactus, could long survive such blighting months. How we prayed for rain!

Manuel Salazar gave heed to Halley's comet as he lay on his tarp, and crossed himself to avert the death-curse which was come upon the land. This weird luminary portended dire events and Manuel began, like a prudent man, to take thought of his religion. There might be nothing in religion, as Chico contended; but a man never knows and it is the part of wisdom to be on the safe side.

Then, one evening when the mountains were taking on their blue sheen and the beauty of those vast stretches smote one with a feeling akin to pain, Archie Smith rode up to headquarters and tossed a human hand on the porch.

"Found it in the far corner of the Zacaton Bottom," he said.

Jim Floyd recognized it at once by the triangular scar on the palm. The hand had been gnawed off cleanly at the wrist. Floyd wrapped the gruesome thing in a sack, wishful to give it decent interment when opportunity should offer.

"It's ol' man Greer's," he said. "You-all remember ol' man Greer? He used

17

to dig postholes for the Lazy L. Where's the rest of him, Smith?"

"I aim to go and see. Ki-yotes et him up, don't you reckon, Jim?"

"It sure looks that way. Pore ol' Greer—he could dig postholes right good," the boss answered.

What Archie found of the digger of postholes established nothing of the manner of death. Both arms were gone and wolves had dragged the body; consequently there was no real argument against the theory that old man Greer, who indulged a tase for *tequila*, had sustained a fall from his horse and had perished miserably within sight of the ranch. Yet Archie found this hard to believe. Wolves do not crush in the skull of a man and it was the cowboy's conviction that anyone could fall off Hardtimes, the digger's mount, twice or thrice a day with no other injury than the blow to his pride.

Two days later Manuel Salazar brought in Greer's horse, shockingly gaunt, and swelled as to the head. But what interested the outfit when the saddle and bridle had been removed from Hardtimes, were long, parallel wales along neck and flank. Archie pronounced them to be the marks of a horse's teeth.

"That don't show nothin'. He wandered off and got into a fight with another horse," Floyd asserted. "Yes, sir; it's like that he done just that."

After which he dismissed the unfortunate Greer from his mind. The outfit shook its head and expressed sorrow for the digger, but opined that his fate surely went to show how injurious steady application to *tequila* could be, more especially in cruel weather. The Mexicans, and the nesters in outlying parts, were not satisfied with the explanation put forward. They discussed the mystery during pauses in work and in the dark of the night. When two men met on a trial and halted to pass the time of day, Old Man Greer was the subject of talk. There were rumors of a snug fortune the digger had amassed and buried—sixty-six thousand dollars in gold, it was. Joe Toole, who made a nice, comfortable living by systematic theft of calves from the cattle company, did not hesitate to hint that Greer had died a victim to its professional gun-fighter for reasons best known to the rich corporation; but then Joe was prejudiced. Soon the death grew to a murder and no man not of white blood would ride the Zacaton Bottom after nightfall.

Tommy Floyd talked of these and other matters to his father as the boss was feeding Apache.

"Pshaw!" Floyd said contemptuously. "Don't you put no stock in them stories, Tommy boy. Some people in this here country can smell a skunk when they sight a dead tree."

"But what do you reckon killed him, Dad?"

18

"I don't know, son. I sure wish I did."

He punched Apache in the ribs to make him move over. The huge jack laid back his ears and his tail whisked threateningly, but he gave place with an awkward flop and Floyd laughed. Others might fear Apache, but he knew there was not the least particle of viciousness lurking in that hammerlike head. Of all the ranch possessions—blooded horses, thoroughbred Herefords and cowponies—he liked the jack best. It pandered to his vanity that others should avoid the monster, or approach him in diffidence, with suspicion and anxiety.

In truth, Apache's appearance was sufficiently appalling. Great as was his blue-gray bulk, it was dwarfed by the ponderous head. His knees were large and bulbous and when he opened his mouth to bray, laying bare the powerful teeth, Apache was a spectacle to scare the intrepid. Horses would run at sight of him; an entire pasture would squeal with fear and flee on his approach. Yet there was not a gentler animal to handle in the million acres of the company's range.

Toward the fag-end of a day Tommy was eating *panocha* on the steps of the porch. While removing some particles thereof from his cheek, in the region of his ear, he espied his father riding homeward from the Zacaton Bottom. Something in the way the boss swayed in the saddle brought Tommy's head up. Floyd was clinging to the horn and the reins trailed on the ground. The boy threw his crust away and ran to meet him. A dozen yards from the house the horse stopped, as though he knew that the end of the journey had come for his master.

"That black devil, Tommy!" his father gasped and lurched outward and to the ground.

Two of the boys came running and carried Floyd to his bed. That he had contrived to ride home filled them with wonder at his endurance and fortitude—nearly the whole of his right side was torn away, one arm swung limply, and there were ragged cuts on the head. Tommy hovered near, crying to him to open his eyes. The boss never regained consciousness and died at midnight.

A Mexican doctor was summoned from a border village—his American competitor was off in the Dragoons, assisting at an increase to the population. After a minute examination the man of medicine announced that five ribs were broken. It was his opinion that Señor Floyd had met with an accident, from the effect of which he had passed away. Nobody was inclined to dispute his finding.

"Something done tromped him," Dan Harkey asserted. "It's like one of them bulls got into the Bottom and went for him when he got down to drink."

"No," said Archie, "a bull couldn't have tore him up that way. It looks to me like teeth done that."

Then Tommy awoke from the benumbed state in which he had moved since the tragedy and repeated his father's dying words. They were very simple of interpretation. A black man had drifted into the country from eastern Texas and lived, an outcast, on a place not fifteen miles from headquarters. It was well known that Floyd had had trouble with him, being possessed of an aggressive contempt for negroes, and twice had made threats to run the newcomer off.

"A nigrah could easy have beat him up thataway," Dan declared. "A nigrah could do most anything. Yes, sir; he beat him to death—that's what he done. It's like he used that old hoe of his'n."

Word of the killing flew over the land in the extraordinary fashion news is carried in the cow-country. Within twelve hours men knew of it in the most remote cañons of the Huachucas, and a party of nine set forth from headquarters. But somebody had carried warning: the lonely hut was untenanted and the door swung loose on its rawhide hinges.

They buried Floyd on top of a hill where the wind had a free sweep, and piled a few stones atop. Tommy fashioned a cross out of two rough boards: and the boss sleeps there today.

The sheriff was deeply stirred and had notices posted throughout the territory.

$250 REWARD

For the arrest, dead or alive, of the man who brutally murdered James Floyd, boss of the Tumbling D, sixteen miles from here, some time yesterday evening. This man is supposed to be a negro; about forty years of age; black; about six feet in height and weighing close to two hundred pounds. Has a razor scar above the left ear.

He has in his possession a .35 caliber autoloading rifle, No. 5096, and a .32-30 pistol. He may be riding a sorrel horse with a roached mane, branded 93 on left hip.

This crime is one of the most dastardly in the criminal annals of the Territory, and I earnestly urge every officer and other person receiving this circular to do everything in his power to effect the capture of this human fiend.

The above reward is only a preliminary reward, which may be increased later to one thousand dollars, when the governor, with whom the matter will be taken up, is heard from.

Wire me if any suspect is arrested, or if any information is obtained whatever concerning this negro, at my expense.

Two months passed and nothing was heard or seen of the black man. The rains held off. North and east the ranges were deluged. A blight appeared to have fallen upon the Tumbling D. The land grew a shade grayer, the dust spurts

whirled in gleeful, savage dance, and the cattle gave up the effort of living and lay down to die. All that the boys could do was to distribute salt and feed and work frantically to maintain the water supply. The emaciated brutes would eat of the oil-cake and hay and sweat profusely on the nose, then stiffen out and expire with a sigh. Those that clung to life carried swollen under-jaws from the strain of tearing at the short grass.

"Poor bastard!" Archie grunted, tailing up a cow he had already helped to her feet three times. "It makes a man sick at the stummick to see 'em. Here, you doggone ol' bitch! Why don't you try for to help yourself? Up you come! That's it—try to hook me."

It was no use. He shot her where she lay, and skinned her. Then, with the wet hide dragging at the end of a rope and her calf thrown over the fork of the saddle, he set out for headquarters. The orphan was a lusty youngster and Archie made him many promises, accompanied by many Mexican oaths.

"Li'l dogie," he said, "I'll find a mammy for you tonight if I have to tie up the old milch cow. Do you think you can suck a milch cow, dogie? Sure you can. Man alive, feel of him kick! He's sure a stout rascal. You'll be a fine steer some day, dogie."

On a black-dark night flames leaped above the rim of the mountain and the Tumbling D were roused from bed to go forth with wet sacks, and rage in their hearts for the scum of humanity who would fire a range. Twenty-six hours in the saddle and six more fighting the leaping, treacherous enemy; then two hours of sweating sleep on saddle-blankets beside their hobbled horses, and back a score of miles on desperate trails for fresh mounts. Three separate times they beat out the blaze with sacks and back-firing. Once more, rising heavy-lidded and dripping from the stupor of utter exhaustion, they saw it licking hungrily through the Gap. No cigarette-stub thrown amid parched grass, no abandoned campfire, had done this. It was the deliberate work of an enemy.

Orders came to move the cattle down into the valley, lest they perish to the last horn, to the last torn hoof.

"It'll take you three days to move 'em ten miles," the manager said, "But never mind. Ease 'em. Ease 'em careful. The man who yells at a cow, or pushes her along, gets his time right there. The only real way to handle cattle is to let 'em do what they want and work 'em as you can. Think that over, boys."

Manuel Salazar remembered this warning as he moved his tired horse at a snail's pace behind a bunch of sick ones in the Zacaton Bottom. Manuel made twenty dollars a month with consummate ease, working only seven days in the week and only thirteen hours a day and he would not throw his job away lightly.

22

Therefore he permitted the gaunt cows to straggle as pleased them, humming to himself while they nibbled at tufts here and there. If one turned its head to look at him it fell from sheer weakness; therefore he held aloof. So the sad procession crept along.

It was in Manuel's mind to save a mile by moving the bunch through the horse pasture. He put them through the gate with no trouble and was dreamily planning how he might steal back a hair rope Chico had stolen from him, when the quirt slipped out of his fingers. The vaquero got down to pick it up.

"Hi! Hi!" he yelled in panic and ducked just in time.

A black shape towered above him, striking with forefeet, reaching for the nimble Manuel with its teeth. Its mouth yawned agape: Salazar swore he could have rammed a lard bucket into it. The vaquero swerved from under the deadly hoofs and hit out blindly with the quirt. The stallion screamed his rage for the first time and lunged at him, head swinging low, the lips flicking back from the ferocious teeth. Manuel seized a stone put to his hand by the blessed saints and hurled it with precision, striking the horse on the nose. Midnight blared from pain and shook his royal mane in fury, but the shock stayed him and Salazar gained his horse.

"Now," he yelled, pulling his gun and manoeuvering his mount that he might be ready to flee, "Come on, you son-a-kabitchee! You want to fight? That's music to me."

But Midnight did not want to fight. He had employed craft in stealing upon the man and now he moved off sulkily, the whites of his eyes rolled back, a thin stream of blood trickling from his muzzle. Salazar longed to shoot holes through his shiny black hide, but contented himself with abuse instead. Was not the stallion worth five thousand dollars? Who was he—Manuel, a poor vaquero—to be considered in the same thought with so noble a beast?

"Tommy," he said as he unsaddled at headquarters, "I've found who killed your father. Yes, and Ol' Man Greer, too. Don't look so pale, Tommy."

Tommy stalked into the manager's office next forenoon, a very solemn and very determined, if a short and somewhat dirty figure. He was white under his freckles and he talked through his teeth, jerkily, his eyes fixed unwaveringly on the manager's face.

"Midnight!" the manager exclaimed. "Nonsense! Why, he wouldn't harm a fly. That horse would never kill a man. He's worth five thousand dollars. Since we got him from Kentucky, two years ago, a woman could handle him, Tommy boy. Salazar must have been teasing him. You'll have to look somewhere else, Tommy."

"You mean you ain't going to do nothing, Mr. Chalmers?"

"Of course not. Midnight? Impossible. He couldn't have done it."

Tommy went back home very slowly. That night he sat beside Manuel's candle and cleaned and oiled a sawed-off .25-30 rifle, inherited from the man who slept on the hill. Salazar smoked lazily and watched him through drooping lids. The boy finished his task and leaned forward on the stool, staring at the tiny flame, the weapon across his knees.

Of what use to shoot Midnight? Of course it would be easy. Tommy had acquired skill by blowing the heads off chickens whenever any were desired for the dinner-table and he felt assured that at two hundred yards he could pick off the stallion with one pressure of his finger. But after all—had the stallion done the killing? He had only Manuel's experience to go on. Moreover, if he took punishment into his own hands they might throw him into a jail. Midnight was worth five thousand dollars; assuredly Mr. Chalmers would cast Tommy out into the world to shift for himself. He put the rifle back under his bunk.

At sunup next morning Tommy entered the horse pasture and made his way down the mile-long fence toward the corner where the mares usually grazed at that hour. He had a six-shooter in his pocket for an emergency but hoped that he would not use it. Midnight sighted him and stood rigid a full minute, twenty paces in advance of the mares, gazing at the boy. He was a regal animal—Tommy thought he had never seen so glorious a horse. Then the stallion advanced with mincing steps, his head bobbing, the ears laid back. He sidled nearer, without haste, whinnying softly. The boy waited until he was a dozen feet distant, then threw himself flat and rolled under the barbed wire fence. With a rending scream Midnight reared and plunged for him, his forefeet battering the ground where Tommy had fallen. He tore at the earth in discomfiture and wrath and raved up and down on the other side of the fence, his nostrils flaring, his eyes a glare of hate. Tommy watched him in deathly quiet.

The dark came warm, with puffs of hot wind, so the Tumbling D men reviled the discomfort joyously because it presaged rain. Tommy slipped from the bunkhouse for a breath of air, although it was past bedtime and they had told him to turn in.

"Apache!" he whispered, gliding into the stall.

The jack cocked his monstrous ears, knowing well the voice. Tommy put a halter over his head and opened the stall door. It was gnawed and scarred by Apache's teeth and hoofs and the boy wrenched it from the hinges and laid it aslant on the ground.

"You done bust your way out, Apache, you hear me, you ol' devil?"

24

He led him out into the corral and thence into the lane, talking softly as they went. Apache raised his nose and sniffed the breeze. When they reached the horse pasture the boy tore out the strands of wire at a spot near the corner of the fence.

"Now" Tommy quavered, working with nervous fingers to unbuckle the halter, "Go to it. There he is."

The jack required no second bidding. He wrenched free and stepped carefully over the wire into Midnight's domain—Apache never did anything in ill-judged haste. A blur two hundred yards away attracted him and he headed toward it eagerly. A moment, and he stopped; then went forward with caution.

Midnight had seen him coming. He trotted out from his band of mares and halted expectantly. Next instant he had recognized Apache for what he was and blared a challenge. The jack brayed like a fiend and went forward slowly to meet him.

Apache had fought before—many, many times. He made for the foe with circumspection, his head jerking sideways, his tail tucked, ears laid flat on his neck, and his feet barely touching the ground, so lightly did his tense muscles carry him. One evil eye measured the enemy with venomous composure.

Vastly different was Midnight's attack. The stallion had pluck to spare but his temper was overhasty. Rage forever clouded his judgment in battle. He knew only one plan of attack and that was to rush and bear down his opponent. There was his rival: he would kill him.

His harsh scream rent the night silence and the fight was on. Another horse might have circled so formidable an adversary in an endeavor to create an opening, but the black's temper was too imperious for delay. Straight was his rush. He bore down on the jack at the top of his speed, his wonderful, supple body a-quiver.

Then Apache did a remarkable thing, a thing almost human in cunning. Swerving ever so slightly as the black came, he lunged to meet him, crashing

25

shoulder to shoulder with all the strength of his tough sinews behind the impact. Hit sideways, taken off balance, the force of Midnight's own charge contributed to his overthrow. Down he tumbled, scrambling with his feet as he fell. Before his body touched the ground the jack whirled and lashed with both heels into his ribs. With the same appalling speed, Apache drove for the throat of his prostrate enemy, secured his grip and shut his eyes, wrenching frenziedly from side to side and upward.

It is well not to tell further what Apache did to the mankiller. A jack has about as much sense of mercy as he has of fear, and he has never been taught any rules of warfare. When he gets his enemy where his enemy would like to get him, he does his utmost to stamp him off the face of the earth. So it was that next day the Tumbling D men were barely able to recognize the Kentucky stallion in the torn, broken, black pulp they found in the horse pasture.

All night long Apache brayed and screeched. The noise pierced Manuel's dreams and he muttered in his sleep a prayer for protection from the Evil One. The jack pranced around and around his victim and up and down the pasture, wild with the joy of battle, magnificent in his strength and pride of victory. Toward dawn he abandoned the carcass and drove off the terror-stricken mares as the just spoils of the conqueror.

Big white clouds boiled up back of the mountains that afternoon, with a stiff wind from the southeast behind them, and at sunset the heavens opened of their blessed treasure. Manuel and Tommy lay in the bunkhouse listening to the thunder of rain on the sod roof. A burro came to the door and poked his patient head inside, seeking warmth and a friendly dry spot.

"Come in!" cried Manuel cheerily. "Take a chair. Tommy, give him your bed. Ain't that music, though? Hark! Oh, the cattle! Can't you see them soaking in it, boy?"

A yellow mongrel ousted the doubtful burro from the doorway and began nosing about for a place to rest his uneasy rump. The roof was leaking in strong, hearty streams, and Salazar sprawled on his back, letting the water run on to his chest. He was smiling placidly. Tommy snuggled into the blankets and pictured to himself a new land of much grass, and clear-eyed, contented cows and high-tailed calves.

"The curse is lifted," Manuel observed piously. "Yes, sir. The dear God sent the jack to kill that stallion. How else could it be? What do you think, Tommy boy?"

"Maybe" said Tommy.

PIONEER

West Texas

Ben Strusky

Pioneer

A skunk wandered into the Bar P camp during the night, stampeding the staked horses, which made him so nervous that he did his little business on the boss' tarp. The boss had to retreat two hundred yards from his fellows and burn his clothes.

"Why, I done smelt the rascal the minute he hit camp" the cook said.

"Then why the hell didn't you crack down on him?"

"Well, at first I thought it was Shorty comin' to bed."

Some unpleasantness with Shorty further delayed the cook and it was long after sunup before the outfit had finished breakfast and got to horse. They redoubled their efforts to make up lost time and it was not much past the usual hour when the cook descried the dust of the cattle's approach and heard the yelps of the cowboys urging them toward the roundup ground. In a few minutes they arrived and the ropers went to work.

Dust swirled in blinding clouds; the pungent smell of burned hair and seared flesh set the flankers to coughing; a continuous clamor of lowing cows and bawling calves, now and again broken by the thuttering challenge of a bull spoiling for a fight; and piercing the din the high-pitched voice of Hi Garrett, "Hot iron! Hot iron!"

A husky red calf which one of the ropers had dragged out of the herd by the neck foiled the Big Un's heave and knocked him down with a desperate lunge. And while the Big Un was on the ground the calf kicked him in the face.

"Stay with him, cowboy! . . . Hey, look out, Big Un! She's on the prod."

The mother had followed her calf when he was jerked from her side and now stood gazing uncertainly at the scene, her head turning from side to side. At last she came to a decision and bore down on the Big Un to horn him. He jumped to his feet, kicked a spurt of dust in her face and the cow swerved irresolutely and trotted back into the herd.

"Heel them big boogers, Reb. Heel 'em" said the Big Un, wiping blood from a cut cheekbone.

"Hi, Lafe—catch that one again" Garrett yelled from the fire, where he was seeing to it that the branding irons were kept hot. "It ain't earmarked."

Two ropers and four sets of flankers were working at feverish speed to brand the calves brought in by the morning's roundup. Close to four hundred cows were in the herd and practically every one was followed by a calf. The heat was appalling, the ground hard and cracked, the cattle fractious and inclined to break out every moment, but Garrett drove his men as he always did when bossing the job. The sun was straight overhead and the exhausted flankers had begun to curse every little mishap before Garrett took out his fat silver watch and inquired, "What's your tally, Lafe?"

"A hundred and ninety-seven."

"Check! Let's go."

The Bar P outfit mounted and, leaving two men to guard the herd, dogtrotted toward camp. Some of the boys washed before dinner, but sparingly. Water was scarce in that region and what they used was carried in a barrel on the hoodlum wagon. Every time a man took a drink, he had first to fish out the tadpoles.

"How about it, Dave? Ain't you ready yet?"

"Chuck!" yowled the cook. "Come and git it or I'll throw it away."

They had just squatted to eat when a man on a burro appeared in the dry river bed, ambling slowly toward camp. He was leading another burro loaded so high with a pack that nothing except its slender legs was visible.

"Good day, gents."

"Howdy" somebody replied.

"Get down and eat dinner" Garrett invited him, his mouth full of beef.

The man on the burro bobbed his head eagerly and proceeded to take off the pack. Then he staked the burro out to graze.

"Best take the saddle off'n the other one" the cowman suggested. "It's like to gall him."

The outfit watched with broad grins as he clumsily obeyed. The freed burro lay down to roll. His owner stood uncertainly near the wagon-fly, apparently not knowing what to do next.

"Git a knife an' fork an' plate from that box an' he'p yo'sef" the cook told him. "That's beef in one pot an' them are beans in the other. But watch out for that coffeepot. It'll sure enough burn the hide off'n you."

The visitor was a short, rotund man much soiled by hard travel. He had made some attempt to dress according to cow-country modes but the effect was

30

only to accentuate the tenderfoot. Also, he walked as though legs and feet hurt him, and the toes of his boots turned up oddly. Nobody said anything while he was eating. Nobody asked him his name or where he came from or whither he was bound, but they eyed him covertly because his type was strange to that country in those days.

"Vot is it your name, please, mister?" he inquired of Garrett, with a propitiating smile.

"Garrett."

"Mine's Strusky. But everybodies they call me by Ben."

"Yeh?"

"Who owns yet all this country opp by where I been riding?" he next wanted to know.

"I own some."

"But how can anybody tell it where his land begins ent the other land it stops, hey, mister?"

"Fences."

"Me, I stryg only one fence today ent that is easy eleven twelve miles back, I bet you."

The cowman nodded. "Our east pasture fence. Hundred and twenty thousand acres in the east pasture. You're in it still."

Strusky spilled the knife-load of beans he was raising to his mouth.

"Aw, gwan—you're stringin' me, mister, yass?"

The cowman grinned and asked, "Where you bound, young man?" Strusky named a mining camp in New Mexico, a hundred and fifty miles southwest.

"Well, the gait you travel you'll be on my land three more days."

They could see Strusky revolving this statement. Finally he inquired, "How much does that add opp to all told, vot you got it?"

"Oh, maybe four hundred thousand acres."

The peddler got up very thoughtfully and deposited his tin plate and cup with the others in the dishpan. When next he spoke, his manner was nicely compounded of deference and suspicion.

"I also seen it a lot of cows by calves, too, mister. Some cows was he's—fine big fat fellers."

A roar of laughter from the outfit: the Big Un almost choked to death.

"Those were mine, he-cows and all" Garrett told him. "Leastways they were if they wore this brand." And he drew Bar P in the dirt with a stick.

"Oi, oi! How many you got it of them cattle then, mister?"

The boss didn't like the question—nobody ever got him in his life to admit

31

within forty percent of what he owned, more especially the tax assessors.

"Oh, ten thousand, maybe. Maybe twenty" he said brusquely.

"They must of cost it you planty money, yass?"

"You're damn tootin' they did."

"But where'd you get it all that planty money? Ent who owned it all this land foist, mister?"

The cowhands were now taking a lively interest in the conversation and Garrett said in a harsh voice: "What're you doing in this country, anyhow? What's your business?"

Ben saw he had offended and became eagerly apologetic. "Mister, no offence. Me, I am a stranger."

"Peddler?"

"I got by me some nize clothes ent shoes in that peck."

Still out of humor, Garrett said: "You look to me like a Kansas City Jew. I seen plenty . . . If you're so all-fired curious about it, me and a few thousand like me made this country safe for fellers like you to do business in. We never saw hide nor hair of any of your tribe until it WAS safe. Thirty, twenty years ago, you couldn't have rode ten miles across them flats you come over today without losing every last shoe-string you got, and maybe your scalp to boot . . . Come on, boys. Let's go."

The remuda was driven up, they saddled fresh horses and went back to the roundup ground, and Ben slowly set about reloading the pack on his burro. While tightening the rope his glance fell on the carcass of a heifer lying about a hundred yards from camp.

"Say, mister" he said to the cook, "Is this here frash?"

"Killed this mornin'."

The peddler walked over to inspect it. "Vot you do now with this meat, mister?"

"Nothin'. We took the hindquarters—all we can use. And it'll spoil in a coupla days."

Ben looked from Dave to the carcass, in amazement. Here was sufficient beef going to waste to feed half a dozen families and where he came from they never wasted anything, not so much as a crust. He said, "How often now you kill it one like this, mister?"

"Oh, maybe one every other day durin' roundup. It takes a sight of beef to feed thirty men. Why? You want some?"

"You gimme, mister?"

"Fly at it. He'p yo'sef, Ol' Timer."

The peddler cut off all he could carry on the burro and wrapped the meat in a sack. In return he offered to help Dave wash the dishes and they were presently discussing the drought, the science of cooking, the troubles of feeding an ornery bunch who were too doggoned lazy even to scrape their plates clean, and other such life-problems. Dave was in a moralizing mood induced by a prolonged spree which had just terminated with two days in the calaboose in Fort Worth and Ben agreed with him sympathetically on every point.

"This meat now, mister—ain't there by here a place maybe where you could sell it?"

"Nowheres but Doghole and that's eleven mile. It ain't worth the trouble."

The cook felt toward this tenderfoot alien the large tolerance of a man accustomed always to seeing things done on a big scale and he began to talk in millions of acres and hundred of thousands of cattle. The peddler listened in awed silence; but when Dave began to brag about his employer's possessions, Strusky piped up: "He'll brand it seven thousand calves this roundup, you say? Oi, oi! Listen—how did he get it yet, all this land, mister?"

The cook spat about ten feet and replied: "Hell, just grabbed it, you might say. He was here first. Well, Garrett fenced in all he could see and nobody else wanted it then. He done got quite a smear from the Injuns, too—run 'em off or traded 'em out of it. When ol' Hi first come here, you could buy most all the land you wanted for thirty cents an acre. He used to work a smart trick, too—they all did in them days—Hi'd get nesters and bums to take up school land and jist as soon as they'd proved up their claims they'd vamoose and Hi would own it. It was legal. The land's his'n all right."

"But he must had planty money to buy cows with, no?"

"Money? When Hi Garrett done come to this country he didn't even own a pair of socks. No, sir: he come out here to he'p a bunch of hunters skin buff'lo. But Hi was a right smart boy and he done a li'l' tradin' round and got hisself a bunch of cattle. He done stuck his brand on many a maverick, too. They all did those days, with stray calves roamin' the ranges. Garrett'd raise sand if he heard anybody say so now, but he done it plenty those days. Times has changed."

Before he departed, the peddler sold Dave a couple of bandanas the cook would never use. The cook paid him with some of Garrett's flour. And then the peddler disappeared into the broad wastes of sand and red dirt and dry creek beds and mesquite flats.

"Pore ignorant cuss" the cook soliloquized as he dragged his bedroll under the shade of the hoodlum wagon and prepared to take a nap, "It's like he'll die or git killed somewheres, roamin' round like he does. He'd ought to of stayed in the

34

city where he knows the ropes. He ain't cut out for this country."

The peddler sold the beef to the butcher at Doghole for a dollar and continued on his way, and four days later he came upon another roundup ground on a wide flat near the bed of a river. This was in New Mexico and four outfits had combined to work the open range. Strusky stayed for dinner with them and in the afternoon went out to watch them cut the herd, possibly in hopes he might be able to do a little business with the cowboys on the side.

As he sat his burro at a safe distance from the churning, bellowing mass a sudden dispute arose between a wagonboss and a strayman over the ownership of a dogie. The strayman claimed it belonged to a cow bearing his brand; the wagonboss had a very distinct remembrance of its mother having died up in the foothills the previous day. He described the mother in detail, but the calf gave color to the strayman's claim by sticking close to one of his cows.

Before Ben regarded the dispute as even started—not a name had been called, not a threat made—guns were pulled, one of them flashed and the strayman slid slowly from his horse, clutching at the mane and the horn of the saddle as he fell. His mount snorted and pulled away. The strayman died in a few minutes.

"Who was it?" he whispered to a cowboy.

"Hi Garrett—ol' Hi Garrett's boy. He's been gatherin' their strays."

"My, my! Ain't it ter'ble!"

"Well, he drawed his gun, didn't he?—but he drawed too slow."

Scared and depressed, Strusky got away as soon as possible.

"They'll a fine cow leave it rot out on the ground, but they'll kill by each for a baby calf" he muttered as he rode along. "The lowlifes!"

The tragedy had so upset him that he paid no particular heed to surroundings and consequently a nester who had trailed him from the roundup ground was able to overtake Ben and get the drop on him before Ben was aware of his proximity. The nester got his living by rustling cattle and stealing anything he could find; and he robbed the peddler of everything of value that he fancied. Ben carried a six-shooter, but he never dreamed of using it. In fact, he did not know how and was in terror of the weapon.

The peddler saw all his money go into a pocket-sack the rustler carried—even the gold coins he had sewed inside the soles of his boots. Then the rascal rode away, taking the burros with him. Some of the merchandise in the pack he left behind, either because he did not want it or feared its possession might incriminate him.

Ben sobbed and whimpered like a child as he watched him go, but after a while he gathered his scattered stuff into a bundle and resumed his way on foot.

35

It was thirty miles to the nearest town and he had only a canteen of water, the rustler having stolen all his food, but Strusky kept at it doggedly. He shed plenty of tears, yet never once thought of giving up. This was a savage country of ruthless greed and sudden death—but he was there and going to stay.

FIRST MONDAY
East Texas

Brother Schoonover

First Monday

EAST TEXAS

IF anyone had intimated to us that Ringer was lacking in culture, those would have been his last words on earth. Yet it is a fact that certain jealous neighbors to the north and south said behind our backs that Ringer was a sure-enough tough town. They had a nasty way of pointing to its homicide record, just as though cold statistics ever gave a true picture. From these it would appear there was never a Saturday without a shooting or cutting, and the Courthouse Square on First Monday was so apt to yield the coroner a job that the boldest citizen trod it with an eye peeled for a place of refuge.

These critics entirely ignored the fact that we shipped out sixty thousand bales of cotton every season. A lot of people are mean and envious that way.

"It ain't the town's fault," Bill Bobo argued. "The visitors start the rough stuff, dadgum their hides."

He was referring to the regular visits of certain undesirables from Red River Bottom, a wild, inaccessible portion of country on the Oklahoma border. Perhaps the loneliness of the shimmering sand wastes along the river bed and the tense quiet of the wooded tangles farther back—Bill and I once rode ten miles of the Bottom in quest of a stray without seeing a living thing except one bogged cow, two herons and a rattlesnake—perhaps the environment induced in these outlanders a yearning for cheer and the warm contact of their fellow men. At any rate they came once a month to Ringer on First Monday, got drunk with all possible speed, and then set out to show the citizens how bad they were. First Monday is the day for swapping horses and mules, and shopping for the farmers, and general hell-raising.

And they were bad, too. The Kincaids were the worst. The gang consisted of three brothers and four cousins and they all lived by theft. It is true their women grew a little corn and cotton above flood level, but only enough to give a semblance of legitimacy to their livelihood. The men rustled cattle. They would steal a horse also, but that involved greater risks: it was easy to throw a bunch of steers across the state line in either direction. Frank, the head of the clan, was

39

indicted on this charge twice but came clear through the efficient perjury of his clan.

One day there drifted out of nowhere a long, concave-bellied string of a man named Cicero Schoonover, who turned on us the eyes of a stranger within the gates and told us we were a wicked and perverse generation. What Brother Schoonover saw was not the town we saw at all and his opinion was that Ringer made a blot on the fair face of Texas. He announced these conclusions at a revival he started on a vacant lot back of the Fashion Saloon.

"Men," he began, "you've got thirteen saloons in this here town, and three churches. The saloons are full all of the time. How long do you aim to deliver up your sons and daughters to the devil by maintaining his chief agent right at your very doors? Hey?

"Do you know what Seth Rountree died of? Shot, was he? Maybe so; but it wasn't Clint Harkrider's bullet that killed Seth. It was the dirty, rotten booze Clint had drunk. That's what killed poor Rountree. That's what made his wife a widow and his children fatherless. I tell you, the man who sold liquor to Harkrider ontil his wits was gone, ontil he didn't know right from wrong and was crazy for trouble—that man was the real murderer.

"Friends"—his voice soared high and cracked—"the saloon must go. It is the hotbed of corruption. It is the hideous destroyer of morals and homes and souls. It is the greedy god on whose altars we sacrifice our young. It is the yawning gateway to hell. Your feet're on the hot bricks right naow."

Brother Schoonover could rave that way by the hour. We had heard it all before, revivalists being as regular as the circus in our country; so his preaching would have made no special impression had it not been for the personality of the exhorter and the approach of a local-option election. He was uncouth and none too clean, his ears stuck straight out from his head, his Adam's-apple bobbed up and down and he was grossly ignorant—yet somehow the spirit of the Living God flamed in Schoonover when he talked.

"Listen at him!" Bobo said to me one fine June evening. Through the open door came loud groans, sounds of lamentation, the hysterical weeping of women. "He's got all those ol' sisters rockin' right now, ready to stompede up the aisle when he gives the word. I sure do admire to hear the Brother when he's goin' good."

We were in the Fashion Saloon, where Bobo made his headquarters. It was a favorite resort and, being a horse and mule trader, he found it convenient.

"Burn it down!" The raucous tones of the exhorter rose to a howl. "Burn it down! There it stands by consent of your men-folk—stands there high on a hill—

the lair of the Scarlet Woman!"

I glanced at Bill, who said, "Sure! He means Picnic Kate," and twisted impatiently in his chair. After a moment he added: "He won't have to worry about her long. I done met up with Doc Buchanan yesterday and he told me Kate ain't got a week to live."

Old Lon Terryberry, who owned the Fashion, carried a chair over to our table and sat down.

"That crazy fool is doing a lot of harm," he grunted.

"Let him holler. He'll have to quit soon and then it'll all blow over."

"Maybe so, but I ain't so sure, Bill. Doggone it, I wouldn't mind so much if I only got it at meetin', but I git it agin when I go home."

"Willie May is sure strong for him," Bobo admitted.

"Strong?" Lon bellowed. "That gal ain't missed a meetin' since the rascal struck town. And she plays the organ for 'em, too, and sings fit to bust. What do you know about that? My own daughter in cahoots with the very crowd that's tryin' to run me out of town!"

"Leave him roar. He's called me plenty names, too, for gamblin'. But names ain't bricks."

"No," Lon conceded, "they ain't. But you can dodge a brick." He eyed Bill morosely. "What's this I hear," he demanded, "about you giving up twenty dollars to Willie May for the Cause, as she calls it?"

"Shucks! That don't mean nothing, Lon. You know right well I'd do anything Willie May should ask me."

"And there," cried Lon, bringing his fist down on the table, "is where you make a big mistake, Bill. That gal's mean, I tell you. She's just naturally mean-tempered. Why, she thinks she knows more'n her own daddy! I'll bet she figures she's got you tagged."

"Well, ain't she?"

"Aw, to hell with it. Let's have a drink."

"This Schoonover's a small-towner, isn't he?" I asked.

"I reckon so. What of it? So'm I. So's Lon."

"Yeh, but you two're different. Most small-towners are born missionaries—always trying to regulate other people's lives. They like to play God."

"First thing you know, the Reverend'll be pinning your hide to the fence, too" Bill said.

Two days later he called at my house in his Sunday clothes. His suit was black; dead black was his hat; and he wore a white satin tie strung through a gold ring.

"I gotta fix up a funeral," Bill explained in a hushed voice. "Yes. For Picnic

41

Kate. Schoonover done sent for me this morning and I got there just before she died. She wanted to tell me how I could get my money for that hoss she bought offa me—Kate always was a mighty conscientious woman—and while she had us there she done made me and Schoonover promise to see she was buried proper. It seemed like Picnic was afraid they might put her some place where she wouldn't care to be a-tall, or just leave her lie out, maybe."

"Schoonover? How did he happen to be there?"

"Why, Kate, she begun to get scared toward the last and she sent for a regular parson; but he wasn't home. So she sent for another, but he couldn't go on account of a cold—the lying bastard. Finally she got desprit and asked Brother Schoonover would he come. And he went a-runnin'."

"But what can I do?"

"You can come along. That's all."

We buried Picnic with decency and in the Baptist cemetery, too, where scores of departed "good women" surrounded her. Brother Schoonover said the service. Aside from the girls in her house, only Bobo and the livery stable man and myself were on hand.

The town buzzed with the scandal of this all Saturday and Sunday. Meeting Bill in the square, I asked what ailed him.

"I'm in Dutch with Willie May. That funeral—you know how women are."

"Christ, they make me tired! Didn't you explain?"

"I never explain" said Bad Bill.

"It'll all come right."

"Sure it will. Only—we were fixing to get married."

Next day was First Monday. It broke hot. At an early hour dust clouds hung thick above every road leading into Ringer and soon the square was jammed with wagons and buggies and horsemen. They overflowed the livery yards and appropriated every vacant lot.

"Look at 'em milling round" Bobo remarked, standing on the curb in front of the Fashion. "I never seen so many farmers in town."

As we watched, a little cavalcade of five men on cowponies debouched on the Square from the north. They were weatherbeaten, hairy and hard. In close order they ambled past us, their faces wreathed in expectant grins. One of them waved at Bill. Saddles and bridles were frayed and patched. Red dust coated horses and men.

"Isn't that Frank Kincaid in front?"

Bobo nodded, continuing to stare after them. Presently he said: "I wish Thurber was here."

"Where is he? He shouldn't be out of town on a day like this."

"You're damn tootin' he oughtn't. But he done fixed up some business for today over at the Junction—had to fetch a prisoner or something. So he deputized me."

"They should never have elected him sheriff at all, Bill. He's scared of that Kincaid gang."

"So is everybody. I am. And so are you. The sheriff ain't a coward. He's just naturally peaceful."

The Kincaids dismounted in front of the Court House, leaving their horses tied to a hitching rail, and Bobo departed for his lodging house with the explanation that, since he was sheriff for the day, it behooved him to "get heeled."

We did not meet again until late afternoon. Then on my way to the post office I ran into Bill lounging outside the Fashion Saloon. While we were talking, along came Brother Schoonover with his ludicrous, hurried, shambling gait. He had on baggy trousers, a black seersucker coat and a straw hat. The coat was a mile too big for his wasted frame and the hat a size too small for his bulging dome.

"Howdy, men."

"Howdy, Reverend."

As we gazed after him, Bill said: "It's right queer. I've got so I sort of respect that dadgummed fool."

Then the Kincaids came clinking through the swing doors of the Fashion. The crowds had thinned out in the Square and only a few horse traders remained, half-heartedly pulling at tails to test the sorry scrubs left over. Nobody near to rouse their malice or stir them to mischief: they moved in a body toward another saloon.

One of the gang tripped over a basket of vegetables in front of Sid Semple's grocery store. He hauled off and scattered them with a running kick. Cabbages rolled along the sidewalk and with gleeful whoops the Kincaids pounced on them. Sid rushed out with fire in his eye, but when he recognized the gang, tried to join in the spirit of the joke. There was nothing else he could do.

"Charge 'em to me, Semple," Frank Kincaid yelled, shying a cabbage at a farmer just starting home in his wagon.

The grocer gave a sickly smile.

"That's all right, boys!"

The deputized sheriff for the day allowed this disturbance of the peace to pass.

"If Sid's satisfied," he argued, "It ain't up to me to butt in." All the same his irritation made it plain he had not convinced himself.

Leaving the others, Frank Kincaid walked solemnly to the Court House rail-

44

ing, untied his horse, kicked him in the ribs and mounted. We knew what that portended; but, instead of executing his favorite trick of riding along the sidewalks, whooping and shouting, he began a slow circuit of the Square.

At the Cottonwood Street corner Brother Schoonover stood on the sidewalk in the angle formed by the First National Bank and Jim Seeley's barber shop, talking to one of his saved sinners. All the little devils that lurk in bad whisky did a hop-skip-and-jump in the rustler's muddled brain. He took down his rope. A few deft shakes to make a noose, an overhand flip, and he had roped Schoonover around the body. Then Kincaid jabbed his horse into a lope, jerking the revivalist out into the dirt of the Square. He started to drag him. Brother Schoonover never uttered a sound, but tried desperately to hold the rope with his hands.

"Drop him!"

The command came like the crack of a rifle and there was Bad Bill, poised on the curb, left hand high above his head in warning. Kincaid stopped his horse.

"Turn him loose!"

In the hush that came over the Square his voice echoed in every corner of it. "Who'll make me?" Frank jeered.

His kinsmen burst out of a nearby saloon and Bobo drew a long breath, like a man who has passed a crisis.

"Who'll make me?" Frank yelled again, his hand sliding to the gun scabbard under the flap of his overalls.

Bobo said irritably, "You ornery son-of-a-bitch," and dropped him out of the saddle before anyone could flick an eyelash. It was as pretty a throwdown as ever

I saw. The rustler's horse braced his legs but did not move, and Schoonover threw off the rope.

Then Bill ducked behind a telephone pole as the gang cracked down on him. Three bullets plumped into the pole waist-high; a fourth ripped along its edge level with his head. Bobo blazed away with his .45 and got one of them. Then the other Kincaids ran to their horses.

Suddenly little Sid Semple dashed out of his grocery with a repeating rifle and dropped behind a rampart of baled hay. The Kincaids received him with a hail of bullets, but he yelled defiance and triumph. They had humiliated him once, but he was a man again and his spirit soared.

"Good boy!" Bobo shouted. "You sure do handle that gun pretty, Sid. But lower your sights, Ol' Settler—lower your sights."

Experts in such matters declared it was a beautiful fight while it lasted. Perhaps it was. It did not last long. The Kincaids never stood a chance. They were in the open and mounted—ready targets despite rapid moving. Two were killed outright, and within five minutes the fifth member of the gang was in flight for Red River Bottom, leaving Frank and one other badly wounded Kincaid behind on the ground. Whereupon we all emerged blithely from our barrels and cellars and other convenient shelters.

Brother Schoonover held another revival meeting the next night in the tent behind the Fashion.

"Friends," he began in a tone that caused his hearers to sit up expectantly, "Before we sing the next hymn I want to tell you something: The hymn is 'Wash Me and I Shall be Whiter Than Snow.' Brother White will lead us. Shout it out, friends. Let it come from the heart, for if ever the words of this hymn meant anything to us in our lives they should ought to strike deep tonight. Sing it all together.

"This is what I've been fixing to tell you: 'Wash Me and I shall be Whiter Than Snow' were the last words the woman known to you as Picnic Kate said before she died." The exhorter broke off to blow his nose. "She said them to me. And with what a look on her face! Yes, to me—though you-all know how I preached agin her. I was there at her bedside and prayed for her and gave the poor, tortured soul what comfort I could.

"But there is another thing yet I want you to know: These last few days have been a great eye-opener to me, friends, sure enough. Everybody within sound of my voice knows what come off and you-all must have wondered.

"Still and all, I reckon these things could never have come off, only for what one man among us done. What did he do? I'll tell you what he done. She sent for him, Kate did, when she knew the end was near, to ask forgiveness because she couldn't pay him a debt she owed. And she had still another reason. She felt the need of a friend, one to stand by her through fear and uncertainty. I tell you it is a dreadful thing to face the Unknown alone.

"So she sent for a man she was already in debt to—with no more claim on him than on you or me, perhaps not so much—because something somehow let her know that man's great heart. She was scared to die—it is not for me to speak harshly of the departed but she sure had reasons, Kate did. Oh, my friends, the agony, the bitter agony of those final hours!"

He paused a moment, that he might drive home his next words.

"This man was Bad Bill Bobo. She done made him promise to give her a funeral. He paid for every cent of its cost.

"You all know Bill. But how did he git to be Bad Bill? I heard the story for the first time today. It's familiar to you-all—how the Kincaid gang done run off his pet horse when he wasn't more'n a boy, hardly, and he went after 'em.

"There's a text right there, friends—right there in the way he done it. Let us see how he acted: Did young Bobo wait to git help? Did he try to find an easy way? Did he hunt round for the sheriff while they was making tracks with his horse? Not much he didn't, no more'n he sat round for somebody else to do the sheriff's work yesterday. He up and went after the Kincaids. And he done caught three in a nigrah shack over beyond Sandy."

The preacher's voice soared, seemed to take fire.

"Then what did he do? Hey? I'll tell you what he done: young Bill, alone, eighteen years of age, with nothing on him but a knife for a weapon, walked in on 'em where they was playing cards on the floor and just busted the damned bloody scoundrels wide open." Frenzied applause. Willie May, at the organ, wept with pride. "Yes, he did—done cleaned the three of 'em all alone. And when he come back to town that night, all shot to pieces and hangin' onto the mane, and slid off in front of the Palace Drug Store, what did he say? Just what you'd expect that booger to say: 'It was some fight. But here's my hoss!'

"Ever since that night he's been Bad Bill in this county. A poor name for Bobo, friends. What if he does skin a feller now and agin in a horse trade? Wouldn't you? Or you? How about Jacob of old when it come to tradin'? Why, he drove a close bargain with God, didn't he?

"Maybe Bill's a close trader. I've heard it said round town, too, that Bill has got draw poker down pretty near to an exact science." Ripples of laughter. "I hope he has; for I want to tell you folks"—tears were hopping down his sunken cheeks—"that I'm—proud—to—shake such a man by the hand. Let us sing, all together, 'Wash Me and I Shall be Whiter Than Snow.' Shout it out. Brother White will lead."

SHEEPMAN
New Mexico

Uncle Joe

TUMBLING K RANCH
F. Lisby, Manager

Cattle Brand, K ⅂; Left side   *Horse Brand, K; Left Hip*
——County, New Mexico
August 1, 1909

Friend Bill:

Yours to hand and contents noted. In reply to same will say I am feeling fine. Hope you are feeling fine. Hope Ed is feeling fine. How are all the boys? I hope they are feeling fine.

Will expect you as soon as you can make it. Trouble with sheepmen as usual. They try to hog this whole country and if it gets any worse I'll close out and go find me a new range in Arizona. Hurry up. You ain't any fonder of this breed than I am. If we don't run them off now we might just as well give up raising cattle and take to hoeing cotton. Regards.

Frank.

P. S. Jimmy Wilson has skipped the country. Joe Blackburn got bit by a rattler. Horse fell with Lee Haverty and broke his leg. Booger Red is south buying me a bunch of steers. Tom got shot—drunk again. Dave is in the pen. Nothing new since my last.

*   *   *   *   *   *   *

The sun was sinking and twin peaks faced me where I had expected to see Lisby's headquarters straggling over a tableland. Where a cowpath curved upward between the peaks, a dog slouched into view. It stopped and barked. A rider appeared behind the dog: he halted at sight of me.

"Lisby's ranch? My, my, but you done come a fur piece away from it. Lisby's all of forty mile from here. Yessir."

He was old and bleached and listless and his vacant blue eyes fixed themselves on my saddle-skirts and never wavered from them.

"I reckon you'd best stay with me tonight—yessir. Me and Mary Lou will be proud to have you."

"That's kind of you. How far to your place?"

"Only a coupla mile. You cain't see it now 'count of that ol' rock. When we round the bend you'll see it."

The collie followed, off to one side, red-eyed and suspicious and growling. Soon we came in sight of the sheepman's home. It clung to the slope of a hill whose crest afforded protection against the violent storms that swept down from the mountain. At the door of the squat sod-roofed shack a woman shaded her eyes against the sun with one hand and clutched a frying-pan in the other.

"I thought you was going to Pine Spring, Mister Joe."

"I didn't git to go. This genelman met up with me and I done asked him to stay the night with us, Mary Lou."

"Come right in. Come right in. I'll have supper ready in no time. Things don't look none too tidy—I was just fixing to clean up, mister. What'd you say the genelman's name was, Mister Joe?"

"Thatcher," I said. "William Thatcher."

We led the horses inside a gate and turned them loose. My host said he would round them up early in the morning and put me on the trail to Lisby's.

The sheepman's name was Harris. Having been a year in a cowcamp, it astonished me mightily to see them bow their heads when we sat down to supper. He mumbled something that I failed to catch, but his face was serene and mildly expectant when he opened his eyes on the sowbelly and beans, the biscuits with flour gravy, and the coffee. His wife waited on us: she would eat when we had finished, having received a careful upbringing. Mary Lou was also gray and lean of face, but her eyes were keen—one of those angular, alert, flatchested female pioneers who acquire a premature stoop from excess toil. They are always in the vanguard of civilization.

Afterwards we sat in front of an open fire, smoking, whilst the dog curled himself at our feet and started in to have nightmares.

"Kin you sing?" Harris inquired in his soothing voice. "We're kind of fond of singing, Mary Lou and me. We don't hear it much."

For the life of me I couldn't remember anything except Casey Jones and I gave them Casey. They listened eagerly, the sheepman tapping time with his foot.

"That's a right catchy song. But there's one a traveling parson done sung for us when he went by here a month ago. A new thing it was. I wonder if you mought know it."

"How does she go?"

52

"Well, it was something about angels and a choir—a heavenly choir, wasn't it, Mary Lou? I cain't think of the name, but there was a lot about Gee-rusalem. The parson'd got it from Brother Schoonover over in Texas."

"Oh—that one! You mean The Holy City."

"Sure. That's it. The Holy City."

So I gave them The Holy City. They gazed raptly at the fire as they listened, scarcely breathing.

"That's it——yessir. Ain't it strange he should know it, Mary Lou?"

"It's wunnerful. . . . I'll bring you out blankets, Mister Thatcher, and you

can sleep here in front of the fire" said Mary Lou. "I'm sorry we ain't got but the two rooms. Mister Joe, take Rags out and put him in the shed. He has ter'ble nightmares, Mister Thatcher, and he's liable to keep you awake."

An hour before sunup I awoke. It was stingingly cold and I raked up the ashes in the fireplace and put on some wood, then went outside to the well to take a wash. The sky wore a greyish tinge and when I returned to the shack, objects close at hand loomed in ridiculous disproportion.

There was a piece of paper stuck to the door with a knife. The hand that drove the knife must have been strong, because the blade was sunk deep into the wood. No swift blow, but steady pressure, had done that. We had heard no sound and the dog had not raised an alarm.

Drag it NOW. This is the last.

"No use saying nothing to Mary Lou about this" said Harris at my elbow. "She's kinda high-spirited."

He was holding a basin with water in it. I could hear his wife moving about the shack: the crisp whirr of the coffee-grinder reached us.

"What does it mean?"

"Oh, some folks're just naturally ornery—yessir. This is the third one. I don't pay 'em any mind, the lowdown sneakin' polecats."

He volunteered no further information and I watered my horse while the sheepman splashed his face and hands and combed his tousled beard with his fingers. Then we had breakfast.

53

"What's wrong with your hoss? He's limping."

"Looks like he's strained his leg."

"You cain't go on today—he'd never carry you to Lisby's place. It's a bad trail in spots and forty-two mile easy. Leave him rest a coupla days."

"What'd you say, Mister Joe? Is his horse done gone lame? I'm right glad —leastways, we enjoy having you a heap, Mister."

We dawdled about all morning, making repairs on a shed in which he kept a decrepit wagon, a plow, tools, corn and some alfalfa hay. In the afternoon I announced an intention of walking to the Twin Peaks, but Harris said that was absurd as it was all of six miles. However, he was going part way there to see one of his herders and would like my company if I cared to go that far.

We set out, the sheepman on his forlorn dun, his saddle and bridle frayed and patched with rope, the stirrups worn thin. His hat and shoes were white with alkali. A stream brawled across the trail. Here we paused beside two huge rocks that stood perilously on end at the edge of the stream.

The sheepman's gaze rested on them thoughtfully. He slid to the ground and said, "Do you reckon the two of us could move these here rocks, Mister Thatcher? You look right stout."

"We can try. Maybe if we can find something for a lever——"

"I'll go git me a pine limb. I'd like for to switch this stream into that other channel you kin see over there. That crick's gone dry—and it feeds one of my waterholes."

We toppled the rocks into the creekbed and diverted the current. Thereupon he left me and descended the rough slopes to the right. I saw far below what appeared to be an expanse of hill moving in slow undulations—a flock of sheep. There must have been thousands in the flock. Harris had told me he owned thirty-five hundred, grazing near Pine Spring.

Rain was driving down from the mountains in squalls when I shook myself free of the blankets next morning. The door was bare.

"No, I didn't look for one this morning. That was the last, I reckon" Harris remarked while we were washing for breakfast.

We tinkered in the shed throughout the day, repairing a couple of cinches. The sheepman cleaned and oiled a .45-70 rifle, handling it with affectionate care. Just before supper the rain ceased abruptly and in a rift of hurrying clouds the sun gleamed coldly yellow.

"My horse is better."

"There ain't any call for hurry, Mister Thatcher."

"Well, I'll rest him another day if you'll have me."

"I reckon we won't turn you out. Will we, Mary Lou? Will we turn Mister Thatcher out?" Mary Lou came to the threshhold with a dishrag in her hand and beamed on us.

More than once that night, as we stared at the fire, the sheepman rubbed his hands along his overalls and chuckled softly. His wife busied herself darning socks, Rags dozed on the hearth and shuddered in nightmares.

"Would you mind singing that Gee-rusalem piece agin? It is sure comforting—yessir."

About midnight I roused and was turning over to adjust the bundle of coat and trousers that made my pillow, when I was shocked wide awake by the sight of the sheepman at the window, rifle in hand, his dog at his knee. Rags growled at my movement, so I feigned sleep. All was quiet for some time and I was slipping into slumber again when a fierce bark, bitten off sharp, brought me upright. The sheepman turned his face toward me angrily.

"Keep still. And you hush up, Rags."

We listened, straining to catch a sound, but all was quiet outside. Then a blaze of light reddened the window. It wavered and leaped. Something stirred behind us and there was Mary Lou in the inner doorway.

"The shed's afire, Mister Joe."

"If I could only see one of the damned scoundrels! There! I've got you, by God."

The rifle blazed: then he swore and jerked out the shell and banged the weapon's butt on the floor.

"Missed him—consarn my fat haid. They're keeping behind the shed in that rim o' dark. Git back to bed, Mary Lou. Me and Mister Thatcher won't let nothing hurt you."

"I reckon I'm safe enough, Mister Joe. But what about the shed?"

We could see the flames leaping from log walls to sod roof. After the heavy rain the fierceness with which it burned mystified me.

"They done used kerosene," said Harris.

He was calm again, and calmly he walked to the door. Rags whined in a frenzy of eagerness when he loosed the bar, and shot out in advance of his master, his note changing to the snarl of close quarters as he reached the firelight.

"Don't go, Mister Joe! Please don't. Please! Stop him, Mister Thatcher!"

His wife's cry was punctuated by the spat of a rifle and the sheepman staggered. The two of us dragged him back inside the hut. Here he shook me off furiously, but Mary Lou had barred the door and stood with her back against it.

"Best stay indoors, Harris" a voice called from beyond the shed.

Could this be the man who had sat serenely in the firelight, listening with soft eyes to a song of angels and heavenly choirs? The sheepman's eyes were blazing now with unholy fire—sweat poured from his forehead and down his chest—a crimson stain was widening on his sleeve, and in the clutch of his hands on the rifle was revealed the lust to kill.

"Harris!" The call came again with a sort of contemptuous unconcern. "You listening? Then listen good. If you don't drag it outa here before forty-eight hours, we'll come for you."

His answer was a shot at random. Shortly afterwards we heard galloping hoofs. The flames from the shed gave a final vicious leap, then wavered and died.

"Mister Joe, why didn't you tell me? I knowed you was keeping something back." She was trying clumsily to staunch the blood and bind the wound. "I knew all the time, and you thought—oh, they'll kill you, I know they will."

She broke down, her head against his unhurt shoulder, and he comforted her with gentle pats. The dawn found him staring out at the ruin.

"Who were they, Mister Harris? And what is all the trouble about?"

The sheepman laughed bitterly.

"You keep outa this, Mister Thatcher. The less you know about it the better. Your hoss kin carry you today and you'd do well to git on to Lisby's. Besides, you're rightly on their side—you're a cowman."

"Yeh? Well, I'm going to stay, anyhow."

He looked at me oddly but did not say anything. As the morning wore away, his customary preoccupation returned and his voice again took on the gentle note characteristic of his speech. Aloofness from surroundings is frequent among old sheepmen, especially if they have been herders. It usually finds expression in a mild stare, but many herders end up with a wild, furtive eye—and such often go crazy.

We rode over one of the Twins that afternoon to ascertain how his sheep fared. The flock was browsing a ridge with a good set of grass. And on the homeward way we encountered two riders. Harris was for passing them with a civil "Howdy," but the foremost barred his path.

"One of the boys tells me somebody fired your shed last night, Harris."

"Which of your boys done told you that, Mister Loring? News travels fast, don't it?"

"What's the matter with your arm? Somebody cut you?"

"Jist a scratch. Well, adios. We must be gitting on."

Loring's companion was a bewhiskered, massive individual with friendly brown eyes, who sat his horse like a sack of meal. He did not say a word, but

Loring spurred knee to knee with the sheepman.

"Somebody turned the mountain spring. It's running into your waterhole now, Harris."

"Is that so? Do tell! I seen I had lots of water and was sort of wondering. That's mighty curious."

"Damned curious," Loring agreed. "We had to drive the day-herd eight miles to water. The cattle around the Big Tank're in a bad way."

It was very hot and uncomfortable and I gave a hitch to my belt.

"Who's your friend?" he shot out.

"His name's Thatcher. Why?"

"He's got a queer way of playin' with his belt. It ain't a safe way, neither."

"He's safe enough, I reckon." The sheepman spoke so quietly that the other laughed.

"Well, anyhow, you quit foolin' with our water and quit annoying our cattle, or this country won't be big enough for both of us, Harris."

"And say, Harris," spoke up the stolid one in a booming voice, "You keep your sheep off'n the Twins. That's my range."

"It's all gover'ment land, ain't it? And one of the Twins is nearer my waterhole than yourn, Richter."

"You'd better drive your goddamned sheep over across the line" Loring exploded. "Where they crop, no cattle can graze. They destroy the grass."

"Then how about Richter's sheep? Huh? Don't they destroy the grass? And don't he annoy your cattle? He's got fifty thousand head and my pore li'l' bunch——"

"He keeps his off our range."

"I'm a peaceful man, Mister Loring, and I'd like to git on friendly with you-all. There's room for all of us out here. The Lord's been mighty kind in these parts—them ol' mountains and these valleys could keep double your cattle and Richter's sheep and my pore——"

"I tell you there ain't room for both of us."

"Well, here's what I'm willin' to do, Richter. You stick to the big Twin and I'll stay on the other. How does that suit you?"

Richter hesitated, glancing at the cowman as though for instruction. Then he boomed, "All right. That suits me—for a while, anyway."

They rode on their way. The sheepman watched them go and remarked: "That's Loring of the Flying W, and the other's Richter, the biggest sheepman in these parts. Some folks say Lisby and them're pardners—yessir. I dunno, myself. I got an idea Lisby's the boss, though."

Next afternoon we rode out again toward the peaks. Soon we saw a Mexican herder against the skyline. He waved a slicker and Harris responded with movements of his hat. The herder descended the slopes to meet us. Overalls and a jumper clothed him and he wore sandals on bare feet. He came close to the sheepman, took hold of his stirrup and talked eagerly in mongrel Spanish. Harris sat a long while in silence, then replied in the same tongue. When he had finished, the Mexican gave a cackling laugh and started at a swinging stride for the nearer Peak while Harris rode upward to guard the sheep.

"He's gone to see his brothers" Harris explained. "His brothers, they work for Richter."

It was sundown when the herder returned and he wore a wide grin. He said a few words to the sheepman, and as we plodded down the draw toward home the Mexican and his helper with their dogs were gathering the flock into a compact mass.

At supper Harris was restless and extraordinarily sensitive to the minutest sound. By mischance I trod on Rags' foot as we rose from the table, and when the dog yelped, the sheepman's eyes flashed with anger. Next moment he was comforting Rags with endearing words.

Darkness shut us in and I smoked in front of the fire, speculating on how long it would be before they wanted The Holy City again; but neither of the couple seemed in the mood for a song. Mary Lou watched her husband with a puzzled expression. He kept roaming about the shack, occasionally muttering, sometimes shaking his head. Perspiration dripped from his face. Once he beat a fist against his palm. At last he stopped.

"I cain't do it" he said fiercely. "I just cain't go through with it!" And he glared at me as though I were somehow responsible.

"Can't do what? What's the trouble?"

"Yes. What's eatin' on you, Mister Joe?"

"Git your slicker, Mister Thatcher. We're going. You got a six-shooter? Then git it."

"Where? Where you fixing to go this time of night, Mister Joe?"

"The Twins . . . Hurry or we'll be late. We jist got time to make it."

"Lan's sake! What you aiming to do at the Twins this time of night, Mister Joe?"

"I done changed the sheep, Mary Lou—switched one of Richter's flocks to where mine was. But I cain't see all them pore creatures die. I jist cain't. Come on, Mister Thatcher. Let's saddle up."

North of where Harris' sheep were wont to graze on the slopes of one of

the Twins, a landslide had cut away the hill. The precipice thus formed was about two hundred feet deep, the bottom cluttered with rocks and jagged pieces of boulders. The night was black, with promise of rain from the southwest. One of Richter's herders, dozing as he leaned on his staff, came alive at the clack of a horse's shoe against stone. Who rode tonight? With muscles taut, he strained for another sound.

Suddenly a wild shouting broke out and six-shooters flared in the black dark. Half a dozen riders burst upon the rear of his flock. A tremulous bleat from thousands of throats and the sheep were off at a mad run. The cowboys spurred their horses into the press, yelling, firing their guns, working up the flock to a frenzy of panic. The herder bent his head and ran for safety.

We almost rode him down as we raced for the Twins. The sheepman drove headlong forward, plying his quirt. To our ears came a swelling, rushing sound like that made by a huge canvas dragged over stubble. The flock was in stampede. I had a flashing mental picture of them plunging to their death among the rocks.

"Come on!" howled the sheepman, a length ahead.

We gained the rear of the stampede. The sheep were running in a tossing torrent, the punchers forcing them forward with yells and waving slickers. A vivid fork of lightning zigzagged down the sky.

Into the heart of the tumult Harris plunged on his sorry dun. He fought his way to the foremost rider and leaned close and bawled into his ear. The other darted ahead.

"The wrong sheep! The wrong sheep! Mill 'em! Mill 'em!"

The raider screamed his orders, spurring from man to man. And now his cowboys raced to the head of the stampede. A chasm yawned eight hundred yards ahead. Could they turn them in time?

Thudding in front, they fanned the faces of the maddened creatures with their slickers. They fired under their noses. They fired point-blank, dropping the leaders. Four hundred yards and the ground was broken and treacherous. A misstep and life would be snuffed out. They yelled and thrust and cursed as they strove to turn them.

With faultless intuition the sheepman picked the key to the situation and to that point bent all his efforts. The cowboys swooped to his side. Together they swung the head of the horde in a wide curve, and when a horse sent a stone flying from his hoof into the abyss the sheep were running aimlessly in circles and those circles were being pushed back from the brink.

To Harris and me as we sat outside his shack next morning, whittling sticks, there came three horsemen out of the west. One was the Flying W boss; another, a massive individual who sagged all over his saddle. The third rider took one look at me and his eyes bulged.

"Howdy, Harris."

"Howdy, Loring."

"Harris"—Richter scorned to beat about the bush—"You done helped the boys to save me three thousand sheep."

"I reckon so. It did seem as if somebody had made a li'l' mistake."

The taciturn Richter pondered this a while.

"Harris," the heavy voice boomed again, "Lisby and Loring and me come over to shake hands and make up. I reckon there's been a misjudgment some-wheres."

"Sure I'll shake. Put her there, Richter. . . . Oh, here's Mister Thatcher, Mister Lisby."

"I see him" said Frank.

BLUE BLAZES
New Mexico

Blue Blazes

Blue Blazes

His father always had all he wanted to eat and weighed two thousand pounds with his shoes on. His mother never wore a shoe in her life, had to rustle hard for a living, and weighed barely seven hundred and fifty. There are great possibilities in such a union and the colt fulfilled them. From the Percheron stallion he inherited fine bone and magnificent shoulders, and when the sunlight played on his black hide it brought out the identical blue sheen that made his sire glorious. From that he got half his name—Blue. His mother was to blame for Blazes, because from her he inherited his disposition.

His mother was a small scrawny mare of the old Spanish strain, with slender legs and a coat like a brindle pup's. She was so wild that the sight of a fence made her snort, and had anybody shoved a mess of oats under her nose the mare wouldn't have known its use. She was so mean that the boys called her Violet. Violet could whip any mare on the range and once she tore a chunk out of the stallion's shoulder that scarred him for life. With the other brood mares she roamed a two-hundred-thousand acre tract we called the Moon Pasture, which took in a valley and a range of hills.

"She ain't got one kind thought" Uncle Harve said.

"And that rascal with her is just as mean" Rush Ardrey declared. "Look at him hightail it, will you?"

At that moment Blue Blazes took a kick at a playmate's ribs, then dashed madly away, shaking his head and flagging his tail in sheer joy of living.

He was certainly mean enough when it came to branding him. In this job it is possible for two men to hold a young colt with ease—one sits on the head while the other gets back of the colt and draws the tail up between the hind legs and hangs on like grim death. Uncle Harve roped Blue Blazes and it was just my luck to get the tail. As soon as Rush knelt on his head I grabbed the tail and the youngster gave a heave with the strength of a yearling bull, shook Rush off and then kicked me in the stomach, shins and thigh before I could move. Then he lunged away and raced around the corral to join the mares huddled in a corner. Before he could reach them the buster flipped a rope and noosed his forefeet.

65

"You will, huh?"

When Blue Blazes bucked, Sloan gave a jerk that flopped him in the dirt. Two cowboys pounced on him and secured the lashing heels and another burned in the company's brand with a red-hot iron that sent up stinging puffs of smoke. Then they emasculated him. While the colt still quivered from it, the buster knelt with knees on his head.

"Take the rope off" he said. "I got him."

Feeling his legs free, Blue Blazes began to struggle. A sharp pain shot through one eye and he writhed in agony. A voice cried angrily from the corral fence: "That'll do, Cal. Quit gougin' that colt."

"He done tried to bite me."

"Shucks, a li'l' ol' colt like him! Take your thumb out'n his eye and turn him loose" the boss ordered. "The Turkey Track don't wan't any blind stuff."

The buster obeyed, giving the colt a vicious parting kick. And Blue Blazes fled to his mother, to whose side he clung for the balance of the day. That night they were turned out and with the Turkey Track red and raw on his left hip, he went back to the range.

There he had nothing to do except eat and grow and romp with the other colts. At eating and growing he was in a class by himself, but his temper was too uncertain to make him a safe playmate. When he was a year old he could clean up any two of the other yearlings and he let slip no opportunity to prove it.

Frequently we glimpsed the mares as we rode range. Invariably Blue Blazes had stationed himself in front like a stallion leader, nose up to sniff the air, muscles taut to flee. Did a rider approach nearer than four hundred yards the colt would blare a warning and the entire band would stampede to the hills.

"Look at him leg it" Rush whooped. "In three years there won't be another hoss like him in the cow country."

The buster said, "If only he don't grow too big. I'd sure like to top him when he's growed."

He got his wish when Blue Blazes neared four years. In the Fall the boss saw a chance to turn a few thousand dollars by selling his surplus horses to the war buyers and ordered Sloan to break all the broncos three years old and over to take the place of the culls.

There were thirty such and Blue Blazes was easily the pick of the lot—a big four-year-old of perfect conformation, beautifully muscled, and wild as the antelope that roved the valley. He was first to sight us when we rode to drive them in and he led the band in flight toward the fastnesses of the Mules. Rush and another cowboy headed them off and they swept in a wide semi-circle that carried the chase north of headquarters.

"They'll have to fetch up at the fence there" the boss said, "And then swing round by Sauceda. We've got 'em. Close in. Watch they don't break through but be sure not to crowd 'em too close."

When our manoeuvring pressed the broncos toward the open gate of the corral Blue Blazes stopped and faced about. He seemed undecided, looking from us to the stockaded enclosure.

Lyford said, "Go easy or he'll bust through and we'll have it all to do over again."

Somebody drove out the saddle bunch and the broncos mingled with them, whinnying greetings. The trained horses trooped into the corral and the others followed fearfully—all except Blue Blazes. At the gate he whirled out of the press and made a dash for liberty. A rope whined.

"Good throw, Sloan" the boss shouted.

The buster raced his horse some distance alongside Blue Blazes lest too sudden a jerk break his neck, then swerved to halt him. The pressure on his windpipe maddened the black. He plunged and kicked and bawled, but the noose shut off his breath and he desisted, facing his captor with legs a-sprawl. His nostrils flared red, his eyes bulged as though they would pop from their sockets. Instead of easing up, the buster deliberately tightened the noose by a steady pull and Blue Blazes collapsed to his knees.

"Give him slack" the boss ordered. "Do you want to kill that hoss, Sloan?"

"No, but I aim to learn him what this means."

A deep intake of breath, and the black recovered. He lurched to his feet, but he was still shaking and followed meekly enough when Sloan led the way through the gate. Another rider moved behind to encourage him.

Thereupon we perched gleefully atop the corral fence to watch the buster give the first lesson. The first lesson is often a terrible one, and if a horse be well taught he will ever afterward so fear the rope that he will stand tied to a daisy.

The gate of the smaller inner corral was thrown back, we waved our arms and hats and the black shot through it.

"Gee, I'm glad Mr. Sloan picked him first to ride" Lyford's small son exulted. He was on the post next to mine: the boy was quivering with excitement.

Severity is essential in teaching the lesson of the rope, but it struck me that Sloan was needlessly harsh with Blue Blazes. Time and again he let the bronco run to the end of the rope, only to toss him into the air. Each time the black came down with a thud that jarred him from teeth to tail. Time and again his stout heart nerved him to scramble up and try once more. At every fall Jimmy Lyford howled with delight and stuttered advice.

Then Sloan brought the bronc down with such sickening force that he lay as one dead, whereupon the child's enjoyment cooled. He looked scared, and after Blue Blazes got up and limped a few steps, Jimmy remained silent.

The buster yelled, "Hi, there! Go to it!" and flapped the rope. The black made another lunge, only to be jerked down again.

"Make him quit it, daddy. Make him quit it" the boy begged.

Lyford ignored him for the moment, but when it became obvious that Sloan was teasing the bronc to further resistance for the sole purpose of punishing him, the boss got down from his perch.

"Let me try my hand with him, Cal. It's been such a mighty long time sence I—well, I'd kinda like to see if I still know how."

"Maybe you'd like to ride him, too."

"No-oo, not me. But you go work on the others and leave him rest a while."

The buster said thickly as he surrendered the rope: "All right. You're the doctor. But when a hoss is mean, it ought to be tooken outa him. He ain't hurt. He's only pretendin'."

So ended the day's ordeal for the black. After some desultory trotting around the corral, he was led out and tethered to a log, there to spend the night.

"He's too hard on 'em" Rush Ardrey said at supper. "I've saw Oscar Goodson gentle one so's a baby could tickle his laigs. And Oscar never did touch him with quirt or spur. A hoss ain't just a hoss."

After some thought Uncle Harve remarked, "That's right. No, he ain't. Sometimes he's a mule."

Rush said, "There're hosses and hosses, just the same as there're men and ol' Uncle Harve here."

"What's that you're sayin'?"

"I was sayin' that hosses, taken by and large, are mighty like humans only more so, and what goes for one don't for another a-tall. Some're as steady and gentle as a second husband and have to be drove all the time just the same way, and then agin others'll look back at you out of the whites of their eyes and be terb'le mean and ornery."

"All the same" Uncle Harve said, "I'd liefer any day own a mean one than a gentle no-account."

The boss said, "That goes for men, too. There's some hope for a mean man, because the right sort of handlin' will often straighten him out; but a no-account—hell, he just ain't."

"Well, anyhow"—Rush sopped up the cane molasses on his plate with a crust—"I sure want to be there when Sloan tops him."

"Me, too!" Jimmy said.

The Turkey Track outfit was astir for the day's work a full hour before dawn. In sleepy silence they munched steak and cold bread, gulped some biting coffee, rolled cigarettes and mounted. The mists of early morning hung low as they ambled toward the corrals and there was a tang in the air that nipped to the bone. A herd of steers rumbled and tossed near the corrals.

The boss placed his son on the fence and issued his orders: "Rush, you can help Sloan with the broncos. Buf'lo, you get on the squeezer with Tud, and for Gawd's sake act like you're alive. The rest of you boys do the same as you've been doing. Dick'll earmark and John can handle the irons. Fly at it, hombres!"

A portion of the herd of steers was halloed into the crowding pen where a horseman darted at them with shrill whoops, scaring them into the chute. In the chute they could neither turn around nor stand still: they had to go forward, to be caught by the squeezer, held fast and branded. Some were old longhorn steers which had escaped branding as calves and had been running wild in the brakes. These the boss was unloading on an absentee retiring partner: several plunged up over the backs of their comrades in front and cleared the eight-foot fence into open range.

"Look out! Go get 'em! Go get 'em!"

Riders scampered in pursuit, ropes singing for the throw. In the crowding pen was sweating tumult; at the squeezer the irons sizzled and smoked, Buf'lo grunted and swore, dust welled in choking clouds.

The boss bellowed: "Shove 'em up! Hold him, Buf'lo. Bear down on him. Hot iron! Hot iron!"

Meanwhile the buster was making ready for his own task in the smaller corral. He twisted some strands into a hackamore, tested every part of his saddle, saw to the straps of his spurs.

"All right. Let's go fetch him."

"Which one?"

"Ol' Blue Blazes."

They walked toward the log to which he was tied. The black had lost his barrel-like girth during a night of sweating fear. He was covered with dirt.

"Now, now" Sloan chided gently when Blue Blazes greeted him with a snort. He unfastened the rope and wrapped it around his saddlehorn. All his movements were unhurried, sure.

"Get in behind him."

There was no need. The bronc had learned the first lesson and trotted ahead of his captor into the corral. There the buster turned him loose and Blue Blazes began to prowl around and around the inclosure, hunting for an outlet. Once he tried to nose under the gate.

Jimmy shrieked, "He's tryin' to crawl out. Look at him sweat, will you?"

In a few minutes Sloan picked up the rope and halted the bronc. The black stood with his feet braced, watching the buster as though fascinated while he advanced along the rope hand over hand. As he came Sloan talked to him, holding the horse's eyes with his own. What he said was goodnatured banter, the voice was low and confidential: friendly, also, was the slow, fearless approach. Blue Blazes stood perfectly still. He was quaking. He sensed the mastery under that light touch, the malice back of the caressing voice.

"Fetch the blanket."

Holding the hackamore at the jaw, he laid the blanket gently on the bronc's back. Blue Blazes swerved and lashed out with his heels.

Sloan said without anger, "All right, if that's the way you feel about it."

He snubbed Blue Blazes tight to a post, dropped a rope back of the left hind leg and hauled it up so that he could not move. Then he took hold of the blanket again, but the gentleness had flown. He slapped it smartly across the bronco's back from side to side, crying "You will, hey? Well, then, pull your fool head off."

Two terrific wrenches convinced Blue Blazes that resistance was hopeless and that the blanket did not hurt. He grew passive and permitted Sloan to lay it in place. That achieved, the buster paused for a puff at a cigarette. At last he walked over to his saddle and lifted it from the ground.

"Ear him down, Rush . . . Got him? All right. Watch out he don't swing you off'n your feet."

The cowboy brought his weight to bear on the bronc's head while Sloan was easing the saddle to his back. Blue Blazes did not show a sign of fight and waited without a move, but his body stiffened to rigidity and his eyes rolled back at Sloan. Rush knew those symptoms.

"If you want—to send—any word to your kinfolks in Arkinsaw" he panted,

70

"Now's—the time—Cal."

The buster made no reply, but reached under the bronc's belly with a pronged stick and caught the girth. Only when he had brought it up into place and was ready to cinch did he offer any comment. Then he said lazily: "I reckon you've got it all framed up for me right now, ain't you, sweetheart?"

The girth tightened and Blue Blazes humped himself and tried to swell his body with intakes of breath so as to loosen it. Sloan tugged and pulled as though he wanted to cut him in two. Then he stepped back.

"Let him go and see what he'll do."

Blue Blazes promptly lay down.

"Goddamn it" the buster said, "That's one thing that makes me mad—just awful mad."

He slashed at the black's head with a quirt. The thong raised a wale but the bronc did not bulge. Again Sloan struck, but the black merely blinked. "You won't, hey?" The buster kicked him in the ribs. That also failing of results, Sloan raised his foot and jabbed him in the nose with his spur. Still Blue Blazes would not get up.

Rush said, "Let me try."

"Are you breakin' this hoss, or am I?"

"I only thought——" Rush began and at that moment the black lurched to his feet.

"And a right good thing you did, too" the buster told him, "Else I'd have skinned you alive."

Then Sloan adjusted his spurs, gave a hitch to his belt and made ready to mount. Jimmy shrilled in genuine solicitude, "Best throw that chaw away, Mister Sloan, or maybe you'll swallow it."

Sloan swung into the saddle. It was done so defty that the black hardly realized he was there, his attention being focused on the man clinging to his ear. But when Rush let go his hold, Blue Blazes awoke to the fact that a rider was on his back; he felt the cautious pressure of the knee as the buster slid his feet into the stirrups. Even then he did not offer to move—simply tilted the saddle at a more acute angle. Sloan flicked him with the spur. The bronc winced.

"Well" the buster said, "I'm up here."

The black turned his head for a peep. Thinking he meant to bite his leg, Sloan swung the quirt at his muzzle. Instantly Blue Blazes reared straight up and threw himself back.

"Look out!"

The warning was superfluous. As coolly as a man vacating a chair, the buster slid out of the saddle and stepped aside. He did it without the least fluster, but I was close to him when he cleared and I saw a devil leap in his yellow eyes.

Blue Blazes hit the ground with a smack that knocked the wind out of him and he lay there while one could count ten. Then he clambered to his feet, but before he could make another move Sloan was atop him, feet in stirrups and ready.

"Come on!" he mocked. "Try that again, you son-of-a-bitch."

The black reared again, but the buster fetched him a blow between the ears with the loaded butt of his quirt that brought him down, and while his senses were still reeling, started to ply the whip, first on one side, then on the other. A very little of this sufficed. Blue Blazes broke into a stiff, jarring trot.

The buster said, "Here he goes! He's coming unwell right now."

Right upon his words, the black leaped. With mouth agape, bawling like an angry calf, he bounded high in air, head sunk low between his knees. In the same instant he hit the ground he whirled and pitched blindly across the corral toward the fence, hindquarters weaving. The buster was raking him with the spur. There came an instant's loss of poise and Sloan grabbed the horn and righted himself, but for the moment he felt too insecure to use the quirt. Blue Blazes bucked in tremendous jumps all around the corral, his tail clamped like a vise. The jar of his impact was terrific. It sent the buster's head snapping back, blood began to trickle from his nose. Then he gulped and the bulge disappeared from his cheek.

"He's swallowed it" Jimmy yelled. "He done swallowed his chaw."

Blue Blazes made a frantic leap and turned back so fast that he barely missed his own behind. Sloan stuck to him. Then abruptly as he had begun, the bronc quit. Sloan seized the opportunity to alter his position and get a firmer grip on the hackamore rope. His face was pallid.

"Now we'll see who's—" he began and choked, because the bronc got into action. With a harsh squawl he pitched straight ahead—straight for the fence.

"Jump! He's going into it!"

Apparently Sloan thought so, too. He kicked one foot free for the dive and it was his undoing. When almost into the fence, the black swerved. His side actually scraped the boards and Sloan's leg was knocked backward. He let out a groan and toppled off into the dust.

Blue Blazes whirled like a snake and jumped for Sloan's middle, striking with his forefeet like a stallion. He missed by the fraction of an inch and the buster squirmed away. Once more the black sprang. Sloan managed to elude him

72

and started toward the fence on hands and knees. Blue Blazes seized the seat of his pants with his teeth and took a piece out of them.

"Hi, you devil!" yelled the boss, who had come on the run at Jimmy's outcry. He hurled a red-hot branding iron at the bronc's head. It caught Blue Blazes on the neck, inflicting a long burn. The black retreated.

Lyford puffed, "I've seen a mule tromp a man, but that's the first time in my life I ever seen a hoss that mean."

Sloan was dusting his shirt and testing his limbs for breakages. Now he said in a low, unnatural voice: "I'm a-goin' to kill him for this."

"No-oo, leave him go, Cal. He'll never make a cowhorse now and we'll get shet of him with that army bunch. They don't mind 'em mean."

Now, it is an unwritten law in cowland that no man shall interfere between a rider and his horse. The buster stopped short and stared at the boss.

"Do you mean to say you ain't a-goin' to let me ride him?"

"What's the use? He ain't worth the risk, Cal."

Sloan said, "Then I'm through. You can have my job right now."

"Please yourself. That suits me. Let's go over here and I'll give you your time. You're too rough, Sloan."

"If you want to baby 'em, go git somebody else" the buster said contemptuously as he followed the boss to the gate. There Lyford wrote out a check with the stub of a pencil.

"You can have Snake to get to town" he said. "Leave him in the company corral there. Well, adios. Take care of yourself."

The buster said, "Same to you."

He started off without a word of farewell to the boys with whom he had worked for six years. It needed only a spark to explode his rage, so nobody ventured to address him—with the exception of Jimmy. Jimmy could not for the life of him repress a grin when Sloan rode past the post he straddled and he cried to the buster, "Did that chaw make you sick, Mister Sloan?"

"If you was my boy" Sloan said, "I'd sure enough tan you good."

Jimmy stuck out his tongue and shrilled, "But I ain't your boy, and if you ever lay a hand on me, my daddy'll kill you."

Meanwhile Rush Ardrey had engaged the boss in talk. When Jimmy joined them, his father was saying: "Shucks, that hoss wouldn't even leave a grease spot of you. You don't want Blue Blazes."

"Leave me take him and see, Lyford. Don't send him off to the war. I'll pay you sixty dollars for ol' Blue Blazes—ten a month off'n my pay."

The boss said, "You've bought somethin'. But if he busts you wide open, don't come bellyachin' to me."

Rush never gave the black a chance to bust him open. He kept Blue Blazes at headquarters in a pen used in bad seasons for sick cows and for a fortnight doled out only sufficient food and water to sustain life. Having always been a hearty feeder, Blue Blazes lost weight with surprising rapidity. When a block of hay was tossed into the pen, he fought shy of it because he had eaten nothing except grass since babyhood. However, hunger conquered; but there was a vast difference between hay and green grass and the block did not fill the void. The black was troubled in mind, too. Rush had left the hackamore on his head, with about ten feet of rope. It worried him.

"Why'nt you take it off?" Jimmy demanded. "His head is all swelled up."

"You run back to the house to your ma. Don't you see I gotta wear him down?"

Gradually Blue Blazes became reconciled to his surroundings and began to show curiosity about the source of his meals. Rush left him severely alone. Never once during the period of diet did he give the black cause for distrust. The result was that one night Blue Blazes came sniffing at the hand that held out the hay to him. Next morning, although he blew like a grampus, he permitted Rush to touch his nose. Blue Blazes seemed to sense friendliness in the fingers and shortly after this relation was established he began to nicker at Rush's approach. Later still he allowed Rush to rub his neck as he nibbled at the hay.

One of the outfit jeered: "Sure. He'll let you do that now because he's starved and weak. But wait till he's got his stren'th back—he'll throw you into the next county. That hoss is like a mule, I tell you. I knowed a mule once that acted gentle as a lamb 'til she got this feller where she wanted him—and then I had to break the news to his widder."

Not until the bronc had grown gaunt and listless did Rush take him out of the pen. Then he led him down to a sandflat beside the creek. There he saddled him without assistance and Blue Blazes did not resent it.

"That wind sure cuts like a knife" Rush told himself, trying to think it was the chill that made his teeth chatter.

He stepped cautiously into the saddle: the black remained quiet. He humped his back a little, but the cowboy gave him time to think it over. He clucked at him and talked in a low voice. Soon Blue Blazes ventured a few steps as though to find out what would happen. Nothing happened, so he jerked his head down and pitched about twenty yards. His rider sat undisturbed, employing neither quirt nor spur. The black gave it up, perhaps as a waste of energy. He began to trot. Still nothing hurt him.

An hour later Rush made our eyes pop by riding the dripping bronco up to the door of the bunkhouse.

"He's broke" he said, giving Blue Blazes' neck a friendly slap to prove it. "In a month I'll have me a ropin' horse. He'll be eatin' out'n my hand."

"Out of your laig, you mean" Uncle Harve said. "He won't stay like that, Rush. One of these days that hoss'll turn right around and bite your ear off."

"Shucks, no. Him and me understand each other."

It did look that way. Although Rush increased the bronc's feed so that Blue Blazes regained his barrel-like body, the black made no serious effort to throw him. Now and again he did a little "goating," but it was half-hearted and seemed to spring from a conviction that it was expected of him.

Winter set in and he was turned out to pasture. In a week he had almost forgotten his recent experiences. Then one sparkling morning three horsemen surprised Blue Blazes and some companions in a box cañon and cornered them against a sandstone cliff. While two stood guard, the other stretched a rope barrier.

"Take 'em all except the black."

"But he's the pick of the lot, Cal."

"I know—but we don't want him. I've got a li'l' score to settle with that gen'l'man on my own account."

Blue Blazes pricked his ears when he heard Sloan's voice. The buster threw his rope with an overhand flip and cried: "I've got you where I want you now. And there ain't nobody here to play the baby. Me and you can have it out."

They threw Blue Blazes and hogtied him, and Sloan went to work to get even. His weapon was the stout limb of a mesquite tree and he flailed with it on head and neck and ribs until his arms ached. So savagely did he punish the horse that one of his companions was moved to an oath of protest.

The buster snarled: "You keep out'n this. He's my meat. And I'll kill him—after I've learned him to——"

"Look out! Here comes somebody."

There was a rattle of wheels on the rim of the cañon. With a scared look at his confederates Sloan removed the ropes from the black and ran to his horse. Then they scattered the other captives and galloped off.

Presently the Turkey Track boss and his small son arrived in a buckboard, wending homeward from a trip to a windmill. They passed the mouth of the cañon.

The boy piped up, "What's that, daddy? Look beyond those trees. Looks like a dead horse, ain't it?"

76

Lyford peered at the object on the ground and said, "Let's go see." His astonishment knew no bounds when he recognized Blue Blazes.

"What the Sam Hill!—I never seen anything like it. Who's been beating you, ol' feller? Hey? Fetch my rope, son."

"Is he dead, daddy? Is he dead?"

"No-oo, but he's sure tore up a fright. I never saw a worse beating. Let's see who's been round here."

"Did he have a fight, daddy?"

The boss scanned the trampled ground and then nodded.

"Sure, Jimmy. That must have been it. Ol' Blue Blazes got into a fight with another hoss and the other hoss give him the worst of it. What else could it be? That's what we'll tell Rush, hey, son?"

"Them're right queer marks for a fight with a hoss" said Uncle Harve that night. "Looks to me like—how the tarnation did you manage to bring him in, Lyford?"

"Just eased him along. He come to life right after we found him."

Rush Ardrey was at a division camp fifty miles to the south, riding fence and tending windmills, and did not learn of the occurrence for nearly a month. By that time the black's wounds had healed beyond betrayal. Nevertheless he was suspicious.

"A fight, huh? Hell's bells, there ain't a hoss on the range Blue Blazes can't lick the whey out of."

"Maybe the stallion——"

"How could he get out? Besides, Blue Blazes wouldn't fight him. He's got more sense. That hoss is goin' to be marked for life, Lyford. As soon as he's well enough to move, leave me take him to my camp and grain him the rest of the winter. How about it?"

It was at the division camp high up on the back of the Mules that Rush trained Blue Blazes in the work of a cowhorse. The black was quick to learn. Keen and powerful, he early developed into a crack roping horse and he could outrun anything the cowboy had ever topped. For mountain work an especially surefooted animal is required and Blue Blazes was like a mule in that respect. He could slide down a shale slope on his rump and bring up in stride, and he could whirl faster than any calf on the Turkey Track.

The winter wore away. The boss said to Uncle Harve, "Those sons-of-bitches're getting bolder every day. That makes twenty-two head since December."

Uncle Harve bit off a hunk of tobacco and tongued it meditatively.

"Why'n't you have the varmint arrested? You've got proof."

The boss said: "What's the use? You know as well as I do we can't get a jury to convict a man for stealin' hosses or rustlin' cattle in this country. And Sloan——"

"He'll slip up yet. Him and them Hightower boys is drinkin' heavy and it's only a question of time, to my notion."

Lyford said: "Well, if we can't stop it legally we'll do it our own way. Saddle up and take this over to Sloan's place for me, Uncle Harve. Maybe you'd best make sure he ain't home first though."

"I ain't scared of Sloan" Uncle Harve protested.

Nevertheless he took pains to ascertain that the buster was in town before starting to deliver the letter. A quarter of a mile north of the ranchhouse he passed the reservoir Lyford had built to irrigate the farm lands on which he raised his feed. Jimmy was sailing a paper boat in the water running from the sluice.

"Git away from there, cowboy! What the tarnation you doin' out here, anyhow? I swan you make me nervous, always pokin' in that ditch."

"Where you bound, Uncle Harve? Take me with you."

"No, sirree. You git on your pony and go home to your ma this minute. Ain't there no place else to play 'cept a six-foot ditch? And look at your clo's, cowboy—and you most a man growed, too."

"Aw, take me with you, Uncle Harve. I'll be awful good—honest."

Uncle Harve waved his hand and ambled on. Of course he had to pretend that he expected to find Sloan at home when his wife came to the door.

She said, "Cal's went to town . . . And I don't much care if he never comes back."

"Oh, now, Miz Sloan! . . . Has Cal been mistreatin' of you?"

"Mistreatin'? Huh!" She stopped herself, then asked, "What's that you got there in your hand, Uncle Harve? Anything for us? Some mail?"

Uncle Harve said, "Just a letter for Cal. Want to give it to him?"

"Depends on what's in it." She fingered the envelope doubtfully. "I do hope this won't make no trouble. It ain't a warrant or something, Uncle Harve?"

"No-oo. What'd I be doin' with a warrant?"

"Well, jest leave it and I'll see he gits it whenever he comes home."

Uncle Harve coughed.

"Do you mind mentionin' to Cal, ma'am, how come I brung it over? Just happened to be ridin' this way and Lyford asked me to. I don't know what's in that there letter any more'n you do, Miz Sloan."

"Then it IS trouble."

The letter threw Sloan into a terrible rage when he read it next morning. His wife asked no questions but prudently kept out of reach; and after breakfast he saddled a horse and rode off toward the ranch.

At the kitchen door of the manager's house he asked, "Where's Lyford?"

The Chinese cook said, "Him no home. He go light away to town soon as he et."

"Well, I'm here to see him and I'll stick round ontil he gits back. Will he be home for supper, Chink?"

"I no know. Maybe. Maybe no."

Sloan walked over to the cowboys' quarters. He found nobody there except Miguel who was making a hair-bridle in the saddleshed.

Miguel told him, "All gone. No one here but me and little Missus, and she is sick of the head and sleeps. So I am minding the baby. Hey, Jimmy?"

"I ain't a baby, you big ol' fool, you! I'm five years old and goin' on six."

With that, the boy abandoned play in the saddleshed. He was afraid of Sloan, and as soon as he saw Miguel's attention wander he slipped away to the house. There he dug up his toy boat from a heap of playthings and went down to sail it in the big ditch below the reservoir.

Sloan pulled a bottle from his overalls and took a long swig. He offered Miguel a drink, but the Mexican declined. In a few minutes the buster took a second pull.

"It's time Lyford learned this is a free country" he mumbled. "Folks is just as good as people, any day."

Miguel paid him no attention. It was very quiet in the saddleshed and not a sound came from the ranchhouse, where Mrs. Lyford was sleeping off a headache and the Chinaman was peeling potatoes. A couple of hours passed, but still the boss did not return. Sloan kept on taking nips. Now and again he cursed, his gaze on the road winding over the mesa toward town.

"Ain't he ever comin' back?" he asked Miguel. The horsewrangler said he didn't know. "Well, I don't aim to sit here all night. The sorry scoundrel! You tell him, Miguel, that if he thinks I'm stealin' his horses or rustlin' his cattle, why'nt he come out like a man and say so to my face 'stead of sittin' down and writin' a dirty li'l' letter? You tell him just that, unnerstan? We've got courts, ain't we? Well, tell him to prove it on me in court. The Turkey Track can afford to hire them a lawyer."

He left Miguel and went to the bunkhouse where he remained about an hour, drinking alone. His wrongs began to boil; the more he brooded over them, the more contemptible and cowardly seemed Lyford's treatment of him.

79

Glancing up from his work, Miguel saw Sloan riding away and flogging his horse as he went. The Chinese cook was plucking a chicken on the back porch when the buster rocketed past the house, sawing his horse's head from side to side for some fancied fault. The cook paused to watch. Sloan soon got straightened out and slowed to a trot. The Chinaman saw him cross the foot-bridge over the reservoir ditch: then he lost interest and went on plucking feathers.

The buster came upon Jimmy at play in the muddy water. The boy was prattling to himself, giving orders to the crew of a merchant ship to keep a watch out for submarines. The paper boat stood proudly erect, the ditch's banks being so high and steep that no breeze reached it.

It was on the tip of Sloan's tongue to hail Jimmy and tease him to hear him cuss, but a puff of wind at that moment sent some water lapping over the rim of the reservoir. Sloan looked at the sluice-gate and an odd, furtive expression came on his face. He turned in the saddle to stare back at the ranch-house, the stables, down the valley, away to the distant hills: he stood up in the stirrups to make sure. Then he moved his horse to higher ground, tied him to a mesquite tree and walked to the sluice.

Engrossed in naval tactics, Jimmy neither saw nor heard him. Sloan examined the lock a moment, then tugged at the gate's lever. It came readily.

The roaring rush of the flood sobered him. Possibly in that instant he would have turned to rescue the boy had not fear driven him. He ran to his horse and fled.

The animal headed toward home. "Not that way, damn you!" Sloan cried, sluing him around. He struck south toward the Mules. In their cañons he might find a place to hide until a chance offered to slip across the border into Mexico. For four hours he urged his jaded horse up steep slopes, nor would he recognize its condition.

"You're throwing off on me" he railed, striking it over the ears with the quirt. "You ain't give out—you're actin' this way a-purpose."

On a jutting crag he turned to look back. The whole valley was spread out below. Midway between him and the clump of green that marked the ranch-house was a swirl of dust. Tiny dots moved under it.

"They're after me already."

At nightfall, with the purple shadows creeping up the shaggy sides of the Mules, Sloan clattered down a rocky trail into a cañon. It was very quiet and green and peaceful. There was a log shack at one end amid trees, and to the right of it a pen.

80

He panted, "Maybe Rush'll lend me a fresh hoss. If he don't—he'll have to, that's all. I'll make him."

He eased his gun in its holster. Then he halloed. There was no response except a neigh, which came from a saddled horse near the shack. With a cry of relief the buster kicked his feet free and sprang down. Here was salvation—hope soared in him. The beast he abandoned wavered a moment and sank to the ground.

The horse beside the shack shied away at Sloan's approach.

"Hold still, you son-of-a-bitch" the buster yelled, frantic at the delay.

He managed to grab the loose reins, but the brute dodged and pulled. Sloan cursed again and jumped to seize the cheek of the bridle. The answering tug jerked him off his feet and he fell flat in the dirt.

A blaring screech and a great black shape rose above him and smashed down, striking with iron-shod hoofs. Sloan tried to roll clear. The horse landed in the middle of his back. He reared and struck again.

"Hi! Hi!" Rush came stumbling out of a clump of post oaks back of the shack with an axe in his hands. "You, Blue Blazes! You! Quit it!"

With axe and voice he forced back the maddened horse and dragged Sloan into the shack. Shortly Lyford arrived at the head of five men, their mounts in a lather.

"Has Sloan passed this—" he began, and caught sight of the stricken brute on the ground.

Then Rush led them into the shack, where they stood silently above the broken thing in his bunk. Not a word did the boss say. At last he turned away and went outside and they heard him ascending the trail.

Uncle Harve said, "Well, it wasn't Sloan's fault that Jimmy ain't dead, so I reckon Blue Blazes done saved us a job. But who's goin' to bury this bastard?"

NESTER PARSON
New Mexico

Les Grady

Nester Parson

NEW MEXICO

"I JEST cain't git it through my head how a man who kin cook as good as you, kin think the earth's round, Mister Dave," said the parson.

"Hell's bells, didn't you ever went to school? Well, I did! . . . Gimme three cards off'n the roof, Al."

"I ain't a scholar myself, but don't the Good Book say 'An' the angels stood on the four corners of the earth an' held the winds thereof'? Now, if them angels stood on the four corners, how could the earth be round? It stands to reason it's flat if it's got four corners, don't it?"

Some of the boys were playing poker in the bunkhouse—the strawboss, the blacksmith, the headquarters cook, and a couple of cowhands. Fat Dave threw down his hand in disgust and said: "For Christ's sake, leave me be, parson. I ain't drawed a thing sence you begun to preach at me."

"I ain't preachin', Mister Dave—I ain't preachin'. But when a fine man like you don't know no better'n—"

"Come far?" the strawboss interrupted.

"Oklahoma. My li'l ol' team done walked that nine hundred miles in twenty-four days, pullin' fourteen hundred. You-all started your roundup yet?"

"Sure. The boys is all out with the wagon . . . What d'you say if we call this game off? The flies're ter'ble in here."

They went outside and squatted in the shade of the adobe wall of the bunkhouse and whittled on sticks.

"I'm a preacher, like I told you" the visitor said, "But I'm a right good cowhand, too. My name's Grady."

"Yeh? What sort of preacher?"

"Campbellite. Perhaps you-all done heard of my debate over to Texas with Sinkiller Griffiths. I wrastled four days and four nights with the Sinkiller an' my voice kep' jest as fresh as it is now. I coulda kep' on for another week but Sinkiller had to quit—plumb wore out."

"What was the debate?" Dave asked.

85

"On the impossibility of apostasy."

"Oh, indeed" said Dave.

The blacksmith said uneasily, "I gotta go shoe that ol' bed-wagon mule," and departed.

"Don't you want a good man to work round here?" the parson demanded of the strawboss.

"Where is he?"

"Right here, mister. You're a-lookin' right at him. I ben sort of figuring I might take up a quarter-section somewheres near here if I could git me some work to carry us through the winter."

"Us? You married then?"

"Sure. I done brought the gal along because she's ben sickly an' I thought this climate'd holp her some. She's down with the wagon in that grove of cotton-woods, May Belle is. You kin see the smoke of her fire where she's cookin' dinner."

"This quarter-section, now—where were you figurin' on takin' it up?"

"There's a stretch down near the school-section in the valley struck me as a right pretty place. Near that big ol' pine."

"Yep, that's sure pretty" the strawboss agreed.

Where they sat in the shadow of the roof it was almost cool, but six inches away the sun was cracking the hard-trodden earth into fissures. The bunkhouse stood close to the stockaded bronc pen and beyond the pen were a pond and a grove of trees. Beyond those the ranchhouse showed, gray and red. The huge corral encircling the water-troughs was empty and shimmered in the noon glare: tomorrow it would swelter in the dust and echo to the roarings of two thousand cattle. A pineclad mountain rose at its back. That was The Hatter and it was forty miles away. Between The Hatter and the ranch lay an apparently level expanse which was actually a broken stretch torn by arroyas and draws.

The strawboss got up and stretched. Then he asked with a queer resentment: "You reckon on staying here then?"

"Sure."

The strawboss opened his mouth to say something, then slowly shut it and started off toward the blacksmith shop.

"He's figurin' on proving up a claim in Eden."

"The poor son-of-a-bitch" said the blacksmith.

Meanwhile the Campbellite preacher went cheerily along the wagontrack to where his prairie-schooner rested after its journey across two states—jolting over highways and trails, climbing mountains and fording treacherous rivers. His wife had finished a dinner of dograbbit and was trying to make the dregs of a bucket of water suffice for a cleanup.

"It's all right, gal" he told her briskly. "I kin tell they're fine men, this outfit. They play poker and cuss some and they got fool notions about the earth bein' round, but they're fine men. They done made me stay an' eat an' Mister Dave, the cook, said as how we could have some sowbelly an' beans maybe."

"Lan's sakes! No wonder you was so long comin' back, Les. That's mighty fine. Do you reckon Mister Dave mought give us a li'l' coffee, too? We're gittin' awful low."

"I'll ast him. I'll fetch you some more water an' we'll camp here tonight. You keep an eye on ol' Runt there an' see he don't worry the cattle none if any strays along. I gotta go see the manager to git me a job."

The manager himself opened the screen door at sound of the visitor's step on the porch. Whether on floor or across smooth ground, the parson always walked as though he were stepping over hummocks. The manager took one glance at his wide-open eyes, with their startled, hesitant look, and knew him and his history and his whole character as though all had been charted for him.

"Well?"

"I'm figurin' on takin' up a li'l' claim next that school section in the valley, Mister Loring, sir, an' I wanted for to see you about a job."

"Got more men than we need already."

"But I'm a right good cowhand, Mister Loring. I used to could break broncs too, ontil I got stove up. Worked for the ol' Matador outfit for three years."

"Floyd is the range boss and I never interfere with him. Besides, I happen to know he wants to drop a couple instead of taking anybody on."

"I kin do most any kind of work, Mister Loring. I'm a blacksmith an' could holp there. Or I could grow some alfalfa in that stretch of meadow near the crick."

The manager eyed him a while.

"You say you want to take up a claim in Eden?"

"Eden? Where's that?"

"The boys call that valley Eden."

"I sure would like to. Yessir."

"Well, if you're set on staying, I suppose you've got to live. Maybe you could help in the blacksmith shop."

"I done brought along the gal too, Mister Loring, sir. She's ben some sickly an' I thought——"

The manager frowned. "You mean she's an invalid?"

87

"No-oo. She ain't an invalid. But she ain't strong. Jest fragile like."

"All right. I'll give you twenty-five dollars a month and your keep."

The parson's curiously immature face glowed with doglike gratitude.

"There's a coupla good rooms back of the wagonshed and you can have those for the time being. They'll need to be fixed up, but they're watertight. Where did you say you aimed to take up a claim?"

"In the valley near that big ol' pine. Eden, you done called it."

"Well, see that you prove up your claim. We don't want you here at all if you're going to flit any day you take a notion."

"No, sirree. I intend to stay this time for keeps. An' I'll make sure my li'l' place don't interfere with your cattle none neither, Mister Loring. I'm mighty thankful to you, Mister Loring—mighty thankful."

"By the way" the manager said, "Mrs. Loring needs somebody to help her cook. The hired girl's sick. Is your wife strong enough for that sort of work?"

"Cookin' is her middle name. Why, that ain't work a-tall for May Belle. Shall I go an' fetch her, Mister Loring?"

"Not right now. You might bring her round tomorrow morning."

Mrs. Loring took one look at May Belle and decided to employ her at house-cleaning and moving the heavy furniture, because the "gal" was a florid person of about two hundred and twenty pounds who walked with a hearty sway and had a bass laugh.

"Les, he had a fine claim in Montana eleven year ago" she confided to the manager's wife as they started to work.

"Why didn't you stay there then?"

"I dunno. We done proved up our claim and jest when we was gittin' our first good crop, you mought say, Les, he allowed we'd move. Said he felt a call to go forth."

"Had he?"

"I dunno. Sometimes I think he's hearin' wrong. Anyhow, we went down to Texas and took up a whole section."

"Have you got that still?"

"Mercy, no! We wouldn't be here now, would we? We done left that, too. Les, he sold the farm to a cattle buyer for a wagon and fifty head of cattle and we lit out for Oklahomee."

Mrs. Loring paused to adjust her dustcap and asked: "When was that?"

"Four years ago. The cattle buyer in Texas, he got rich on Les's farm. There's a town there now."

"But what happened to your cattle?"

"I was fixing to tell you, ma'am. We done lost 'em in the Canadian. That was a sure-enough fool thing the way it happened, too, but of course I never said nothin' to Les."

"Then what?"

"Well, we had that place in Oklahomee. Then Les, he hearn as how the claims here was so easy to git and so rich, and he done told me the Oklahomee climate weren't healthy for my trouble. I git spells of heartburn now and agin, Miz Loring. Maybe it's because I'm gittin' kinda stout. Do you reckon?"

"That might have something to do with it," Mrs. Loring admitted.

She told her husband all about May Belle that night and he snorted.

"Sure. They drift from the Arctic Circle to the Gulf, that class of nester. Always following a boom of some kind; sometimes they even go ahead of it. But I never knew one of them to stick at anything. I never knew one to profit from his changes. Usually some other fellow gets rich on the things they abandon."

His wife made a half-hearted attempt to defend the couple. The parson's strange hallucinations about the "gal" appealed to her sentimental side: perhaps his blind devotion touched something in her heart which a sane, safe attachment of twenty years had been unable to awaken.

"Will" she said suddenly, "Why did you let them stay? Did you really want them here?"

"You wanted a cook, didn't you? I couldn't see them starve. They won't be in the way."

"That's what you said about that nester who took up that claim near The Hatter."

"What do you mean?" he said angrily.

She said, not looking at him: "Well, has anything ever been heard of him?"

"I don't know. I guess he went to Arizona. Floyd says he did, anyhow."

"I do hope nothing happens to this pair. They're simply overgrown children, Will."

The manager pushed his cup away with a clatter and rose from the table.

"Don't be a fool" he said. "And I'll trouble you not to talk to me like that again—ever! Understand?"

"I only meant—I mean I hope they won't light out somewhere, too."

Loring did not answer. He clinked out to the porch, mounted his horse and rode away to make surveys with a land commissioner.

Meanwhile the blacksmith was wrestling with a puzzle: the blacksmith couldn't figure for the life of him why the hell the parson had been put to work to help him.

"Don't you go scratchin' your brains out about that" the strawboss advised. "The ol' man knows his bus'ness."

"Yeh. That's just what's eatin' on me."

The parson was untroubled by any doubts and accepted his luck with childish glee. He soon fenced in a quarter-section with a single strand of barbed wire and the days were all too short for him while he toiled with the house. It was to have two rooms and to be made of adobe bricks obtained from the strawboss, and it would be roofed with sod. There were to be two windows in it, moreover. Standing back one evening to survey the results of his labors, the parson's ambition soared skyhigh. Dadgum, he'd have glass windows if only they got one good year's crops. Yes, sirree!

He bored for water and found it at sixty feet—not a few settlers had found water in abundance in a country which the cattlemen had painted for years as an arid desert. Indeed, the flow was so plentiful that the parson was nonplused until he heard from the waterhole man how the Big Spring, ten miles away, had unaccountably fallen off in its output. Not being entirely a fool, the parson kept his mouth shut.

When the boys returned from the roundup in November the parson and his wife were installed in their new home. The cowboys were curious when they rode past the shack, but showed indifference toward the couple. True, at sight of May Belle, Reb Steger offered to bet a month's pay the parson'd never have to shake the blankets to find that gal, but their attitude was friendly enough. Just another nester—here today and gone tomorrow.

Every fortnight the parson hitched up his team and drove forty miles with May Belle to a mining-camp on the slopes of The Hatter. There he held services with six members of his faith who worked in the mine. The parson knew a score of songs, so these meetings never lacked variety. And he was a terrific debater. After one tussle that lasted eight hours, not a man in the camp would tackle him on any subject, from Free Silver to predestination.

"Say" the blacksmith said one day as he and Grady worked over a wheel, "I advise you to stay clear of Hawkins."

"Why? He 'pears to me a fine man, Joe."

"Yeh? Well, let me ask you somethin'—has he ever passed the time o' day with you, parson?"

"No-oo, now you mention it, I don't recollect he has. Come to think of it, he ain't ever spoke to me."

"That's just the way he treated Davis."

"Davis? Who's Davis?"

"Oh, a nester who drifted in here. Big man with a beard and a cut across the jaw. You hearn what happened to him, didn't you?"

"Uh-uh."

"Hawkins done got him. Over in the Gap, it was. They had a quarrel, Hawkins said."

"What about?"

"Well, seems like Hawkins is a land agent or something for the ranch. Anyhow, that's what he calls himself. The boys all know what he is, though."

"What is he?"

"He's gunfighter for Loring. They run him out of Texas, so they say."

They went on with their work. After an interval the parson asked: "How long was that nester here before Hawkins done killed him?"

"Oh, about—how should I know? I don't recollect."

"He'd proved up his claim though, hadn't he?"

"I reckon so."

"Then I don't need to worry none about Hawkins for a while" the parson said.

*   *   *

Several years passed. Although the parson in his frequent visits to the eating-house and bunkhouse became an object of banter to the boys, it was in a kindly vein and he seemed to have won from them a reluctant respect.

Walking out from his shack one summer evening he gazed with pride over twenty acres of corn. He had now twelve head of cattle. They grew fat to bursting on the alfalfa he had grown beside his water-trough—he had already secured four cuttings of alfalfa from this patch during the year. His eyes kindled as he looked on his possessions. They gave him a newborn sense of security, of self-respect. At last he had a stake in the world, a stake worth a lifetime's devotion. Yes, he was fixed for life. He would always stay here; he would be a real farmer, a worthwhile citizen.

A few weeks later he proved up his claim—and within a month his sheds and cattle pen were burned down during the night. The precious wagon escaped by a miracle of which Runt's barking was the medium.

It stunned the parson. For a week he went about in a daze, hardly able to comprehend his misfortune and utterly at a loss to explain it, because that kind of fire was a rare occurrence in the Territory. It seemed to him a visitation.

"I reckon we was too puffed up with pride, gal" he said.

"No-oo. Whenever was you proud, Les? Somebody done us dirt. That's what I think."

"You reckon? If I was sure of that——"

He brooded over this explanation for days. Then one night he took down his double-barrelled shotgun from the wall and started to clean it.

"What you aimin' to do now, Les?"

"Nothin'. This ol' gun's rusty and I want to clean her up—jest in case."

"In case o' what?"

"You never kin tell in this world. There's some mighty mean an' ornery people round these parts, gal."

"Les Grady" she said, "You put that ol' gun away right now. I know what you're fixin' to do. You cain't fool me. Please, Les. Remember what happened the las' time you took to shootin', before you got religion—you and your brothers agin the Jackson boys."

"The scoundrels deserved what they got, May Belle. I'd do the same thing over agin, if I had to."

"A fine Christian you are, ain't you? Time and again I've heard you preach about forgivin' our enemies and how it's better to turn the other cheek'n to fight. Ain't you? You know you have. And how many times have I heard you read from the Good Book—why, only las' month you preached on that at the camp—'He who liveth by the sword shall perish by the sword'."

"Yeh, that's so. I did. But the Good Book don't say a word about shotguns, May Belle . . . Where'd I put them buckshot? I swan I'm gittin' awful absent-minded."

The parson was riding his old mare along a trail over The Hatter one day when he encountered Hawkins at a bend above a gorge. The gunfighter stopped his horse.

"Howdy, parson."

"Howdy."

"Where'd you git them three new calves of yourn?" the Texan demanded.

"Done bought 'em off'n the Blocks strayman."

"Them're Flying W calves."

The startled, hesitant look vanished from the parson's eyes. He stared at the gunman and said: "Hawkins, I reckon you figure on gittin' me this way. Why, I dunno. But first lemme tell you somethin' for your own good. The minute I hearn about that nester Davis you killed over in the Gap, I done wrote my brothers in Oklahoma to look for you if I should happen to die suddent or git the worst of an argument. They ain't like me, my brothers ain't—not near so peaceful. Two of 'em outlaws an' there's five of 'em. Gudger, the name is."

The Texan snorted contemptuously, but looked thoughtful, too.

92

"Gimme the trail then" he ordered. "I got no time to waste on you."

The parson slued his mare around so the approaching horseman might have right-of-way and Hawkins trotted by without even a glance at him.

"Hawkins!"

The voice was quiet, but in it such a note of command that instinct brought the Texan's hands up as he turned. The parson had him covered with a double-barreled shotgun.

"I reckon I oughta kill you, Hawkins" the parson said, "But I sorta hate to do it account of May Belle. You done burned my sheds an' my cattle-pens, an' I figure you run off them young steers, too. But some day you'll be called to a reckoning—yessir—so I kin afford to wait. The Good Book says 'He who liveth by the sword shall perish by the sword," an' you'll find that out before long. Now, listen—you leave me alone, hear me? Why're you after me, anyhow?"

"Go ahead and shoot" Hawkins drawled.

"You jest say that because you know I won't onless I'm fo'ced to. But I'll jest take that li'l' ol' gun of yourn, Hawkins. Oh, yes, I will. Keep those hands up! I kin git her myself . . . Now, you drag it outa here and drag it quick. I feel meanness comin' on me. An' don't forget what I said—there ain't a rathole in the world you could crawl into without findin' a Gudger there, waitin'."

The manager was checking up some account-books when Hawkins clanked in without knocking and banged down a chair in front of his desk.

"What's the matter now?"

"Nothin's the matter. Only I ain't goin' ahead with that feller over in Eden, Loring. Just dropped in to tell you."

"Why ain't you? Scairt?"

"I don't like that kind of talk, Loring. Unnerstand?"

The manager didn't fancy the look in his eye and said hastily: "But what's happened?"

"Nothin's happened. I need a holiday. I kin feel a drunk comin' on—been on this goddamned job now seven years ,and I've got my bellyfull. Gimme a coupla hundred dollars and I'll take a month off. You kin easy get somebody from Tucalari to ramrod things while I'm gone."

"How about Grady when you get back?"

"You kin get somebody else to run the parson off, Loring. Not me. What's more, his name ain't Grady at all. It's Gudger."

The manager sat back and stared at him.

"Not one of that Oklahoma gang?"

"You're damn whistlin' he is—and mean as pizen. All them brothers're bad

94

hombres. Preacher, huh? Well, I don't aim to get tangled with that bunch. Know what he told me?"

"Uh-uh."

"He up and told me if anything happened to him there wouldn't be a rathole in the world where I could hide without findin' a Gudger in it."

"Aha!—then you ARE scairt."

Luckily for the manager his wife came through the door at the instant that Hawkins kicked back his chair.

"Me and you'll talk about this again, Loring" the gunfighter said. "How do, Miz Loring. No, don't go. I'm on my way just as soon as I get my check."

The manager paid him without further words and after the Texan had ridden away, sent a cowboy for the parson.

"What did you want for to see me about, Mister Loring?"

"Well, a friend of mine figures he'd like to buy a few sections in Eden. I thought perhaps you might like to sell. There ain't much left to your place now."

"No-oo, I wouldn't choose to, thanks" the parson said.

"He'll give you two hundred and fifty dollars for your claim."

"Why, that's only a dollar'n a half an acre, Mister Loring. An' there's all that corn an' alfalfa."

"I know that. But it's a bad year—a very bad year—and you could use the money."

"Why, I wouldn't take a thousand for that claim. No, sir. I done worked too hard on it. It's our home—about the only real home me an' the gal ever rightly had."

"All right" the manager said.

While the parson and his wife were absent at the mining camp for the next fortnightly meeting, somebody left a gate open and a bunch of cattle wandered in from the range and devoured his corn and alfalfa. What they did not eat, they tramped down.

The parson stared at the destruction and did not say a word. But he stared so long that May Belle put a hand on his arm and said, "Now, Les. Now, Les."

"It's all right, gal. It's all right. But somebody'll pay for this."

He went straight to see the manager.

"I'm sorry, Grady" Loring told him. "You must've forgotten to fasten that gate good. Did they do much harm?"

"Do you aim to pay me for that damage, Mister Loring? They was your cattle."

"Gawdamighty, no! It ain't my fault if you go off and leave your gate open.

Cattle're bound to wander, and if they see feed——"

"I admit that. It jest depends on how that gate come unfastened."

"Well, you can't blame me if you go off and leave a place to take care of itself and something happens to it. You're away to hell-and-gone from here, over there in Eden—how could we know you'd gone?"

The parson regarded him steadily.

"Mister Loring, this has jest about cleaned us. What May Belle an' I are goin' to do, I don't know. I got to git me a job. Kin you give me one—any kind of job—ontil I git started agin?"

"Sorry, but Floyd has just given three of the boys their time. We've more men now than we need for the work."

"You won't give me a job then?"

"I haven't got one to give you."

The parson remained silent a while, crumpling his old felt hat. Then he nodded and started out the door.

"I'll tell you what I will do, though" Loring called after him. "That friend of mine still wants to buy some land in Eden and he'll pay you two hundred for your claim."

"No, sirree, you won't!" the parson shouted back. "I'm a-goin' to stay right here. Me an' May Belle are like to starve, but we'll stick right here. I'll see you an' your fine friend in hell before you beat me out'n my land, Loring."

As he emerged from the ranchhouse he saw his wife getting down from one of the ranch buckboards.

"What're you doin' here, May Belle? I thought you was at home?"

"So I was, Les. But Miz Loring, she done sent one of the boys for me. She wants me to cook for her—the help done quit. She's a-going to pay me twenty dollars a month, too. Ain't that grand? That'll keep us through the winter. She's a real lady, Miz Loring is."

The parson took her by the arm and led her aside and they argued long and heatedly. What they said the buckboard driver could not hear, although his ears flapped in the effort. It ended in the parson mounting his old mare in surly fashion and riding away, whilst May Belle walked around to the kitchen door.

Next day she was back home. On his return to the shack in mid-afternoon the parson found her lying on the bed, her eyes red from weeping.

"What's the matter, gal?"

"I done lost my job, Les. Oh, oh, oh! And we needed it so bad."

"How come you lost your job?"

"Mister Loring" she said brokenly, "Mister Loring done sent to Tucalari for a man to cook. He got there this mornin'. And he told me—Mister Loring told me I wouldn't do—that I didn't know how to coo-hook. Oh, oh, oh! I never felt so ter'ble in my life."

"Couldn't cook?" the parson cried in an incredulous voice. "Loring done said you couldn't COOK?"

"That's what he said. Boo-hoo. Oh, oh, oh!"

The parson left her where she lay, got his shotgun down from the wall of the adjoining room, and mounted the mare again.

"They done burnt my sheds an' they stole my cattle" he muttered as he rode toward the ranch, "An' they tromped down my corn an' he won't even give me a job so we kin eat. But when he goes to insult the gal—when he says she cain't cook —CAIN'T COOK! CAIN'T——"

As he approached the gate of the ranchhouse yard at sundown he saw a horse tied to the picket fence. The parson recognized it as one of Hawkins'.

He dismounted and freed the safety-catch on his gun. Voices raised in hot argument came to him through the open door of the manager's office.

"You're a goddamned liar, Loring. I got seventy more comin' . . . I've stood all I'm a-going to stand from you . . . And you said I was scairt, too . . . You will, will you? Then take it, you son-of-a-bitch."

The report of a six-shooter followed and Hawkins came running out of the office and down the path. He knocked Grady down as he raced toward the gate and was in the saddle before the parson could get to his feet. A piercing scream broke from the house as he rose to one knee and raised the double-barreled gun.

The parson yelled, "So! Here's where we square accounts, Hawkins." The gunfighter was bending low over his horse's neck as he fled: his slicker and the high cantle of the saddle received the charge. The parson saw the leather rise in strips, saw Hawkins waver, but the Texan recovered himself and spurred forward.

The parson banged the butt of the gun on the ground and cursed fluently.

"After all these years" he mourned. "After all these years this had to happen. Never missed in ten years ontil I wanted most to shoot true."

Then he turned and ran toward the manager's office. The screams continued, and a man and a young girl burst from the house, crying to him for help.

Lying face downward on the floor was Loring's body. And beside it the widow knelt, calling on God for pity in this hour of need. The parson stared at her, then rubbed a hand across his forehead like a man awaking from a dream. Next he looked at his gun as though seeing it for the first time. He went to the door on tiptoe and stood the gun behind it, then knelt down beside Mrs. Loring.

"What happened? Oh, how did it happen?" she asked.

"I don't know, ma'am. But the Good Book says 'He who liveth by the sword shall perish by the sword'. That's Gospel, ma'am."

A GOOD ROOSTER CROWS EVERYWHERE

Mexican Interlude

A Good Rooster Crows Everywhere MEXICAN INTERLUDE

PERMIT me to disagree with you, sir. The fellow showed himself devoid of spirit and you would excuse it because he has had a misfortune. In Mexico we have a saying, El que es buen gallo en donde quiera canta. This means that while any rooster will crow on his own dunghill, a GOOD rooster crows everywhere, regardless.

Did I ever tell you about Dario Pez? By goodness, sir, there was a good rooster! Ignorant, yes—ah, qué pelado!—how ignorant he was! And yet how great in his simplicity and force. He was born to lead men, that fellow, and they would follow him to death.

"These Americans, Don Francisco" he once said to me, "They cannot understand one another's talk, do they? It is impossible. Do not deny it. They must just guess. I have listened attentively and I haven't heard two words alike."

I was an exile and bossing a gang that was clearing a tract of land below the American town of Pharr when we first met. He wanted a job. The pay was from forty-two to sixty-five cents a day. Pez was a fine chunk of a man, so I gave him sixty.

Well, he went to work and he worked hard. We had refugees in the grubbing gang from all parts of Mexico. Some who never pronounced the s, they were from Vera Cruz; a few who added in to everything, they had drifted clear from the Pacific Coast; but Dario talked in a singsong there was no mistaking. He was a Chihuahua man, sir.

"Now tell me the truth, compadre: what are you doing here? A guy like you does not come over for sixty cents a day."

He looked at me and grinned. Then he grew very solemn.

"The derecho de pernada" he replied in a terrible voice.

"What did you do to him?"

"I caught him unawares on the road and tried to choke him with my bare hands, but the soldiers came and I beat it."

"When did all this happen?"

"Four years ago. I have been in the mountains ever since."

You do not yet know what the trouble was about, sir?—you never heard of

101

the derecho de pernada? It was a very iniquitous custom. Not a law—no, it had never been written into the many laws—but in some remote regions where the Indian element is strong the custom was in operation since the days of Benito Juarez and even before that. It is that the cacique or great landowner has the right to take a girl on the eve of her wedding, sir. You marvel that such a thing could be, but consider: the people were so wretchedly poor and ignorant, they were taught to look up to the caciques and rich landowners as superior beings, so the exercise of this right was seldom resented.

But Dario Pez was of different stuff from the humble inhabitants of Baca. The authorities might forget in four years how he choked Señor Balderrama, but he still burned for another chance at him.

"Poor Rosita!" he would often murmur and then he would grit his teeth and cry in a strangled voice, "That viper! Wait until I catch him!"

Unfortunately Dario Pez was always broke. We paid the gangs on Saturday night and he never had a centavo by Monday morning. Most of it went to Manuel Ortiz who dealt monte in a house north of the railroad tracks. Manuel was a very excellent dealer. However, luck must change at last even with Manuel dealing the cards and one night Dario accumulated by the help of Providence eleven dollars and seventy cents. It was prodigious. He spent three dollars celebrating with friends and then bought a talking-machine with the balance. Dario Pez was very fond of music. His favorite piece was They Wouldn't Believe Me. It turned his thoughts to higher things, he said.

Now, Manuel Ortiz had a daughter named Luz. She was very beautiful, sir. She had great, soft brown eyes and her hair was long and silky and she loved Dario. She loved him from the moment she first saw him coming along the street, because this Pez was a fine chunk of a man; by goodness, yes.

At this time there were troop movements along the Border, sir, and a train of pontoons went through, bound for Sam Fordyce.

"Wow!" said Dario Pez, "Look at that, Don Francisco. The gringos bring along troughs to water their horses. What next?"

Then word reached us of sad happenings in our own country. War had broken out again between two factions and there were assassinations and much bloodshed. We were all uneasy. The gangs grew restless.

"I think the gringos intend to invade our country" Dario declared, "Else why all these preparations? In any event, the scoundrels now in power are robbing and oppressing the people. Let us go back. What are we doing here? A band of cranky exiles! It is better to die in a righteous cause.

"Are you willing to shed your blood for your country and the cause of

102

justice? Are you equal to a task dangerous but cut out for men of our stamp? If so, tell me, compadres, and within twenty-four hours we will be on the run."

Sir, there was magic in Dario Pez when he was roused, because the sword of his faith was blind. Seven of us cried with one voice: "We will follow you!"

By goodness, he was a changed man from that hour. He made us put our hands in his and swear never to forsake him. He seemed to be on fire.

However, next day was Tuesday, so we delayed our venture. Why? Because Tuesday is San Martes with us, worse than Blue Monday with you. It is our custom to drink and gamble all day Sunday and consequently let Monday slip by without work. Therefore we feel badly on Tuesday and there is an old saying El Martes ni te cases ni te embarques, which means Don't get married or attempt to travel on Tuesday.

But on Wednesday night we left Pharr and headed up the valley. It was our intention to cross the river farther west, because the patrols near Pharr were maintained with ceaseless vigilance on both sides.

"We will go into Chihuahua" said this Pez. "I do not like the people of Tamaulipas. They are hypocrites and bandits. Are you aware, Don Francisco, of what the rascals do?"

"No, General. What do they do?"

"Why, when a child is born in Tamaulipas the mother throws him up against the wall—and if he cannot cling there with his nails that child is unworthy and tossed to the buzzards."

Well, we sneaked out of Pharr and plunged into the brush. We had five borrowed horses and three we had stolen.

"No smoking" commanded Dario Pez. "Smoking in our business and giving yourself up are one and the same thing."

We went along with much caution, keeping close to the river. Just after dawn there came a crash behind us and we took shelter behind some trees. In a minute a fellow in overalls burst into sight. He was riding a big roan horse I had often seen Manuel Ortiz ride.

"Dario! Don't shoot. It's me."

"What are you doing here?"

"You didn't say goodbye."

"You can't come with us, Lucita" said the general, looking very foolish, sir. "Go back home before harm comes to you."

"No, I am going with you. Where you go, I will go."

"You mean it, Lucita?"

"Try me, Dario."

103

"Then come to my arms, muchachita. You shall not be separated from me. You see before you a man who is a scourge to his enemies but a cloak for his friends —a man who gives all and expects all. Hear me! What I propose is an honorable union—yes, I will even marry you. It shall be performed before the first cura we can find. There will be terrible hardships ahead, my poor Lucita, but the greater shall be your reward. Some day I will give you a palace. What do you say to that?"

"Oh, Pez!" cried Luz and they embraced. Was it not beautiful, sir?

Well, we left that spot and went on. All of us were cheerfuller in spite of the heat and want of sleep because it seemed to us that Lucita's coming was a favorable omen. Riding only at night we moved along the Border for twelve days and at Laredo, Dario Pez married Luz Ortiz.

How did we live? That was a very simple matter, sir. Our people are numerous in the Rio Grande counties and we had no difficulty obtaining shelter and food to eat. They never asked any questions.

At last we reached the point where Dario Pez desired to cross. It was at nightfall on the sixth of June. He halted us and made a speech.

"Listen, my children. We go to fight for our country, is it not so? But how shall we know that the side to which we lend our support has its real interests at heart? There are traitors and rascals everywhere. Therefore we will bide our time. Ours is the Army of Deliverance. Let us therefore act independently, ready to seize the favorable moment when it comes. Death to all traitors! Viva Méjico! Let Fortune guide our Cause."

We cheered him, then my friend Carlitos had a thought.

"Mi general" he said, "If we do not fight the Federals, or side with the bandits, who is there to fight?"

"All oppressors of the poor" replied Dario Pez. "Them we will bring low, whatever their affiliations. And we will start with Señor Don Carlos Balderrama."

I could not help smiling, sir, at the way he was mixing up the Cause with his desire for revenge. But Luz, she did not smile. No—she knew all about Rosita and Señor Balderrama and she by no means entertained the same hostility toward him.

About ten o'clock that night we emerged from a thicket and forded the Rio Grande, Dario Pez leading the way on the big roan Luz had turned over to him. We had just climbed the opposite bank when we heard noises and hid ourselves. Along came a patrol of about thirty Federals heavily armed. Some of them were singing and they passed without noticing us. Yes, they passed by a bunch of men who were destined to destroy them later. Human justice was near to us, but divine justice stretched forth her hand to save.

But by goodness, sir, what a start for a revolution! For provisions we had one pound of coffee, two pounds of sugar, three small sacks of salt. That is the naked truth. And we were striking into a desolate land, we knew not whither, nor what enemies and dangers might be lying in wait for us. Yet Dario Pez was cheerful.

Well, we headed south into our beloved Méjico and about two in the morning we watered our horses at Rancho de Flores. Then we went on. We crossed a railroad several times. The horses were very restless. They seemed to sense danger. We rode gun in hand, expecting a shower of bullets any moment.

In this fashion we moved until dawn broke and we found ourselves in front of Sierra de los Medanos forty miles below the order. Not a bite of supper the night before, yet Dario Pez said there was no time to eat so we kept going. In a little while we struck a sandy desert. The sun was terrible. We had water in our canteens but we had to be careful with it because there was no drinking place within thirty miles. Luz and Carlitos and I, we were not used to such hardships and in the afternoon we began to show signs of sunstroke. I swayed in the saddle and had to hang on by the horn. Carlitos was as bad. The girl held up better.

"Hello, muchachitos" said Dario Pez, who was perfectly fresh, "You are thirsty, are you not?"

Carlitos and I, we were ashamed and tried to smile and we said, "No, General."

"Then let me see how far you can spit."

We tried and by goodness, sir, we could not spit at all.

"You boys—and you, my poor Lucita—are not used to this. Here"—he took out the bullets from three cartridges that would not fit any gun we had—"here is desert water. Put the lead in your mouth and think it is a piece of ice."

We did so. It is a wonderful remedy, sir. Carlitos and I, we could spit.

Just before nightfall we came on a cow at a pool of dirty water in a cañon and shot her. Then we made camp.

"Hombrecitos" said Dario Pez next morning after breakfast, "We're going on. But before we set out, let me make plain to you that the only law to be respected here is the law of the rifle. Have your guns ready all the time. And never forget: The man who hits first hits twice."

We filled our canteens there and started to climb some mountains. We climbed and went down again, climbed and went down, and at last came out into a valley. Soon we met an old man. He was bowed by more than eighty years, sir, and his clothes were all of them filthy rags. When he saw Dario Pez he bent almost to the ground.

"Blessings upon thee, uncle" Dario Pez said.

"In the name of God, have them yourself."

"Why don't you buy some new clothes, Tio?"

"How can I buy clothes, Excellency, when I have not the means even to clothe my grandchildren, who need them so badly?"

"What? What is this? What, then, do you do with the money you earn?"

"Oh, señor, señor" the old man wailed, "When I was eighteen years of age, Señor Balderrama's father, whom God bless, lent me one hundred pesos for my marriage with Juanita, who is the mother of my nine children. We have all been working since then for this plantation and his son, Don Carlos—my sons and their sons. Still we have not been able to pay it because of the interest which makes it grow. How then, Excellency, can I buy garments if they will not give me credit in the plantation store?"

His words filled us all with rage, but the effect on Dario Pez was dreadful to see, sir. The veins swelled in his neck and his eyes began to roll.

"What?" he said in a choked voice, "That old crow again?"

Then he sat up straight on his horse and cried: "Hear me! In the name of my beloved mother and the protection I have received from the Unknown, I will never rest until I have punished this Prince-Albert-coated robber. I will never rest until his gold atones and his houses have been turned into headquarters for my army."

With that, he handed over to Tio an American dollar. The old man was overcome: he bowed low again and we went on.

After a while we came in sight of the plantation and town of Tres Hermanos. It was a lovely spot with fruit trees and gardens and among them a kingly mansion of white. On its towers and on the dome of the church gleamed in big gilt letters, C. B.

"So" said Dario Pez, "We will now have an accounting with Don Carlos Balderrama."

He asked for a volunteer to spy out the plantation. Carlitos and I, we spoke up at once but Luz cried out louder than both of us. Dario Pez smiled and told her to get busy. And guess what that girl went and did, sir! She pretended her horse was running away and galloped right through the middle of Tres Hermanos. A crowd of soldiers in the barracks ran to the gate and laughed and jeered when they saw Lucita with her arms around the horse's neck, but they would have laughed on the other side of their mouths if they had seen her make a detour on the other side of town and rejoin us.

106

"Dario, more than a hundred men occupy the town and they are well armed."

Our position seemed desperate. The horses were worn out and we were famished and in need of water. We had to get relief somewhere. So although there were only nine of us, and a hundred seasoned troopers in the place, he led us boldly into Tres Hermanos and halted in the plaza.

"Captain Ochoa" he ordered in the hearing of the citizens who had come running to see, "Take two hundred and fifty men and deploy up into those hills. And you, Colonel Zapien, take a hundred more and seize the church. Carlitos, you and Major Ortiz follow me. I want to send a courier to let the General know that I am here with eight hundred men."

By goodness, sir, we did not know whether he had gone crazy or not, but we all rushed to do as he commanded and the people fled in all directions, carrying the news.

"Where is the owner of all this splendor?" he inquired of a group of open-mouthed inhabitants.

They all tried to tell him at once. El Señor Don Carlos Balderrama was not at home but had gone to another plantation he owned farther south. From there he would proceed to the capital city for the marriage of his only daughter.

"So!" Dario Pez exclaimed. "And what is the day?"

"The tenth day of September, Excellency."

"We will be there."

Then he commanded them to fetch the administrador and that official was brought before him mighty quick. Dario Pez demanded fresh horses and food. The overseer swore that every beast had been run off and none were to be had; yes, the last had been stolen by the American filibuster, Kid Porras.

"Well, well" the general murmured, "That is very sad. Get your affairs in shape, hombre. We're going to have a hanging."

The overseer, he implored the saints. He called on some whose names we had never heard before he stopped for breath. Then he experienced a sudden change of mind.

"All right, boss. I have eleven horses here, one belonging to Señor Balderrama himself."

"Good. I will take them all. And now for something to eat."

"It may be I could get you some tortillas, Excellency."

"Tortillas, rascal?" bellowed Dario Pez. "Is that all you have to offer distinguished guests? How about yonder palace?"

Without waiting to bandy any more words he set out toward the house. There he established headquarters and those of us who had been given those false commands joined him under cover of darkness. The administrador sent plenty to eat and by goodness, we needed it, sir. The nine of us remained in the mansion until midnight, playing cards and enjoying ourselves. There was a talking-machine and we kept it going without a stop.

All the while the garrison remained shut up tight in their barracks in town, with the doors and windows barricaded and everything in readiness to repel attack. They could discern no troops but they feared that this might be only a trap. Was it not droll?

Just after midnight we got to horse and slipped out of town. Seven men of Tres Hermanos joined us and we had eleven fresh horses and all the provisions we could carry. We had hardly left when the garrison woke up to the trick that had been worked on them and they fired a few shots after us, but they did no harm and none of the soldiers had the nerve to follow us in the dark.

Dario Pez rode along laughing and singing.

"Oh, muchachitos" he said, "Learn human nature. Learn how to handle yourselves against danger. You can draw its fangs if you know how. I am a doctor in human affairs—a doctor without a drugstore."

Well, we kept going south and came to a swampy region infested by bandits. It is known by the name of Cienaga de los Ladrones. There we rested in a village and gained recruits every day. The news of our exploit had spread like wildfire and men joined us every hour. All were desperate fellows accustomed to hardships and danger. Several small bands arrived under their own jefes, until Dario Pez had four hundred and forty-five men.

We stayed there a week to organize our forces. The general kept sending couriers to all the leaders operating in that region, urging them to throw in with us for mutual defence. I wrote these messages myself and riders carried them all over that country.

And now another problem confronted Dario Pez. The higher you go the more the problems, sir, and he now needed money badly. So long as we were a small band we could rustle enough to eat and food for our horses and we had the ground to sleep on, but with hundreds of soldiers to provide for, much money would be required. We lacked clothes and blankets and shoes and rifles and ammunition, not to mention provisions and medical supplies. Poderoso caballero es Don Dinero—A powerful gentleman is Mister Money. By goodness, yes. But where was this money to be obtained? Listen, and I will tell you.

About four o'clock on the morning of July Fourth the bugle sounded "Saddle Boot" to start a march of a day and most of a night. We were trotting along through the dark when the general halted us. Then he shouted in a wild sort of lunatic way: "Faster, boys! We're going to capture a train." What do you know about that! We were in the heart of the mountains. Where could there be a train? Nevertheless he ordered us to deploy, designating a small peak.

"Grab your guns!"

Then he ordered a charge. There was no enemy to be seen, nor a sign of human habitation. However, that was none of our business. Dario Pez commanded us to charge and we charged over broken ground toward that peak. We galloped around a curve and there before us was a railroad and on it a passenger train at rest because some rails had been torn up. In two winks we had it surrounded. Some of our boys climbed into the engine, others into the cars. The general and Luz went through each coach, examining all the travelers. Those people were astounded, as you may suppose.

The treasure we seized was prodigious, sir. The scoundrels had hidden it carefully but we smelled out their hiding places. In the water tank of the engine we discovered a bar of silver bullion weighing one hundred and eighty pounds; then another and another. All told we found a hundred and twenty-two bars of bullion and three bars of gold that weighed forty pounds each. The conductor was an American named Webster and he told us that the shipment had been consigned to the United States to be changed into those darling dollars which assert "In God We Trust."

Dario Pez ordered the treasure transferred to our horses and we rode until three o'clock in the morning, when he took pity on his poor boys and called a halt. Have you ever slept with a treasure, sir? Carlitos and I, we never had and the thing caused us agitation. We could not sleep a wink. The spot where we were camped was a most beautiful one. With mountains all around and the greenery and bullion it was very beautiful, sir, but we could not sleep.

However, we might have spared ourselves the trouble of staying awake to think about the treasure, because early in the morning Dario Pez took a few trusted followers and went off into the forest with it. Yes, they rode away with every bar of that bullion. On his return, Dario Pez informed us that they had hidden it in the forest and would come back sometime to dig it up. But guess what, sir! Later he informed us that some rascals had removed and carried off the whole pile. The treasure was gone, we did not know where. It was very strange. What is your opinion of this mystery, sir?

Well, we went toward Bachiniva. Bachiniva is a paradise. It lies in a valley of pine and oak and the ground is reddish and the rocks are green and red. The entire region is famous for fruit and there are apple and peach trees by thousands.

And the girls! By goodness, the prettiest girls in the whole of Mexico are in

Bachiniva. My, what glorious violet eyes they have!

No conquering heroes could have received a warmer welcome than our little army there. They strewed flowers in our path. They brought baskets of them to the general's office and heaped the perfumed masses on the floor. Dario Pez would smile at them and rub his hands and cry "Gracias, muchachitas. Gracias, muchachitas." And the pretty little girls, they would blush.

What pleasant hours we passed there, forgetting our fatigue and privations in the lovely violet eyes of the nice girls. Their presence was a happiness and a solace for us poor boys. We had music, too. One band would relieve another and there was always a minstrel to sing. Tunes dear to Mexican hearts enriched the air.

But it had to end: there was work to do. At four o'clock one morning "Saddle boot" sounded and in less than an hour we were moving out of Bachiniva. Carlos and I, we surely did hate to part from the family of Señor Chavez. We were booted and ready when his three nice girls appeared, wearing blooms at their breasts.

"Take these flowers" they said to us, "from our souls."

Oh, sir, we were transported. Also, they gave us some cakes of their own making. We did not eat them. No. That would have been sacrilege. Hungry though we often were, we wore their cakes next our hearts as a token of their heavenly association.

At the mining town of La Boquilla we were accorded a splendid reception, particularly by the foreigners resident in the place. They hailed Dario Pez as a great man and prophesied that he would soon become governor of the entire state. Instead of pleasing, this made him angry.

"I am not seeking office" he told them. "I am working for a Cause—the Cause of Justice. Colonel Ochoa, go open up the church and summon the people."

When they heard the bells ringing they came from all directions. They gathered in a crowd in front of the church and the general sat on his horse and addressed them. He swelled out his chest and cried: "Hear me! You see before you Dario Pez, the dark cloud of evildoers. Here is a humble peon like yourselves, but the man who has been lifted up to become the Emancipator of our oppressed people.

"I come from the mountains. My home is where the eagle builds its nest. My soul soars aloft with its flight. You are listening to the words of one who dwells in everlasting touch with the stars.

"I come to you with a message. I am here to listen to your wrongs and to right them. Here, people, is the army with which I aim to fight tyranny. Those who have grievances, let them speak freely."

110

The crowd shouted and pressed close to him. Complaints began pouring in. Some Indians reported two of their villages had been destroyed to make more room for a dam. Dario Pez flew into a rage and summoned the manager of the mines.

"What are you?"

"A Canadian."

That puzzled the general. He frowned.

"Don Francisco" he said to me, "Where is the fellow from?"

I explained that Canada was part of the British Empire.

"No matter. Now, listen to me, hombre: I'll give you fifteen days to rebuild those villages—and to make amends for their sufferings with money, also. And you will build them brick houses instead of adobe."

"But, General, this concession was granted by Porfirio Diaz."

"By that rascal, you say?" he bellowed. "Then I don't wonder that you ill-treated them. It is the same with all you foreigners. But what can you expect from a pig but a grunt? Get out of my presence or I will give you a pill of my making."

By goodness, the Indians who heard this speech stared at Dario Pez as though they saw a god. Here was one of their own kind defying the rich and powerful foreigners. That same day four thousand men in the mines offered their service, but he could not equip them and so told them to be patient.

One day there came a courier from Señor Balderrama, who was growing uneasy because we were near another property of his. This courier brought a message full of compliments. Don Carlos stated it was hopeless to express half of his admiration for General Pez and he had been deputized by the governor of the state to offer the general acknowledgment of his rank, command of the military operations in the Northern District, and the sum of one hundred and fifty thousand silver pesos.

But listen to what he put at the end: the sting was in the tail. In case of refusal, said this Balderrama, they would dispatch three thousand men from the capital and speedily finish the general's business.

Dario Pez, sir, liked to send off letters and he dictated to me an answer:

Viper! Do you not then know me? I am the man you persecuted.
I am the man whose sweetheart—poor Rosita—you stole on the eve of our
marriage. Think you such a man forgives?

Your money would be far better employed for the widows and
orphans of your rascals that I will kill. So far as your three thousand are
concerned, I will meet them all and hope to see Balderrama at head of
same. I would enjoy to see your back.

Dario Pez.

After sending this he got into communication with several other leaders operating to the south and an agreement was arrived at for concerted action. Small bands continued to join us and preparations went forward with a speed never dreamed of before in any Mexican army, because Dario Pez, sir, worked like a fiend. He put his shoulders to the wheels of the gun-carriages and wagons; he heartened the loafers with blows and abuse; he kicked the mules and lashed the horses. Never a moment's rest did he give his poor boys—but at the end of thirty days we had two thousand men ready for fighting.

We moved on from there to the rich plantation of El Carmen. And now we were hailed everywhere as the Army of Deliverance. El Carmen is on a railroad north of the capital where Señor Balderrama had a palace and where his daughter's wedding was going to be celebrated. Many lesser jefes reported to Pez at the plantation and a council of war was held.

On the eighth day of September an unexpected blow was delivered that almost destroyed us, sir. While the greater part of our army was getting a bath in the river, a heavy cannonade was opened on our camp and shells began bursting among the bathers, too. A large force of the enemy had treacherously sneaked up behind us by a wide detour.

The confusion was terrible for a few minutes. The soldiers ran in all directions and only for Dario Pez, the Army of Deliverance would have melted away right there. Gathering a few hundred of us he rode to meet the enemy and engaged them with ferocity. That gave our men a chance to recover from their bewilderment and they reorganized and returned.

By three o'clock the enemy was in retreat and two hours later we had captured four hundred prisoners, three hundred horses and several machine-guns. This was in the center. The fight was progressing favorably on the left also, where Ochoa and Carlitos had soundly whipped the scoundrels.

Then here came a train of reinforcements from the city, steaming at full speed. It became necessary to stop that train. Luz Ortiz, sir, she did it. Yes.

When she saw that troop train coming toward us, Lucita did not wait for orders but ran to a siege cannon we had captured and aimed it and fired. Now that train was fully two miles distant and Luz had to point the gun up in the air. Moreover, the poor child knew nothing of artillery except what she had seen the boys do. But mark what happened: the shell hit the cowcatcher of the engine and there was a tremendous explosion. It spread the rails and the train ran off the track. That settled the enemy's business. They piled out and beat it back to the city on foot.

We started closing in on the city. Our grip was tightening. Their artillery opened a bombardment of our positions and directed their fire on a dam we were utilizing. This later proved to be the rascals' undoing, because when they tried to retreat they could not get their wagon trains across it. But by goodness, sir, although we were winning, our army was in a terrible fix. Our ammunition was practically gone. We were down to five cartridges each, which was hardly enough to protect a retreat.

Carlitos and I, we could see nothing but complete rout and disaster. In this terrible emergency Dario Pez went off to a little hill and there he sat down. He began to weep like a child. We had never seen him weep, sir.

"Beloved Ruler of the Universe" he prayed, "If my end is to be here, send it to me. Beloved Mother, do not desert thy son."

Then he jumped up and yelled to all of us who were watching him: "Boys, we have come here to conquer or die. On to the city! Let us make a whirlwind of our foes. Who reaches the place will be lucky. Who dies in the task will be blessed. Forward, boys!"

As we were forming up, the flare of a conflagration appeared against the sky. The enemy were retreating and had set the city on fire. Yes, the prayer of Dario Pez had been heard. How else can you explain it, sir?

This was on the ninth of September and it was the biggest victory we had ever won. The booty consisted of two million dollars' worth of cotton, hundreds of cars of beans, barley and cereals, thirty-eight cannon and a hundred and fifty machine-guns. Also thousands of horses and saddles and blankets. What pleased the general very much was the capture of a huge quantity of medical supplies and surgical instruments; but five thousand rifles they were compelled to abandon escaped our clutches. The perfidious enemy saturated them with kerosene and set them ablaze.

But better than all else, sir, was the capture of Señor Balderrama. The greedy old miser had delayed to hide his wealth and the general himself overtook Don Carlos fleeing on a mule in the wake of the army.

"So, old crow, we meet again!"

Señor Balderrama threw a frightened look at Pez but it was apparent to me that he did not recognize him at all.

"Take him back to his house and keep him prisoner there" the general ordered.

Not many hours afterwards some of our cavalry he had sent to harry the foe's rear returned with booty and prisoners. Among them were the daughter of Don Carlos and her intended husband. As soon as he learned their identity, Dario Pez sent for the prisoners to be brought before him at headquarters.

"What is it now?" Balderrama inquired. "Do you seek the life of my children as well as my own?"

"Not at all, Señor Don Carlos" answered Dario Pez in a sort of cat's purr he used when most dangerous, sir. "Not at all. But I am now cacique here—and the derecho de pernada is mine."

By goodness, everybody was amazed and scandalized when they heard that. The beautiful daughter of Señor Balderrama screamed and her intended husband made a jump at the general, but the soldiers pushed him back and held him. And then Luz Ortiz pushed through from the back of the room.

"No, Dario" she said, "You shall not do this great wrong."

The general flew into a terrific rage.

"And why not?" he bellowed. "Tell me that. Why should I not visit on this viper the evil he did to me?"

Everybody there trembled before his rage because Dario Pez was like a madman when angered—Death stood at his elbow in such moments. But Lucita was not scared at all. It is my belief, sir, that few wives are afraid of their husbands.

She looked him straight in the eye and said: "Because, general, the innocent would suffer with the guilty. Do what you will with Balderrama, but his daughter has done you no harm. Therefore you must permit her to go—her and her sweetheart. And that she may do so in safety, you will also send an escort and provide them with what money and necessaries they will require on the way. What would the world say if the commander of the Army of Deliverance were to act now like an ignorant savage?"

By goodness, what do you know about that! We all turned pale when we saw the veins in the general's neck start to swell up and his eyes to roll. Then suddenly he gulped as though swallowing a pill, and when he spoke again his manner was calm.

"You are right, Lucita" he replied in a hoarse tone and he nodded at her. "I am not a savage, and the world must learn that Justice guides us. Don Francisco, you will detail an escort of twenty men for this lady and gentleman and send them safely on their way. In addition you will fill their carriage with food and whatever personal possessions they desire to take. Should they desire money, Señor Balderrama will give it to them."

The fiancé attempted to thank him.

"Get out of my presence" thundered Dario Pez, "Get out before I repent and give you a pill of my making."

I tell you those two beat it from there! As for Don Carlos, I hurried him away immediately lest the general take it into his head to string him up on the

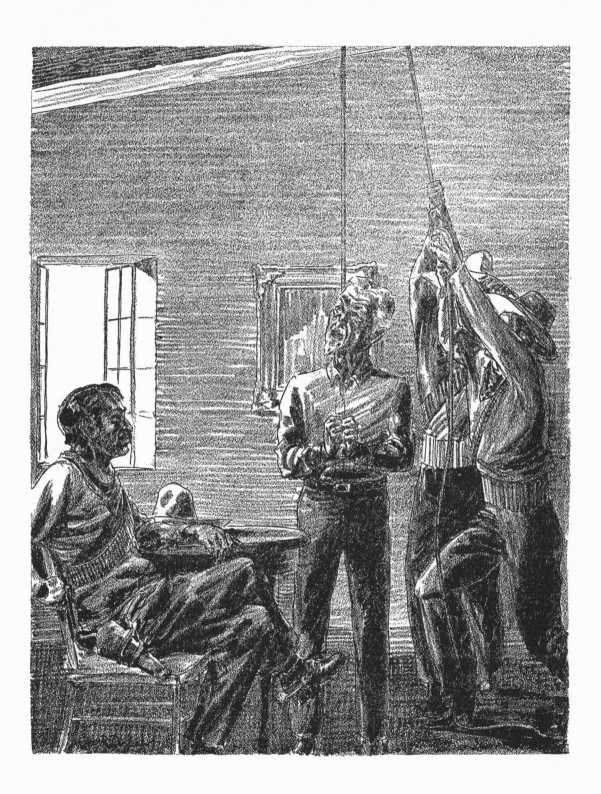

spot.

Dario Pez evidently pondered this affair during the night, sir, and hit upon a plan to get even, because he sent a trusted agent next morning to Balderrama's palace demanding a loan to the Cause of one hundred thousand pesos. Don Carlos flatly declined to hand over any such sum.

Back went the agent again, and this time with a request for two hundred thousand pesos. The second application received the same answer, yet the general kept his patience, which surprised us all. On the third visit the demand was for three hundred thousand pesos and in case of refusal, the messenger had orders to bestow on Don Carlos five strokes with the back of a sabre every ten minutes until he complied.

These instructions were carried out, yet still Don Carlos declined to part with his money. He was exceedingly stubborn, this Balderrama, and after a while the officer returned to report that the punishment would not produce the desired result and seemed likely to culminate in the death of the prisoner.

"Go back to him tomorrow" Dario Pez said, "And ask him for a loan of four hundred thousand pesos, hombre."

It was done. The officer appeared at the home of Señor Balderrama and delivered the general's message, but perceiving that the man with the sabre did not accompany him, Don Carlos firmly declined.

Such ungrateful conduct finally angered Dario Pez, sir. He determined to break his enemy's resistance at any cost and himself went to the house. The two stared at each other a long while. The prisoner's head and hands trembled, but he stared right back at the general.

"I have come, viper" said Dario Pez "to secure a loan of one million pesos for the cause of justice."

"It is absurd. I haven't a cent. I am a man of no wealth."

"Very well, señor—very well. But I cannot go away empty-handed. As you haven't a cent, it is only fair to give you the opportunity of working a miracle."

At a sign from him the soldiers threw a rope over a big beam in the ceiling. The loop was placed around the neck of Señor Balderrama and Dario Pez gave the word to hoist him off the floor. Don Carlos let out a terrible shriek. They lowered him, but still that stubborn old man would not surrender. With his very first breath he cursed the general. Dario Pez did not regard this as a friendly sign and a second lift upward was given the prisoner. That was enough. Don Carlos became reasonable.

"Wait!" he begged. "Wait just a minute. Possibly I could put my hands on a hundred thousand pesos if you turned me loose."

"A million."

"I haven't got it."

"Up with him again, boys."

Before the command could be carried out, Señor Balderrama screamed: "Don't, sir! Don't do it! It may be that I could raise two hundred thousand."

"Not a centavo less than a million."

"But where could I find so much money, general?"

That was a question Dario Pez was not disposed to trouble his head about, sir.

"Finish the miracle. You have started very well indeed. Get the loop ready again, boys."

They were on the point of stringing him up again to the beam when Don Carlos burst out with, "One second, please! Would five hundred thousand pesos suffice for your army?"

Satisfied that he was on the right track, the general shouted "On the job, boys!" The squad heaved on the rope and hoisted Don Carlos from the floor. But he could no longer withstand the ordeal. He signaled that he was ready to give in and they let him down.

Well, when they gave him air Señor Balderrama revealed the hiding place of a treasure he possessed. The miracle was performed. And was it not a beauty, sir? The treasure amounted to four hundred and eighty-five thousand dollars in five and ten dollar gold pieces and was hidden in a hollow column in the Banco Minero. Don Carlos had feared the greed of his friends as much as his enemies.

We took a blacksmith to the bank to open the column. He did his job quickly but when the yellow hoard poured out he was seized with panic and ran off, leaving his tools on the floor. That blacksmith did not even return to get his pay. Perhaps he was scared at knowing a secret that might prove dangerous—or it might have been superstition. The natives have a saying that gold pieces are the coined tears of the poor.

"And now" said Dario Pez "we will send Señor Balderrama to jail. He has not yet expiated the crime he committed against me."

When news of what he had done spread throughout the city, Dario Pez received the adulation of the inhabitants. They crowded to his headquarters to flatter and sing his praises. Some presented requests for favors. Others importuned him for the pardon of relatives caught with arms.

Women were always at his door, waiting for sight of the hero so that they might kiss his hand and ask for aid. Their numbers were so great that they filled the street to the corner and those who had to wait long for their turn squatted on the sidewalk against the wall.

I was always at his elbow while this line of females passed through the room. The general listened to them all. He was very quick to separate the wheat from the chaff and he righted many wrongs, sir.

One morning there appeared in the doorway an enormous fat woman. She had on a black cotton dress made all of one piece, with a string around her middle. By goodness, that was the only way you could tell where her waist was, sir! Moreover she was barefoot and had a shawl over her head. A ragged little boy clung to her skirt and there was a baby in her arms.

I have seen Dario Pez in battle and in situations that would daunt the boldest heart, and never once did he flinch. Yet now he turned a peculiar greenish color and looked scared half to death.

"General!" cried this creature in a booming voice.

"Rosita" he stammered.

"Yes, Dario—at last" she responded with a ludicrous simper and waddled toward his table. The niñito toddled after her.

Dario Pez, he cast down his eyes and rubbed his hands together with a discomfort.

"So! It is long since we met, Rosita—and many things have happened. Great changes, Rosita."

"Alas, it is true" she said, sighing like a bellows.

"I take it that you are married?"

"Of course, Excellency. But my husband is dead."

Dario Pez remarked: "You must not repine for him, Rosita. God knows what is best." Then he cast a glance of disapproval at the brat beside her. "The niñito, Rosita, he is very dirty."

"La cascara guarda al palo" she answered, making the usual excuse that the bark preserves the wood. It was evident to me, sir, that the lady was disappointed in her reception.

"To think, general, that after all these years—"

"Yes, yes. What can I do for you, Rosita?"

"Do? Why, Excellency!"

Dario Pez turned sharply to me.

"See that the señora has everything she needs, Don Francisco. And give her ten pesos. Adios, Rosita. God have you in His keeping."

Before the bewildered creature could grasp his intention I hustled her out, sir. When I returned, the general was sitting at the table and gazing into the courtyard. He looked very glum.

"And that" he said to me with a bitterness, "is what I've been fighting for all these months. It is the way of life, Don Francisco. Nothing turns out as you expect—neither love nor marriage nor ambition."

And in that moment his great hate of Señor Balderrama died. The next day, indeed, he ordered his release and provided him with an escort.

From the interview with Rosita, sir, Dario Pez went slowly into the court-yard where Luz Ortiz was sewing one of his shirts beside a fountain. His head was bent and he seemed tired. Also, he voluntarily kissed his wife, which surprised her greatly.

"Chula" he said, gazing around him at all the magnificence that was now theirs, "I have given you the palace I promised. Are you satisfied?"

"So long as you are here, Dario."

"Oh, aye" said the general in a weary voice. "But NOW what is there to do? I am very miserable, Chula. For see, my work is done. And I do not enjoy all this plotting and scheming."

"Not done!" cried Lucita, "No, not done, Dario! It is only begun."

"Perhaps you are right" he replied and was silent a while. "Anyhow, Lucita" he added, brightening suddenly, "We can buy a talking machine at last and play They Wouldn't Believe Me all day long."

ROMANCE OF TOMAS DOZAL

Mexican Interlude

Tomás Dozal

Romance of Tomas Dozal

MEXICAN INTERLUDE

I HAVE often heard Americans say that Mexicans are ungrateful lovers who soon grow cold once their love has triumphed, but, by goodness, I will prove to you how a Mexican can love and how generously he remembers the object of his adoration even though years and years have rolled past. Wait, sir, until you hear the story of Tomás Dozal and little Antonia.

This Tomás Dozal was a fine chunk of a man with bowlegs and a squint in one eye which rendered his countenance of a ferocity when angered—a dashing, fiery fellow with rough harsh ways. Moreover, he was possessed of a terrible temper which made him feared by the other young men of the town. But Antonia did not fear him—no.

Antonia was nothing short a child when her mother noticed with much restlessness how often a man of very doubtful behavior walked on front of the house, gazing unceasingly toward a window. Her curiosity demanded an explanation as to whom that devil was promenading on front of the house for and with the instinct of maternal defense she got a heavy short pine club and waited.

The clock of the cathedral was lugubriously stroking ten o'clock when Antonia started to unfasten the rusty and massive irons which barricaded her windows. Tomás, concealed under the shade of a weeping willow near the corner of this shrine, began to advance toward his goal stealthily. He had grasped the hand of his idol and was sighing to express how beautiful that night appeared to him—yes, the hands of the two innocent and unsuspecting lovers were still tightly interlocked, their hearts fluttering with a delightful sensation, their breath held and a heavenly scenery in their minds, when a swift blow on the ribs of Tomás Dozal broke the sepulchral silence.

Taken at the cruel surprise Tomás grunted and broke loose from the fingers he had been so reverently kissing. He intended to run and save his hide, but a contact between his head and the club delayed him. Justly fearing a third aggression this modern Romeo applied to his aid a pair of legs that moved quicker than the needle of a sewing machine and the old woman, disappointed at the now inactivity of her club, abused at the top of her voice the daring interloper who was already fleeing beyond the limits of the city.

This Antonia was very beautiful. She had thick, silky black hair and eyes of a velvety softness which seemed to ask everybody "You like me, do you not? Well?" And they were violet in color. By goodness, violet eyes are nice. Do you not think so, sir?

Her father, Ynez Jiminez, was a steady honest laborer who had placed himself in a rather independent position through hard toil and economy. He was the owner of a carpenter shop and had about fifteen skilled workmen under his eye and he owned a small adobe house with a fruit grove and red roses, nards, jasmines and carnations scenting the air with their perfume of luxury. Also, he had a buggy drawn by a mare as old as her master and a cow which fed in the stable very pleasantly.

Yet in spite of all this, Señor Jiminez was cursed with a wife of much virtue and disagreeably religious and fond of cleanliness, who entertained ambitions not at all in keeping with his own ideas. She had a mad desire to elevate her daughter to a position far above the one they occupied; indeed, she had nothing else in mind but that the girl should ensnare some rich landowner who would give a polish to their name. For these reasons she had no use for Tomás Dozal, who was not a bit the sort of husband she wanted for her sweet wild-flower.

"What if Antonia does have a sweetheart?" demanded her husband displeasingly. "Have you forgotten how young you and I got married?"

"But in the name of Heaven, is there any comparison to be considered between you and that—that—?"

"That what? If Antonia's sweetheart has not come clad in a duck's-tail coat, you are the only one he offends. To you he is just a common pelado, not worthy of consideration. But I don't think the same as you do—no. In accordance with my steady principles none but a hard-sweating workman shall ever take Toñita from this house. So you had best quit your foolishness, woman, and come to bed. Trying to give another course to a stream! If our daughter's heart is conquered you might scratch your head to the extent of digging your brains out, but you could not bring her back to us."

The mother shed tears of mortification, sir, and retorted that this Dozal was nothing short a bum and never held a job, anyhow. So they argued back and forth and did not arrive anywhere; but similar scenes to that which had resulted so disastrously to Tomás' ribs were enacted with frequency because the obstinate fellow would not easily give up the girl who loved him. He came back night after night and the cranky old woman went without sufficient sleep to wait in ambush.

Perceiving at last that she could not change the course of a stream, Señora Jimínez thought up a devilish scheme to make trouble between the lovers: she determined to encourage the advances of one, Miguel Gonzales, whose father owned a great plantation not far from the city.

"He is a moustached woman and a fool" the shy young creature declared. "He makes me sick the way he looks at himself in the store windows all the time."

"But his father owns El Fresno and a palace in Durango."

"I'm not thinking of marrying the father."

Nevertheless she was flattered by the attentions of young Gonzales merely because they made the other girls jealous. So whenever Miguel appeared outside on front of the house, she rewarded him with a smile or perhaps a motion of the hand from a window. And Gonzales strutted up and down, sticking out his chest and thinking what a havoc of love he was working up in Antonia's heart. What do you know about that!

"Who is the hombre I saw promenading on front of your house last night?" Tomás demanded.

"Oh, just a cousin of mine."

"Huh!—these cousins! He had best take his walks in another part of the city, else there will be a vacancy in your family, girl."

Antonia was well pleased and laughed, sir, but she had to stroke his chin and look at him with a very lovely expression before she could coax Tomás back to good-humor. And the very next night an unfortunate thing happened. As Dozal was hiding in the corner of a ruined wall, watching the window of his girl with the intent and anxious gaze of love, who should come strolling along but this Miguel Gonzales. He was dressel like a stiffneck and smelled very sweet because of the plentiful perfume he had sprinkled over himself. Tomás sniffed and then gritted his teeth.

"Aha!" he muttered. "What is that wretch of a cousin doing there?"

It soon became apparent what Miguel was doing. He promenaded past Antonia's window several times and just as it grew dusk he began to sing. Toñita, poor child, being unaware that Tomás was lurking near like an evil spirit bent on destruction—you see, sir, the treacherous scoundrel had told her he was going away into the country for a few days to gather some goats—the unsuspecting Antonia opened her window ever so little and let drop a flower.

125

All that Dozal could discern was her slender white hand and the window closed again immediately.

Gonzales was transported with delight and ran to pick up the flower, and in that moment Tomás Dozal leaped from the gloom like a mountain lion right upon the back of Miguel. They struggled a moment there under her window, but the scented son of riches was no match for the bowlegged pelado. Tomás wrested a knife from Miguel's grasp and stuck it into his ribs very advantageously. Then he grabbed the flower from the ground and ran. By goodness, yes, he beat it!

Now, Dozal knew that the sword of authority would fall and chop him to pieces. His rival enjoyed privileges accorded to plutocrats exclusively and the judges would do the bidding of his powerful father. Therefore Tomás did not let the grass grow under his feet but traveled as fast as he could out of that city and into the wilds.

He aimed to go into Chihuahua and live the life of an outlaw, near to Nature and our only Maker. Once he saw a bunch of his pursuers ride past while he was hiding under some rocks and another time an old woman from whom he begged a tortilla and some beans told him that soldiers were out searching for a murderer thought to be skulking in that vicinity. But Dozal was a tiger in stealth and daring, sir, and he eluded them.

He penetrated far into Chihuahua. By a fortunate chance he was able to steal a horse from a small rancho and, shortly afterwards falling in with a charcoal burner who was out hunting for a revolution he might join, Tomás felled him by an unexpected onslaught from behind and possessed himself of a rifle and fifty-five cartridges. Being now fully armed and equipped he was sure of obtaining food and shelter wherever he might find himself and he went forward with a stout heart.

General Dario Pez had his headquarters at Tres Hermanos plantation, sir, when this Dozal rode into camp.

"Tell your general" he bellowed to the first soldier he saw, "That a lion of the mountains has arrived to aid him."

We now called Dario Pez El Capitan Encantado, sir—The Enchanted Captain. When Dozal was marched into his presence the general eyed him a moment and gave a big grunt.

"What do you want? You look to me like a tough guy. What're you doing here?"

"I have come to join you" said this Tomás as bold as a lion. "I am here to show this Chihuahua bunch how the men of Durango can fight."

126

Dario Pez, he grunted again. "Listen, hombre—to tell the color of a mule, I've got to have the hairs in my hand. We will soon find out about you. Take charge of him, Don Francisco."

Well, I put Tomás with my command and inside a month he was a sergeant. Whenever any soldier disputed what he said, that son-of-a-gun beat him up. He was a fine worker, too, and it became apparent to all of us that he was cut out for higher things.

Meanwhile Toñita was left desolate. She had heard the scuffle outside of her window but could not guess the cause of it. How could she when the perfidious Dozal had assured her he was going out into the country for a few days? By goodness, what a liar! Her grief was terrible when she learned next morning that her sweetheart was now a fugitive from a justice that cried out for his blood.

Pity poor Toñita, sir, in her hours of remorse and anguish. Yes, she bitterly regretted the girlish impulse that had prompted her to encourage Gonzales whose memory she now hated, because with the instinct of her sex she blamed Miguel for all the trouble in which she had landed herself. Perhaps if he had died, pity might have entered her heart, but the knife glanced off one of his ribs so the luckless fellow suffered nothing worse than a slight wound of which he was well in no time.

Months went by and then on a night The Enchanted Captain swooped upon Mezquital with myself and two thousand men. The garrison was taken by surprise. Many of them were stupefied by the poisonous drink known as sotol and were dancing with their women when they heard our thundering shouts of "Viva Pez!" The wretches rushed pellmell into the streets with their frantic females clinging to them.

Terrible scenes ensued. The night was exceedingly dark and cloudy. A mild wind kissed the blossoms, scattering their fragrance and scents and whispering to the sighing leaves of the trees, indifferent witnesses of the tragedy. By goodness, we drove them headlong before us so that they could not rally. There were no superior officers present to lead them: the commander was in bed with his sweetheart when the alarm sounded and he fled out of the city in his underclothes on a burro. We were in undisputed possession of the town before dawn, with seven hundred prisoners, five cannon and twenty machine guns.

Awakened by the firing and the screams of the neighbors, Antonia jumped out of bed and dressed. Just in time! Hardly had she got her clothes on when here came a big thump on the front door and a harsh voice commanded, "Open up! Open up!"

Toñita shook in her little shoes, sir. What fate lay in store for her behind that frail barrier? She knew well what a captured city had to expect from the outlaws and she trembled expectantly. They call it a fate worse than death. What is your opinion, sir?

The marauder on the outside continued to shout, emphasizing his words by pounding with the butt of a rifle against the wood, so at last Señor Jimínez decided he must admit him.

"What do you want?" he quavered, opening the door about half an inch. "We are peaceful folk here who have never harmed nobody. Only my old wife and myself are in the house, Excellency, and we have nothing worthy of your trouble."

But the soldier was not to be put off in that manner. He stuck his foot inside the door, pushed it wide open and, paying no attention whatsoever to Ynez Jimínez, strode straight toward Antonia's room.

"Hi, wait a minute!" begged the agonized father. "You cannot go in there. Oh, my poor Antonia! She is lost."

His daughter heard him, but she had also heard the footfall of the bold soldier; and suddenly her door was flung back and she stood revealed in the lamplight.

"Tomás!"

"Toñita! Toñita!"

The lovers rushed into each other's arms. They embraced, shedding tears of joy. By goodness, was it not beautiful, sir?

"But how—did—you get here?" panted the lovely girl when she could catch her breath after the so terrible force with which that son-of-a-gun hugged her.

"I have captured the city."

"What? You? Alone? Or are you in command of the army whose shouts I hear?"

"Well, not exactly that" Tomás answered, very slow to admit it. "A man named Pez is the actual general just now. But I am a sergeant and the best fighter in the bunch."

Well, the old man was quite as glad to see Dozal as his daughter could be. It meant protection and safety for his home and he wept as he patted the honest fellow's back the while Toñita caressed him with her nice violet eyes.

"And you will never run away from me again?" she asked with passion.

"Never. We will never part, I and you. I swear it."

Neither she nor her father dreamed of what was in his mind when he uttered these fateful words. However, they learned before the day was out. At

128

noon Dario Pez sent for me and said: "Get together all we can carry with us, Don Francisco. The rascally Murguia is coming up from the south with four thousand seasoned troops and we must beat it quick. This place is easy to take but hard to hold."

Accordingly I took a bunch of picked men and made the rounds of all the shops and residences named in the list the general gave me. We collected a huge amount of booty, consisting of grain and food and merchandise of the better sort. Also jewelry and household things that could be converted into money.

At four o'clock in the afternoon we were all set to go and this Dozal presented himself at the house of Señor Jimínez, leading a sleek gray mule he had appropriated from the stable of the father of Miguel Gonzales. He had been drinking beer and he gazed about him like a jefe.

"Where are you bound?" inquired the Señora Jimínez.

"We leave for the north in an hour."

"But what is to become of me?" Antonia wailed. "You promised we would never be separated again."

Tomás looked at her and answered very importantly: "And I intend to keep my promise. Get ready to go with me. This mule is for you. See how gentle he is and how easy is his gait."

The doting parents were now almost beside themselves. "What? Take her from us? And with the army? You are mad, Dozal. She is only a child. Think what you are doing. Think what danger——"

They made more noise than a bunch of parrots and Tomás bent his brows on them, thereby acquiring a more fiery countenance.

"Peace, old crows. She belongs to me. When I was poor and in distress you repulsed me from this house with beatings and harsh words. And now I come as a conqueror to claim my own. You see before you a man of humble birth and no education, but a man of heart and indomitable will. I will not tolerate to be given orders by no one on earth. What do I care about the dreaded future? Not any! Power! Power shall be mine! Hustle and get your clothes, girl."

This Dozal had certainly drunk too much beer, in my opinion. What is your opinion, sir?

129

"Yes. I will be the factotum of this entire state some day—perhaps of the world some other time. So hear me: Listen to the words of one who is going far from here and may never return, but who bears in his soul truth and honesty. I will take good care of your fair Antonia. She shall be a fine lady when we have swept this scum from the face of the earth. That's the kind of a guy I am."

There stood the weeping mother, wringing her hands as she saw her beloved child about to be torn from her arms—there stood the distressed father, divided between his love and his fears—and there sat Tomás Dozal on his horse, watching them and perspiring comfortably. The spectacle moved him not at all.

"Go get your things, Toñita. I have got to beat it. We leave in a few minutes and this guy Pez does not wait for nobody."

And little Antonia, sir, never hesitated. She ran swiftly to her bedroom and rolled some clothes into a bundle. Then out she came, carrying it and a broken doll in her slim arms.

"What's this?"

"Mine." She turned all red, Toñita did. "Let me keep her. I can never give her up."

The sergeant made no reply but helped her to get up on the mule and then motioned to the father to let go the bridle and get out of the way.

"My child! My child! Give me back my child," shrieked Señora Jimínez.

But that son-of-a-gun paid no attention. He started dragging the mule along by the reins before the weeping parents had half finished caressing their lost lamb. Antonia did not cry out nor forbid it. No: she settled herself in the saddle, tucked the doll in the hollow of one arm and wiped away the tears that were streaking her face.

"Now you are mi jefe, Tomás" she said gaily, yet with a sort of sob in her voice.

"Sure" said the sergeant, swelling up like a rooster. "I'm the boss."

So Antonia went with Dozal and the army and became a camp follower. How is that for devotion, sir? She cooked for Dozal and washed his clothes now and again when they really needed it, and mended them also. And on the march Toñita trudged along with the other women when we were in adversity and did not have railroad trains. She carried all her own belongings and most of this Dozal's too, because no sooner did Dario Pez clap eyes on the mule she rode than he formed the opinion the beast would make an excellent pack animal for ammunition.

The girl did not complain. She soon lost a good deal of her prettiness, what with the hard work and carrying very heavy loads for miles and miles, but the other women were doing it, so why not she?

We had about nine hundred women with our column, for women play an important part in every Mexican campaign. If thrown on his own resources I doubt if the Mexican soldier could get along. We had no commissary, as you understand that word. If the army was in luck, each soldier received some flour and grain when on the march. He was supposed to cook it himself, do his own washing, and rustle his own food in the towns.

So the soldiers bring their women and sweethearts along and they do all this work in order that their men may be of tranquil mind and free for the fighting. Yes, the women are the slum carts and they are also very often the chief means of transportation for supplies. On the march they can shame most men. When an army is about to start for a new camp the women hit straight across country, walking day and night under their loads of bedding and pots and food and children. Often it means a march of thirty miles, but by the time the soldiers get there the fires are going and the frijoles are at the boil.

Sir, our women are always beside us to help. Afoot, over the highest mountains, taking routes where no water can be found—earthen pots on their backs or in their hands, a pan for baking tortillas, a tin of water, bedding and clothes on their heads, children toddling at their heels or clinging to their skirts—they toil along to keep up with their men. Often I have seen one give birth on the march where no medical assistance was possible, and several times in disastrous retreats we have left a broad trail of dead women and horses. Our camp followers are ignorant and dirty—yes—and they fight about their men and pull hair, but by goodness, sir, I salute them!

Now, Toñita was a dandy cook and Tomás received so many compliments on his wife that he grew surly at last and several fights took place, because he was of a mean and selfish nature. But Toñita never gave him cause for jealousy any more: the affair with Miguel Gonzales had taught her a lesson.

It was a brave sight to see Antonia and the other women when General Dario Pez captured some trains and the camp followers were able to travel like grand ladies. We loaded as many as fifty into one freight car but they did not appear to mind a little crowding. When there was not enough room inside, they rode on top. Toñita grew very expert at this. She could sleep peacefully over the roughest roadbed and she rolled off only once. That happened when the train came to a sudden stop at a bridge the treacherous enemy had burned, so she was not left behind. Yet this Dozal reproached her.

"You must be more careful" he said crossly. "If you should fall off and be killed, I would have nobody to cook for me." Toñita promised to take better care.

131

She was very proud of Tomás, because that son-of-a-gun was very plucky, sir. Whenever Dario Pez asked for volunteers to scout out a dangerous position or blow up a house with dynamite under enemy fire, or throw some bombs, up stepped this Dozal.

"I'm the bravest one in the whole bunch, mi general. Let me go."

By reason of his fearless spirit he rose to be a lieutenant and Antonia was the proudest woman in Mexico that night. She had a fight with the wife of Rafael Fraustro because the wife of Rafael Fraustro laughed a nasty laugh when Toñita went by in some brand new clothes Tomás had looted at the capture of a passenger train.

His great specialty was roping machine-guns. You think it cannot be done, sir? Well, Dozal did it, not once but a dozen times.

However, he tried it once too often for his own good. That was in the battle we had with Murguia's forces at the beautiful plantation known as La Loma. The enemy held the church and had sharpshooters on the roofs of all the houses, but what caused the most havoc in our attacking column was a machine-gun placed in front of the church. This commanded the street up which we had to advance.

They raked us cruelly with this weapon and we were driven back to take shelter. Every attack we attempted was instantly broken up so that Dario Pez flew into a wild rage and yelled: "What? Must I lead you myself? Come on, then. Follow me."

At that moment Tomás Dozal spurred forward and saluted.

"I myself will put that gun out of business" he yelled at the top of his lungs.

"Good. Here's a man of my own kidney. How many men will you need for the job?"

This Dozal laughed and said: "Keep your toy soldiers, General. I can do this trifling job myself."

"Is the man crazy?" asked Dario Pez. "Now I am more than ever convinced that this hombre uses marihuana."

"See for yourself."

Tomás, he dashed off, coiling his fifty-foot rawhide. We lost sight of him for a few minutes and some of the officers began to laugh, thinking it was all a big bluff, but by goodness they soon had to laugh on the other side of their mouths for suddenly Tomás darted out of the lane beside the church and into the square where the machine gun was.

"Viva Pez! Viva Dozal!" he shouted, his rope circling his head in wide loops.

Whish! The rope sped toward the machine-gun and fell fairly over it. Then that son-of-a-gun dug the spurs into his horse and dragged that weapon clean

away from the rascals who were operating it. A rain of rifle bullets greeted him and the next thing we knew Dozal was down. He was down on the ground with his horse heaving and lashing out in the death agony.

I looked toward Dario Pez, who seemed to be measuring the distance between our forces and the church, but as he hesitated a woman ran out of the lane from which Tomás had himself emerged and sped to where he lay. Her hair was down and streamed in the breeze. Yes, it was Antonia.

Not a glance did she give to the enemy soldiers sweatily reloading their rifles at the church door and fumbling in their haste, not a thought for the sharp-shooters on the roofs, whose weapons were crackling from every side. Probably Antonia did not even see the spurts of dust that flew up all around her as she ran. All her eyes beheld was the still form of her man there under his horse. She reached the spot at last and threw herself on top of him, offering her young body against the enemy bullets. And the dear God reached out His hand to turn them aside, sir. How else could Toñita have escaped without a scratch?

Now mark what happened. The instant Dario Pez espied the girl his face lighted up and he gripped the mane of his horse.

"Charge! Conquer or die, boys! Let's make a whirlpool of brothers and enemies."

By goodness, we did it! We fell upon those devils and scattered them like chaff. We killed over one hundred of same. Then The Enchanted Captain came riding back to where Antonia knelt beside her lover.

"Are you hurt?"

"Oh, no, Excellency. But Tomás is dead. Oh, he is dead!"

"Nonsense. Do not talk foolishness, child. They could not kill Dozal. The beloved Ruler of the Universe takes care of fools. Besides, a pretty girl like you should not spoil her eyes by weeping. There're just as good men left alive."

He spoke no more than the truth, sir, still I think that the general erred in mentioning the fact. However, Antonia did not resent his words. She paid no further attention to Dario Pez but continued to stanch Dozal's wounds with a piece of cloth from her waist.

And Tomás did not die in the least. He had been hit in five places but none of them was fatal, and such was the strength of that pelado he was on the road to recovery within a month.

For this feat the general promoted him to be a colonel and gave him a separate command of six hundred men and the town of Saucito and all the surrounding region. Then Dario Pez moved on with his army to more important things. So Dozal was now a jefe and lorded it over miles of country.

But the change in his circumstances wrought only evil, sir, as is so frequently the case. The majority of men behave respectably when poor and humble because they cannot well do otherwise, but the mettle of a man is tested when riches and power are given into his hands.

Control of a big population seemed to turn the head of Tomás. Surely it must have been that, because common gratitude should have bound him to Dario Pez who had raised him from the dust to the heights. Rumors reached us that he was conspiring to seize leadership from the general. At first Dario Pez just laughed and paid no attention, then one day he sent for me and ordered me to report to Colonel Dozal for duty. You discern his intention, sir? He wanted to keep an eye on that hombre.

On arrival at Saucito I found that Tomás was very popular with his men because he fed them well and paid them when he could find the money. Now, it was the unfortunate custom among Mexican officers to appropriate a considerable portion of the soldiers' pay for their own use and the result was disaffection and disloyalty. Often, right in the midst of a battle, I have seen a whole command desert the Federal flag to ally themselves with us.

But this Dozal knew human nature. He would say to his soldiers: "Let it be realized for once and always that for the striving bunch there will always be plenty of dough. Never forget, muchachitos, to observe the everlasting practice of the wise—namely, to provide for themselves with their neighbors' belongings."

However, relations between him and Antonia were becoming very strained. The colonel was rightfully ambitious to have a son to whom he might pass along the possessions he was rapidly accumulating, but Antonia presented him with no children whatsoever, sir. Being of a surely temperament, Dozal did not hesitate to reproach her on this point and many unpleasant scenes took place.

Also, Toñita was extremely jealous. Her own beauty faded fast, which is a misfortune that overtakes women of her class at an early age, and it was inevitable that Tomás should find temptation in his path now that he was undisputed lord of the countryside.

Barely a year had elapsed since his promotion to a separate command when he gave a ball in the big white house which served as his headquarters. To this were invited all the people of consequence. And guess who this affair was in honor of? Not Toñita—no—but the Señora Rosa Ruiz.

This Señora Rosa was the widow of a rich plantation owner who had bequeathed her vast estates in those parts, stocked with cattle and fruit orchards and fine barns. She was very beautiful and ambitious beyond telling, so she set about ensnaring the affections of the powerful Colonel Dozal. The presence of Antonia in his house did not deter her in the slightest. You see, sir, owing to the wild and precarious life Tomás had lived with our forces, no ceremony had ever been performed over himself and little Antonia. Therefore it is likely that Señora Ruiz regarded the business as an everyday escapade of a dashing soldier.

Antonia attended the ball in a dandy dress like a fine lady. She had taken care to bathe and make herself nice and clean. Also, she had rubbed glycerin on her face and then rice powder, so that Toñita was far sweeter in her simple costume than the Señora Rosa in all her finery.

Alas, all her coquettish arts accomplished nothing: the infatuated Dozal had no eyes for anybody but the wealthy widow. He danced with her a dozen times, to the neglect of Antonia, and after the ball a dreadful scene took place. There were tears and shrieks and a little harmless knife play which Tomás easily frustrated.

However, it ended in a break between them. So violent did Antonia become that the colonel ordered her from his house and when she would not budge an inch he got on his dignity and said: "Very well. I will go then."

Antonia raised a great outcry after he had gone, but it did not bring Tomás back to her. No: he took up his headquarters at a place forty miles distant and pretty soon Toñita betook her grief to the capital city and dropped out of sight.

It wasn't long before Tomás Dozal repented of his harshness, being prompted thereto in part by the Señora Rosa Ruiz running off with a young bugler who had pretty legs. He tried to find his Toñita, but the capital city was in the hands of the Federals and none of the men there with whom the colonel corresponded could obtain any news of her.

"Keep a close watch and let me know the instant she is located" were his orders.

I do not think that this solicitude was altogether due to repentance or any wish to make amends. By no means. Tomás knew well the temper of his sweet Antonia and wished to keep informed of her whereabouts that he might be on guard against her revenge. What is your opinion, sir?

However, nobody could get any trace of her. Neither did her parents know what had become of their daughter. When Colonel Dozal inquired, they truthfully replied that they assumed she was in her proper place at his side. To this Dozal answered that Antonia had deserted him. By goodness, what a lie!

There the matter rested. Colonel Dozal continued to administer the country under his control to the satisfaction of General Dario Pez and continued to grow in influence and power.

Meanwhile Toñita was bathing dishes and doing laundry work for the wife of a telegraph operator in the capital city, who had given her a job on sight. To this excellent creature she confided her story and the two would sit together of nights and scheme how they might bring the terrible Dozal to his knees and accomplish the downfall and humiliation of the wicked Señora Ruiz.

In this fashion two years passed. Then this fellow Dozal won so great a victory near Canatlan that the enemy became completely demoralized and resolved to evacuate the capital city itself. When the people heard of it, some rejoiced and others fell into a frenzy of fear. The telegrapher, being in the employ of the government, very naturally expected no mercy and was for fleeing with his family immediately, it did not matter where.

Then Antonia spoke up: "No, you must stay. They will not harm you. Remain here and I will answer for your safety. I swear it."

You may well believe that the telegrapher placed no faith whatsoever in such assurance, sir, but his wife persuaded him and they stayed.

"All right" he grumbled, "But you keep your snout out of this affair of General Dozal, woman. He is a tough guy and if he should catch me mixing up in his business, he would maybe cut off my ears as a warning not to listen to idle talk."

The next morning the army of General Dozal entered the city amid tumult and rejoicing. A proud man that day was Tomás, full of importance and gin.

When we had organized the place, Dozal ordered me to admit those who wished an audience to present their petitions, because it was his policy to listen to all, no matter how humble. In this he had taken a leaf from the book of Dario Pez.

You may well suppose who headed the line of applicants for his favors. Yes—none other than Antonia. By goodness, I was glad to see her again, yet I considered it unwise for her to approach the general without a little preparation. The truth is, when I saw the poor appearance Toñita made, it occurred to me that Dozal's feelings might have to be worked on through other channels than tender memories.

I regret to say, sir, that Antonia had taken on bushels of fat and was no longer the ravishing creature whose freshness and vivacity had charmed all who frequented Colonel Dozal's house in Saucito. No amount of glycerin and rice powder could conceal the ravages of her years of hard work. Moreover, poverty compelled her to wear a loose, sacklike cotton dress devoid of waistline, and a large, cheap black shawl. Consequently I determined to employ diplomacy in advancing her cause.

Among the applicants for an interview with the general was a young woman

137

who had a complaint to lodge against a member of his staff. She claimed to be the abandoned wife of Captain Urbina and she wanted redress in the form of provision for herself and child.

"What?" roared Tomás when he heard her story. "He would treat a woman in this fashion? Send for the captain at once, Don Francisco, and if what the poor creature says be true, I will give that bastard a pill of my making."

I ran like an antelope to execute his orders.

"Captain Urbina" said the general sternly, "Have you ever seen this lady before?"

The captain looked and turned a greenish yellow color, sir.

"She is nothing to me, Excellency. I swear it. When I was sick, she deserted me."

Dozal transfixed him with a dreadful glance. "Will you answer me this, hombre? Have you ever seen any animal deny his own blood? Will you answer me that?"

"Why—that is a surprising question—I don't know what you mean, mi general."

"Answer without evasion! Have you ever seen an animal deny its blood?"

"Well, Excellency—but——"

"There is no 'but'. Isn't that your child?" And at a sign from him the unfortunate mother drew back her shawl, revealing a baby. By goodness, it surprised this Urbina.

"Mi general, I have been calumniated! Hear me, I beg."

"Silence, you big son-of-a-bitch, you!—who have the outward appearance of a civilized man yet are lower than any animal. You have denied your own blood. Wretch, I am going to have you shot."

"But, Excellency, I will make amends."

"Don't waste your breath. But first tell me, viper—are you not the father of that child? Why do you try to deny it?" thundered the general. "Look at his ears."

We all did so. Sure enough, the boy's ears stuck out exactly like the captain's. This Urbina turned ghastly pale. He was plucky, but he saw death staring at him from Dozal's eyes.

"Don Francisco, make the necessary arrangements. Captain Urbina is about to go on a long journey."

This was the moment I judged it opportune to intervene and I whispered discreetly in the general's ear. At first he listened reluctantly, saying "What's that? What's that? You forget yourself, Don Francisco." But after a while he

138

began to twist in his chair and grumbled: "Oh, all right—all right. Have it your own way. Go fetch a priest and let all the bells be rung. We will have a wedding instead of an execution. Now get out of my sight, you!"

You may be sure the captain needed no further urging. He beat it from there as fast as his legs would carry him, with his new-found wife at his heels.

"And now" said Tomás Dozal with the complacence of a man who has performed a meritorious act, "Show the next one in, Don Francisco."

Never shall I forget the general's face when he recognized that next one. Mostly he looked very foolish, but suspicious too, for he discerned a trap.

"Aha, so it is you, Antonia" he said at last with an attempt at lightness. "And where have you been all this while? I have hunted for your everywhere. It seems to me you have treated me very badly."

Antonia tried to say something, but the words would not come. At sight of her old lover she forgot the carefully prepared speech she had rehearsed so often with the telegrapher's wife and could do nothing but stare at the magnificent soldier. The contrast between them was painfully marked, sir. Tomás was attired in a gorgeous uniform with all the insignia of his rank, and the habit of authority had grown so natural to him that it was obvious to the most unobservant that an impassable gulf separated the triumphant rebel chief and the poor peon woman who stood dumbly in front of him, looking just like all the other slatterns who waited outside for a word with the new ruler of the state.

"Excellency" I ventured to murmur, "Knowing your sense of justice and how strongly you feel for all helpless women, the Señora Antonia has dared to appear before you to request that some provision should be made for her out of your munificence, in order that she may live."

It was a bold step to take in view of Dozal's fiery temper, but I calculated that he could not reverse his attitude on top of his treatment of Captain Urbina. Moreover, I wished to provide him an opening to escape the importunate pleas of Antonia, for our conversation had revealed to me that she entertained no less an ambition than to assume her former status with the general.

"So that is it?" exclaimed Tomás Dozal and he took a deep breath of relief. "And what are the poor woman's circumstances, Don Francisco?"

"She is destitute, mi general—dependent on the charity of an excellent creature who is wife to the telegrapher at the railroad station."

"So?" said Dozal displeasingly. "But her parents in Mezquital are comfortably situated? Surely they can provide for their only child, Don Francisco?"

"They are both dead, Excellency. The plague carried them off last winter and every bit of property belonging to Señor Jimínez was seized by the rascally

139

Federals."

The general drummed on the table with his fingers. Antonia did not utter a word—just stared at him like a faithful dog waiting for a word from its master. At last he rose and, advancing to her, took her by the hand and said very gently: "My poor Toñita, you have judged me right. You will see that the heart of Tomás Dozal is ever loyal to those who have loved him. I cannot forget the years when we were all the world to each other and I am going to reward you and make provision for your future."

Antonia clung to his fingers, sir, but before she could formulate the words that were in her heart, the general turned hastily toward me and continued: "Don Francisco, you will escort this lady to a suitable place of residence and then report to me for further orders."

And with that he turned back to the table and I hastened to usher Antonia outside. She wished to remain and continue the audience and I had almost to drag her from the house.

Yes, Tomás Dozal did not forget at the pinnacle of his triumphs the woman who had sacrificed so much for him. By his command she shortly received a responsible post under the city administration, a post which removed her from the fear of want and offered steady employment. Antonia was put in sole charge of the largest and busiest comfort station in the capital, sir.

DRYCHECK CHARLIE

Arkansas Oilfields

Drycheck Charlie

Drycheck Charlie ARKANSAS OILFIELDS

SEVEN men with nineteen diamonds sat in a poker session in a squalid bedroom of a ramshackle hotel far out amid the pine sticks of Arkansas. The game they played is known by many names but they called it Black Annie—a variation of the classic Down the River, two cards buried and five up, with black cards in the hole wild. Six of the men wore shirts ranging from red corduroy to army khaki and every time a player fingered his cards there came an eight-hundred-dollar gleam or a dazzling two-thousand-dollar flash.

Only Drycheck Charlie was devoid of ornament, having hocked his four-carat headlight that afternoon. There was nothing drab about Drycheck, however: he sported a linen collar and a silk shirt with yellow and green stripes. Both had passed through a punishing week, but Charlie felt they sustained his reputation as a dressy man.

They played silently, each player watching the dealer with the intentness of a terrier at a rat hole while jealously holding a paw over his two buried cards.

"Listen, you birds," said Drycheck, after he had been dealt a card, "I'm playin' five hundred behind this stack, see?"

"Put up the money then."

"I'll have to write a check. I ain't got any more cash on me."

The others laughed.

"You'll cash my check, won't you, Abe?" Charlie asked.

Abe replied he'd be damned if he ever seen such gall, especially after he'd given Drycheck four hundred on a phony ring. Perceiving the subject to be unpopular, Charlie dropped it. They played out the hand and were starting another deal when the door opened stealthily and Old Man Tracy shoved his head inside.

"Mimms!" And the head disappeared.

Mimms instantly cashed in and hurried away, leaving the others glancing uneasily at the door. Old Man Tracy was a veteran oil scout who had worked every field opened in the last forty years.

"Shucks," Drycheck snorted, "It ain't nothin'. Tracy's just heard where he can get a bottle of hootch for thirty-five dollars."

"The last bottle I got from Tracy," said Abe, "tested about forty-four degrees Baumé gravity and he soaked me thirty dollars for it. Why, I feed my flivver better stuff'n that at twenty-four and a half cents a gallon!"

Despite this talk, it was plain that Mimms' departure had everybody worried. An oil scout or a lease hound has only to see a couple of men conferring in a corner of a hotel lobby to make sure a new wildcat has been brought in and go scurrying madly over the countryside to buy leases. Old Man Tracy might be only plying his murderous sideline, but again he might have brought some news.

Mr. Rosenfelt was first to quit the game. He yawned and stretched and announced that he had had enough and was going to bed. Hardly had the door closed on him than a third cashed in.

"Hell, let's call it off and get some sleep," Drycheck suggested.

Two minutes later they were trooping downstairs. The lobby was deserted except for a nigger bellboy snoring in a chair close to the gas stove and the floor was littered with old papers and cigar and cigarette butts left by the swarming lobby lice who made the place hum with their trading until past midnight seven days a week.

"Well, adios, fellers," said Drycheck heartily, "Pleasant dreams."

"Good night."

"Good night."

They went out into the street and separated. Not a man of them had the faintest intention of going to bed. Each headed for his car or a place where he thought a car could be obtained. Drycheck did not own an automobile, so he started at a run through the stinging sleet toward a garage.

"Hey, buddy," he shouted, pounding on the office door, "I wanta get a car!"

"Where to?"

"Jenkins Number 2."

"You're locoed, brother. You couldn't make it in a thousand years. Some of them holes are full of mule teams right now."

"Fifty dollars."

"Not for a million! On a night like this?"

"But I just got to get there. Seventy-five!"

"You drag your ass away from here before I smear you, and leave me sleep."

Drycheck turned away and went slopping through the puddles and mud back toward the hotel. In front of it now stood an empty flivver chugging industriously: Charlie could see the driver warming himself at the lobby stove while the fare counted out his money. Without a second's hesitation he hopped into the machine and the roar of the engine drowned the shouts raised behind him.

It took only two minutes to clear town. For a mile beyond, the road was graveled and going was fast, then he dropped off into the blue mud but the flivver never faltered.

"Just because a mule can't make it don't say this ol' mudhen can't," he remarked hopefully and opened the throttle. The mudhen responded with a spurt that sent a pool of water cascading over the hood and windshield.

During the first six miles of his trip Drycheck was never out of low gear except to let the engine cool when the water boiled over. At such times he took a bucket he found in the tonneau and poured in fresh water from the rills running beside the road.

"The guy who owns this ol' mudhen sure knows his business," he remarked approvingly. "A hatchet, a bucket and some balin' wire—shucks, I can go any-wheres with this outfit."

Sometimes the wheels were groping for bottom without the car moving an inch because the rear axle was resting on the ground. Other times Charlie realized there was no bottom to reach and his mudhen simply swam out. He climbed a hill which a truck couldn't have pulled going down, so deep was the thick, clinging mud, and beyond it crossed a brawling stream on a temporary bridge of pine boughs. Off that he dropped sheer a hundred and ninety feet. This is indisputable because Drycheck swore to it himself later and crossed his heart on the statement. He said he kept falling and falling—down, down, down—and finally brung up on a stratum of Annona chalk with the mudhen spittin' and r'arin' to go, so he just held his breath good and fed her plenty gas and she come bustin' out of the mud and clay like a hog out'n a wallow.

He slid off into ditches twice after that, but lifted her out and kept on. And once he wandered off the road into a shallow lake because he couldn't tell which was road and which was lake and come nigh to gettin' lost in the woods, windin' around and around among the trees thataway. And all the while the sleet pelted him, driving straight against his face, and his hands and feet grew numb with the bitter cold.

About twelve miles out he had to cross a bayou in flood over a narrow dam. The footing was slick and treacherous because the dam was of dirt and he hadn't more than a foot to spare on either side. The night was pitch black, his lamps covered with mud. About two-thirds of the way over the car started to slip and Charlie turned her head and made the motor roar in an effort to climb out, but the mudhen slid sideways down into the bayou and expired in three feet of water.

The hood being entirely submerged, Drycheck foresaw there might be difficulty in starting her again and so waded out and continued on foot. The loss of the flivver neither daunted nor worried him. They would find her tomorrow or next day and snake her out; and as for the theft of the machine, hadn't he once hauled off all the tools and rig from a well on which work had been stopped owing to the cold when the driller was on a spree in town?

Now up to his knees in mire, now making a detour through the flooded woods, he kept on. An hour before daylight he arrived at the Jenkins Number 2 in a small valley in the heart of the pinewood hills, where a hairy person rose up with a double-barreled shotgun and told Drycheck to get the hell back where he come from and be damned quick about it, too.

"I gotta have a look! We done heard in town tonight you'd brought her in."

"You stick your nose any closer," the guard warned him, "and I'll blow your guts out for you."

Charlie laughed wearily and sat down on a log.

"Listen, Ol' Timer," he said, biting off a slab of plug, "I've had a helluva time gettin' here and I don't much care if I never get back. So shoot. But I gotta see that well."

His earnestness impressed the guard and after a long inspection of Drycheck by the light of a lantern he assured him it was a false alarm and they weren't down more'n eight hundred feet. Charlie jeered at that and offered to bet him five bucks he was wrong. To win this bet he permitted Charlie to look for himself. The sluice pit revealed to the latter's experienced eye that the guard spoke the truth.

"All right, buddy," said Drycheck, "I reckon I took the wrong trail. And if those other birds've struck a gusher they're welcome to it—all I want is some sleep."

"Go down to the bunk house," the pacified guard told him. "Yonder it is— you'll have to jump that crick though. Maybe you can horn in with the rough-necks."

"What's worrin' me now is how I'm goin' to get back to town. My car's stalled back in that ol' bayou."

The guard opined that this difficulty would be easy, for it was like there'd be a dozen scouts out in the morning. So they parted on good terms and Charlie went to sleep.

When the driller woke he cussed the guard and was for throwing Drycheck out on his ear, but fearful of what an enemy might do to his well he let him sleep. One of the roughnecks gave him some dinner when he finally crawled out.

Not a man in the poker party got anything out of the night's work except pneumonia. The report Old Man Tracy brought to Mimms turned out to be

146

mere rumor: yet it still persisted next afternoon although the new well had not been located by any of the scouts, and when Charlie returned to town in a lease-hound's flivver he found brisk trading in acreage. More than forty thousand dollars' worth of leases changed hands in two hours at prices ranging from five dollars an acre to two hundred for close-in stuff.

That's the way they do business in an oil field boom. Speculators turn loose hundreds of thousands of dollars in a single evening, with only a blue print for guide, on the strength of a fairy story a newspaper reporter would hoot at as a joke.

Drycheck loafed in a pool hall where they were working up a market for some condemned stuff by means of wash sales, and there finally ran across Abe Rosenfelt. The two mingled with the crowd until the supper hour, bidding when there was no prospect of a purchase or offering for sale a stock they did not own at a figure they knew would be prohibitive.

"Say, Abe, I gotta scheme. You own any acreage?" said Charlie as they sat down to table in the Mecca.

"Uh-uh—and no money neither."

"How come? You had thirty-four thousand dollars last month."

"Sure I did. But I dropped it in Othello. When Number 3 come in a gusher I shot the whole roll and you know what happened."

"It was a plenty," assented Drycheck sadly. "I've saw enough salt water out there to make me sore on the ocean, ain't you?"

"What I aim to buy in future," Abe replied, "is condemned acreage. What's the good of sinkin' money in a well? If it's a real well I can't afford that high-priced stuff. No, sir. But if she's a duster I'll buy all the leases I can lay my hands on, Charlie. Look what I done up in New York with Happy Days. The minute they started pullin' the pipe from the second dry hole, I jumped in and bought all the acreage they had at fifty cents an acre and then I hit for New York and sold it like hot cakes. Cleared thirty-four thousand, that's all!"

"I know. I reckon there's more suckers in Wall Street than in the whole Sabine River."

Drycheck was mighty thoughtful during the rest of the evening, which they spent in hanging about the pool rooms.

"What ails you, anyhow?" Abe inquired.

"I'm just studyin'."

Early next morning Charlie hied him to a garage and rented a car for the day. While waiting for it to be filled with oil and gasoline and water he gave sympathetic ear to a driver who had a hard-luck story about a dirty skunk who had snaked his flivver from right under his eye at the hotel and later abandoned it in

Wildcat Bayou.

"If ever I meet up with that bastard" said the driver, "It'll jar his kinfolk in Oklahoma."

"I don't blame you. It's gettin' terrible in this town—looks like a feller with gold fillin's dassent go to sleep with his mouth open nowadays."

Drycheck drove ten miles out into the country. He had no special destination. One place would do as well as another for his purpose, provided it was sufficiently far from any drilling to make leases cheap. Deep amid the pine woods he stopped to fill the radiator and a flathead belonging to a gang engaged in felling trees hailed him. The flathead wanted a chew. From him Charlie learned that a thousand acres of this timberland belonged to a Frenchie by the name of Laferrière.

"They call him Cayuse."

"Why?"

"What do they call a mule a mule for?" retorted the flathead, and on reflection Drycheck perceived the logic of this argument.

He found Cayuse in a flimsy frame shack of two rooms on top of a knoll. The old man was taking a nip of homemade corn whisky when he knocked at the door and hid the bottle before responding. Bleary-eyed and with matted hair and beard he was an unlovely object, but Charlie speedily discovered that he had cut his wisdom teeth early in life.

"Five dollars an acre? Why, I can buy all I want around here for fifty cents. Your land's nine miles from the nearest producing well."

"There's oil on this place," Cayuse declared.

"How do you know?"

"A lady done told me I'd strike it."

The oil speculator does not live who won't fall for a fortune teller, but Drycheck contrived to laugh.

"Shucks! If a fortune teller told you you was goin' to be hung, would you believe her?"

"I'd be right oneasy."

They dickered a while and at last Charlie said: "Well, I'll tell you what I'll do. I'll take a look round your land and see for myself. I'm some pebble-pup on my own account, and if there's oil near here I reckon I'll locate it. She said the northwest corner, didn't she? Fine! I'll just go over it with my finder."

The following three days he spent in carefully stepping off the entire northwest corner of Cayuse's property. Jealously cupped in both hands he held a small metal instrument on which he kept his gaze. Drycheck would stop and eye this mysterious contrivance from time to time, shaking his head and betraying an excitement he could not repress. Once he stopped and seemed to be muttering an incantation. His face grew red, he clasped his forehead convulsively. These signs were not lost on Cayuse, who trailed him every minute.

"What did I tell you?" he demanded excitedly.

"It's wonderful—wonderful! How she knowed beats me, but there's a pool here. I can feel it. Mr. Laferrière, you're a rich man. A millionaire and then some. Now I'd like to see the rest of your land."

This inspection did not take long. Evidently the other acreage in the tract failed to show the symptoms he was seeking, because Charlie walked faster and faster, occasionally shaking his tiny instrument and giving vent to exclamations of disappointment. Cayuse never took his eyes off him.

"How many acres in that northwest corner, did you say?"

"A hundred and forty."

"All right. I'll take it—five dollars an acre."

"It *was* five. It's fifty now."

A long and bitter argument followed, Dry-check calling Cayuse every name he could think of that wasn't a fighting word. However, it ended in his yielding.

"Oh, hell, all right—it's out and out robbery but I'll give you fifty dollars an acre for this north-west corner and one-eighth royalty."

"And you'll put down a well?"

"I said I would, didn't I?"

They went back to the shack and there Charlie filled in a lease form, B-P, and wrote out a check on his bank for seven thousand dollars. It was more money than Cayuse had ever dreamed about in his life. He signed and the deal was closed.

"Better put it in quick," suggested Charlie, laughing.

That seemed to reassure Cayuse. He answered: "I'll go to town soon, but I reckon this paper's good."

At that precise moment Drycheck had a dollar and eighty cents in the bank and four hundred and fifty in his pockets. An oil speculator of his type is wary of bank accounts: a bank account can give lots of trouble, what with garnishees and other devices employed by soreheads.

"Well, now that it's all over," said Charlie, tilting his chair comfortably as he rolled a cigarette, "I don't mind telling you somethin'. I got a confession to make. I didn't buy this land for myself: I'm chief scout for the Toro Comp'ny."

Old Cayuse cackled and slapped his leg.

"I knowed it. I knowed all along you didn't want that for yourself, or you'd never have paid me my price."

"Listen," Drycheck continued, placing a hand on the old man's knee. "I gotta proposition to make. You'll admit I've done right by you, won't you?"

"I ain't complainin'."

"Well, then, why not give me a chance to make a li'l' piece of money for myself?"

Sensing a touch for a commission, Cayuse became aloof.

"What I ask of you is very simple, Mr. Cayuse. I won't make a nickel out of this deal except my pay, so I'd kinda like to pick up some acreage on my own account. Why not sell me the balance of your land here? It ain't good for nothin'. The pool's in the northwest corner, like I outlined."

"Then what do you want it for?"

"Well, I thought maybe I could find some sucker who'd pay me a li'l profit on it after this northwest corner come in."

As this was in line with what Cayuse himself would have done under the same circumstances, he felt a friendly respect for the lease hound's shrewdness.

"What'll you pay me?"

"Aw, shucks! Why not throw it in with the other, Cayuse? There's been a dry hole on it already. You know as well as I do it ain't worth a nickel."

"Maybe it ain't and maybe it is. Anyhow, it'll be worth somethin' to you. I want fifty cents an acre for that land."

They disputed a while over this price, but again Drycheck gave in. He made out a lease on eight hundred acres for a cash consideration of four hundred dollars and the usual one-eighth royalty. No other consideration was mentioned and there was no reference in the lease to the first transaction.

"I'll just pay this in cash," remarked Charlie. "I got that much on me."

"Suit yourself. I never refuse real money," Cayuse chuckled and he felt so good over the day's work that he invited his guest to a drink.

Of course Charlie's check was turned down at the bank next day and Cayuse went looking for him.

"The comp'ny throwed me down," Drycheck told him. "They said I'd been done and they wouldn't pay the price."

"You've got to pay it. You got the lease and I got your check," shrilled the old man.

"And you still got your land, too, ain't you? If I don't cover that check, then the lease is dead and you can sell it to somebody else."

"But you've got a lease on eight hundred acres of my land too. I'd have asked

150

five dollars an acre for it only for this other deal."

Charlie surveyed him tranquilly.

"I can't help that," he said, "They was separate transactions."

And so they proved to be when Cayuse consulted a lawyer. A couple of days later he filled up on white whisky, saddled a mule and rode to town again. Meeting Charlie on the street Cayuse attacked him with a knife, yelling that he'd whittle him down to his size. Before they could pry the old man loose he had carved Drycheck in half a dozen places.

The younger man refrained from pulling his gun. Any time Charlie killed a man he wanted to be in a locality where the victim's friends did not make up the jury panel. It took a doctor a couple of hours to sew Drycheck together and he retired from the marts of trade for a week to give his wounds a chance to heal.

While visiting his injured friend, Abe Rosenfelt learned something of the events leading up to the ruckus.

"What," he said, "do you aim to do with that wildcat stuff, Charlie? Tain't no good. It's been condemned twice."

"I'm fixing to organize a comp'ny and drill a well."

The other scrutinized him silently for a minute. "I see," he said. "Let me in on it, Charlie. How much capital stock'll there be?"

"I calculated to organize a twenty-thousand dollar comp'ny."

"With eight hundred acres?" cried Abe in horror. "You're nothin' but a busher, Charlie, and won't never be nothin' but a busher! Why, all that acreage is good for a coupla hundred thousand easy. Let's make it a hundred thousand at the lowest."

"All right, fix it to suit yourself. But how'll we raise the dough to drill?"

Abe flapped his hands scornfully.

"That's easy. I know the very bird we want. But we'll have to put up a few hundred in advance and let him in on the clean-up."

"Fair enough," Charlie said and the bargain was struck.

They decided to name the company the Roosevelt Oil and Gas Company, after Abe. To be sure, his name was Rosenfelt but he said he would change it for the good of the project and if any investors were misled, Abe and Charlie could not be blamed.

"Nothin' illegal, mind!" was the former's parting caution to his partner. "I'm not goin' to get in bad when there's so many ways of makin' money without."

"You never had to bail me out, did you? No, and nobody else did neither."

The driller to whom they put their proposition came down to cases at once.

"It'll cost pretty near as much to fake as it would to drill. I got to pay my crew, ain't I? If you can get the derrick, like you say, then the main expense'll be the pipe. And Abe can rustle that—or steal it. A few hundred feet'll do."

"How much?—your lowest figure."

The driller figured on an envelope a few minutes and then announced that six thousand dollars would be the very least they could get along with.

"Zowie! Why not say six million?" cried Mr. Rosenfelt.

"Because I know you've got six thousand. Yes, you have too. No use bellerin' because I know it." And when Abe hooted at the very idea and denied it with profane heat, the driller sprang a surprise by naming the exact total of his bank balance. Driven into a corner, Abe finally agreed to lend the new company six thousand dollars at ten per cent, taking a mortgage on all its assets as security.

"Well," the driller said, "That's settled. And we split three ways."

"It's a holdup!" Drycheck bellowed, looking as though he could cheerfully strangle him.

"It's that or no dice."

So they signed.

The trio decided on a location as far removed from Cayuse's shack as the limits of the property would permit, and a derrick one hundred and twelve feet high went up in short order. The old man was for running them off with a shot-gun, but in the course of an afternoon's persuasion the three of them managed to make him see the immense value a well would be to his property.

"You got everything to gain by lettin' us go ahead, Mister Cayuse," Abe argued, "and everything to lose if you don't." And Laferrière sullenly withdrew.

The driller had a crew of five roughnecks, a rotary rig, and all the necessary tools. They spudded in and the clanking grind of the grief-joint soon gave daily assurance to the inhabitants for miles around that work on Come Eleven was being pushed. During the first month after drilling began, Drycheck and Abe returned to their regular calling and made no attempt to sell any of the company's stock. They joined the swarms from all parts of the continent who filled the sidewalks of the oil town and made a babel of hotel lobbies and pool rooms and lease offices. With the opening of new fields in the Southwest, adventurers had flocked there by the scores of thousands like flies to sugar.

They traded in the streets, in flivvers out on the roads, at meals, and in their sleep. They talked, ate and breathed gushers. If a well came in it was always rated in the thousands of barrels by the rumor mongers. In a new field, a "thirty-thousand-barrel well" will usually register about six thousand in a genuine test and is then likely to dwindle in a short time to a few hundred, after which they put it on the beam or pump. And whenever you hear about a two-thousand-barrel gusher, it's safer to rate it at three hundred and then keep your money in the bank.

Oil gamblers are the most credulous people on earth. They will believe anything and tell anything. What's more, they will risk real money on what a wild-eyed stranger hoarsely assures them he got from a flivver pilot who heard a couple of geologists talking in the back of the car. And the woods are full of geologists, or rock hounds, or pebble-pups, as they are variously known. Genuine geologists are scarce. About fifty per cent of the lease experts who talk glibly of Arkadelphia clay and Nacatoches sand and the worth of close-in stuff never saw any oil except when it was being poured into a motor and couldn't distinguish between a sluice-pit and Red River. Not many months ago they were earning their living behind a counter somewhere or juggling dishes in a beanery, but living off the other fellow has a stronger appeal than work, in which respect they assuredly run with the majority in the United States today.

Drycheck and Abe bought and sold leases at no risk on a commission of ten per cent. They were strictly curb dealers without any investment or sources of information except rumors, and no responsibility whatsoever. They belonged to the hordes of parasites on the oil business. Far removed from this sort of activity is a legitimate oil business, highly organized and engaging the services of trained, experienced men both in production and leasing. Indeed, the real oil business is as efficiently organized as the best industry in the country, but the men engaged in it don't ballyhoo the public with wild promises of fabulous profits. They raise the money they need in the same way a manufacturer would raise it.

Equipped with maps and blue prints, the pair nailed every stranger who entered the hotel's portals. Appearance was no guide in spotting prospects. A redneck in topboots and soiled cotton shirt might be in better shape to take a flier with thousands than the smooth, overly groomed person of prosperous air with the marks of the city all over him.

The place crawled with lease hounds, both men and women. The latter's competition was a serious handicap, because their sex aided them in plying their business. Nevertheless Charlie and Abe had a fair run of luck, due to a couple of false rumors stirring up a market. Each made several thousand dollars out of commissions on sales.

At the end of thirty days people started to talk about Come Eleven. It was wildcat territory, but rumor had it they had obtained oil showings at a depth of fourteen hundred feet. The next report was that gas had been struck. This was considered a favorable omen and Abe and Charlie received bids on small blocks of stock.

"Let's sell some," said Abe. "I want that six thousand back and it'll give us the money to keep on drilling without putting up any more of our own."

Accordingly they sold a little stock at two for one. With the proceeds of these sales they were able to make the advances the driller required.

As time went on and the clank of the grief-joint at Come Eleven was only stilled when they had to pull the pipe—and they're always pulling the pipe to fix something or put in a new bit—the countryside was set tingling with expectation. From nobody knew where seeped wonderful tales of Come Eleven. They were right on top of the oil sand—they were purposely holding up the work until they could grab more leases in the vicinity—they had struck oil and only needed to blow the well in.

Scouts made the road to Cayuse's place impassable with their flivvers in a couple of days. They reported that there was some oil in the sluice pit—not much, but some.

"Go easy on that stuff," Drycheck cautioned. "I knowed a guy once who put oil in with the bailer, Abe, and he et next Christmas dinner as the guest of Uncle Sam."

Abe started to protest and bluster.

"All right, all right—but quit it. We want to do nothing illegal—didn't you say so yourself? Besides, leave it to me. I know a trick worth two of that."

His claim was justified by action. Under his orders a high stout fence was built around the derrick. Guards were hired to keep off visitors: day and night they watched the well, repelling with automatics the hardier scouts who persisted in the face of threats.

The result was a riot of excitement. If the Roosevelt Company didn't have a real well, why did they take such precautions to keep people at a distance? There was some big mystery here! It was going to be a gusher, sure—probably the biggest in the history of the oil fields—and those shysters, Abe and Drycheck, were holding it back until they could get leases on the whole parish. Didn't the way they clung to the company's stock prove something was up? Only a few had been able to buy any shares—friends of theirs, you might say—and even they had had to pry it off'n 'em.

Followed a mad scramble to buy. Abe and Charlie were out at the well when it started and the first hint they had of the trend of popular favor was when Madam Tabasco, the copper-haired owner of the leading poolroom, met them in the road halfway to town and stopped her car. She said she was out to take a squint at Topsy Number 7, but of course they knew she was lying and she knew they did. Very casually she referred to their well and inquired what progress had been made.

"Oh, we're movin' along."

"Well, I been thinkin', boys, we might work up a market for that stock. What d'you say? Suppose I start a buyin'-and-sellin' campaign and turn my girls loose on it too. Hey? And we'll split three ways."

"No-oo, thanks, Miz Tabasco," answered Drycheck respectfully. "We wouldn't choose to sell any right now."

The poolroom queen eyed them sharply a moment and her thin lips met in a straight line.

"Oh, cut out that bull!" she snapped. "D'you think you've got me fooled too? I ain't been doin' business with my eyes shut all these years and I got you boys' number, don't make no mistake about that. Now come on and loosen up. I can boost that stock up to a hundred for one if you do what I tell you—and we'll split three ways."

A polite cough behind his bediamonded hand and Abe intervened.

"We ain't anxious to sell right now, Mrs. Tabasco," he said firmly. "But when we do we'll be glad to pay the regular commission—no more and no less."

She cried furiously: "All right! Just wait and see, that'll all! You two'll be sorry!"

"Good-by, ma'am," they chorused in honeyed tones and continued glee-fully toward town.

"All the same, Abe, we'd best sell," said Drycheck. "I reckon now's the time, or that ol' buzzard wouldn't have made us an offer. And besides, it's like she'll get after us now and blow the works."

The hotel and pool rooms resembled a mob scene in a movie, for a scout had come in with hot news from Come Eleven. It would be a thousand-barrel well at the lowest estimate—she had run three hours at that rate and then they had shut her off. High grade oil, too, testing forty-one degrees!

"Here they are now!" the crowd yelled when Charlie and Abe stepped out of their flivver.

There was a rush for them. Men fought to be first with bids for the stock. They clawed their way through the press of struggling humanity to get at Drycheck and his partner. A woman broker fainted and Come Eleven stock instantly rose fifty percent a share. The hotel lobby became a howling, surging, smoking welter.

The pair managed to force their way to the stairs and escaped to Abe's room, whose door they locked. Then they sat down to plan the campaign.

"Ol' Timer," said Drycheck in a hushed religious voice, "We're millionaires —if we play it right."

"Charlie," Abe cried, shaking his hand and almost weeping with excitement,

"You're the best friend I ever had. You're the best friend any man ever had. You done this for me. I think more of you, Charlie, than I would of my own wife if I still had one of them. If ever—"

"All right, Abe, all right. We'll let it go at that. But don't cry—it'll make your nose red. What we got to do now is get busy—get busy and let some of the boys turn loose our stock."

All that afternoon and late into the night Come Eleven stock was sold at prices ranging from four to ten for one. Four for one—six—eight—back to seven —nine—back to six—up to ten. With wash sales and the dissemination of rumors they forced the figures upward and ever upward. By one o'clock in the morning they had disposed of the bulk of it and had cashed in close to five hundred thousand dollars; and then the driller arrived in a profuse perspiration with an automatic pistol in his hip pocket. He had got wind of the boom and came to claim his share before the two could decamp.

Efforts to stall him off were futile. He was a plain-spoken individual and after he had shoved the automatic against Abe's vest, the partners admitted the justice of his contention and turned over what was due him from the spoils.

"And now," he said, "If you take my advice you two'll blow. The bottom is goin' to drop out of this thing by mornin' and then people will begin to ask questions. It's like I'll have to come out with a statement of the truth—or leastways tell em we ain't struck oil yet."

Abe gave vent to a jeering laugh.

"And I suppose they won't do a thing to you—oh, no! You'd best join us, Bull."

The driller placidly lit a cigar.

"Why should I? They don't know I've any interest in the deal. Besides I aim to begin real drillin' tomorrow."

They gaped at him.

"Go on! What you givin' us? Who'd pay you for it?"

"Well, the parish has offered twenty thousand dollars to anybody who'll bring in a well over there. I figure it won't cost me more'n eight thousand additional to go twenty-nine hundred feet—and now I got the money to do it I feel like gamblin'."

The partners exploded into boisterous hilarity.

"Well, well, well! Ol' Bull's fixin' to get out on a limb at last. Why, I never thought a driller done such a thing, Bull. I always thought they played it safe."

"Don't you guys worry about me none. I'm fixed for life," retorted Bull, grinning amiably as he patted his wallet pocket.

It still lacked three hours of dawn when Drycheck and Abe climbed into a hastily purchased flivver and departed for parts unknown. They took the least frequented road and Drycheck drove. Their way carried them close to Come Eleven. The last thing they saw in that parish was the twinkle of the light at the tip of the derrick.

Next day the town regained a wisp of sanity. The driller came out with a denial that any oil had been struck and a statement that they were not yet deep enough to warrant any guesses, so the shorn speculators started to unload. Come Eleven stock slumped from ten to one to par. Within twenty-four hours it could be bought for fifty cents on the dollar and a lot of it changed hands at that figure, being taken up by farmers living in the vicinity of the well. And for three months the Come Eleven scarcely figured in the talk. Bad weather set in and drilling in that region was frequently shut down.

One sparkling May day Drycheck Charlie rode a freight into a new oil town not sixty miles from the scene of his former activities. He looked seedy. His clothes were frayed, he wore an unkempt beard and there hung a general air of desperation about him.

Charlie was now an enthusiastic booster for intervention in Mexico. Having no wife to persuade him to go to a city and horn into society, he had bought a peck or two of diamonds, the largest and reddest automobile money could command, and had taken up residence in El Paso. There he distributed diamonds with princely hand among his lady friends and frequently crossed to Juarez, where he spent days and nights playing the wheel, guzzling booze, and trying to prove American superiority to the Latin in the science of stud poker.

After nine weeks he ended up in the cuartel, following a losing night, a fight and considerable big talk. In the jail they frisked him of everything he had on him and before he won freedom, his bank account across the bridge was written in red.

So now he was back in the oil fields to pick up another fortune if luck proved kind. As he entered the hotel with a furtive watchfulness vastly different from the breezy confidence of his old manner, there was a sudden commotion and a hatless farmer burst through the crowd with a wild yell. His eyes were rolling, his vest was open and he waved a telegram on high.

"Hooray, fellers! Yip-yip-yip—yowie! I've struck it! Come Eleven was brung in this mornin' at seven o'clock. Twenty thousand bar'ls a day if she's a bar'l! Blowed the tools to hell-and-gone and is pourin' over the crown-block. Whoopee!"

BARREL-HOUSE BEN
Arkansas Oilfields

Sol Callahan

Barrel-House Ben ARKANSAS OILFIELDS

ON the flat car ahead, piled high with pipe, a couple of hijackers were frisking a drifter. The victim yelled and fought. In a vivid flash of lightning Ben and the Big Un glimpsed the struggle. Then one of the thugs lost patience with such obstinacy and hit him on the head and they rolled him off the train. He made a big splash.

"It sure has rained here," Ben remarked.

Drifters and boll-weevils perched precariously on every car of the heavy freight. None of the train crew came near them; after one look they had unanimously decided to leave those guys alone. So the long line of tank cars, and flats loaded with boilers and gas engines and supplies, went careening through the blackness toward Smackover at twelve miles an hour with a passenger list inclusive of the choicest scum of oilfield society.

The rain drove down in sheets. Suddenly a dull glare lit up the night and the sky ahead pulsated with billowing flame—a tank in the swamp had been struck and fifty thousand barrels of oil were blazing.

It took them three hours to go fifteen miles, the engine feeling its way cautiously over the water-soaked roadbed, with many fierce anxious blasts of its whistle and frequent stops for nobody knew what. Just before they reached Smackover the rain eased up momentarily and then they could see dozens of tiny lights gleaming like low stars above the trees—the lights on the crown blocks of the derricks where the work went doggedly forward night and day.

The freight pulled into the station about ten o'clock and everybody dropped off. As a late passenger train was about due, there was a crowd on the platform —and whom should the Big Un and Ben Gober bump into but Drycheck Charlie.

"Howdy, men," he said cheerfully. Then sinking his voice to an earnest whisper: "Listen! I want to do the square thing by you boys, so before you start to knock 'em over, gimme the name of your next of kin and where you choose to be shipped."

"What's eatin' on you?"

"Every mornin' they lay out the stiffs whose home town is east on this side of the station, and them that goes west lays over there. Some mornin's there's only one or two, and then ag'in there'll be a good night and Ed'll ship three or four, maybe. Pick your spot, gents."

"Let's wrastle with a T-bone steak first," suggested Ben and they crossed on a narrow plank over a sea of mud to the business section of Smackover.

The place blazed with lights. Blare of jazz orchestras and the thump and swish of dancers in the barrel-houses—dance halls earned that name originally because they used to knock 'em on the head and roll 'em out. Barkers for movie shows were yelling at the swarming throngs. Every soft-drink place was jammed. Fortune tellers, sitting at the entrances of their booths, invited them to learn their luck. A troupe of performing dogs had a ring of spectators around them on a platform close to the sidewalk; a carnival with merry-go-round and Ferris wheel was in full blast on a vacant lot; yells and squeals and laughter; half a dozen grimy roughnecks were sternly striving to knock over dolls, with balls.

A few women and young girls mingled with the crowds. Nobody spoke to them. Smackover is the wildest and woolliest town in the history of stampedes; gamblers and adventurers and every species of strongarm gentry abound there and parasitic women appear to number about 80 per cent of the feminine population, yet a woman is seldom treated with disrepect on the streets. Indeed, an unescorted girl is safer from annoyance in Smackover than in Boston. The explanation probably lies in the fact that a mistake in Boston means nothing more than a rebuff to the masher, whereas the lady's closest male kin is very apt to bump him off with great suddenness in the oil fields.

Less than a year previously Smackover had been merely a wide place in the road. Now it was a roaring, surging camp of ten thousand men. The buildings were mere box shacks, the two main streets rivers of muck through which horses waded. In the fine, free, pioneer fashion, the citizens swept nearly everything out of the front door. For that matter they do the same in large areas of New York, where some of our fellow citizens from the ghettos and gutters of Europe still cling to the dear customs of the homeland, but at least they clean it up now and again in New York. In Smackover it sinks. The mud swallows it, but the soul of that garbage does not die. In the rainy season the stench reeks to the skies. Close to the most odorous corner an open chile stand was doing a flourishing business.

"Well," Ben said as soon as they had eaten, "Let's go see the town."

Drycheck led the way to the most popular barrel-house. It was a long low frame structure with a door at either end, a soft-drink bar in one corner, a fine jazz orchestra in another, a lady cashier perched above a desk, and benches along the walls. These were occupied by men and women spectators, with a sprinkling of snowbirds who sat with eyes glassy and gibbered to themselves. Dancers filled the floor.

"Turn it over," yelled the floorman as the trio entered, "They like it." And another dance started.

Followed by his friends, Ben pushed his way through the groups. A trim little girl in knickerbockers, sweater and tam-o'shanter picked him for a sure prospect at once, glided into his arms without a word and away they went.

"Look at that ol' boy strut his stuff" exclaimed Drycheck admiringly. "Show 'em up, son!"

Ben was certainly "showin' them Arkinsaw guys up." Mr. Gober's style was not especially graceful, but he had a lot of showy steps a man can acquire only by a wide experience in the very best barrel-houses, and the way he clicked the joints of his knees straight after each step made everybody take notice.

Umph-ah-umph-ah-blah-blah-blah went the orchestra and stopped. All the men stepped up to the cashier's desk and put down a quarter. Their partners each received from her a check good for ten cents to be cashed in at the end of the evening; and "Turn it over. They like it," bellowed the lank floorman. Once more they were off.

In thirty minutes Ben had spent four dollars and was just beginning to warm up. The Big Un and Drycheck held aloof among the spectators because Charlie didn't dance and the Big Un was bashful. The Big Un was six feet four and broad in proportion, with a face like an ox, massive and patient; also, he had warts on his hands; but his soul was shy as a poet's, so he shrank from subjecting a partner to clumsy footwork.

Pretty soon Gober's labors provoked a thirst and the three adjourned to a drug store where Drycheck assured them they could obtain right good corn liquor.

"She ain't brand new, is she, doc?" Ben asked.

"Hell, no. This is good old stuff. Made her myself day before yesterday," the druggist assured them as he filled a half-pint bottle from a pitcher. They paid two dollars for it and returned toward the dance hall.

"Let's step up here and take a shot," said Ben and they followed him into the alley beside the building.

"Here, Big Un—fly at it."

"After you."

"No. I tell you what—let ol' Charlie try it first."

"Give it here—I ain't scared of that stuff," Drycheck declared. Nevertheless he carefully shook the bottle before drinking. "That's to take the fusel oil off'n the top," he exclaimed. "Now and agin a feller drinks some of that and it puts his lights out."

When it came Ben's turn he swallowed a mouthful, shuddered, and then listened intently.

"It's O. K. I can hear it drop," he said. "But you need a sody pop for a chaser."

After a hearty swig of corn liquor, the barrel-house ball took on a different aspect to the Big Un. Somehow the girls looked younger and prettier and he began to feel confidence in himself. The majority of the ladies wore ballet skirts and low V-shaped bodices: some of them had bare legs and some had gone in for elaborate costume effects.

Not a few were exceptionally pretty. Their ages ran from seventeen to anybody's guess, but the majority were very young. The Big Un's heart warmed to a tiny girl in green ballet dress, a sprite with bobbed hair and a shy ingenue manner. Her large violet eyes were as innocent as a calf's—wistful, appealing—and when she glanced at him questioningly he tightened his belt and stepped out onto the floor.

"Go to it, Big Un! Atta boy!" Gober whooped.

That was along about half past eleven and by midnight the Big Un had spent seven dollars and fifty cents without ever changing partners. It seemed to him they barely turned around before the floorman bawled, "Turn it over. They like it."

"Well, how does she dance?" inquired Drycheck.

"Swell! But, say, that pore kid hadn't ought to be here."

"How come?"

"She don't belong in a place like this a-tall, Ben. Honest, she don't. Her father lost all his money in oil and she's tryin' to earn enough to go to college."

"Sure. I suspicioned right away she was a boardin' school gal just out for a lark. Say, if I was you, big feller, I'd send her some American beauties tomorrow."

"Who're you boys talking about?" queried a spectator standing beside them.

"That gal in green—the right pretty one with short hair."

"Yeh, Myrtle's all right," was the judicious comment, "but her daughter's got her beat a mile."

Just then the floorman bellowed—"Pick your partners for the waltz, gents—the prize waltz. Let everybody dance this one," and there ensued a scramble for the most desirable. The Big Un secured Myrtle. Ben stepped out with the girl in the knickerbockers and sweater. This was to be the final event of the evening and the orchestra didn't abbreviate it.

They danced and they danced. The judges seemed reluctant to come to a decision. It soon became apparent to all beholders, however, that the contest was narrowing down to Ben Gober and a gentleman from the hinterland of Arkansas, a rangy youth with long hair and adenoids who had fortified himself for the struggle with choc beer. Now choc beer is all right up to a certain point, despite its oily taste, but it carries a delayed fuse and after a few quarts something happens.

Not a minute passed but one or the other introduced some new stuff. They simply put all the rest in the shade. True, the Big Un was still going strong, but he found difficulty in making the turns and only overcame this by banging full-tilt with his back into the far wall, which gave him a sufficient start to carry him to the other end again.

Meanwhile the Arkansas youth was tossing back his mane and bending back almost to the floor, and doing solo stuff and flinging his legs around in such amazing gyrations that all the spectators were agreed the freckle-faced kid was the mustard sure enough. Outbursts of applause greeted each new astounding effort and perhaps Ben divined that he was beaten. At any rate he suddenly quit, paid off and rejoined Drycheck Charlie. Shortly thereafter the dance ended.

"Shucks!" Ben panted as he mopped his face and neck. "Only for these here rubber boots of mine startin' to smoke, I'd of showed that bird up."

"Sure you would!" agreed the Big Un. "You would of been barrel-house champeen easy. But nobody can't dance good in rubber boots. Let's take another shot. What say?"

They did so in the dark alley and then stood near the door, watching the dancers come out. Among the last to emerge was Myrtle, snuggling against a hard-visaged man with a cauliflower ear. The Big Un's eyes bulged.

"Did you see that, Ben?" he asked hoarsely.

"Uh-uh."

"Why, that gal of mine give all her money to that big bum."

"Well, what did you expect? They've all got pimps livin' off 'em. Har, har!"

Next moment the laughter died on his lips, because the girl in knickers brushed past him and he perceived that a pasty-faced kid to whose arm she clung was carrying her bag.

"Come on," he said hotly. "Let's go."

"Where you headin', Ben?" they demanded as they followed.

"Stick right close and you'll see."

Arrived at the end of a street he drew them into a dark doorway and said, "Here's where she lives—she done told me so. We'll wait at the foot of the stairs and when this pimp comes in with her—well, leave it to me, that's all."

166

"What do you aim to do, Ben?"

"Get my money back—that's what I aim to do. Do you think I'm goin' to dance my fool head off all evenin' for that sonofabitch? I reckon not!"

"Maybe I can git mine too."

"No-o, we couldn't grab off both, Big Un. They'd be too many for us. Besides Myrtle lives in another part of town. You hold 'im for me, Big Un, while I go after the money, and I'll split fifty-fifty."

"Let's see—I done spent eleven dollars and twenty-five cents. Her share of what you spent would be—what would it be, Ben?"

"It'd be a-plenty, I know that much. Sh-h! They'll be along pretty soon."

"Well, so long, you boys," Drycheck said.

They urged him to stick around.

"This ain't my funeral," Charlie argued, "and I don't aim to be mixed up in it. What's more, if you take my advice you'll lay off'n this bird. Most of these boys is hijackers, too, and all of 'em pack a gun."

"They ain't got nothing on me. Besides, the Big Un will take care of that."

Thereupon Drycheck Charlie departed and the two took up position at the foot of the dark stairs. At last the couple arrived, strolling leisurely. A sharp scuffle, a scream, a grunt, and then perhaps thirty seconds of quiet. Two figures —one huge and the other short—dashed out from the doorway and sped into the night, followed presently by shriek after shriek of, "Thief! Thief! Murder!"

The pair came to rest behind some freight cars on a siding and sat down to regain their wind.

"Suppose she sicks the law on us?"

"How can she? She don't know who it was from Adam. Besides, all I did was git my money back and he'd of tooken it off her anyhow. Do you reckon you hurt him much, Big Un?"

"No-o. Just choked him some."

"She tried to bite me when I put that newspaper in her mouth. What d'you know about that?"

"There's a lady for you, ain't it!"

"I'll say so. Well, let's mosey along and find ol' Drycheck. We got to get us a place to sleep soon."

They found Charlie in the drug store where Doc dispensed corn liquor.

"What's on your mind now?" he inquired.

"How about a game of craps? Anything doin' in this burg, Doc?"

"Any sort of game you want. Stud, red dog—take your pick. The sky's the limit."

"I ain't flyin' high tonight. But I feel lucky and I crave action. A Christmas tree couldn't hold me down, the way I feel."

He got action. Drycheck conducted them down a side street and a narrow, brightly lighted passage and there in front of them was an open door. A man stood on either side of the entrance and patted each arrival on the hips as he went in. Anybody with a gun was relieved of it: the house took no chances. The friends surrendered their artillery without protest and were presently lined up at a crap table.

It was not a large room, but filled to overflowing. Two or three tables of poker were silent and intent, the table where the big game was in progress being cut off from the herd by a railing.

"Now play careful, Ben," the Big Un cautioned. "Every time you win, don't shoot the whole works but cut down. You know your weakness."

"Sure. I got to play careful. All I've got is fourteen dollars. How much you got?"

"Seven or eight maybe."

"Might as well shoot it. We ain't got enough to do any good and tomorrow we'll be workin' anyhow."

The Big Un didn't take kindly to the theory and he had no special taste for gambling, but he was as clay in Ben's hands and stuck to him loyally. Gober was one of those natural-born crap shooters who know the language and can talk to them, but of course he never stood the ghost of a chance against a house game. At one period he had more than a hundred dollars stacked up in front of him, and ten minutes later was flat broke.

Then he emptied the Big Un's pockets and lost that. Meanwhile Drycheck Charlie wandered around, watching. He did not play. Having been a gambler for years, Charlie never took part in any game where he had to buck the house. His cold eyes did not miss a thing. His swarthy face wore a half-scornful, half-amused expression.

"Say, lend me ten dollars, Drycheck."

"All right. But not here."

"Why not? I can make it back in two shakes."

"It'll go like the rest. Call it a day and come home and I'll lend you ten."

"All right," Ben grumbled, the glitter still in his eyes. "Let's go. How much've we spent tonight, Big Un?"

"Search me. I had twenty-one dollars when I hit this burg and now I got a dime."

"That makes nearly fifty bucks. It's me and you for a job in the morning, boy. Got a bed for us, Charlie?"

"I got some blankets and you can bed down on the floor, I reckon. Had enough for one night? Then let's drift."

They received back their artillery and went out into Broadway. It was long past midnight, but a few of the restaurants were still open. They turned toward the railroad. Passing a café Ben perceived at the lunch counter several of the girls who had been at the dance, still in costume. All had escorts and he recognized two of them. The group looked tired but content, like business partners who had had a hard but profitable day and could now relax.

It was too much for Gober. He stuck his head inside the door and shouted: "All right. You've got our money. But let me tell you somethin'—a year from now all you gamblers will be playin' solitaire, and all you wild women a-takin' in washin'." And he slammed the door and went on his way.

"A hophead," they concluded and laughed. But one of the girls, perhaps more exhausted than the rest, gave a little shiver.

Drycheck Charlie lived in a two-room shack next to a warehouse a few hundred yards from town and they had to walk eastward along the railroad tracks to reach there. Rain was still falling and the night was black. Drycheck snapped on a flashlight.

"Stick close together and keep your eye peeled," he warned. "They got a coupla of the Hocot boys along here the other night. If you see anybody snoopin' around, go to the gat."

Just as they were leaving the tracks to follow a road that ran into the woods, Gober descried a head peering round the end of a flat car.

"Well," he yelled, pulling his gun and dropping behind a pile of ties, "What you got on your mind?"

No answer. They heard running feet.

"Unless they get the drop on us before we see 'em, they'll leave us alone," Charlie said as they went along. "I reckon it's safe enough from here on."

Gas torches were flaring amid the trees: the moving figures of men against the light looked like denizens of another world. The air vibrated to thud and thump. Gas engines were coughing and fussing as though they had a lot of unfinished business and it was worrying them. A gusher was booming against its flowbox, somewhere in the night a gas well roared, and the drills were grinding their way down into the bowels of the earth with an irritable rackety-clank of griefjoints.

Here was the real Smackover field—not the noisome camp they had left behind. That was merely an excrescence. The muck and squalor, the vice, the crimes of sudden violence—those are phases of every great pioneer effort in the United States when men stampede to sudden riches. Out there in the gaunt, oil-blackened, bedraggled swamps a titanic achievement was going ceaselessly forward. Topping the highest trees were hundreds and hundreds of derricks. The roughnecks and roustabout crews were toiling and sweating and cursing and getting maimed and dying, and figuring on a little choc beer and a fling with the girls on pay night. Each day may take its toll of maimed and dead, but the work goes on. A steady stream of horses and mule teams and patient oxen strain through the muck from dawn to dark with supplies. Nothing stops them.

"We need a new boiler on that Murphy lease," a gang pusher reports.

They put it there. It may mean risk of life—it invariably involves struggle and hardship that would daunt an army commander—but they never hesitate. They lay the stuff down where it's needed, in spite of hell-and-high-water. There's no job on earth they're afraid to tackle. By just such breeds of men are empires built.

The Smackover field at night is superb, colossal. There in the raw one sees the human race's endless battle against Nature. Perhaps a glimmering of this reached Drycheck Charlie because he stopped once and, gazing at a group of derricks rising ghost-like above the glare of torches, exclaimed: "And yet there're guys back East who spend good time paintin' A Lady With a Teacup or something."

His guests slept on the floor and rose early to go to town.

"I got to git me a job right now," Ben announced.

He found it harder than they had anticipated. The heavy rains had halted work on quite a few leases and every contractor the pair approached made the same reply—"Not right now. I ain't turning round."

So they bummed around town all day watching the incoming trains disgorge their hundreds of new arrivals and the puffing freights arrive with supplies. A team of horses bogged down in Broadway and one of the animals nearly drowned before they got him out. They walked over to Griffin and back and contrived to spend on drinks what was left from Drycheck's loan.

While idly dangling their legs from the porch of a store in late afternoon, they perceived a tall individual at the edge of the sidewalk gazing fixedly at a spot in the liquid street. He stared so long that the Big Un grew restless.

"What you see there, Ol' Timer?"

"A guy on a horse just slipped off and went under in that deep hole yonder."

The Big Un jumped up excitedly, crying: "Then why the Sam Hill don't somebody snake him out?"

"Oh, Ed'll be up directly."

The Big Un would have pursued the conversation had not Ben nudged him. There fell a silence.

"Many get drownded here?" Gober asked civily.

"No-o. A span of mules got drownded in Broadway last week and only yesterday a nigger went under with a sack of oats and never did come up, but I wouldn't say there was many got drownded."

"A nigger—" the Big Un blurted out but again Gober's elbow stayed him.

"A nigger with a sack of oats."

Neither had any comment to offer now.

"Yessir, a big buck nigger with a sack of oats," the stranger repeated hopefully. As they steadfastly repressed any interest in the sack of oats, he asked, "You boys come from Texas, don't you?"

"Yes, and we're dadgummed sorry too. But our jobs blowed up on us there, so we up and got passports and come to Arkinsaw."

"Roughneckin'?"

"We aim to."

"Real roughnecks, or just boll weevils?"

"There ain't two better floormen than us in the business. Yessir, we learned roughneckin' when it took a man to be a roughneck. You ain't talkin' to any brake weight now, mister" Ben told him.

"Fine. Well, I'm a contractor."

"The hell you say!"

"Yessir. My name's Simmons—Joe Simmons. Used to work for one of the big production companies and finally got me a horseback job, but shucks, you know how that is—a few years and it'd be a service card and a boiler station for me. So I up and started in contractin'."

"Give us a job?"

"Right now I ain't turnin' round, but maybe I can put you in the way of landing one. Did you ask Sug Carraway?"

"Never heard tell of him."

"Well, let's go find him."

Whilst they were hunting, Mr. Simmons remarked that to look at the mud now you'd never suspicion it was so dusty last summer that automobiles had to keep their lights on in broad daylight in Smackover. He also confided to the pair that the best job he had ever done was a buttermilk well in Oklahoma. The only response he drew was an inquiry as to whether it was a turnkey job and what was the gravity of that there buttermilk?

Unable to find Sug Carraway they parted from Simmons and went down to the carnival to take a whack at the dolls. Somebody had built a derrick back of the lot where the Ferris wheel was located and had then stopped work. About five o'clock a carnival performer in spangled tights climbed up to the top and after due preparations and ceremonies to fix the attention of the crowd, made a flying trip down on the guy wire by hanging to a sort of pulley. He scored quite a hit.

"Shucks!" Ben grunted. "I used to could slide down one of them wires standin' up on one foot. Here—hold my coat, Big Un."

Full of scorn and choc beer, he went swarming up the ladder to the crown block. Arrived there in no time at all, he stood on his head in the middle of the gin-pole projecting a hundred feet above the ground. Then, before the fascinated gaze of the spectators, he came down the guy wire hand over hand. They cheered him to the echo and raised a hat collection of seven dollars and thirty cents. And —"Say, you want a job?" inquired a fat flabby gentleman in a check suit.

"What kind of job?"

"I'm fixing to put me down a vell."

"Promotion?"

"You mean vould I sell stock in it? Listen at him! My Gawd, yes. But it is going to be a real vell. This is straight business I am giving you."

"Sure I want a job. My friend here wants one too. We'll be glad to work for you, Mister—what is the name?"

"Callahan. Sol Callahan."

"Well, Mr. Callahan, you've bought something. When do we start work?"

"You come with me now, yes, and I vill eggsplain everything. Me, I mean real business. But I need joost the sort of men what it is you are. Unnerstan?"

"I ain't sure. But if it don't mean goin' to jail, we're on. Let's go."

They adjourned to a cafe, where Sol explained as much as he thought they needed to know.

"What's that guy up to, anyhow?" the Big Un speculated at supper. "I don't git the idee of that one acre."

"What Sol's fixin' to do," replied Ben as he rolled a cigarette, "is this: he's bought that one acre close to production, ain't he? Well, he bought only one because it came high—real money. Then he'll go away out on the bald prairie somewheres, twenty miles from a well, and pick up a whole lot of wildcat acreage for nothin' almost."

"Still, I don't see—"

"Why, he can advertise that he's drillin' a well a few hundred yards from some producing wells, can't he? And if he strikes oil, which is likely, he can advertise that he's got a gusher. How'll the suckers know he's only got one acre there

172

and that all the rest of his stuff is twenty miles from nowheres? They'll see only that well and they'll figure all his acreage is A-1."

"Anyhow, we should worry."

"That's what I figure. All he pays us for is to drill a well. The promotion end ain't any of our business. And it's good pay, too, Big Un. We had ought to save a right smart of money."

They ran into Callahan later in the evening, loitering near a fortune teller's booth. In front hung a curtain painted blue and on it in red letters:

> Look Whose Here. Madam La Valleyer and her temple of Mystery. The One with a Master Mind. Reads your life like an open book. Tells past, present and future. Consult her on love affairs, marriages and divorces Change of business Law suits Lost and Stolen articles. Tells who your enemies are and how to combat them. Also tells what you are adapted for and how to be Successful, in the future. This Wonderful Woman has lately came here to inform the public. Come on in, boys.

"Wow, aindt it the limit?" said Sol. "A graft, that's all it is. Suckers is what she takes us for—oi, oi!"

"Sure. There's nothin' to that bunk."

"Besides, she'd charge it us a dollar, I bet you."

"What's a dollar to you, Mr. Callahan? You go in. You've got more'n me."

"No, I vill tell you, Ben—one of you boys go in first, y'unnerstan, and find it out vot luck I vill have with the vell, see? And I put up the dollar."

"I don't wanta know nothin' about my past," the Big Un declared, "and I don't wanta know nothin' about my future neither."

"Besides, it's like she wouldn't say a word about a well, because we don't own it, Mr. Callahan."

Sol stood in indecision, eying the sign and jingling his money.

"The only good luck vot I got me in five years was brung by a fortune teller," he remarked.

"Then take a chance. We'll wait here."

"No. You boys come with me and I vill go, y'unnerstan, but not alone by no means."

Madam La Valleyer, a small, thin woman of gypsy type, with a baby at the breast, did not relish the arrangement but finally consented to the presence of Sol's friends in the vestibule of the booth while she was unfolding the future to him in the inner sanctum. They could hear everything. She put the child on a cot, seated Callahan on a soap box and asked him for a dollar. Then she went into a sort of trance, from which she only partially emerged once to glance at the baby when he grew fretful.

She told Sol a lot about his character that impressed him with her powers of divination. For instance, she said he was warm-hearted and foolishly confiding and inclined to spend money recklessly. Then she dubbed a shot: she told Sol he fondly imagined that his married life was happy and his wife true to him, but in reality he had best watch out because a tall fair man who posed as his friend would prove a snake in the grass. Sol could identify the tall fair man, but which one of his wives Madam La Valleyer had in mind troubled him for days.

Next she requested that he place all his money in his hand. He turned his back to do this.

"This all you got, gentleman?" she whispered, fingering the odds and ends of small bills and silver.

"S'help me, m'am."

"Close your hand on it tight. You got more than that," Madam insisted, eying him sharply. "Don't be afraid, gentleman. You are nervous. I no want your money. But you must trust me and tell me all you got. Else if you don't, how can I tell your fortune right? Where is it? Where do you keep it hid?"

"In the bank. I ain't got it any more with me," Sol insisted. He was resolved to die before revealing the seven hundred dollars he had in an inner pocket.

"You have, too. I know you got more and a lot more. Where are you stopping here?"

Callahan swallowed hard and replied, "The Waffle House."

"These friends of yours, are they stopping with you?"

"No, ma'am."

Despairing of extracting any further information of a financial nature out of Sol, Madam La Valleyer proceeded with his fortune.

"You are in the oil business," she declared in the course of it. "I see a derrick and oil running out. You will be successful in what you undertake. I see you rising very high, but I do not see what happens when you get up there. You must—"

The baby breaking into a wail at this juncture, madam abruptly terminated the séance.

"Say, that's jake about the well, hey, Mr. Callahan? But what did she mean about risin' very high?"

"Me, I do not bother my head vot she means. But vot did she mean when she asked me where was it I am stopping? Huh?"

Ben told him: "It's like she'll pass it along to her gang so they can lay for you."

"Wow, let them lay it for me, the moiderers. I should worry—I pull out of here tomorrow morning, boys. Besides, I aindt staying at the Waffle House—tee hee!"

Long before city dwellers are astir the trio were many miles from Smackover, headed eastward in a flivver. The day was cool and sunshiny, the dogwood and flowering peach were blossoming amid the pines and all Nature seemed to smile. It was a sweet country they traversed and the road they were on was exceptionally good for such a district.

"Say, you won't never get oil in a country like this, Mr. Callahan," Ben assured him in all sincerity.

"No? Why?"

"It's too pretty and the road's too good. If you want to strike oil, you got to go way out in the sticks where there ain't no roads and nothin' but mud or sand."

"Who said anything about oil?"

"The best place of all, you might say, is right next to a nigger graveyard, Mr. Callahan." It was the Big Un who delivered this opinion and Sol displayed keen interest.

"Vot you say? That's queer, boys, I tell you. Because, y'unnerstan, my location is smack up against a nigger graveyard."

"You mean that acre of yours?"

"Sure. Vot else?"

He showed them a number of long and short forties he had under lease many miles from any field proven or prospective, and then an entire section. All told, Sol owned leases on about a thousand acres, for a total outlay of as many dollars.

"I reckon you aim to sell this stuff with a rubber map, don't you, Mr. Callahan?"

"Vot you mean?"

"So it'll look like close-in stuff."

Sol threw back his head and laughed uproariously. It was plain that he liked Ben.

"Now let's hurry so I can show you my location."

The acre on which he proposed to drill was within reasonable distance of production and right in line with all the rock hounds' prognostications. Also, it adjoined a negro cemetery. The prospect looked all right to Gober and they settled the arrangement on the spot. Callahan would have a derrick put up im-

175

mediately and also buy a good rig and pipe: it was up to Ben to get a drilling crew. This was to be a daytime job because Gober would not take the risk of delays due to rain, even had he been finanicially able.

The derrick went up as though by magic. They connected up with a gas pipe from another well to run their boiler, spudded in, and very soon the Kelly and the Maude were hard at it. Once the work was under way Sol bothered his head no further about that angle of the business. He had every confidence in Gober and while Ben fished for tools he got busy on another kind of fishing.

In a score of newspapers throughout the country he was advertising the Golden Torrent Oil Company and guaranteeing a gusher. How a man can guarantee a gusher is a nice point, but Sol did it. Moreover, in addition to the gusher his experienced driller was now drilling, the Golden Torrent Oil Company would own a thousand acres under lease.

"Think of what this may mean! What will your answer be to yourself, to your children, and possibly your grandchildren, in the coming years if you fail to take advantage of this present offer?" demanded his appeal. "What will your answer be if you see the Golden Torrent Oil Company stock at $50 a share, then $100 a share, and possibly $500 a share, if you have failed to take advantage of your present opportunity to buy at $10 a share? When I say 'present opportunity' I mean just exactly that, because before many morning suns have cast their bright rays over Arkansas' oceans of oil, it is my opinion Golden Torrent stock will be advanced to $100 a share and I believe it will steadily rise.

"Again I ask you: What will your answer be? What will your answer be to the children and grandchildren when the history of petroleum wealth is written and the name of the Golden Torrent Oil Company stands at the top for producing dividends for investors? When your children say to you: 'Why didn't you make a fortune out of the great oil boom, daddy, as did Rockefeller and others in the days of long ago?' What possible excuse can you make to yourself, my dear friend, when the door is closed and this offer is withdrawn? The enclosed subscription blank is for your prompt answer."

These advertisements carried half tones of several famous gushers. Sol did not claim that the Golden Torrent Company actually owned the gushers, but below these decorative pictures he ran a photo of their derrick and the implied association became indissoluble. Moreover, a derrick looks like a well to lots of people.

So while Ben Gober and his crew were wrestling with the maddening delays and shutdowns inseparable from a drilling job, Sol gathered in the shekels. The Smackover field was enjoying a heyday and any prospect in Arkansas gleamed like a rainbow. Widows by the dozens, doctors by the hundreds, schoolteachers, preachers, stenographers, ribbon clerks and other shrewd investors sent feverish wires to Sol, begging not to be shut out as special-delivery letter with cashier's check was following in the mail. Washington took note of the volume of his correspondence, investigated, and requested Mr. Callahan for an explanation; but he now had enough money to hire a good lawyer and obtain a delay from the Post Office Department on a technicality. This gave him time for fresh activities.

Meanwhile Ben and the Big Un worked like terriers at a rabbit hole and spent their earnings regularly in town. The Big Un now had a crush on one of the Broadway Belles, a vaudeville troupe playing the town, and wanted to save her. She was making the saving process expensive.

He and Ben and the others of the crew lived in a farmhouse a quarter of a mile from the derrick and boarded there also. It got so that they would bet fifty dollars to a nickel they could name what sort of meat they would be served at the next meal. Nobody would ever risk the nickel because they knew it would be pork.

Sol dropped in on them regularly, more for the purpose of paying them and keeping them contented than from any anxiety about the progress of the work. The outcome of the drilling was now a secondary consideration unless the Government should bear down on him about that guaranty. He had his pile and was already laying plans to get out from under responsibility.

One night the three attended a movie show in town. They never try any highbrow stuff on the oil fields. It's all good honest drama there, with the villain a blackhearted devil and the hero arriving at the head of a bunch of cowboys just in time to thwart him and save Daisy from a fate worse than death. The audience yells itself blue in the face when those gallant punchers swoop down from the mesa and, as the fight progresses and the villain's ruffians bite the dust, they rise up and yell: "That's proddin' it to 'em! Stay with 'em, cowboys!"

On this occasion it happened to be a story of New England life, one of those wherein the village miser gets possession of the old Joyce homestead and the outlying acres by fraudulent deeds, and the Widow Joyce and her tender young daughter are thrust out into the snow while the orchestra plays Hearts and Flowers. Sol just couldn't stand it. He sat there and cried like a child.

"The lowlife!" he sobbed when they regained the street. "Boiling in oil, it vould be too good for such a bum."

As they separated Ben said, "We're down nineteen hundred and twenty feet and right above the Nacatoches sand now, Mr. Callahan. Best come out tomorrow and see what happens."

"Sure, boys. I'll be there."

Something had halted work, and Gober and the crew were at dinner in the farmhouse when Sol arrived next noon at the well, so nobody could afterwards tell what happened. Probably he was dipping into the sluice pit, after his usual habit. Suddenly the whole world rocked to the thunder of an explosion, the heavens seemed to fall, and when Ben picked himself up and ran to the door a large section of the county was shooting toward the sky and the day was dark with falling debris. Tons of sand were showering down all around the house.

"What's happened?" the Big Un shouted in his ear.

Derrick and rig and nearly two thousand feet of pipe had been blown to heaven knows where. Their nine-thousand-pound boiler had gone up like a rocket. When it came down, the gas geyser caught it and sent it up again, whirling it around like a fountain tossing a ball. Finally it was flung far to one side.

The gas well's rumbling shook the earth. It had torn a crater more than a hundred yards in diameter and fifty feet deep.

As for Sol, he never did come down. After all the earth and rocks and trees had settled and the air somewhat cleared, they discerned away up in the sky a faint moving speck which some asserted to be Mr. Callahan. But this was never really verified.

The colored population of the region declared the place was directly over hell and ha'nted by ghosts from the graveyard, so they moved out. The gas well ran wild for a week, pouring better than sixty million feet a day. Then lightning set it ablaze and a pillar of fire matching the beacon for the Israelites of old rose to heaven. The fire went out, but still the well roared and rumbled. It continued to shoot gas for months, then finally subsided. The bottom of the crater filled with water which churned and seethed like the geyser pools in Yellowstone Park.

"Well," Ben remarked as he surveyed the wreckage, "We've got to go find us another job, Ol' Timer. This one has blowed up right in our face."

The Big Un nodded.

"Maybe you won't be so ready to laugh at fortune tellers after this, Ben," he said.

"Why not?"

"Well, that lady done told Sol she couldn't see what happened when he got up there, but she could see him rising very high. And he sure enough done it."

TAR AND FEATHERS
East Texas

Uncle

Tar and Feathers

EAST TEXAS

THE rain lashed the windows, the wind whistled and shrieked, buffeting the frail structure until its ribs rattled. Blinding flashes of light, a splitting, rending sound, then the crashing detonations of heavy thunder. At every peal Charity would throw up an arm as though to ward off a blow; but she continued to prepare for bed, the whites of her eyes rolling. She made sure the black cat's skull bone which she wore in a pouch suspended from her neck was in its place, then knelt down and prayed. The thunder and lightning growing even worse after she rose she unlocked her trunk, extracted a pint-flask and took a hearty swig of bootleg gin. Charity had faith in prayer, but she had found gin quicker in results.

A knock came on the door; somebody tried to turn the handle. Fumbling with the button of her flannel nightgown the cook stood for a moment in chilled terror, staring at the moving knob.

"Who—who's 'at?" she demanded in a harsh, cracked voice.

"Open the do', gal," came the quavering reply. "I cain't hold out much longer."

"You git away from there, you no-'count nigger, you!" Charity bawled in tones that would have carried a mile on a clear night. "Drag it now and lef' me alone or I'll bust you wide open! Git goin'!"

"Don't shoot! I don't aim to hurt you, gal. Ise—Ise sick."

Something in the quality of the voice—thin and feeble—stayed the cook as she reached for her six-shooter. She glanced irresolutely toward the door; the handle turned again. Then a thud as of a body falling against it. Very cautiously she turned the key, opened the door no more than an inch and peeped out.

A flash of lightning revealed a huddled figure on the step. No longer fearful, Charity seized it by the slack of its coat and dragged it indoors; then she had to exert all her strength to shut the door against the wind while the rain drove through and soaked her. When she turned she saw a little dried-up old darky lying on his side, unconscious, his hat fallen back from his gray kinky head.

At prevailing prices it would have been criminal to revive him with gin. She laid him on the bed and then dashed water in his face. As he was already dripping

181

rain it seemed a superfluous form of first aid, but presently he made a sound and opened his eyes.

"How'd you git here? Huh?" Charity inquired, standing above him with arms akimbo.

"I seen your light."

"What ails you, anyhow?"

"Ise got a misery. I'm bad, I tell you, gal—awful bad."

"You been prowlin' raound in all this rain?"

He nodded.

"It looks like you'd have better sense."

"I didn't have no place to go."

"What? You ain't got no place to sleep? When did you eat las'?"

"Yiste'day mornin'," he said faintly.

"Good lan', no wonder you got a misery!" the cook scolded, her finer nature stirred. "Vittles is what you need. How come you don' eat since yiste'day?"

"You cain't eat what you ain't got none of."

"D'you mean to tell me nobody wouldn't give you nothin'?"

"I didn't ask. I ain't never begged yet, and somehow—"

"Here! You lay right where you is while I go fetch some vittles."

With her back turned modestly toward the bed she put on stockings and shoes, donned an overcoat, threw a shawl over her head and sallied out into the night. It was only thirty yards to the kitchen of the house, but she had to fight the wind every foot of the way.

"Is that you, Charity?" her mistress called from upstairs.

"Yassum."

"What on earth are you doing in the kitchen at this hour?"

"Ma'am?"

"I said what on earth are you doing in the kitchen at this hour?"

"I ain't feelin' good, Miz Gudger, and I aim to make me some coffee."

She heard the judge grumble something, then a tart reply from his wife. Evidently the explanation satisfied them, for she was left undisturbed. With cold pot roast, corn bread, a jar of cane molasses and a pot of coffee wrapped in her shawl she returned to her room in the garage.

"All right," she announced, "here 'tis. Let's see you fly at it, oncle."

He flew at it, she watching with professional appreciation. Uncle's chewing apparatus consisted of only three worn black stumps of teeth, but what he did with those was a caution.

"You sure do take hold!" she remarked admiringly.

They were an odd pair: Charity, nearly six feet high, angular, loose-jointed, with long arms and flat chest, her sparse woolly hair twisted into tight checkerboard squares, and uncle, on the bed, small, slight, gray of head but otherwise black as the ace of spades.

"What's your name?"

"Dan'l."

"Dan'l what?"

"Just Dan'l. I did have another name once," he replied, scratching his pate like a tired child, "but I just don't recollect what it was."

"How come you're in Liveoak? Huh? I never seen you raound this town befo'?"

"No-oo. I used to work a li'l' farm down in the river bottom but Mr. Lemmon, he done run me off las' Monday." He spoke uncomplainingly. "Took my mule too—the onliest one I had. Yassum. He sure did me mean."

"Well, I reckon maybe you didn't make a crop down there in the bottom, did you?"

"No-oo. But I'd of paid him if he'd give me time."

Charity snorted at this. Hers was too resolute and resourceful a soul to sympathize much with failures.

"How old mought you be?"

"Ninety-four." He raised his head with a sort of infantile pride. "Yassum, ninety-four. Ol' Miz Shortridge done owned me till I was thirty-six."

"Well, what d'you know about that?" Charity murmured, regarding him with an altered expression. She was much impressed and the news added to her responsibility. With that clannishness born of slave days when to stick together meant life or death, she was resolved now to make some provision for uncle's maintenance. This feeling among the negroes explains why they usually guard each other's secrets so jealously.

"Oh, it was ter'ble—ter'ble!" exclaimed Uncle Daniel suddenly, as though he had just remembered, and he wagged his head.

"What was ter'ble? Huh?"

"I seen a white gen'l'man shoot another white gen'l'man right through here tonight. Yassum; he done shot him right through here." He indicated a spot on his abdomen. "Killed him, too, I reckon. Must of."

"Huh?"

"It's troof I'm tellin' you, gal. Right in front of that bank on the corner of the square. There was nobody round, and one white gen'l'man stepped out of the bank just as I come along, and then another gen'l'man done stepped out of an automobile and shot him—right through here."

The cook began to breathe fast and her big eyes blazed. She reveled in mystery, and a murder fascinated her even more than a funeral.

"What's 'at you say? Huh? Your misery done made you see things, oncle."

"No, ma'am. I seen it all right, every bit. He lifted him into that car and then I drug it away from there. Done shot him right through here, 'thout sayin' so much as howdy neither."

Charity scrutinized him closely, undecided whether he was laboring under hallucinations or was merely seeking to repay her hospitality. But nobody could doubt uncle's sincerity or question the horror still upon him. She said abruptly, "Don' you tell nobody about this. Hear me? Don' you dare!"

"What would I go and tell for?"

"Well, sometimes a fool nigger ups and shoots off his mouf, and it always lands him in trouble. You know what us gits when we meddle into white folks' business, don' you, oncle?"

"I sure do!"

"Then you keep quiet. Where'd you say he shot him?"

"Right through here. It was dark, but I seen him grab at it—like this."

"Did he groan much, or take on?" demanded Charity hungrily.

"I didn't hear. No, ma'am, I drug it away from there right now."

She was disappointed that he could not supply more of the gruesome details; still it was a choice morsel and she felt well repaid.

"Where do you figure on sleepin'?" she inquired, after turning things over in her mind.

"Anywheres, so long as it's dry. I feel right sleepy."

"Maybe so, but you cain't sleep where you is. What's mo', if I was to keep you here they'd think you was my comfort maybe." And she cackled with glee.

"Ninety-four ain't so old, gal," Uncle Daniel said darkly.

"Ain't it the troof? Men just naturally don't know when to git ready for the day of judgment." After staring at him a while she announced, "Well, you cain't stop here, and there ain't no bed or nothin' in the yardman's house. We don' keep a yardman regular now—just hire somebody to cut the grass."

"I kin sleep anywheres it's dry."

"Could you sleep in the automobile if I done give you a coupla blankets? Huh?"

"Sure I kin, gal. Sure I kin."

"Then come on. But mind you wake up befo' the judge gits down, else he'll skin me alive. You hide out somewheres till after breakfast and maybe I kin fix it up so's you'll have a place to stay."

When Charity rose next morning Uncle Daniel had disappeared according to instructions. She set about getting the breakfast ready. Returning from the garden with some strawberries, she halted in amazement to stare at an object coming slowly up the driveway. It was a tiny brindle pup, so young he could barely stagger along; his face was black and flat and wore an expression of unutterable woe; every few steps he would stop to let out a treble yelp of misery. In a dozen long strides the cook was upon him. She gathered him up and pressed him to her breast, then glanced defiantly about to ascertain whether anybody had seen her do it.

"You come to your mammy," she cried. "Good lan', but you is thin! All haid."

She had always wanted a dog, but the judge had declared he would not have one on the place. Now Providence had intervened.

"I sure would like to see him git raound this," she muttered.

A minute later the brindle was gulping down a bowl of corn bread saturated with gravy, whilst the cook watched.

"He sure do go after it," she observed approvingly as the pup swelled and swelled. "It's like he'll bust if he don' quit."

So far from having any such intention the brindle tried first to lick the pattern off the bowl, then began a mournful nosing about the floor, smelling for bits he might have overlooked. Charity gave him some more.

"I reckon I'll call you Pahson," she said thoughtfully, "after the rev'end. You'se so hard to fill."

The judge always went through a regular routine on rising—first to the front yard for the morning paper; then a slow tour of back lawn, garage and garden by way of inspection whilst he skimmed the news heads. Despite his preoccupation the cook often declared it was surprising how much meanness he could discover. He spotted the pup at once, of course.

"Where did that come from?"

"The storm done brung him, judge. Anyhow, he was here when I got up this mornin'."

"How often have I told you I wouldn't have a dog about the place? You brought that pup here yourself—don't try to tell me you didn't! You've been scheming how to get round me for years."

"No, suh! Honest to goodness, cross my heart, I never!"

"Well, you can just get rid of him anyhow. I won't have a dog digging up my flower beds."

His tone was final, but the effect was spoiled by his wife's inquiry from their bedroom window—"What's the argument now?"

"Ma'am?"

"What's the trouble down there?"

"Why, the judge won't let me even give a little bitty food to a pore starvin' pup, Miz Gudger."

"Who said anything about food?" the judge fumed. That was an old trick of hers, to twist what he said—she had probably picked it up from his wife. "I've told you many times that I won't allow a dog on the place and I won't."

"Would you turn away a starvin', helpless critter from your do'?" demanded Charity, fixing her eyes upon him with extraordinary intentness.

"What's that got to do with it?"

"Would you? Huh? I'm askin'."

The judge felt in his bones that Charity was laying the predicate for something else, and a grin lurked back of his stern query—"What are you driving at anyhow, you old rascal?"

Mrs. Gudger's arrival on the scene saved the cook the necessity of reply.

"Where is this pup you-all are talking about?" And then she glimpsed Parson. "Oh, isn't he cunning! Look at that little black face, Jim! You darling, you! Look, Jim, did you ever, in all your born days, see anything look so sad? Oh, oo is so cute—ess, oo is!"

The instant she started baby talk Gudger knew it was all off, and with an exclamation of disgust he started into the house. His wife was cuddling the brindle now and she cried after him, "Indeed, we will keep him! The idea of turning away a poor little helpless thing like this! Oo is mother's 'ittle dumpkins, isn't oo?"

"You wouldn't let me keep Pete on the place—made me send him down to the farm——the best bird dog in the county," her husband shot at her through the window.

"What? That great, tearing wild thing! I should say not—that's different."

"The only difference is Pete's got sense and is good for something."

"I'm going to keep this one anyhow."

"All right. It's a bargain." cried the judge eagerly. "You can have the pup and I'll bring Pete back."

"Men are such babies," Mrs. Gudger exclaimed, and although Charity maintained a discreet silence it was plain that she was in hearty agreement.

Her first precaution was to jerk a couple of hairs out of Parson's stubby tail. These she buried under the back stoop.

"Now he won't never run off," she said with perfect confidence.

186

On tenterhooks to learn whether the newspaper contained anything about the killing Uncle Daniel had described, the cook loitered around the breakfast table so aimlessly and hovered so close to the judge that he felt her breath down the back of his neck and brusquely inquired what the mischief was on her mind.

"Nothin'."

"You're up to something."

"No, suh."

He made no mention of any shooting, which he would certainly have done had there been anything in the paper about it. And then Charity remembered that the newspaper was published in a city a hundred miles distant. She determined to go down to the grocer's the first thing after breakfast and learn all about it.

Just as the judge was about to leave for his office the telephone rang and he answered it. Charity had a phone in the kitchen in order that she might take calls; she promptly took down the receiver and listened in. What she heard made her eyes pop.

"Good God!" exclaimed the judge, and he said it again in a lower tone when he hung up.

"What's the matter, dear?"

"Jeff Harkrider killed Fletcher Dawes last night."

"No!"

"Earl Smith just phoned. It's a bad business, Miriam—a bad business."

Mrs. Gudger turned pale. She knew both families intimately. "Where did it happen? And what did he do it for?"

"Earl says Jeff won't talk, but he did say when he surrendered to the sheriff that Dawes had broken up his home."

"Oh, what a lie! I'll never believe it. Never!"

"Neither can I. Fanny isn't that kind. Why, I never heard the slightest whisper about her in my life. I'd as soon believe it about—about—"

"About me?"

"Well, you know what I mean."

"Of course. I feel exactly the same way. It's all a lie, Jim, a contemptible lie. He's trying to hide behind her skirts."

"Queer," the judge mumbled, staring at her unseeingly. "I happen to know—" But what he happened to know he kept to himself.

"And I suppose Fanny will stick by him—that's the sort she is. She'll sacrifice herself for that miserable—"

"Easy there, honey, easy! This is a bad business and the less we talk about it the better."

He stood looking out of the window for a few moments, lost in thought. At last he turned away with a grunt of contempt.

"Protecting woman's honor!—and all that bunk. This country's just full of it, Miriam. If a woman carries on with a man her honor's gone anyhow. A husband doesn't guard it—he doesn't bring it back—by shootin' the other fellow. All he does is drag her name through the dirt in every newspaper in the country. Shucks, it makes me sick. Every cowardly killer who wants to get even with his enemy goes and drags his wife in, and juries fall for it."

"Well, if Jeff Harkrider—"

The telephone rang again. After a minute Mrs. Gudger heard her husband say with unusual emphasis, "No, I will not! You tell him for me I won't touch it."

"Who was it?"

"Jeff's brother. Wanted me to take the case for him. Not me! The less we have to do with this business the better, Miriam. Both families are friends of ours, so let's keep our mouths shut."

Charity had been hovering near the door. She now cut in with, "Where at did you say Mr. Dawes got shot, judge?"

"You been listening?"

"No, suh. I couldn't help but hear some."

"He was shot in Mr. Harkrider's house."

The cook opened her mouth to say something, thought better of it and retired precipitately into the kitchen.

"What's the matter with her now, I wonder?"

"Search me. She's a crafty old bird, Miriam. What made her look at me like that, do you suppose?"

"You were going to say something about happening to know—and then you stopped. What was it, Jim?"

"Oh, nothing."

"Now don't be foolish. I wouldn't be as mean as you for anything. The idea of not telling me!"

"Well, you promise never to breathe a word of it?"

"Of course."

"Your word of honor?"

"I'll never tell a soul."

"You'd best not, or the fat will be in the fire. Well, I happen to know that Jeff Harkrider owed Fletcher quite a lot of money and Fletcher has been pressing him for payment."

"Oh!"

"They had trouble over that lumberyard sale and—honey, it looks to me like this was nothing but cold-blooded murder and Jeff is trying now to crawl out by using his wife."

"The low-down sneak!"

"They usually are. But you keep quiet about it and so will I. It's a bad business." And reiterating this opinion the judge went downtown.

Charity could scarcely wait for Uncle Daniel to arrive. He finally put in an appearance about ten o'clock by way of the lane.

"Where at was that killin' you saw las' night? Be careful now."

"Down by the square, near that bank on the corner. One gen'l'man done shot the other right through here."

Uncle Daniel looked scared, but he did not deviate from his facts.

"Then how come they found the body in Mr. Harkrider's residence and Mr. Harkrider says he was tryin' to bust up his home? Huh?"

Uncle scratched his head.

"Maybe there was two killin's," he hazarded.

"Uh-uh! It's the same one."

"Well," he replied, vaguely troubled, "all I know is I seen him do it—right through here."

The cook seized his shoulder and administered a gentle shake to emphasize her warning—"Don' you say a word! Hear me? Don' you ever let on you saw nothin'! And I won't neither. If we do, the Ku-Klux will come and fetch us maybe. So mind!"

"I ain't seen nothin' and I don't know nothin'," Uncle Daniel promised.

Charity did not bother her head about work that morning. Neither did any other cook in Liveoak. They gossiped over fences and visited; the whole town was agog with the news. By noon every detail of the story was public property, and persons meeting on the street, in the stores or at the post office, would supply the latest tidbit that had developed in the gruesome affair. Miz Harkrider and Fletcher Dawes had been carrying on secretly for more'n a year and all the time her singing in the choir that way and the families such close friends! Jeff Harkrider had come home unexpected from downtown and caught Fletcher Dawes in the hall and he shot him right through the heart the very first shot.

Well, they never would have thought it of Fletcher Dawes or of Miz Harkrider either, for that matter, because she always seemed a right nice lady; but you never could tell and he only got what was coming to him. A man had a right to protect his own home. Was it true that she admitted it and would testify for her husband at the trial? They had heard that Hunter McLemore told somebody she would. Yes, McLemore would defend Harkrider, so it was a cinch. The smartest criminal lawyer in Staple County, if not in the whole state. Yes, as smart as they made 'em. What he couldn't do with a jury wasn't worth trying. Look how he had got Joe Bass off that time, and Lee Terry and the Tarwater boys! Why, Harkrider was as good as a free man already, but McLemore would sure shake him down. There wouldn't be much left of the Harkrider black-land farms when McLemore got through with Jeff. He was smart, sure enough.

What a bomb Charity could have thrown into all this welter of gossip! How she could have made their eyes pop, and to what a pinnacle of glory she might have won at a jump! Her mouth watered over the chance. The temptation was almost more than flesh and blood could bear, but never once did she weaken to utter the slightest hint. She gathered all the gory details she could, but of what she had heard of the tragedy from an eyewitness of it, not one syllable. However, she kept Uncle Daniel carefully under cover, not yet persuaded of his discretion.

To her disappointment the judge did not speak of the case when he came home for dinner and she got nothing for her trouble of hanging about within earshot. He and Mrs. Gudger went upstairs right after they had eaten, and probably talked it over there. And at supper the only references he made to the murder concerned features with which the cook was already familiar. Like everybody else he thought Harkrider would get off; but unlike the vast majority he thought he ought not to get off. Although refraining from any opinions in her hearing, the cook could tell that the judge had his own ideas about the killing and did not believe what was popularly supposed to be Harkrider's story of defense.

He gave her a momentary fright as she was putting the milk bottles out for the night.

"Charity," he said, "was the garage locked last night?"

"Yassuh. I done locked it my own se'f."

"I found some burned matches on the floor of the car this morning. I wonder how they came there—I don't smoke."

"Good lan'! Matches? Well, what d'you know about that!"

"Do you reckon somebody got in and stole something?" Mrs. Gudger interjected.

"Everything seems to be in its place. Have you missed anything, Charity?"

"Nossuh, not a thing; but I ain't looked. I'll go make sure right now."

"And be careful to lock up too. I don't like to think there're thieves about. We've never had one in twenty years."

As the cook gave uncle his supper she delivered an impassioned lecture on carelessness in smoking that ol' pipe of hisn and he contritely assured her he would be more careful in future. There was no difficulty about feeding him; she already surreptitiously supplied several kinfolks from the Gudger larder, and hers were generous employers—real quality—not disposed to pry into the fate of a knuckle of ham or raise a question about the remains of the fried chicken from supper, or get mean about a paltry bowl of black-eyed peas. But she had to exercise caution about keeping him out of sight until the judge and Miz Gudger had gone to bed. As for getting out before dawn, uncle assured her he had been accustomed to do that all his life.

The murder proved a nine days' wonder. Harkrider enjoyed his liberty on trifling bail and the preliminaries to trial moved along about as they always do. He simply entered a plea of not guilty and Hunter McLemore kept in reserve the sort of defense he would make.

"Charity," said the judge at breakfast one morning, "how's Mr. Thompson?" By that name the cook always referred to a fifty-year-old beau she sometimes entertained.

"All right, I reckon. I ain't saw him lately, judge." And Charity exploded into coy laughter.

"Surely you haven't got another lover, then—at your age?"

The cook regarded him with bulging eyes, fearful of what was coming.

"I thought I saw somebody sneaking off down the lane about daylight."

"That Stella woman next do', maybe," suggested Charity with dry lips.

The judge eyed her strangely but did not press the matter. To uncle, when he arrived for breakfast, the cook burst out: "Now you done it! Didn't I tell you to git movin' before the light come? We got to think up somethin' mighty fast."

"I'll just up and move along, gal. If I stay here it's like to make you a heap of trouble."

"Oh, shut your mouf and leave me think," the cook snapped, her nerves on edge. "I'll tell you what we'll do: When Miz Gudger comes out this evenin' to mess raound her rose bed you happen to be on hand and help her. That'll fix it."

So it was arranged. Straightening from a rosebush around whose roots she had been digging, Mrs. Gudger was surprised to see an old darky grinning at her from ear to ear.

"Well! Where did you come from, uncle?"

"I just happened by, ma'am. I thought mought be you would need a yardman?"

She glanced at his puckered face and shriveled limbs and smiled.

"No, we don't. And I'm afraid you're rather old for that sort of work, aren't you?"

191

"No'm, I can work good. Just let me dig that there bed for you and you'll see. These niggers nowadays, they don't know nothin'—just no 'count, that's what they is."

Charity had joined them and stood watching in silence.

"All right. Let's see how you do it. But take care not to tire yourself out. Charity, go and show him where the fork is."

The long, lank cook led off toward the garage, and as she went muttered to Uncle Daniel out of the side of her mouth, "Didn't I tol' you I'd fix it?"

Mrs. Gudger talked to uncle while he worked. He went at the job with surprising vigor and no inconsiderable knowledge of rose culture, but would pause every few minutes to give her a chance to applaud. Within a quarter of an hour she had made up her mind.

"Charity, uncle says he has no place to stay. The idea! Isn't the yardman's house all cleared out and clean?"

"Yassum."

"Then get somebody to help you fetch a bed down from the attic. We've got plenty of bedding and he can sleep there." Turning to Uncle Daniel she added, "You come right along and live here, uncle. Charity will give you your meals."

"I'll earn 'em, ma'am. I kin work."

Again she smiled.

"Well, you can watch the puppy and see he doesn't run off and you can help me with the rose bed, of course. You're really wonderful with roses, uncle."

"Yassum. I reckon there ain't a man in the county knows more 'bout roses than what I do," replied Uncle Daniel, swelling up importantly.

By the time the judge arrived home the business was settled. On first hearing of the proposal he put his foot down hard against it—he wouldn't have a lazy old nigger idling round his place—but after looking uncle over, after listening to his gentle old voice, the judge experienced a change of heart.

"Poor old fellow," he said to his wife. "That man Lemmon treated him like a dog. I tell you, Miriam, some of these landlords are nothing but bloodsuckers. Of course we'll let him stay. Charity, you feed him up, and mind you treat him right too."

"Yassuh," the cook assented; but such was the depth of her guile that she grumbled audibly on her way out to the kitchen, "I didn't hire to cook for every stray nigger what comes along."

A night's reflection seemed to give the judge another angle on the arrangement, for he remarked with a slow grin at breakfast: "Charity, you ol' rascal, I believe you had this whole thing framed up the day you adopted that pup."

"No, suh! Cross my heart!" cried Charity, then broke into peals of laughter. The judge joined in. They understood each other thoroughly.

In such fashion did Uncle Daniel become a pensioner of the judge's. He settled down to a fine, lazy life, because the weather grew very hot and Mrs. Gudger would not permit him to work. He had everything he wanted to eat, could doze in the shade whensoever he felt like it, and often the judge and his wife had him up on the back porch to tell them about slave days. In return he made an admirable guest; never gave them the least trouble and took excellent care of the pup, which adored him. On only one point was he stubborn, but on that he would not budge an inch. He refused point-blank to give the brindle a bath. No pup had ever had a bath in his day and it was all foolishness—like to give him distemper and a misery—so the job fell to Charity.

At supper one night the judge remarked to his wife, "Reese Kemp was in to see me today."

"What did he want?"

"Asked me to join the Ku-Klux."

Mrs. Gudger put down her fork, her face a picture of astonishment.

"The very idea! So it's true they've got a Klan here then? I heard they had, but I wouldn't believe it. Seems so childish. But, of course, Reese—he's just a natural-born joiner. What did you tell him?"

"Told him I'd think it over."

Charity, who usually managed to overhear important scraps of conversation, ejaculated, "Good lan'!"

"That will do, Charity," said her mistress. "You can stay in the kitchen. We've got everything we need."

The cook departed reluctantly. She hadn't a high opinion of her sex anyhow and this confirmed her judgment.

"What do you mean by you would think it over, Jim?" demanded his wife when the swing door had ceased to sway. "Surely you wouldn't dream of joining the Ku-Klux! Why, I've heard you say a hundred times how dangerous they were, and how they were tearing down law and order and setting man against man."

The judge fidgeted uneasily under her eye.

"Yes, that's true—to some extent. But they do a lot of good too. They're putting fear into the niggers and teaching 'em where they belong. And about time. Some of the niggers round this neck of the woods were getting mighty uppity."

"Well, I never expected to hear you talk like that, Jim Gudger!"

"And they're putting a stop to a lot of crime, too."

"We've got police and courts and everything for that."

"Yes, but the courts and police don't reach 'em. Look at the bootleggers! Look at the gambling going on right in this town! And there're crimes it's hard for the law to get at—men chasing after young girls and other men's wives and all that."

"You mean that Bascom case over in Windy City?" his wife retorted. "But nobody's sure even now he did anything wrong. They done tarred and feathered him and ran him out of town but the only evidence I ever heard against him was the word of that Tom Jenks, and everybody knows what he's like. They say he and Bascom have been enemies for years."

The judge fretfully pushed his plate away.

"I suppose they didn't do a good job when they took the Tarwater boys out and gave 'em a whipping, hey? Maybe you'll claim they made a mistake there."

"Those two boys who beat up and robbed old Mrs. Rosenberg, and Hunter McLemore got them off?"

Her husband nodded.

"And they went and robbed another the very next week? Then why don't they take that Hunter McLemore out and whip him? They'd have gone to prison, where they belong, only for him and his jury."

"Why, he's a lawyer!" the judge exclaimed in horror. "You talk like you're crazy, woman."

"Maybe I do but let me tell you this, Jim Gudger: You don't join the Ku-Klux as long as I'm above the sod!"

At this juncture the argument was cut short by Charity who entered with a plate of hot biscuits—the kitchen acoustics were poor and she simply couldn't stand the suspense any longer. They waited until she had gone, then the judge said, "Would you like to take a walk downtown tonight?"

"What's going on?"

"Well, tomorrow's election day, and there'll probably be some fun."

The sidewalks were filled when they reached the square just at twilight, and the crowds grew denser every minute. Many country people mingled with the townspeople and everywhere they encountered an atmosphere of expectancy.

194

"What does it mean?" Mrs. Gudger inquired as they tried to worm through. "What's up?"

"They expect something to happen, I reckon."

The crowd moved slowly up and down, alert and eager, yet singularly subdued for a pre-election gathering. It grew dark, but still they lingered, ignoring the movie theaters which generally drew them. At half past nine all the street and shop lights went out and a sudden hush came over the square.

"They're coming!" the whisper ran. Everybody strained forward to stare in the direction of the opera house.

In its doorway there suddenly blazed the fiery cross and as they watched, a ghostly procession debouched into the square, the Ku-Klux emblem at its head and drooping beside it the Stars and Stripes. Silently they came, six hundred and fifty sheeted, hooded men, and through silent ranks of thousands they moved, the only sounds the muffled thud and soft dragging of feet. In the middle of the parade flared a couple of torches, lighting up banners carried back of them. These banners bore such mottoes as "Supremacy of the White Race," "Criminals and Degenerates Must Go," "Protect Our Womanhood."

Some few applauded, but they were instantly hushed and the Klan continued its silent circuit of the square. At the opera house corner they turned down the street, instead of re-entering the building, and marched into Nigger Town. Most of the spectators followed.

The district appeared to be deserted. Every shack was dark. A group of colored children gaped through the pickets of a fence but scurried into hiding before the head of the parade reached them. The attendant throngs were disappointed and some of them yelled warnings at the darkened houses, but no sound came from the Klansmen's ranks except the steady tramp of feet. They marched along under the liveoaks and cottonwoods, right through the heart of the district, then about-faced and marched back. Having reached the square again, they disappeared into the opera house and were seen no more that night.

In the revealing light of day it would have looked like a burlesque troupe advertising their night's performance. Darkness made it eerie, tingling, impressive: one felt the sinister power back of those voiceless ranks. And next day not one colored citizen of Liveoak cast a vote.

Mrs. Gudger watched it all without a word. When the last sheeted form had vanished she gave a slight shudder. The judge drew a deep breath. In spite of his good common sense he had been impressed.

"They're stronger than I thought," he said in guarded tones.

People were discussing it excitedly on every hand, yet there was no loud talk. An odd, uncanny restraint marked the comment. Men eyed their neighbors cautiously when they spoke. It was plain that nobody cared to take chances.

"What did you think of it?" the judge whispered.

Mrs. Gudger made an effort to shake off the spell it had cast.

"It was all right until I saw their feet and then they looked ridiculous. Didn't you recognize Reb?"

"I didn't recognize anybody. Neither could you."

"Nonsense! I'd know his feet anywhere. He helped carry one of those banners."

"Well, what about it?"

"You surely don't expect me to take anything seriously when Reb belongs to it, do you? If that's the kind of organization it is, the sheriff ought to put the whole crowd in jail."

The judge replied quietly: "I'm afraid it wouldn't hold them. And no matter what you say, Miriam, there're some mighty good men in it. Some of our closest friends belong. Some of the very best citizens of this town are high officers, so it won't do to talk about the Klan at all."

"Well, anyhow, you're not going to join."

They had entered their own street now, dark and deserted, and could speak with freedom.

"They've done a lot of good," he insisted.

"How?"

"They've given to the hospitals and quite a lot to charity—you remember that widow woman, Miz Jester, and Charlie Moss when he was sick last winter?"

"Sure! That's all a part of the racket. Tammany Hall started that. I've heard you say so yourself."

This unfortunate reference nettled the judge; it was so like a woman to turn some forgotten utterance of the past against you.

"But there's a real need of an organization like this just now, Miriam. This crime wave is serious. Where it will end nobody knows. Something must be done to stop it and these men mean to do it."

"We've got courts."

"But the courts don't punish as they ought. You know yourself how the very worst class of criminals—murderers and highjackers—get off every day."

"Yes, and whose fault is it?" she countered hotly. "You're a lawyer—whose fault is it?"

There was no use trying to reason with a woman and the judge gave up in disgust. As they prepared for bed she took a final shot at him.

"Men make me tired," she mumbled through a mouthful of hairpins. "Always wanting to join something. If they can wear an apron or a sash and a dinky little sword they're in the seventh heaven. And give 'em a bed sheet and a mask and—why, they just come a-runnin' like a pack of small boys to play Indian."

Every married man will know by now that Judge Gudger did not join the Ku-Klux. He was tempted, but soon perceived which way his duty lay; and after coming to a decision it was not long before he reverted to his original opinion of the peril which the organization constituted.

Events drove him in this direction. Encouraged by their strength and success in gaining new members—it was reported that the sheriff and all the peace officers belonged, and Bob Upham came out openly as a Klansman in his race for Congress —the Klan acted vigorously. One night a party of them in seven automobiles took out two colored bell boys from the Hotel Alamo, drove to a secluded spot, and there tied them to trees and whipped them. What the darkies had done to bring down this punishment was never made public, but various rumors went round.

Their next victim was a white man, the manager of the local flour mill. Him they enticed onto his front porch by sending a stranger to his door to inquire for a house number, then kidnaped him under the eyes of his wife and daughter, who made a great outcry; carried him to Red River Bridge and there administered a coat of tar and feathers after the leader of the party had delivered a rambling lecture on morality. What the specific charge was did not transpire, according to the reporter for the Liveoak Booster who accompanied them on invitation. They dumped the unfortunate wretch out into the middle of the square just as the moving-picture theaters were disgorging their audiences and drove off. All were hooded.

Next day the mill manager left town, taking his family with him. He assured the Booster editor that he wasn't afraid and had done nothing wrong, but he could not face the disgrace.

"I don't know anything about him," cried Mrs. Gudger, "But if he did wrong, why didn't they bring him to trial? And his wife and daughter are just as nice as they can be. They simply idolize him too. What was the trouble, Jim?"

"Oh, I've heard a lot, but it may be nothing but gossip. Best not talk about it, Miriam."

"Indeed, I will, whenever I feel like it! They may have you scared, but not me."

*   *   *   *   *   *   *

Old Colonel Allen came stumping up the stairs into Gudger's office one morning and, taking a chair without a word of greeting, tossed a letter in front of the judge.

"Read that," he said. "My boy received it last night. Is it genuine, do you think?"

The judge scrutinized the missive carefully.

"Hard to say, but it looks like it to me."

"Then I know what to do," declared the veteran, with his chin whisker thrust out.

"I wouldn't do anything violent, colonel," the judge cautioned. "What's the trouble about your boy, anyhow?"

"No trouble," snapped his client. "I know that boy inside out. So should you, Gudger. He's never done a thing but talk; but he will say what he thinks, in spite of hell, and he's been talking mighty strong against that bunch."

"Where're you going now?" Gudger asked as the colonel rose with the help of his stick.

"Over to Bob Upham's office."

"What for?"

"Well, I don't know exactly who belongs to this here Klan and who doesn't, but I know Bob does because he come out flatfooted and said so. And I aim to tell Bob this"—the colonel's voice grated—"If anybody harms that boy, or so much as lifts a finger against him, I won't bother to hunt down the particular men who did it. What I'll do is kill on sight the members of the Klan I happen to know, regardless of whether they were in on this particular job. And I'll start with Bob Upham and Hunter McLemore, who's the Imperial Gizzard, or Head Beagle, or whatever they call him."

He went out and down the stairs and he told Bob Upham just that. The colonel had a reputation for having been quick on the trigger in his youth. They never came for young Allen.

Meanwhile the Klan was winning sympathy in various ways. They offered to build a hospital for babies and they put up the money; they attended Clem Maddox's funeral in a body in full regalia and pensioned his widow; their mere existence induced a renewed attitude of respect in the negro population toward the whites; and undoubtedly they put the quietus on a lot of evils with which Liveoak had become infested since the war—gambling and loose road-houses. And a number of shady characters, who saw the handwriting on the wall, drifted.

"All the same, they ought to be suppressed," Mrs. Gudger declared. "Are we going to have our lives regulated by a bunch of men who meet in secret and hide behind sheets? This town isn't a bit the same since they started. Everybody's suspicious of everybody else and afraid of they don't know what. Why, what's to prevent them coming some night and taking you out and giving you a coat of tar and feathers?"

"Nothing but my good behavior," answered the judge with a smile.

"But supposing somebody in the Klan's got a grudge against you and makes up a lot of lies? That could happen. You might not even get a chance to find out what they were."

"Ye-es," her husband admitted, "that's the bad feature of it, of course. It's not likely to happen, but it could."

In the autumn the Harkrider case came to trial, relegating other sensations to the background. Its result was, of course, a foregone conclusion. Hadn't he simply protected his home? And what man worthy of the name would not? Besides, the South has an abiding aversion to hanging white men, and Hunter McLemore was defending Harkrider—a smart lawyer—the smartest criminal lawyer in the county. McLemore would get him off—yessir—he would have the jury crying like babies in no time. Nobody could do things with a jury like Hunter McLemore did. They chuckled over his smartness.

The trial dragged along several days but that was only because McLemore wanted a chance to display his forensic talents. So far as the result was concerned, it could have been wound up in a forenoon so everybody could go to the ball game. The prosecuting attorney did not extend himself—the dead man was very dead, his murderer had numerous and powerful friends and the sympathy of the great mass of the public—the prosecuting attorney intended to run for office again the following year. Well?

Mrs. Harkrider took the stand and admitted misconduct with Dawes. Her appearance made a profound impression and evoked no little pity. Never once did she raise her eyes, and she gave her evidence in a low voice frequently broken by sobs. Toward the end of her story she broke down utterly and buried her face in her hands, her body racked.

"Oh, I can't! I can't!" she cried wildly.

The jury displayed emotion and the courtroom began to buzz. Some of the spectators shed tears. McLemore hurried to her with a glass of water and whispered in her ear. She straightened and went on with her story. The incident proved favorable for the defense as showing that she was not lost to all sense of shame, but had simply yielded to a man she loved deeply. By implication, of course, he must have been a sorry rascal to have taken advantage of such a woman and McLemore made the most of this later.

The prosecuting attorney addressed the jury half-heartedly. Had he asked for acquittal his wish could hardly have been plainer. Then Hunter McLemore got slowly to his feet and began. He started quietly, temperately, as a finished orator should; but gradually the deep, vibrant voice for which he was famous began to thrill with passion. He soared to oratorical flights. He shook his fist; he trembled; he pounded the table and tossed back his leonine mane from his eyes; he adjured the jury to consider the facts as husbands and fathers, and render a verdict which would enable them to go out from that courthouse and look God in the face; he painted Mrs. Harkrider in such warm colors as a poor, deluded, trusting woman that the audience cried openly; he pictured to them the wrongs and terrible mental anguish of the confiding, deceived husband, his desire to protect his wife's honor at all costs and preserve an unsullied name and happy home for those little helpless children. He wept.

Never had McLemore been in better form. It was masterly, wonderful, overwhelming—if you happened to be such an ignorant saphead that you were moved by such claptrap.

The jury was out eleven minutes and returned a verdict of Not Guilty. Everybody crowded about the Harkriders to shake their hands and pat them on the shoulder. McLemore, too, was the center of an admiring throng. The couple left the court together, Harkrider's arm around her waist as the last dramatic touch. Once in their car, she shook it off and did not speak to him all the way home. Two days later she went to her mother's in Windy City, taking the children with her, and Harkrider flitted for parts unknown. He was never again seen in Liveoak.

"And he done shot that gen'l'man in his own house?" demanded Uncle Daniel as he and the cook were discussing the trial over their supper.

"That's what he done."

They exchanged glances and went on with the meal. If the white folks wished it that way, well and good. It never paid to monkey with white folks' business.

The riffraff of Liveoak were now making efforts to join the Klan, perhaps as a precautionary measure. To what extent they succeeded was not generally known, but rumor had it that a number of the more prominent members, who had enrolled with the idea that the organization was needed as an emergency weapon, did not relish some of the company in which they found themselves. They were becoming dissatisfied and fearful and only awaited a favorable opportunity to withdraw.

And unscrupulous individuals outside the Klan did not hesitate to utilize the terror its name inspired to work out their private grudges. At least a score of warnings to leave town were sent to citizens and signed with the Klan's name, whose authorship the Klan publicly repudiated.

"What's this I hear about you and the parson, Charity?" the judge asked at dinner one day.

"Suh?"

"The reverend says he got a letter signed by the Ku-Klux warning him to get out—and he says you wrote it."

"What!" Charity blared. "That no-'count rascal done said that?"

"He sure did. What's more, the Klan wrote a letter to the Booster today saying they had nothing to do with this warning. Some people thought perhaps they wanted to get rid of the church in that neighborhood, but I don't see why—there're no whites within half a mile."

"He says I wrote that letter?" The cook's indignation seemed to the judge a trifle overdone.

"He did. What's more, I say so."

"No, suh. Cross my heart!"

"You can't look me in the eye, you old schemer, you! Now listen to me, Charity. The reverend showed me that letter, and it was pounded out on that old typewriter of mine upstairs. I'd know those *e*'s anywhere."

"Why, judge, suh, you do me wrong! You do, sure enough!"

Gudger laughed and his wife watched Charity with delight.

"What's the matter between you and the rev'end, anyhow?" she queried. "I thought you were a pillar of the church."

"And so I is," insisted the cook stoutly. "But that ol' robber done come raound here two weeks back and claimed I ain't paid my building dues. Why, Miz Gudger, I had the receipt, only I couldn't lay my hands on it right then. So I up and run him off'n the place. I sure did."

"Well, you be careful or the Ku-Klux will get you."

Charity came as near turning pale as her hue would permit.

"So he said that, did he? Well, I intends to git even with the rev'end."

She hurried through the dishwashing and vanished for the remainder of the afternoon. It was half past five when she returned and she was breathing fire, but triumphant.

"Where you been?" Mrs. Gudger asked. "And what've you been up to?"

"I done went down to see the rev'end, ma'am, and I made him take back every word of it. Yes'm; I made him admit he was a liar, right to his own face."

"Charity! You ought to be more careful."

"I was, ma'am. But he was sure enough scared. His conscience must of smote him, Miz Gudger. It's the troof."

When the judge came home he brought some news.

"Whatever have you done to that parson of yours now, Charity?"

"Suh?"

"What happened today? His wife took a razor to the reverend about two hours ago and cut him up bad."

"She did? Sure enough?" cried the cook with unholy glee. "Well, I declare!"

"Come on, now, what did you do to him?"

"I ain't done nothin', judge, suh. Cross my heart!"

"Well, what did you say, then?"

"Why, all I said was how come the automobile the congregation give him for Christmas was kep' standin' in the lane back of that Cora woman's house most every evenin'? That's every word I said."

"Did his wife hear you?"

"Maybe she was listenin'—you cain't never tell."

Two days later the town was electrified by news of an attack on a ten-year-old girl at the Gracey farm southwest of Liveoak. Suspicion fastened on a young negro boy by the name of Blair who had formerly worked on the place. A search for him began, but he had flown.

The news ran like a prairie fire, and everywhere men dropped what they were doing to pile into automobiles and join in the man hunt. Within a few hours practically every male resident of the county was engaged in tracking down the fugitive—in cars, on horses, afoot, with dogs—all armed, every man of them desperately resolved to catch the fiend. Rumor had it that he had been seen on the outskirts of Liveoak, but this chance was scouted by the local police officers. They were of opinion Blair would hardly run his neck into the noose in that fashion, but would likely strike into the wild country along Red River near the boundary and hide out there until the pursuit grew cold.

Uncle Daniel ate very sparingly that night and Charity remarked it. He seemed worried and restless; yet when she returned from a trip to the dining room most of the food was gone from his plate.

"Where at has all that beef went?"

"I done et it."

She opened her mouth to say something, but changed her mind. For a long minute they stared into each other's eyes. Then Charity went on with her work and uncle retired to his shack.

The judge did not reach home until nearly ten o'clock, and then he was so worn-out and depressed that he went immediately to bed.

"Did they catch him?" Mrs. Gudger asked.

"No, but of course they will."

"Why don't the Ku-Klux run him down? They're always so anxious to show off."

"Maybe they will."

Shortly after midnight the couple were wakened by the noise of automobiles in front of the house. Some men alighted and, led by one carrying a searchlight, went straight to the servants' quarters in the rear.

"What is it, men?" demanded the judge. "What do you want on my premises?"

"You stay indoors and mind your own business, Gudger. It'll save you trouble."

His gorge rising, the judge went padding in his bare feet to get his gun. Nobody could invade his home in this fashion. His wife threw herself in his way and by twining herself about him and clinging to his arms prevented the accomplishment of his foolhardy purpose. She begged him to be sensible.

The judge heard violent knocking on the door of the yardman's house, then somebody kicked it in. A shout, cries of exultation, and Uncle Daniel's high-pitched tones raised in piteous entreaty. Before Gudger could break free and descend, the party returned along the driveway to the waiting automobiles, half dragging, half carrying two figures with them.

"You turn me loose right now, Miriam," her husband said in a deadly quiet voice.

"I won't! I won't! You'll go and get yourself killed!"

"If you don't take your hands off me this minute I'll strike you, so help me!"

She fell away from him then, gazing at him in horror. What was this beast she had roused in her man? Was he like all the others?—like those out there in the road? She could hear their cars starting.

A window opposite went up and a voice shouted, "What is it, boys? Got him?"

"You bet we got him!" And then the boom of motors as the procession raced toward the square.

The judge, very pale, went to the bureau drawer, drew out his revolver and started to dress.

"I promise you nothing will happen so long as they don't harm that old man," he said before descending the stairs. His wife did not reply—merely gazed at him with wide eyes, the tragedy outside dwarfed now by her own.

A glance into uncle's shack revealed that it was empty, and the judge walked out into the street. Men were hurrying from every direction; doors flew open, letting out broad shafts of light and running figures, all headed toward the square.

Voices cried to know whether they had caught the nigger, others answered jubilantly. Women leaned from bedroom windows to watch the excitement; they talked from house to house; some of them joined the rush. Scores of boys, racing to be first on the scene, passed the judge.

"Have they caught Blair?" he cried after a fleeing urchin.

"Sure!" replied the boy over his shoulder, not recognizing the judge. "They done run him down in ol' Gudger's yardman's house. He was hidin' aout there."

The posse was returning from Nigger Town when the judge reached the square. They had driven all through that quarter to exhibit the prisoner. Every car had its lights burning full; some of the occupants carried torches.

Where was uncle? The judge could not discern him in any of the cars; but, try as he would, it was impossible to get near them. The crowd was so dense, and surged and barged so wildly as they pressed to get a view of the prisoner, that he had all he could do to keep his feet. Nobody had time to look at whom he was shoving, nobody paid any attention to queries. They pushed and shouldered, bellowing into one another's flushed faces without recognition, heedless of everything except the terrible business in hand.

He persisted in his efforts. Man after man he asked about Uncle Daniel. Had he seen a very old nigger in any of the cars? At last he won close to a man in a hood. To him he put the question also.

"What business is it of yours?" was the answer. Then the fellow turned to look at him and, seeing who it was, edged closer and tapped the judge on the chest.

"We've had about all we want to hear from you, Gudger," he said with deliberate emphasis. "If you're looking for trouble you can get it right now. I choose you!"

The crowd swept them apart. Realizing the futility of coping with this horde of men gone mad, the judge went home. Thereby he escaped the sight of the dreadful ceremonies which followed.

The little girl who had been attacked was led up in front and asked to identify the negro. The child stared at him in horror and then said she couldn't say —he might be, but she wasn't sure.

"He's the man!" somebody yelled, and word went around that it was her father who had said it. On the strength of this they proceeded with the lynching.

They tied the boy to a hitching post, then castrated him. After that they piled planks and scantlings around him to the level of his neck and saturated them with kerosene. Several took shots at his head as he writhed and screamed amid the flames.

When it was all over, somebody dragged Uncle Daniel out of the tonneau

of an automobile and flung him to the ground.

"This ol' nigger hid him!" he shouted.

With that they tied uncle to the courthouse fence, took off his shirt and lashed him across his bare back until the old man hung senseless. Then they cut his bonds, placed his limp form in a car and drove to the Gudger home. Arrived there, they dumped him out onto the lawn and sped away.

The mob broke up and dispersed to their homes. Some went in high excitement, filled with a species of frenzy; others hurried off, almost in panic, as though just waking to what they had done and terrified by it. Soon the square was empty, and when the sun broke fiery red through the mists of dawn Liveoak seemed at peace.

Hearing a low moaning from the lawn after the car had departed, the judge went out to investigate. He found Uncle Daniel huddled on the grass, whimpering like a child. His back was covered with welts and blood; he could not stand on his feet. Summoning Charity, he carried the old man to his room and then telephoned for a doctor.

"Did you hide him, uncle?"

"I won't lie to you—yes, suh."

"What for?"

"Well, he come sneakin' in here just after dark—and he is my onliest gran'son. What could I do?"

A short silence; then, "Did they—did they kill him, judge, suh?"

The judge nodded. Uncle Daniel broke into weird, wailing cries. "Oh, he never done it!" he cried, rocking to and fro on the bed. "He never done it! I just know he never done it!"

Within twelve hours his conviction was proved correct. The Gracey child happened to meet in the road a half-breed Indian horse-trader who was working the county and instantly identified him as her assailant. He was arrested and, under a severe grilling, confessed. The prisoner had a large amount of money on him and claimed to own several farms in another state. He engaged Hunter McLemore to defend him and McLemore obtained his speedy removal to a city a hundred miles distant in order to escape possible mob action.

The precaution was unnecessary. Popular rage had exhausted itself in the night's lynching and there was not even a demonstration, although some loose talk was heard.

"The doctor says you'll git well in no time a-tall, uncle," Charity announced as she brought him a bowl of chicken soup.

"I don't care whether I do, gal," was the dispirited reply. "I'm all broke up

206

—and he's dead—my onliest gran'son."

"Shucks, you'll soon be steppin' raound as lively as ever. Here, eat some of this."

As Uncle Daniel made a feeble effort to do so she added: "The judge, he says as you're one of the fam'ly after this, Uncle Dan'l. And when your time comes to die he says yours'll be the biggest funeral what ever was in Liveoak. Yassuh, he told me it would be a mile long, if he had to hire every automobile in the county."

Uncle Daniel looked up eagerly from his soup.

"A mile long?" he mumbled. "You mean that, gal?"

"Yassuh, that's what he done said. And if the judge says a mile, it'll more like be two miles long. He don' promise much, but when he do he generally always does more'n what he promised."

Uncle closed his eyes and lay back with a happy sigh. A funeral two miles long!

"And I been payin' dues to the Daughters of the Mornin' Star fifteen year," continued Charity, not without chagrin, "and mine won't be half a dozen cars hardly."

The old man grinned up at her with a sort of triumph. In his mind's eye he could see the long line of automobiles wending toward the cemetery, the flower-bedecked hearse, the staring spectators on the sidewalks asking who it was—and himself providing the reason for it all. Perhaps they might even have a band.

His poor bruised body relaxed. The negro's haunting dread that he may die friendless, and fill an unmarked grave, dropped from him. He sank to sleep, waking once to murmur "Two miles long!"

Next morning he was so much improved that he betrayed traces of impatience with the soup.

"You done heard the judge say as I could have all the liver and onions I wanted from now on, didn't you?" he remonstrated.

"I sure did."

"Then you cook me up some tomorrow, gal. I feel like I could eat some right now," he commanded in a stern tone.

"All right, Uncle Dan'l. I will."

The judge was extremely busy at this time. From one office to another, from one store to another, he went, and often he was closeted with the president of the First National Bank and Doctor Ashcraft and Rufus Page and other citizens of their caliber. In small towns there is always an element which forms the backbone of the community. They may not bulk large in the sensations of the day or be much heard of when the big bass drum is thumped, but in any crisis it is to them that the town turns. And the judge was now rallying these stalwarts.

The result of his labors was a mass meeting in the old town hall, which was packed with the sober element of Liveoak. An overflow meeting adjourned to the baseball park. Many speeches were delivered and some tall spellbinding was done, but it remained for Judge Gudger to deliver the talk that counted.

"Men," he said, "there is no profit in blinking facts. We stand disgraced in the eyes of the world. We have put a stain on the name of this state. But there is no use going into that now. What is done cannot be undone.

"Tragedies like this have happened before. They are liable to happen again. They are peculiarly liable to happen so long as we have in our midst an organization whose purpose is to terrorize behind mask and shroud."

Some of the audience began to stir uneasily. The Ku-Klux had publicly denied any connection with the lynching and some hissing broke out.

"You all know what organization I mean," the judge continued, taking a step forward and raising his tones. "The Ku-Klux Klan! Some of you may belong. Many honest, God-fearing men are enrolled in its membership. I have friends among them. But I say to you that these men have made a great, a tragic mistake. They have been blinded to the perils by their hopes of achieving good. The Klan may do some good—I don't deny it—but consider the menace they constitute.

"Not one of you outside this organization knows when it may become his turn to be dragged from his home and whipped and degraded without so much as learning what his fault has been. There is no longer any sense of security. There is whispering and dread.

"A power calling itself the Invisible Empire skulks behind sheet and mask. It would usurp the authority and powers which belong to government. It would substitute its dictum, its night riders, its whip, for the legally constituted courts of our country. Are you going to allow that?

"Let me tell you, men"—his voice rose like a clarion, shaking with passion—"let me tell you that any group of citizens who band together behind masks, for any purpose—any purpose, mark you—strike at the very roots of our government and free institutions. And they must go!

"You may say that the Ku-Klux fills a need, that our courts fail to deter crime by too lenient treatment of criminals. The latter contention I freely admit. There have been numberless failures of justice. Men have killed in cold blood and come clear. They have robbed and pillaged the helpless and the ignorant, and have been allowed to escape with the spoils. An offender who possessed sufficient money has been able to take advantage of the law's delays and technicalities, and to laugh at prison. These things have made justice a byword among us, so that the criminal stalks boldly about his work, sure of immunity or at most a trifling punishment.

"Why? Why this state of things? I am a lawyer. Coming from me, what I have to say may surprise you but it is the truth. More than half the troubles that have brought our courts into disrepute, that have made the administration of justice in portions of this country a farce, that have taught our people the contempt for law which my own profession has been so loud in deploring—more than half these troubles can be laid at the door of the legal profession.

"The lawyer who saves clients from prison when they deserve to go there—the lawyer who takes advantage of every technicality to thwart justice—the lawyer who manages by appeals to false and maudlin sentiment to turn aside from a criminal the punishment that is his due—the lawyer who quibbles and twists, and packs juries and keeps his own talesmen available for emergencies, who exhausts every resource of the law so long as there is money in it for him—he it is who has undermined respect for law in this country. And he must go!"

A moment of startled surprise, then a clamor of applause cut in on him.

"We must see to that. The day is coming when these parasites will be relegated to the limbo in which they belong, when all the petty technicalities and hair splitting will be swept aside by the courts and only the simple justice of the matter considered. Too long we have given paramount consideration to the rights of the accused. The time has come to consider the rights of the injured—and the public.

"You all can help. You can do your duty as citizens by faithfully serving on juries instead of dodging that duty. We must set aside appeals to mawkish sentiment. We must steadfastly steel ourselves against pity for the man who has earned punishment. For I tell you, men, until you have hanged a few of these killers and jailed evildoers wheresoever caught or whosoever they may be, there will never be respect for law. Try it! Hang a few white men who have been guilty of murder and see how quickly this country returns to law and order.

"But we can never have real law and order while a strong organization exists which is destructive of every principle on which law and order are based. The Ku-Klux must go. I have done."

He sat down. There was a ripple of applause, but the audience seemed at first to waver. A few continued clapping. It grew and grew, swelled to a roar, until the old town hall rocked with the plaudits. Here was one who talked out like a man—no sob stuff or windjamming or flag waving—just talked plain sense. And he was the first man in Liveoak who had dared to attack the Klan publicly.

"Good boy, Gudger!" they yelled.

When he could make himself heard, Rufus Page stood up beside the judge and announced he had resigned from the Ku-Klux. He had joined, he said, because he had felt that such an organization could do a lot of good. There had certainly been need of drastic action, but at joining he had failed to see the possible uses to which the Klan's power might be put. He felt no hostility against its members as individuals, but he hoped many others like himself, whose expectations had been disappointed, would follow his example.

Doctor Pierce, the dentist, followed him and said practically the same thing. Solid men of public spirit, both, who enjoyed the respect of the community. So, one after the other, ex-members of the Klan rose in their places and came out openly against the continued existence of the order.

Somebody proposed a resolution condemning the Klan and it was greeted with a whoop. But the judge stayed the enthusiasm with uplifted hands.

"Men," he cried, "I don't think that will accomplish anything. It is plain that the sense of this meeting is overwhelmingly against the existence of the Klan. Let it go at that. Why stir them up and provoke a fight? That's what this resolution would do—it is a challenge to battle. And no manly man takes a challenge lying down.

"Let every man within sound of my voice, who may belong to the order, think over what he has heard tonight and go to his Klan's meeting and there resign. Then he acts as a free agent and not under coercion. Let him talk to his comrades and persuade them they have been mistaken, as we are profoundly convinced they have been."

Much quiet work was done in the way of canvassing during the following week, so nobody was surprised when a rumor went round that the Liveoak Klan would disband. With nearly all the leading citizens withdrawing, the element which clung to the organization grew uneasy. They were fearful of how continued membership might affect their businesses and jobs. The same considerations that had driven them to join now drove them to desert it. One of the first to get out was Hunter McLemore.

A gathering of the Klan took place on Saturday night, and on Monday the Booster published a formal notification that the Klan had disbanded.

However, that there were still some in Liveoak who clung to hooded operations was proved a few nights later when an automobile containing six men, in the full regalia of the Klan, drove to Hunter McLemore's house and the occupants marched solemnly up to the front door in pairs. It was nearly eleven o'clock and

Hunter was in bed, but he rose quickly and came down to them.

"Hello, boys," he exclaimed in an eager whisper. "What's up?"

"There's work to do," replied one of the shrouded figures in sepulchral tones.

"Fine! You going after that scoundrel at last? Now you're talking! If we'd only taken care of Gudger in the first place we wouldn't have had all this trouble. Wait until I put on my clothes."

"It ain't necessary, McLemore. You can come right along as you are."

"Why, what do you mean?"

"Well," replied the night rider who had spoken before, "we been studying over all that's happened and we figure maybe we been going after the wrong men. Looks like we might have put the tar and feathers on the wrong parties."

"Ain't I been telling you that? Just what I've told you all along! Who do you aim to take out now?"

"You! Grab him, men!"

SHOTS IN THE DARK
East Texas

Miz Wilkerson

Shots in the Dark   EAST TEXAS

A MOCKINGBIRD was testing its voice in the chinaberry below the Wilkersons' sleeping porch. Every night its liquid warblings soothed Lee to sleep, so when the bird suddenly stopped he woke with a jerk. Somebody was stealing on tiptoe up their walk.

The intruder crossed the lawn and eased through the hedge into the Bantys' front yard, where he hid behind a tree. Then he flitted back to the Bantys' gate, opened and closed it with a bang and walked boldly toward the house. The manoeuvre brought instant results. There came a subdued scurrying at one of the lower windows and something dropped onto the lawn. Then a spurt of flame and the crash of a .45. Leaping from bed, Wilkerson reached the porch screen in time to descry a dim figure scale the picket fence between the two back-yards and go streaking towards the lane. The man on the walk dashed in pursuit and started to clamber over the fence, but a woman's scream stopped him. He turned and fled. Lee could hear him running swiftly down Live Oak Street.

"Well," said his mother, padding out in her bare feet, "who's killed now?"

"Nobody, mamma. Don't be scared."

"Scared? Don't talk foolish! Who did that shootin'?"

"I don't know. Some drunk, I reckon."

Up and down the street, windows and doors were being flung open and people called to one another to find out what the trouble was about.

"What're you staring at, anyhow, Lee?" demanded Mrs. Wilkerson.

"Seeing if I can see anybody."

"I thought I heard somebody run off."

"So you did. Somebody ran down Live Oak Street as fast as he could leg it."

An unsteady voice called to them from the house next door: "Didn't you hear a gun, Mr. Wilkerson?"

"I sure did, ma'am."

"Where was it? I was sound asleep but it sounded like it was right close."

"Not very far off."

His mother whispered "Listen at how funny she talks."

"Anybody hurt?"

215

"Not that I know of."

A short silence. Then, "I wonder who—did you see anybody?"

"No-oo."

"Do you reckon it was burglars?"

"Well, I reckon he was after something—yes, ma'am."

He waited for a reply but none came.

"Lee," said his mother, "you're keeping something back from me."

"Nonsense! What makes you say that, mamma?"

"Then what makes your voice so queer?"

"Cold, I reckon. Best get back to bed, mamma. This is bad for your rheumatism."

Muttering that nobody ever told her anything, and with shoulders humped up and hands thrust inside the sleeves of her nightgown, Mrs. Wilkerson shuffled back to her room where she switched on the light to take a look at the clock. "Way after midnight!" she exclaimed. "Looks like folks could do their shootin' in the daytime!" And she quickly fell asleep.

That was just before the clock in the courthouse tower struck one. In the same minute Clyde Odom started to close his Kandy Kitchen. He was two hours later than usual because a party of motorists had dropped in for some chili as a counter-irritant to the gin they had drunk on the road. As Clyde turned the key of the front door the screen door at the back opened and a man plunged in, carrying most of his clothes.

"Well, I swan! Been to a party, Ad?"

"Pull down the shades."

While Odom was doing it the newcomer hurriedly donned his trousers and shirt and shoes.

"This society stuff sure has its drawbacks, don't it?" remarked the Kandy Kitchen man.

"Forget it and gimme a drink."

"What kind of a drink?"

"Shucks, something with a wallop—none of that belly wash."

Odom produced a bottle and Rucker took a shuddering drink. "Ain't as good as the last batch, Clyde," he observed critically. "Don't take hold the same way."

"What can you expect? They're working that guy to death. Give him time and he can make as good corn whisky as you'd choose to drink, Ad. But they won't. First thing you know, he's going to get sore and go back to Tennessee."

"Uh-uh! The sheriff won't let him. He'd lose his graft."

Somebody rattled the doorknob.

216

"Don't let him in!" Ad exclaimed, but the man on the outside called out, "It's me, Clyde. I want a cigar."

"It's Joe Banty. I've got to let him in, Ad."

Rucker stepped behind a showcase and seemed ready to run as Banty entered the store. Yet the latter did not appear formidable—a heavy man of middle age, of the plodding, wheel-horse type.

"'Lo, Clyde," was his greeting as he set down a suitcase on the floor. "'Lo, Ad. You're out late."

"How about yourself?" rejoined Odom. "Been away?"

"Just got in on Number 8. Gimme one of those panetelas. What's the matter with you, Ad? Been runnin'? You're breathin' hard."

"I'll say he's been runnin'! The dust ain't settled yet."

Banty glanced at Rucker in some surprise. The latter laughed uncertainly and said: "He's kidding you, Joe. Did you say—did I understand you to say you'd just this minute got in? Just now?"

"Sure. And I'm dog-tired too. Well, I must be going. Coming my way, Ad?"

"Reckon I might as well."

And they went out together, Ad deep in a recital of the shooting that had alarmed the neighborhood. The Kandy Kitchen man watched them go with an odd expression.

"Well, I'll be goddamned. Guess I must of been wrong," he muttered as he turned out the lights.

The same idea occurred to Lee Wilkerson early in the morning as he was peering over the hedge into the Banty place and Joe came out on the porch.

"Why, hello!"

"Looking for burglars?" inquired Joe with a grin.

"Well, I thought they might have left a trace or something."

"Must have been your place they were after, I reckon. I ain't got anything here worth taking. Ha-ha!"

Wilkerson studied him curiously. He always felt a species of contempt for Joe—the fellow was so blind, so slow. He always rubbed Lee the wrong way.

"Were you home last night?"

"Got back about one o'clock."

"Oh," said Lee, "I see."

His mother, who had been pottering among her flower beds for an hour, now summoned him to breakfast.

"If it ain't one thing," she grumbled, "it's another. First they go shootin' in the middle of the night and now Stella's got a black eye."

The cook confirmed this with proof.

"He'll never do it agin," she announced in solemn accents as she waddled in with the hot biscuits.

"Doc?"

"Yassuh. Who else would it be?"

"Well, he gave you a beauty—I'll say that."

"Yeh, but I done learned that no-'count nigger that he cain't lay a hand on me!" shrilled Stella. "He's in the lockup right now. I done called the law."

"All right, Stella. Fetch Mr. Lee's eggs," said her mistress and the cook departed to the kitchen.

"So Doc's in jail, is he?" Lee asked when Stella returned. "You remember what happened last time you put him there, don't you?"

"He can stay there till he rots for all of me."

"That will do, Stella. Please, Lee!"

They went on with breakfast. The old lady's consisted of a large glass of milk. She never ate more than a few bites of anything and enjoyed amazing health.

"Well, what did Joe Banty have to say?"

"Nothing much. He got home early this morning."

"He's a fine man. I feel awful sorry for him."

Lee made an impatient gesture. "I reckon you understand, mamma, that the less said about last night the better?"

"Talking is a waste of time. And talking in a small town is downright dangerous," his mother answered.

Having finished her glass of milk the old lady rose and picked up a basket and a pair of scissors.

"Going to cut some flowers for the church social," she said. "Minnie May is coming with me."

Just after she had gone out, the doorbell rang.

"There's a man outside wants to see you, jedge. Do you want I should fetch him in here?"

"Of course. Who is it, Stella?"

"I didn't get his name."

The visitor entered with an air of repressed excitement. He was a long, lank, badly nourished individual, with an indefinable suggestion of aristocratic forebears—the type is not uncommon in the Southwest.

"Morning. Is this Lawyer Wilkerson?"

"Yes. What can I do for you?"

"It's my boy, judge."

"What about him?"

"He's in trouble."

Instantly assuming the portentous manner he reserved for prospective clients, Lee cleared his throat and inquired: "Why didn't you wait and come to my office?"

"I just couldn't wait, judge. The sheriff come this morning and done took him off to jail. It about killed his mother."

"What's he been up to?"

"Nothin'. So help me God, Mr. Wilkerson, sir, he never done it!"

"Never did what?"

"Took that money from the bank. Why, that boy could no more steal than—well, he just couldn't, that's all. It ain't in him."

His voice sharp, Lee demanded, "What bank?"

"The First National. He worked there. It's like you know him, judge. Larry Kane? Well, I'm his father . . . What's the matter?"

Lee had pushed back his chair and stood up. Vanished was his professional expression, nicely blended of judicial dignity and sympathetic encouragement. He looked at Kane with a cold and impersonal eye.

"So he couldn't do it, hey? Humph—in my profession, Mr. Kane, we soon learn that anything is apt to happen. I can't take the case. I'm sorry, but it's impossible."

"Can't take it? Why not, Mr. Wilkerson? I'll meet your price. I'll pay you. I know you're expensive and we ain't got much, but we'll sell the home, Mr. Wilkerson. I'll—"

"It's not that."

"Then what is it?"

"I don't care to take the case—that's all."

His tone was hard and final, but Kane was too stunned to comprehend.

"But I told her I'd get you. 'I'll go get Judge Wilkerson, mamma, and he'll be free in no time'—those're the very words I used. Why, everybody told us to get you, judge. 'You hire Lee Wilkerson and he'll come clear easy'—they all said that. For God's sake don't go back on us! He didn't do it, sir—I tell you he didn't do it. He couldn't do it! We'll give you everything we've got, but that boy—it'll kill her, I tell you. It'll kill her."

He took a step toward Lee as though he would use force.

"Stella," said Lee over his shoulder, "Bring me my hat."

"Then you won't?"

"No."

"But what'll I tell her? What'll I do?"

"You can get somebody else. I'm not the only lawyer in town."

"No, but—who'd you recommend, judge?"

"Do you know Judge Tarwater?"

Kane grunted angrily. "Him!" he exclaimed. "He's no good. All he does is pound the table."

"That has won many a jury case."

"So you won't? That's final?"

"That's final."

His visitor turned slowly and started out. "Maybe you'll live to regret this, judge," he said with a certain dignity.

"That's no way to talk, sir."

Kane admitted it with a slight inclination of the head.

"No-oo, I reckon not. But we're in trouble—bad trouble. And you could've saved us."

The door had hardly closed on him when Mrs. Wilkerson entered from the garden.

"Well, what was all the ruckus about?"

"His son's in jail."

"Well?"

"And of course he is innocent."

"What do you say it that way for? Maybe he is. Ain't you ever defended an innocent man?"

"I can recall a few. But I'm not going to defend this one."

"Why not?"

"Because the First National is prosecuting—that's why."

"You're not their attorney."

"No, but I'm going to be—some day."

His mother regarded him steadily.

"What's this boy's name and what's he done?"

On learning, she said: "And you refused to help these poor people, although the boy may be innocent, just because you hope to get the bank business some day?"

"You don't understand these things, mamma."

"No, but I understand you, son. You're exactly like your father."

"I only hope I leave behind me as good a reputation as he did."

"What's reputation?" retorted his mother. "Any scalawag can build up a reputation if he sets out to do it. It's what you are that counts. I'd like to hear

220

from the wives of some of these reputations."

"That sounds pretty hard on father, doesn't it?"

"Your father was all right. He was a good man—according to his lights. But he never could think straight. And neither can you. Maybe it's the legal training does it."

"Goodby."

"Where do those people live?" his mother called after him.

"Down near the cotton mill somewhere. It's in the phone book," he answered from the gate.

"Don't be late for dinner."

She was talking to herself when Minnie May Daniels arrived. Every morning Mrs. Wilkerson carried on a monologue in the living room to the accompaniment of vague, muttered threats against Doc from Stella in the kitchen. It relieved their feelings and was a bond between them.

"Good morning, Miz Wilkerson. Ready?" asked Minnie May. She was a tall, slight girl, already beginning to fade.

"Just as soon as Stella packs the basket. How's Boly?"

The girl's face clouded. "He's all right, I reckon."

"You mean he's been at it again?"

"Oh, I do wish he could get away from here, Miz Wilkerson. He goes with the wrong sort of people all the time and ——"

"He'd do the same thing anywhere else. Folks just naturally drift to their kind, Minnie May, no matter where they are."

"I can't bear to hear you say that."

"No, of course not. The trouble is, Minnie May, you spoil Boly. You have ever since he was a baby."

"Perhaps I have. But how could I help it? He's all I've got. And I raised him, Miz Wilkerson—I feel like a mother to him. And now every time he does anything wrong—well, you know how it is—I think maybe it was my fault, maybe I didn't raise him right."

"Humph!" said the old lady. "What's he been up to now?"

"I don't know. Something's come over him. He acts like he isn't in his right mind sometimes."

"Maybe it's a woman."

Minnie May clutched her chin. "That's just what's been worrying me. It *is* a woman, Miz Wilkerson."

"Who?"

"I don't know. Some creature, of course."

221

"Just like his—Minnie May, you make me lose all patience. It don't matter what that boy does, you always find excuses for him. And it ain't like as if he was a boy any longer. He's a man growed."

"Not to me! He can never be that to me."

The older woman regarded her with a softening expression.

"Do you know," she said in a low voice as though thinking aloud, "I do believe half the trouble in the world is caused by good women—women like you—and me."

"But you don't spoil Lee. You've always been hard on him."

"Hard?" cried his mother. "Oh, don't I wish I could be!"

"How is he getting along?"

"All right, I reckon. He makes a lot of money."

"You say that in such a funny way. I don't think you're fair to Lee. You ought to be very proud of him."

Mrs. Wilkerson smiled. "Of course, I've got a whole lot to learn about my own son."

"I didn't mean that. But so often you say things that hurt."

"Hurt? Of course they do. Common sense always hurts. I declare, Minnie May, it looks like most people just can't stand to hear the truth. They'd rather listen to mush and go along fooling themselves—oh, I've no patience with you, child!"

There was a long silence, broken at last by Minnie May.

"I'm scared, Miz Wilkerson."

"Shucks, what's the matter now? Boly's weak, but there's no meanness in him."

"You haven't seen him when he's—after he's drunk a lot of that awful stuff. This morning he was talking to himself up in his room and I went up and peeped in and ——"

"Well?"

"He was cleaning a gun."

"And tomorrow when he's sober he'll be so meek he wouldn't dast say boo to a jackrabbit."

"Boly's not a coward. Don't you dare say he is!"

"Oh, well, if you're fixing to cry about it."

"I'm not going to cry."

"Then let's talk about something else."

They switched to the sensation of the previous night, Mrs. Wilkerson listening in silence to Minnie May's speculations as to why the burglars should have picked on the Banty house.

"And who would have dreamed that woman had the nerve to use a gun!" the girl exclaimed. "I wouldn't have, would you?"

"It was her who did the shootin' then?"

"Of course. Who else could it have been?"

"I didn't know but what Joe might've been home. Does she admit she did it?"

"Her husband told Jeb Spivy that she did."

"Then that settles it sure enough."

They also talked of young Kane's arrest, news of which had reached Minnie May through her cook. On the way to the church, in fact, there was hardly a local happening of recent date which they did not roll on the tongue—who was going to get married, who was going to split up, who was expecting, the servant problem and household tribulations. Much as Mrs. Wilkerson despised tittle-tattle, it was amazing what comfort she seemed to derive from this. By the time they reached the church both women seemed soothed and uplifted.

Returning home about noon, Mrs. Wilkerson was met by the cook with the announcement that the jedge had telephoned and wanted her to ring him up at once.

"What does he want, I wonder?"

"I don't know, ma'am. He done talked kind of excited, but when I up and ast him he cut me off."

Mrs. Wilkerson called the office.

"Is Minnie May there?" he barked.

"No, she's gone home."

"I've been trying to get hold of her. Something's happened."

"What is it?"

"Ad Rucker has been killed."

"Killed? How? When? What's that got to do with Minnie May?"

"It looks like Boly shot him. I want to ——"

"I'll go to her right now," said his mother and hung up while he was still trying to tell her something.

Lee turned from the instrument to the abject figure cowering in the chair across the table.

"Mother will break it to her."

"This will be the death of Minnie May," Boly burst out, his face twitching.

"I hardly think so," remarked Wilkerson dryly. "But it may be the death of Minnie May's brother."

"What're you trying to do? Scarce me? Well, you can't! The hound deserved to die."

223

"I realize that is your opinion. The difficulty will be to convince a jury of it."

"I was only protecting a woman, wasn't I?" His voice rose, high and cracked and hysterical.

Lee stared at him in wonder. "If I were you, Boly," he said, "I'd cut out the booze."

"What's the matter? I'm all right."

"Right now you need an alienist more than a lawyer. Why, man, you're talking foolishness! Protecting a woman! She was another man's wife, wasn't she? And you were crazy jealous about Ad. That'd be a fine story to tell a jury, wouldn't it?"

"I done warned him! I done told him to keep away!"

"Sh-h!" Lee cautioned, getting up to make sure the door was tightly closed. "Forget it. That won't go. We'll have to find something else."

"Have I got to go to jail?"

"No. I can arrange to get you out on bond. But first you've got to promise me to lay off booze, absolutely—not a drop, mind—and not so much as open your mouth about this business."

"I ain't such a fool as that."

"All right. Remember, now, don't you do a thing except what I tell you. And after I've fixed it up about bail, you'd best stay home and see nobody. Understand?"

Boly readily promised and they called in the sheriff who was waiting in an outer room. Then the three hastened across to the courthouse, the sheriff forcing passage through the crowd of curious spectators that had gathered outside of Wilkerson's door and on the stairs and sidewalk to see Daniels come out.

Afterwards Lee took him home. Minnie May met her brother at the door. She was perfectly composed until Boly uttered a broken cry and threw his arms around her; then she gathered him close to her bosom and began comforting him with her face pressed against his hair.

"Hell!" Lee muttered as he drove away, "It's always the no-accounts who get the sympathy. But I reckon they're the ones who need it. The rat!"

His mother's first words were, "Where is he?"

"Home."

"Home? Why, I thought—don't he have to go to jail? Minnie May was fixing to go down to see him."

"I couldn't get her on the phone. We've fixed bail—ten thousand dollars— three of his father's old friends offered to go on the bond."

"Why," exclaimed Mrs. Wilkerson, watching him wonderingly, "you act almost as if you were glad about something."

"Don't talk nonsense, mama! But then, of course it *is* a great opportunity—isn't it?"

He began to pace up and down the floor, now and again running his fingers through his long black hair. His fine eyes—the eyes of an actor—were glowing, and his mother knew he was mentally rehearsing the court scene already.

"So Boly's home, is he?" she remarked in an odd tone. "And Doc's in jail."

Her son stopped abruptly. "What's that got to do with it?"

"I was just thinking. Boly done killed a man—and that poor ignorant nigger gave his wife a black eye."

"Oh, let's talk about things you understand."

"I reckon that Kane boy is in jail too. Ain't he?"

"He is. And what's more, it looks like he'll stay there. He's short thirty thousand dollars and he couldn't raise bail."

"Thirty thousand dollars? Lan's sakes! What would that boy be doing with thirty thousand dollars?"

"Search me. But it's gone. And there may be more—they haven't finished checking up yet. By the way, I've been retained as special prosecutor."

He watched her jealously for signs of disapproval and found them in every line of the tall bony frame as she turned away and started straightening the sofa cushions.

"I reckon I ought to have turned Bland down, hey?—and thrown away all the bank's business?" he sneered.

"Does this mean you're going to be their attorney now?"

"That's what it does. Bland came to see me this morning."

"What was the trouble between Boly and Ad Rucker?" she asked.

"I—that's something I can't talk about now even to you, mamma. You see, he's my client."

"But how did it happen? It'll be self-defense, I reckon—won't it?"

A troubled look came over Lee's face and he shook his head.

"No-oo. That is what's worrying me."

"How? Why not? Surely he can find somebody who heard Ad make threats! And Boly is bound to've seen him make a move to pull a gun."

She spoke so simply that her son did not suspect sarcasm.

"Boly" he said, "is in a tight place, I'm afraid—a mighty tight place. He met Ad on the square this morning and without saying a single word took a shot at him. Well, he missed and Ad ran—ran down the lane back of the Red Front

Drug Store and hid in a barrel. Boly shot through the barrel."

"Oh-h-h! That's murder!"

"It'll make it harder."

"I feel right sorry for Miz Rucker. She's a good woman."

"Of course," replied her son impatiently. "I've noticed you always confine your sympathy to the women."

"Well, they're generally the victims, ain't they?"

"In this case," he burst out, "it was a woman who ——" and stopped short.

"Well?"

"Nothing. Let's not talk about it."

His mother went on tidying up the room.

"Lee," she said at last, "there's something I think you ought to know about."

"What's that?"

"Joe Banty done brought over Boly Daniels' hat this morning after you'd gone—said he thought it might be yours."

"Where did he find it?"

"In their front yard."

For the first time Lee betrayed uneasiness.

"How do you know it was Boly's hat?"

"Think I wouldn't recognize that old brown felt? I've seen him wear it often enough."

He walked nervously up and down; then, halting in front of her, said with intense earnestness, "Mamma, you must never breathe a word about this to anyone. Understand? You do understand, don't you?"

"I understand what you're driving at—yes."

He waited, wondering what was coming next.

"I'm just a plain old woman, son, and I'd like to get this law business straight in my mind," she continued. "Do lawyers—do they aim at seeing justice done? Or is their job to get their clients out of trouble, no matter what?"

"What's come over you tonight?"

"Nothing."

"Then what do you talk that way for? Are you going to promise? Or do you want to send young Boly Daniels to the scaffold?"

"If the hat's got anything to do with it," she persisted stubbornly, "it seems to me like it's your duty as a lawyer to tell about it."

"It does, does it? Well, if you won't do it for Boly's sake, maybe you will for Minnie May. Do you want to kill her? You know as well as I do she'd never get over it."

226

"I never said I was going to tell."

"No. And you never promised you wouldn't."

"What's the good of my promising if Joe Banty talks?"

"I hardly think that Joe will talk. No, I've got an idea he'll be glad to keep his mouth shut and mind his own business."

"Oh, all right—I promise. But it strikes me, son, you've got a job on your hands this time."

"Don't I know it? It's the greatest chance of my career!"

The deeper he delved into the case the blacker it looked. It is usually fairly easy to clear a murderer in the Southwest, but the fact that the victim was hiding in a barrel at the moment he was shot complicated the defense.

Lee was quick to sense that public feeling would run against Daniels. Generally the people of a small town are apt to be lenient and side with the killer in a shooting case because he is alive and can talk for himself and he has kinfolks and staunch friends to back him. Besides, they entertain a rooted dislike to imposing the death sentence on a neighbor. Yet sentiment soon set in strong against his client. Many people openly denounced the killing as cold-blooded murder and a blot on the town's good name, and even from conservative quarters Lee heard the wish expressed that they would crack Boly's neck.

In vain he pumped his client for something that would help his case. Again and again he went over every detail, every happening between Daniels and his victim. He threw out suggestions, explored every possible avenue of escape. By innuendo and implication he tried to stir in Boly's numbed brain some excuse that would be possible as a defense. No use—there was nothing in the wretched business on which even the most remotely plausible defense could be hung. He was growing desperate. Time was flying, and a rich uncle of Mrs. Rucker had engaged the ablest jury lawyer in the state to assist the prosecution.

And then he heard something; and when he went to see Boly at his home— they held all their conferences in his bedroom for secrecy—he had already formulated the hazy outline of a plan.

"Well, it's all up now," he announced grimly.

"Why, what's happened?"

"Clyde Odom's been talking. It's all around town."

"What does he know about it?"

"He says Ad Rucker came into his Kandy Kitchen about one' o'clock the night before he was shot and all he had on ——"

"So that's where he hid, hey?" Boly cried, clenching his hands. "The bastard!"

"Well? Is that all you've got to say?"

227

"I don't see what all this has to do with my case?"

"You don't, hey? Well, I do. Listen. The prosecution must have heard about this because it's all over town, so they're bound to run it down. See?"

"No."

"Why, look where it puts us! We've got to explain it somehow. If we don't, they'll put two and two together and the truth'll come out. And if it does—if the jury ever hears why you shot Ad Rucker—well, your neck is as good as cracked, boy."

Daniels said in a frightened voice: "That's the third or fourth time you've said that! What're you trying to do—scare me?"

"No. But I want you to help. Think."

"I've seen a lot of killings in this town" Boly whined, "But I never saw a man strung up for one yet. Why should I be the goat? What's the matter with you anyhow?"

"Let me tell you something, Boly. Just forget what happened in other cases. This one is yours and it's different. I warn you here and now, if we don't find some good defense pretty soon, you're as good as done for."

There were beads of perspiration on his client's forehead: they ran down his cheeks and onto his clasped hands, but he took no notice.

"What is it you want me to do, anyhow? Come clean. You've got something up your sleeve. I can tell."

Still Wilkerson hesitated, dubious as to how he should begin.

"Well, why don't you say it? For God's sake, say it and get it over."

In proportion as Boly grey hysterical Lee grew calmer.

"Now, boy, pay attention. You admit they've got us in a tight corner. Clyde Odom is going to go on the witness stand and tell all he knows—and they'll connect that business up with you somehow or other."

"Let 'em. I warned him—done warned him three times."

"Who the woman was in this business," Lee continued, coldly emphasizing each word, "must never come out. If it does you're gone."

"But how'll we prevent it? Maybe Clyde Odom——"

"No, it's too late for that. Clyde has done the mischief already."

"Then what'll we do?"

"Find another explanation."

"I don't get you."

"It's simple enough. They'll prove there was a woman in the case. And the sheriff'll go on the stand and tell what you said when you surrendered. Well, we've got to accept a woman as our defense."

"But the only woman in it——"

"I told you to forget her."

"Then I give up. What the Sam Hill are you driving at, Wilkerson?"

"Listen carefully to what I'm going to say. A plea of self-defense is barred. You can see for yourself it would be ridiculous. Keep quiet, will you? Well, if you can't see it, everybody else can. The only thing that can possibly get you off is to prove you were protecting your home."

Boly looked puzzled.

"My home?" he repeated. "But I'm a bachelor."

"Sure you're a bachelor."

And then his meaning flashed on young Daniels. All the deep-rooted pride his kind take in the women of their families boiled up and he leaped to his feet, sending the chair flying.

"Damn you!" he cried. "You take that back! Take it back, I say, or I'll——"

"Shut up!" Lee warned, gripping him by the wrists, and they stood thus a moment silently straining. Then the older man pushed him down on the bed and stood listening.

"Well, I'm through," he said, with pent-up rage as he straightened his tie. "If that's the way you're going to help, you can swing for all of me." He went out and down the stairs, but he was grinning as he walked homeward, thinking "I'll give him a day or two to let the medicine work."

It required four sleepless nights to break Boly down. In normal vigor, given the choice between death and casting a blot upon any woman of his family, he would probably have met death without hesitation; but what he called his pride, and what little remained of his self-respect, could not stand long against his jangled nerves. Booze had sapped his resolution and terror finally mastered him.

"But YOU'VE got to ask her," he sobbed to Lee. "I won't."

Lee surveyed him with a contempt he was at no pains to conceal.

"All right," he assented. "How about this evening?"

At first Minnie May did not understand in the least what he was driving at. Probably he did not intend that she should, because beyond a vague hint he contented himself with implanting in her the gloomiest possible view of the outcome of the trial. Every feature of the tragedy that would count most heavily against her brother he emphasized—and heaven knows there were enough of them!

"Oh, why do you tell me all this?"

"Well, we've got to think up some line of defense."

"Yes," she replied, "of course."

For a couple of days he left her alone to brood over the prospect he had limned and then the three had another conference. Minnie May came to it wan and haggard. Lee felt an impulse of pity, but time was pressing and the business had to be arranged.

Very slowly, always indirectly and with consummate adroitness, he led up to his plan of defense. He spoke with deep feeling of her late father and mother, whom everybody in the town had respected and honored; he described the agony they would have suffered over their son's plight and probable fate. As to what that fate would be he did not mince words. He told her brutally.

"No, no! Not that! Not that!" she cried wildly. "It mustn't be that! Oh, stop! Please!"

Her agitation was so pitiable that Boly could endure it no longer. He had been sitting between them, in a cold sweat of shame and apprehension, but now he jumped up and rushed from the room. So he did not hear how his lawyer finally broached the plan.

In her dazed condition Minnie May failed entirely to catch his drift, so that he had at last to state his proposal much more baldly than he had intended. When she did understand she rose from her chair, white and shaking. Never, as long as he lived, could Lee shut out the memory of her eyes.

"And you—*you* ask that of me?" she whimpered like a hurt child and went out of the room.

Wilkerson walked up the street as though in a trance. Halfway to his own house he stopped and cried in helpless rage: "Damn him! He makes me feel like a skunk!"

Minnie May went to her room and stayed there, refusing the food which the cook carried up. She did not see her brother again that night—not until the early hours of the morning, when she crept to his door without any real idea of what she was going to do.

He had fallen asleep with the light going, a trick of his boyhood. It may have been complete exhaustion, or it may have been that he felt sure of her help—at any rate, Boly was enjoying the first sound rest he had had in months. The lines of worry were gone from his face; against the pillow he looked boyish and innocent.

Gazing at him through the door, his sister began to cry softly. After a while she tiptoed back to her room and went to bed. In the morning she telephoned to Lee.

"Something's the matter with Minnie May," said his mother at supper.

"How?"

"Well, when I went over this evening she wouldn't see me at first. And when I went upstairs anyhow, she acted awful queer."

"Maybe she wants to be alone," said Lee uneasily.

"The poor child needs somebody. What're you going to do about Boly's case?"

"That's something I can't talk about, mamma."

"Stuff and nonsense!"

He had enjoined on Minnie May the need of the utmost secrecy. The warning was hardly necessary, but he was dubious of what his mother's sympathy might make the girl reveal and if Mrs. Wilkerson ever got an inkling of the line of defense, he knew she would smash the plan regardless of any consequences. But he might have spared himself any forebodings. The girl found it an ordeal now even to see Mrs. Wilkerson and remained almost tongue-tied in her presence.

Meanwhile the life of the town went on much as usual. Doc got out of jail after payment of a forty-dollar fine which Stella borrowed from Lee. And then the fall term of court opened and young Kane's case came to trial. Wilkerson prosecuted. Witness after witness piled up evidence against the boy. The testimony of the bank's president gave the finishing strokes, so that Kane made a miserable showing when put on the stand in his own behalf and contradicted himself half a dozen times under Lee's cross-examination.

A considerable body of public opinion hoped that Wilkerson might be content with a nominal victory and ask for clemency, in view of the offender's youth and hitherto blameless record. Instead, he vigorously demanded the maximum sentence. If this boy, he urged in his argument to the jury, were allowed to go scatheless, the insidious poison corrupting the mind and conscience of our country would spread. He denounced the contempt for authority one met with on every hand. A wave of lawlessness was sweeping our cities and towns and hamlets and penetrating to the remotest corners of our fair land. And why? Because men of criminal tendencies felt confident of immunity from punishment.

Were they going to encourage this notion, let it engulf all they held dear? If the trend of today toward contempt for law and the courts were not checked, red revolution lurked around the corner. They must make an example which would act as a deterrent to evildoers.

President Bland of the First National listened with rapt attention, squirming about in his chair. Twice he leaned forward and whispered to Wilkerson during pauses, and when the lawyer sat down shook him warmly by the hand.

The jury gave young Kane a term in the penitentiary.

"She's sure taking it hard," remarked Mrs. Wilkerson as they sat down to supper.

"Who? Minnie May?"

"No, Miz Kane. I went down there this evening and she wouldn't let me in."

"You'd best keep away from those people."

"Oh, well, they're in trouble. And she's been sick ever since they locked him up. It's right pitiful. She says you could have got him clear—if you'd wanted to."

"Well," Lee admitted complacently, "I certainly could have done a better job than his lawyer did."

"Why didn't you let him off, son, after you'd won?"

"Because justice has to be done. It's my duty——"

"Oh, I see! So you're going to help 'em hang Boly then, I suppose?"

"Mamma," he exclaimed, pale with rage, "I never want to talk about these things with you again! You don't understand."

"No, I reckon I ain't got the legal mind."

From that night until the day of the trial they never once exchanged a word about the case.

The lawyers had the usual long wrangle over preliminaries and the selection of the jury; but when the panel was complete the Daniels case moved swiftly. The witnesses for the prosecution told their stories and stepped down. As they were all swearing to undisputed facts Wilkerson did not bother to cross-examine them but contented himself with a few seemingly casual questions to Clyde Odom and the sheriff, who provided the only testimony he feared. The Kandy Kitchen man told of Rucker's visit to his place the night before he was killed and the sheriff recited how the prisoner had said to him when he surrendered after the shooting, "I gave him fair warning. He'll never go tom-catting nights again."

Some surprise was expressed that this testimony should have been presented by the prosecution inasmuch as it pointed to a line of defense; but the prosecution had no alternative. Both men had talked freely and what they knew was common property. So the prosecution introduced this evidence in the hope it might lead to some damaging disclosure.

It did, but not what they had expected. Lee's defense staggered them. Not a whisper of it had gone out and when Minnie May went into the box the towns-people could scarcely credit their ears. Never had such a sensation been sprung in the history of the county. Minnie May Daniels, of all people!

She began her story calmly, almost as though reciting something she had learned by rote. Her face was white, but she did not falter—not until the tense hush in which they listened grew unbearable. Then she paused, gulped and looked down, clasping and unclasping her hands. Lee waited. At last the girl raised her head and glanced despairingly from judge to jury, her lips moving soundlessly and such helpless appeal in her eyes that Lee thought she was going to faint and hurried to her side with a glass of water. As she took it from him he began to shake and spilled some of the water on her dress. Then Minnie May recovered and with a little squeak in her throat, resumed her testimony.

This bit of drama made a profound impression on the jury, as did Lee's manifest agitation. They had expected him to show emotion in his efforts to excite it, but nobody had anticipated the difficulty he evidently had in going on at all. Two or three times he stopped in the midst of his low-voiced questioning of the girl and once seemed on the point of abandoning the task, but he mastered himself and carried her story to its conclusion.

"No questions," said the prosecutor suavely when it came his turn. He was too old a hand at the game not to realize when he was beaten.

Lee rested his case there. Like the finished actor a successful trial lawyer must be, he knew the precise moment to stop, and the way the jury sat back and the buzz of excitement throughout the court room bore witness to his judgment. Yet when he rose to make his argument to the jury he seemed unable to summon those tricks of voice and manner and appeal with which he had so often moved a court-room to pity and tears. He had prepared for this as the supreme moment of his career—and the swelling periods he had so carefully rehearsed came haltingly, coldly. In place of the deep, vibrant tones which had wrung the heartstrings of so many juries, he spoke in a strangled voice that barely reached the first rows of spectators; and once he stopped and fumbled at his collar as though it choked him.

True, the sob stuff for which he was famous did show finally but not as a calculated effect. He was picturing the wronged sister, and suddenly his voice broke and he could not go on for a moment. It was the poorest effort of his life and yet the strongest, because the jury sensed that the man was fighting against every decent instinct in him and attributed it to his life-long friendship for the Daniels family—which both explained his behavior and confirmed their belief in the girl's testimony.

Two hours later they returned a verdict of not guilty and Boly Daniels walked from the court a free man. He tried to thank his attorney but Lee pushed him aside.

"Get out of the way, you rat! I never want to see your face again."

"Is that so! So I'm a rat, huh? Say, I'd sure like to know what YOU'VE got on me!"

There were a few who congratulated Boly on his acquittal, but the majority showed plainly they wanted to avoid him. The altered demeanor of people did not rebuff him; after weeks of suspense and silence he wanted to mingle again in the places he had formerly frequented, and he stayed in the Kandy Kitchen most of the afternoon, perched on a stool.

About dusk Joe Banty entered and sauntered up to him.

"I was only waiting to see if they'd save me the job," he remarked and shot him dead.

When Lee reached home the house was dark. Stella met him in the hall.

"She's upstairs, jedge, a-lookin' after Miss Minnie May."

"Minnie May? Does she know?"

"Yas-suh. Most everybody does by now, I reckon. Your ma went and brung her over here and she's in the spare bed, with cold towels round her haid. She was talkin' to herself awful wild, jedge. The missy was scared to leave her alone."

And then his mother called him upstairs.

"She's been asking for you," she whispered.

"I can't face her," said Lee, turning toward his own bedroom.

Mrs. Wilkerson followed him. Switching on the light she closed the door and sat down in a rocker, all very deliberately.

"Well, son," she began slowly, "Looks like they'll have it all to do over again."

"Don't! Please!"

"Maybe if you had let justice take its course in the first place——"

He made no answer—just sat gazing at the floor, his face drawn and gray.

"Lee," she said, "I'd like to know just how far a lawyer thinks he's justified in going for a client."

"Don't, mamma. Don't bring that up again."

"I'm ashamed of you, son. I never thought I'd live to see the day when—— No wonder you didn't want to talk about the case!"

"Well, it's too late now."

"Best go in and see her, anyhow," said his mother. "She wants you."

*   *   *   *   *   *   *

Next morning the town received another shock. The First National Bank closed its doors. Lee hurried home with the news himself, both he and his mother being depositors; but if he expected agitation he was disappointed.

"What's the trouble?"

235

"Bland."

"Looted it?"

"Looks that way."

"That's bad. So many poor people."

Later in the day a mob led by Kane swept down the street from the square, clamoring for Bland.

"He's in here," the furious depositors bellowed when they reached the Wilkerson gate. A roar and they surged forward, smashing down the fence and sweeping across the lawn. Lee hurried out onto the porch. They greeted him with boos and jeers.

"Bland isn't here," he shouted above the din. "I have not seen him and I don't know where he is."

"You're a liar—a dirty low-down liar!"

"I tell you he isn't here!"

"And I tell you he is. Where else would he come?" yelled Kane, turning to the mob with upflung arms. "Where else would any thief come if he had the money? This man is attorney for the bank. Let's make him deliver up the scoundrel."

A deafening babel of voices: in vain Lee tried to make himself heard. And now Kane was denouncing him again, half to his face, half in the form of a harangue to the crowd.

"This," he screamed, "is the man who sent my boy to prison for what another man done. And this is the man who got a murderer clear yesterday, though he was guilty—and he knew it! He talks about justice. Justice? What does he know of justice?

"You've all heard him spout. He done sent my innocent boy to prison and he said this country was going to ruin because people wouldn't respect the law and was tearing down the authority of the courts. What've you got to say now, Lawyer Wilkerson? Huh? What've you got to say now?

"Do you know what's tearing down respect for law? Lawyers like you! Do you know why there's so much crime? Because every thief and killer in the country figures he'll come clear with some shyster lawyer to help him. Do you know why there're lynchings and mobs? Because people have learned they can't trust the courts to punish criminals. Law? To hell with the law the way you lawyers use it!"

Each period he drove home with a bang of his fist against his palm. The mob howled approval.

"Let's ride him!" somebody yelled.

236

Willing hands tore off a scantling from the picket fence and a rush was made for Lee. He stepped back, prepared to fight, and at that moment his mother appeared at his side.

"Well," she demanded in her incisive voice, "what's all the ruckus about?"

Then, without waiting to hear, she concentrated on the leaders.

"What does this mean, Tud Kane? You'd ought to be ashamed of yourself, with a wife sick in bed at home. It's a fine way to treat me after the way I've nursed her, ain't it?"

Kane backed up, looking foolish. He tried to say something but the fire was gone from him.

"And the rest of you there! You, Marsh Runk! And you, Reb Jones! What's come over you, anyhow? You-all know me."

They most assuredly did. The yelling stopped and the mob moved back a few paces. She ran her eye over their ranks slowly, as though identifying the individuals and gauging their spirit.

"What is it you-all want?" she snapped.

"We done come for Bland, ma'am," somebody piped up. "We want our money."

"What's that got to do with us? He ain't here."

"We heard he was hiding out here."

"Well, he ain't."

The leaders looked askance at her and one another, reluctant to be balked.

"Then where is he, Miz Wilkerson?"

"How should I know? Won't you men take my word for it when I tell you solemnly that Bland ain't here and hasn't been in this house for a month?"

No answer. A voice cried, "Yeh, and he'll git plumb away, I bet you. Your son'll fix it. That's what he's paid for."

She held up both hands for silence.

"Now listen to me, men. Whatever has happened in the past, my son will not help Bland in any shape or form. If he can help you catch him, he'll do it. Why wouldn't he? We had seven thousand dollars in that bank. Did any of you lose as much?"

They swayed uncertainly.

"I promise you my son will do everything in his power to help you get back your money. You-all know me. Ain't you going to take my word for it?"

"Oh, all right. Come on, boys," somebody cried. "We're losing time here."

"And before you go," shrilled the old lady, "you men clean up all that mess you've made of my front yard. Do you hear me, Staples Fuller?"

237

UNSPANKED THIRD
East Texas

Jake Raines

Unspanked Third

═══════════════════════════════════════

OLD JAKE had his offices on the third floor of the Raines Building. When Sid Bassett entered, there was the usual bunch of borrowers awaiting their turn in the anteroom but he brushed past them with the assurance of a privileged character.

"The boss in?"

"Sure. Go right in, Mr. Bassett," said the secretary. "Those lumber guys've just left."

From the inner sanctum a heavy voice boomed, "Hello, Sid. Come on in."

The cowman grinned as he pulled up a chair, because Mr. Raines was making entries in a small notebook with an indelible pencil and paid no attention to him. At last he sat back and inquired, "Well, what's on your mind?"

"Nothing much, Mr. Raines. But I been wondering what I ought to do."

"Making some medicine?"

"No-oo, not exactly. What's worrying me is whether I ought to buy more cattle or sell what I've got."

"You get around among the cattlemen, Sid. What do they say?"

"Well, they all say now's the time to buy, Mr. Raines."

"Then you sell, Sid."

"All right—if you say so. Well, I must be drifting. See you next week."

"When you going out to inspect that land?"

"Tomorrow."

"He wants a loan of eighty thousand on it. I don't believe it will carry that, Sid."

"That's right good land. And he owns thirty thousand acres in one piece. But I'll let you know Wednesday."

Bassett went out and a stream of callers kept Old Jake busy all day. At noon he ate an apple and at five o'clock a couple of his cronies dropped in. Mr. Raines leaned back in his swivel chair behind the glass-topped table and relaxed—a broad man of heavy build who radiated force.

"Hello, Jimmy. Hello, Judge."

"How about a drink?" Jimmy suggested.

"Well, there's a lot of flu around, and that's a fact."

They had a drink and then the three sat smoking comfortably and trading local gossip.

"Say, boss," said Jimmy, "can't a man pull the leg off a Dominicker rooster?"

"I don't know. What would he want to pull it off for?"

"Then you didn't hear about Joe Clark?"

Jake grew alert. He had no use for Joe Clark.

"Well, it seems," Jimmy continued, "that Joe hooked Tud Tarwater on that Braybook Addition deal and Tud was waiting for a chance to get even. Well, the other night they were having a few drinks and Joe began to brag about how strong he was. You know how he brags. So Tud up and offered to bet him a thousand dollars he couldn't pull the leg off a Dominicker rooster."

"Did he take it?"

"Sure—they had a coupla more drinks and put the money up with Bob Laprelle. The bet was to come off last night but Joe never showed up."

"Forfeited a thousand, hey?"

"Yep."

"That's queer. I wonder," mused Mr. Raines, "whether a man can pull the leg off a Dominicker rooster." Then he added: "Shucks, what a fool way to throw money around. That sort of business is too loose for me."

Half an hour later he descended to the street to go home. The instant he set foot on the sidewalk a newsboy on the corner ran up with the evening papers.

"Well, boy," said Mr. Raines, "how's business?"

"Fair to middlin'."

"Say, how much can you make at this job a day?"

"You the income-tax man?"

It tickled Jake, whose blood pressure was wont to shoot up at every mention of taxes.

"Say, kid, how do you happen to get this corner every evening?"

"Why, we own it."

"Who's we?"

"The guy I work for. He pays two hundred and fifty a year for this corner."

"He does, does he? Who gets that money?"

The boy named the firm which rented the lower floor of the Raines building.

"Well, well, well," remarked Jake, fishing out his notebook. "We'll have to see about this."

Then his driver appeared and Mr. Raines followed him to where the car was parked.

"Bright boy, that," he muttered as he got in.

His house was in the older residential section of the city. The fashionable districts were now far out in the suburbs, but the Raines place still held its head up proudly in the midst of apartment and boarding houses—a great brick structure set far back from the street. The grounds covered an entire block.

On arrival home Jake's first care was to inspect the gasoline gauge. Then he started on a round of the place. First, he had to see how the garden had been plowed. He knew it—he ought to have come home to stand over that nigger. Of course he hadn't plowed deep enough.

"Sam!" he bellowed.

"Sir?"

"Why didn't you spread that fertilizer?"

Sam had five good reasons and some more in reserve and Mr. Raines demolished them all. When he had got this out of his system he moved along to the stable and garage; from there to the chicken yard, where he found a gap in the wire fence. Then he took a look at the cow and at an ancient buggy-horse he maintained. Sam trailed along behind, fearful of the worst.

"This saddle needs oiling."

"Well, I thought you never used it any more, Mr. Raines. Why, you ain't used that saddle in five years, Mr. Raines."

"Is that any reason to let it rot?" Jake snorted. "Just like a nigger! You oil that saddle regular, understand? It don't matter if I never throw it over a horse again—I want it ready."

It was a relief to Sam when the old man went into the house. He had worked for him ten years and bragged continually of the fact, but he just couldn't feel at ease with Mr. Raines at home—no, sir, sort of couldn't let down and be comfortable a-tall. Oowee, how that man did love to find work to do!

"Mamma!" Jake shouted from the foot of the stairs.

"Well?" replied Mrs. Raines, looking over the banisters.

"How soon'll supper be ready?"

"At half-past six."

"But I'm hungry."

"If you'd only eat some lunch you wouldn't be half starved every night. Besides, the children are coming."

"Then that means seven," growled Jake and went into the living-room, where he settled down to read the paper. First he turned to the market page to see the cattle and sheep prices; then scanned the quotations for government bonds and did some figuring on an envelope; after that he read through half a column on the state of the lumber industry and grunted. What did that fellow know about lumber anyhow? As he read, his lips soundlessly formed the words. So far as everyday news was concerned, Mr. Raines contented himself with an indifferent glance at the headlines.

He was fuming by the time the family began to dribble in. First came his eldest son and his wife. Clay was strikingly like his father in appearance. He kissed his mother affectionately and said, "Hello, papa."

"Where're the children?"

"Oh, they'll be along in a minute, I reckon."

"Why can't they get here on time? I suppose we'll have to wait supper for them, too. We didn't pay such attention to kids in my day."

They knew his stomach was talking and nobody replied. Then Jake Jr. arrived, accompanied by Mrs. Jake and a nineteen-year-old daughter. Mr. Raines rumbled good evening and twisted fiercely in his chair.

"Where's Ida?" he demanded.

"She said she might be a few minutes late," answered his wife in her gentle voice and the old man blew up. Fine state of things this country was coming to, he opined, snapping his big chime-watch open and shut. People nowadays seemed to think time meant nothing—within half an hour was punctual for people nowadays. Well, he wanted to tell them time was money, time was the most valuable thing in life. They had only a certain amount of it to use and yet people nowadays thought nothing of wasting it, like they had all eternity to spend.

"If those kids didn't have their own cars," he fumed, "they'd have to come when you do. How d'you expect to control 'em, huh? Why, in my day a kid was lucky if they'd let him hitch up the horse on Sunday night to take his girl for a ride. Yes, sir, he was; but nowadays every brat of a boy has to have his own car.

"And money? A quarter on July Fourth was a fortune to me, but a twelve-year-old brat nowadays carries a roll that would choke a cow. Say, do you know what I saw yesterday? Why, a girl was tearing along the Elmwood Road at fifty miles an hour and if she was a day over fourteen, I miss my bet. If we hadn't turned out, she'd have run clean over us."

It was after seven o'clock when the last of the children straggled in and that

244

last one was Jake's own namesake, Clay's eldest son, who was home from college at the request of the faculty. Jake 3rd arrived with long, cheerful blasts of his siren, parked his roadster so that nobody could get in or out of the driveway without first moving it, and then entered through the kitchen in order to have speech with the cook. Lina adored him, but her cackles of delight did not appease Mr. Raines' hunger.

None of the grandchildren bothered to make excuses. They merely remarked in casual tones "Are we late, gran?" and without waiting for an answer, sprawled their lengths somewhere. Jake's blood pressure must have touched two hundred; but after a while everything was ready and they went in to supper.

Tribal gatherings like this were of frequent occurrence. Never a week passed without the children paying their respects to their mother and father two or three times; but it required special inducements and strong parental pressure to bring the grandchildren.

Mr. Raines started in to carve the turkey. It was his custom to serve the men first, then the women, and work down through the others according to age; but in about a minute the youngest grandchild began to pout and whimper and at last he let out a howl.

"Help Claude, dad," said Mrs. Raines. "The poor child is hungry."

"So'm I hungry. Say, when I was his age, kids didn't get helped first. They were lucky to get the neck."

Nevertheless he cut off some breast for the boy. It was easy to see from the way he eyed him, however, that Claude provided no solace to his grandsire's declining years. After everybody was helped, Mr. Raines took no further part in the talk but once the main purpose of the gathering had been achieved, his face cleared, and when they rose from the table he settled down to his smoke in the living-room with considerable content. The men bunched on one side of the room, the women on the other. As for the grandchildren, Jake 3d began to make vague references to a date he had and presently drifted away without answering his father's query as to where he was going. Clay's two girls were bound for a movie show, and at the sound of their escorts' siren in the street shook off the apathy which had kept them dumb and bored throughout supper and fairly sparkled as they ran out.

"You be sure to get home by eleven o'clock, girls," called their mother.

They shouted back, "All righty. Don't sit up for us though." Then one laughed and the other muttered something.

Mr. Raines glanced from one to the other of the parents in stern surprise. That was a fine way to let kids run loose, wasn't it? In his day—but the supper had been good and he refused to spoil it. Instead, he addressed his son-in-law.

"Well, how's business?"

Charlie shot a swift look at him but Mr. Raines' face was imperturable.

"Only fair," he replied. Why had the old fellow asked that? How much did he know, anyhow? One could never tell what he might be up to. "Pretty fair. Why?"

"Oh, nothing." His next question was directed to Clay. "Well, did you play golf today?"

"Yes, I got out late for a little round."

"Humph! I reckon you manage to get in that little round most every day, don't you?"

"But Clay needs the exercise, papa," Mrs. Clay put in. "He's getting fat."

"Exercise? If I want exercise, I can get it chopping wood."

"Why, everybody plays golf nowadays," protested his daughter-in-law.

"Don't I know it? That's just the trouble. Who's going to do all the work that needs to be done in this country? That's what I want to know." As nobody offered to settle that point Mr. Raines changed the subject. "Did you close that deal for the Shortredge piece?"

"Not yet."

"Then when the Sam Hill do you aim to do it, hey? I want that done right now. Old H. H. never stood hitched in his life and if he gets half a chance to think it over, he'll back out."

"I'll see him tomorrow," Clay promised. His face was red, his manner apprehensive. Jake Jr. came to the rescue.

"Well, dad," he began, "What do you think of the market?"

"Too high. Nobody can tell me steers're worth all that money."

"I meant the stock market, not cattle."

His father removed the cigar from his mouth and turned full on him. "What're you doing in the stock market?" he demanded gruffly.

"Nothing much. I just took a little flyer."

"What in?"

"Kite Motors."

"Where'd you get the money?"

"Oh, I got it all right. Don't worry."

"How much did you buy?"

"A thousand shares," said Jake, beginning to feel regrets.

"A thousand shares? Well, of all the—— Say, how could you buy a thousand shares? You speculating on margin?"

"Of course. Everybody does it."

"And everybody's a blamed fool!" cried the old man. "What do you know about the stock market anyhow? Nothing! Less than nothing! That a son of mine—— Why, boy, it's just plain foolishness. Would you play poker here with somebody away off in New York dealing the cards? . . . I never bought a share on margin in my life."

"But things're different now, dad. Everybody——"

"Human nature ain't. I've watched it forty years. When the bottom's dropped out and things're cheap, not one man in a million will touch a share of stock with a forty-foot pole, but just let 'em skyrocket a stock and—— Say, it looks like the higher the price, the more they want it. You leave that speculatin' alone, understand? You aren't going to shoot any of my money away like that."

"Who's shooting your money? This is my own."

"You borrowed it, didn't you? And do you suppose they'd have lent you a dollar if I wasn't back of you? Huh? You never earned a thousand dollars in your life unless I throwed it your way."

Strong talk, but the family was accustomed to it and presently the conversation drifted into other channels. Old Jake brooded and smoked. So the bank had been lending that boy money to gamble with, huh? Well, he'd see about this monkey business in the morning.

"What did you want to scold that way for?" demanded his wife after the children had gone.

"Because they need it, that's why. They'd be in a pretty shape, wouldn't they, if I didn't keep an eye on them?"

"But you didn't need to get mad about it. They're good boys."

"That Clay's a lazy no-account——"

"He's nothing of the kind. There never was a finer boy."

"That's just the trouble with him," Jake persisted. "He's so nice he ain't good for anything. Look at the way he lets that wife of his run it over him. Why, he daresent open his mouth."

"You don't like Claire. That's the trouble."

"Yes, I do. She's all right but she's too bossy. That woman would try to run the whole world if she got half a chance. Why don't Clay stand up to her?"

"Well, he likes to have peace, I reckon."

"That's just what I've been saying. Clay has no more will of his own——"

"Well, supposing he hasn't. Whose fault is it? If he'd had a will of his own, how would you and he——"

"Let's go to bed, mamma."

"No, I want to talk," she insisted. "It's a wonder to me Charlie ever comes near the house, the way you sit and eye him."

"Shucks, I do nothing of the sort. I've got nothing against Charlie."

"Well, you ought not to have. Everybody except you says he is a fine young man and——"

"You can never tell how a man'll turn out till he's thirty-five" Jake rumbled, limping as he got up from his chair. His rheumatism was bad tonight.

Mrs. Raines did not pursue the discussion. She usually got her way with her husband but she did not get it by nagging.

During the night a norther blew up and when Mr. Raines opened the back door at six o'clock next morning a gust of wind buffeted him, biting to the bone. He looked at the thermometer hanging on the porch—two above zero. Then he put on an overcoat and prowled around until signs of life in the servants' quarters indicated that the cook was up. They breakfasted at half-past seven. Jake rose from the table and shouted from the kitchen door, "Sam, bring the car around."

"For goodness' sake, dad, you aren't going out in this weather?" protested his wife.

"Why not?"

"Well, it's Sunday, for one thing."

"I want to look at those cattle."

"But you can go tomorrow just as well."

"No," Jake said, "I'm going today. If Newt feeds 'em this kind of weather, he's feeding 'em regular."

A few minutes later he was headed for town. The feedlots were just off the Elmwood Road fourteen miles west of the city and he had to traverse the business district. Nobody was out: the streets were silent canyons of brick and mortar—great office buildings twenty, twenty-four, twenty-eight stories high, and traffic lights at every corner. Jake chuckled as they passed a building under construction, a new sky-scraper which would overtop them all.

"See that building?" he inquired of Sam. "Well, thirty years ago I used to put up my horse in a corral there. It was way outside of town, too. And the only traffic signal I ever heard of," he added, as the car came to a halt at a deserted corner in obedience to the red light, "was when some fellow pulled a gun. That meant 'Go'."

"Well, I declare."

"Why, I've brought herds of cattle across country where these streets run—— Say, see that hotel?"

Of course Sam saw it. He could hardly fail to do so because it covered most of a block.

"Well, ol' Gus Rutter used to keep an eatin' house where that stands. We used to tie our horses to a hitchin' rack outside; and you could buy as fine a steak as a man'd want, for a quarter."

"Well, I declare," said Sam again. Then he had a thought. "But in them days a quarter counted more'n it does now, didn't it, Mr. Raines?"

"Not with me," replied Jake. He added, "It took longer to earn it, of course. That's why it bought more; but a quarter's still hard to get, Sam, and don't you forget it. It means work. All money does. Whenever you spend a dollar, you're spending time—somebody's time."

Sam made no reply. He wasn't worrying over time except when he wanted to get the afternoon off.

"Drive by the building," said Mr. Raines.

His glance took it in with fond pride. No better located piece in the city—no, sir—worth eight thousand a front foot if it was worth a cent. And only twenty years ago they had laughed at him for paying less than three hundred a foot. Nothing but nigger shacks there then, with the business district all at the lower end of town; and everybody saying with pity that he'd been a good cattleman but now he was going broke sure enough, when he put up that building. Well, perhaps they thought differently about it now. Yes, he guessed they did. Old Jake smiled complacently and rolled his cigar in his mouth.

About the hour when most city dwellers are coaxing themselves to get up for Sunday breakfast, he arrived at the feedlots. Newt showed no surprise. The boss rumbled, "Good morning. How are they?" and the two started on an inspection of the steers.

"Not so bad," remarked Jake gruffly as he noted the cottonseed meal in every trough.

"They're in pretty fair shape," Newt admitted.

"We'll ship Saturday, eleven o'clock. And don't forget to tell Clyde what I told you. I want them cars here on time."

"Yes, sir."

Next morning Mr. Raines' secretary was amazed to receive an order to sell short a thousand shares of Kite Motors in his own name. Jake did not offer the least hint of explanation—it was not his habit to explain anything. After he had cleaned up his correspondence and disposed of the most pressing callers he walked down to the bank, where he remained an hour. Just as he was going out he ran into his son-in-law, bound for the cashier's desk. Charlie looked worried and he hesitated when he saw Mr. Raines, but the old man paid no attention to him. All he said was "Good morning" and passed on.

Sharp at half-past ten the following Saturday Old Jake drove up to the shipping pens, where he first inspected the arrangements and then stood impatiently snapping his watch at minute intervals until Clyde's arrival. The steers were in A-1 shape—there was no fault to be found on that score—but he discovered a dozen things which could be improved. There were three loose doors in the train; one of the cars needed cleaning out; a chute gate was too frail; and why had Clyde neglected to take the tips off the prod poles?

But at last all things were ordered to his satisfaction and the work of loading went forward. Mr. Raines superintended operations from the top of the corral fence, clicking away with a tally machine as each bunch went into the chute, and yelling at the helpers not to be too rough—to quit prodding so hard and tearing them—and say, Newt, wasn't he loading that last car too light? They'd get down if they had too much room.

For an hour he contented himself with bossing the job. Then the fever of work overcame him and he took off his coat and pitched in with the men on the swing gates. Perhaps they appreciated his help and perhaps not, but he certainly speeded the pace.

"Seventy-two years old," said Newt as he borrowed a chew of tobacco from Clyde, "but lookit the way he flies at it."

"That ain't nothin'," Clyde assured him. "Did you hear what he done last Fall? Well, he climbed aboard a broom-tail and rode three days in the rain and mud to look over a timber tract he was figurin' on buying—seventy thousand acres—that's what he done. An expert had made a report on it but the old man wanted to see for himself."

Newt nodded. "Sure. He don't pay any mind to guesswork. He's got to *know*."

At this juncture the boss paused in his labors to wipe the sweat from his face. A car had just been filled and he seized the momentary respite to take another look at the cattle.

"Say," he called to Newt, "What do you reckon these steers'll average?"

A holy joy filled Newt—he and Clyde had weighed a bunch of those steers to settle an argument of their own.

"Well, it's hard to say offhand. They's hog fat, most of 'em," he began as a lure; but Clyde interrupted under his breath, "Let me do the talkin'. Here's where we get even, me and you both."

"What's your own idea, Mr. Raines?" he inquired with crafty frankness.

"You say first, Clyde. Tell you what I'll do. I'll bet you each a box of good cigars—ten-centers, mind—that I can guess 'em closer than you can."

"We get two guesses?"

"Say, you don't want much, do you? Of course not—one guess for both of you."

He was beaming. His soul was always at peace in a feedlot and he felt a glow when inspecting a range; but it took the turmoil of the branding ground and the shipping pens to make Old Jake exultant. This was work for men. Here was life, surging and furious. He grinned from ear to ear at those two longhorns.

Newt led Clyde aside. "Let's see—the average of that bunch was 1164, wasn't it?" he whispered.

"Yeh, but we didn't weigh only a few, Newt. And they've put on since."

"The whole lot'll run mighty near that figure. But if we guess 1164, the old man is sure to smell a rat and won't bet. Suppose we say 1155 and let 'er go at that. That's near enough."

"Shucks, yes."

They walked over to where Mr. Raines was perched on the fence.

"Well," he asked, "how about it? Is it a go?"

"We'll take you—a box each, ten centers."

"What's your figure?"

"1160," said Newt, improving on the agreed estimate.

"Well, I believe you're mighty close to it," remarked Jake, looking over the cattle in the corral again, "but I think you're a little too low. This stuff is in fine shape—best we ever shipped, Newt."

"What's your guess?" demanded Clyde.

"I'd say these steers'll average 1175 pounds, allowin' for shrinkage. Yes, sir, that's my guess."

"You're on," they chorused.

All three made memoranda of the bet and throughout the remainder of the day Mr. Raines would punch and feel of each animal that passed him up the chute. Yes, they were in fine shape; he saw no reason for changing his estimate.

A couple of days later Sid Bassett called to see him. He found the boss in a bad humor.

"What's troubling you?" asked Sid.

"Old Zed Muma was in to see me a while ago."

"Yeh? What did he want?"

"Wanted to buy my building."

Bassett whistled. "He sure must've cleaned up."

"I reckon so. I declare," exclaimed Mr. Raines irritably, "It beats me how men get rich nowadays."

Sid replied: "Why, less'n a year ago, Zed used to sit out there waiting his turn to borrow money from you. And now he's got millions. I hear his income is three million a year."

"Sure. And there's a dozen others almost as rich in this town. Here I plan and work and save all my life to make my money, and one of these fellows grows rich overnight because he strikes oil on his ranch. It don't seem right to me."

Bassett, who had hopes of one day finding an oil field on his own property, remarked comfortably: "Well, that's life."

"Everything's changed. The prices they ask for real estate these days are just ridiculous, Sid. And look at the rents. I tell you business can't stand 'em. If they keep on gouging like they're doing——"

"They're a fright, sure enough."

"Do you now why I renewed that lease for the Spiegel store like I did? A lot of people tell me I could've got fifty percent more rent. Well, I'll tell you. I wanted to hold 'em here. If a store like Spiegel's was to decide they couldn't pay such rents and get up and move half a mile farther uptown, they'd take the whole retail district with 'em. And then where'd all my stuff be?"

"It'll always be good."

"Not if I don't take care of it."

*   *   *   *   *   *   *

It was exactly eight o'clock when he strode into his office next morning.

"Get Newt on the phone," he told his secretary.

"Say," he rumbled, when Newt answered. "How about those cigars? You fellows ready to pay?

"What did they weigh, Mr. Raines?"

"Eleven seventy-three. Just got the report."

"I might've knowed it."

Old Jake turned briskly to the morning mail. He had barely started on it when Clay entered. His father glanced up in surprise, for none of his children was accustomed to be down at such an hour.

"I've been trying to find you for the last hour, papa."

"I left the house early to drive by and take a look at some property. What's up?"

"It's Jake."

"Young Jake?"

"Yes."

"What's he done now?"

"He's in a jamb."

"What kind of a jamb?"

"Well, his car turned over on the Elmwood Road last night and——"

"He ain't dead?"

"No, he isn't dead. He isn't even scratched."

"Then what's eating on you? Quit wiping your face that way. You carry insurance, don't you?"

"Sure. But——"

"Anybody else hurt?"

"Yes. That's just it."

"Who is she?"

"How did you know it was a she?"

"Anybody could guess that. Besides, that boy's been running wild lately. Of course *you* don't know it, but everybody else in town does."

"Well, he had a woman with him—a Mrs. Griffith."

Old Jake nodded. He knew who Mrs. Griffith was.

"Hurt bad?"

"Pretty bad. The car turned a somersault near the bridge at the bend. It knocked Jake cold at first, but when he got his senses back he dragged her out and carried her a quarter of a mile on his back."

"Good for him!" said his grandfather.

"It's like she'll sue for damages—a hundred thousand at the very lowest," Clay said. "And her husband'll sue Jake for alienation of affection—if he doesn't shoot him."

"He won't shoot him."

"No, I reckon not—from all I hear. What can we do?"

"How do I know? It's not my affair. Jake has got himself into this fix and he can get himself out. Those people won't get any of my money—no, nor a bunch of shyster lawyers either." The old man's voice rose angrily.

"Well, I just wanted to tell you about it before you heard it from anybody else," said his son, getting up to go. "I've got to hustle now."

"If you had raised that boy right, this'd never have happened."

"Aw, shucks, papa. How could we help it? It was an accident."

"Accident? It was a certainty. If you'd ever tried to discipline him—— Was he drunk?"

"He says not. They had a coupla drinks at the Chicken Farm but that's all. The car——"

"Coupla drinks!" snorted his father. "I know what that means. Of course he was drunk—stewed to the gills probably. You and Claire'd never know it if he was drunk. You're both blind. Why, everybody in town knows what kind of a young rooster Jake is, except his own father and mother."

When Clay had gone, Mr. Raines told his secretary to call up Jake Jr. and ask him to come over at once. So Jake 3d was in trouble, hey? Well—— A pang shot through him at thought of his grandson's plight. He loved the boy; despite his wildness and irresponsibility he saw in him every day the fighting qualities of his own youth. All the same they weren't going to shake him down just to square up a jag. No, sir. But while he was at it he would straighten out the whole bunch.

Presently Jake Jr. hurried in.

"What's this I hear about Bertine?" Mr. Raines demanded.

"Well, what about her? You're always hearing things, papa."

"I'm not like some folks—I don't shut my ears and eyes. Don't you know what happened out at that picnic Wednesday night on the Upshur farm?"

"Pshaw, you can hear so much idle gossip nowadays——"

"There's no gossip about this. You'll admit Bertine was there, won't you?"

"Yes, she was there."

"Well, old Upshur was at the house to see me last night and wanted to know what he ought to do about that crowd. Seems like he was afraid to prosecute because a lot of 'em are swells."

"What's that got to do with Bertine?"

"How about the way they acted at that picnic, huh? How about gettin' drunk, and a lot of 'em going in swimmin' in Upshur's lake without any clothes on?'

"I don't believe it," said his son.

"Upshur says he caught 'em—caught 'em cold. And you know Bertine drinks, don't you?"

"She takes a cocktail now and again—yes. Everybody does."

"They didn't in my day. A nineteen-year-old girl didn't get stewed when I was young. If she did we knew where she belonged. But Bertine——"

"She doesn't get stewed, and I won't stand for your saying she does."

"That's all you know about it then. Didn't you have to take her home from the country club New Year's Eve? And didn't you have to load her into the car like a sack of meal? . . . You see, I keep up with things."

"But the way you tell it makes it sound——"

"I'm giving you the facts, ain't I? And just because they hurt, you can't stand hearing 'em. Answer me this: Did that girl ever do anything in her life she didn't want to do?"

255

"Of course."

"I'd like to see you call one instance."

He waited, but Jake Jr. made no reply. He was fooling uncomfortably with a pencil.

"The way these children have growed up, I don't wonder they turn out like they do," Mr. Raines continued. "They've never had to do without. They never had any discipline. Why, you and their mother haven't even bothered to learn 'em manners. They act like they were raised in the kitchen."

"Oh, shucks," exclaimed Jake in disgust, "I'm not going to sit here and listen to this."

"No, but you'll be sitting somewhere and regretting it the rest of your life if you don't watch out, young man."

His son flung out of the office without replying. Didn't his father know about Jake 3d yet? Well, *there* was something to worry about! What did all this fuss about Bertine mean, anyhow?

He went home and told his wife. Mrs. Jake remarked: "Oh, he's just having one of his fits, that's all. Bertine's no angel, but she's a good girl. Your father doesn't understand how times've changed."

"That's so," Jake agreed. "That's exactly it."

At the end of the day's work Mr. Raines drove out to his stock farm where he tried to forget family worries by looking at the Shorthorns and sheep. He would walk around an animal for half an hour, prodding its ribs, feeling its back, inspecting it from every angle. He stayed there for supper and did not start home until long after dark and it was almost ten o'clock when the lights of the city came into view. The boss was tired and dozed a little, awaking with a jerk each time his head sank forward.

"Take the short cut," he said sleepily.

"Through Lovers' Lane?"

"Yes, I reckon that road'll be all right, don't you?"

"Yassuh."

The car went purring along between rows of bois d'arc. Suddenly their headlights picked up a coupé parked at the edge of the road.

"That's what the automobile does," growled the old man. "It's ruined the morals of this country."

They passed the coupé and Sam remarked hesitantly, "Say, boss, that looks like our car."

"Our car? We haven't got a coupé, boy."

"I mean Miss Bertine's," said the darky.

256

The words stabbed Old Jake like a knife. "Back up," he shouted; but Sam was rattled by the tone and did it awkwardly. Before he could reach the spot the coupé was in motion and went tearing past them at fifty miles an hour. Mr. Raines tried to get a look at the occupants, but the shade next to him was jerked down.

"Go after 'em," he ordered.

Sam did his best, but he was accustomed to a leisurely gait and the coupé had turned into a paved highway before he could catch up. In another ten seconds it had vanished in the stream of traffic.

In a steady and casual tone—"I reckon we were mistaken, Sam."

"Yassuh. We musta been, sure enough. What'd Miss Bertine be doing out there this time of night?"

Yes, what was she doing out there this time of night? To think that a grandchild of his—his own flesh and blood—— And who was it with her? He would have given a thousand dollars to know. Well, he'd soon find out. He'd have it out with Bertine and—yes, her parents too. They were to blame. If they looked after their children properly, this could not happen.

"What's the matter?" inquired his wife when he reached home. When he had told her, Mrs. Raines declined to be upset. "Well, I don't see what you're making such a fuss about. They just went for a ride, didn't they?"

"Went for a ride?" Jake stormed. "Do you call parking the car in Lovers' Lane at ten o'clock at night goin' for a ride? Why, in my day it'd mean shootin'! In my day——"

"In your day," she rejoined calmly, "young people went buggy riding, didn't they? And I've heard they used to stop the horse now and again too."

"What's that got to do with it? This is different."

"No, it isn't. You just think it is, that's all."

Mr. Raines grew purple in the face and started in all over again to tell her about the drawn shades but realizing the futility of it, shut up abruptly and went into the living-room to get a cigar. It was all very well for mamma to take that view of it—that was just like her, she always stuck up for 'em—but he knew how these kids cut up nowadays and tomorrow——

On the morrow his son Jake called him on the telephone before seven o'clock.

"Well?"

"Got some bad news."

"How much've you lost?"

"It isn't money."

"Then what is it?"

"It's Bertine. She's married."

"Married? When? Where? Who told you? Why didn't——"

"She just phoned from the Junction. They were married there at six o'clock this morning."

"Who's they? Who did she marry?"

"Tommy Rutter. From what I hear, he's been hanging round her a lot lately but we never dreamed——"

"How could they get married this early in the morning? Where'd they get the license?"

"It seems he got it yesterday, papa—sort of on a chance, I reckon. She seemed excited when she came in last night but we never dreamed—— She was gone this morning."

Mr. Raines opened his mouth to utter his mind, but words were inadequate and he hung up with a savage jerk of the receiver. So Tommy Rutter was his granddaughter's husband, hey? Tommy Rutter, whose first wife had been a street-walker. Old Gus Rutter's grandson—he trembled with impotent wrath.

"There was never a one of 'em worth killin'," he exclaimed, gritting his teeth. "Not a one, from ol' Gus to the last loafer in the fam'ly. Tommy Rutter—sure I know him—know all about him. And she will, too, pretty soon."

The others of the family were inclined to accept the marriage philosophically. They conceded Bertine ought not to have run off that way and maybe Tommy had been a little bit wild, but of course he would settle down now. And she was bound to marry somebody, wasn't she?

"But how're they going to live?" demanded the old man.

They glanced at one another. Finally Jake Jr. summoned up sufficient nerve to hint vaguely at giving them an allowance—nothing permanent, but enough to take care of them until Tommy could get going for himself.

"Yes, and you'll have him on your hands all your life. Mark my words— you'll rue the day you ever heard his name. What's more, you're going to ruin that couple if you give 'em money, Jake. Young people should paddle their own canoe."

A baffling silence was the only response. Mr. Raines could endure no more. He announced that he washed his hands of the whole business and they need not come to him for any help; and if people thought he was going to fling away his hard-earned money keeping up a pack of idle loafers—well, they'd mighty soon find out. Then he departed and the family relaxed with a sigh of relief. The first shock and rush of forebodings past, they even derived a measure of pleasurable excitement from the elopement. As Claire said, it was so romantic.

Old Jake drove downtown. His thoughts seared like fire. For the first time in his life he was beginning to feel helpless, impotent to direct or combat the stream of his life. What could you do with people who wouldn't do anything for themselves?

And what was the use of working like a dog to lay up riches for others to squander?—others who had never done a hard day's work in their lives, who did not know what it was to make a sacrifice. And only to ruin them, too. Soon after he was gone they'd be scattering his money uselessly and fighting among themselves over it—yes, whole families of 'em—people whose names he didn't even know at this moment. The Rutters were in already. Who could say what trash might not tie up with his blood, with all these grandchildren coming on? With his granddaughters carrying flasks at sixteen, what would they be like at twenty?

"Let me out at this corner," he commanded Sam. "I'll walk the rest of the way. Take the car home and wash it. Wash it good, mind. And don't let me catch you doing any riding round on your own account either. How much gasoline've we got? Nine gallons, huh? Well, I'll remember."

He was surprised to find his son-in-law waiting for him at the office.

"I just wanted to thank you," Charlie began awkwardly.

"What for?"

"Oh, I know all about it—that money I borrowed from the bank. If it hadn't 'been for that, I'd have blown up. And now I find out it was you who let me have it."

"Shucks, that's all right, Charlie. I've seen some pretty sick kittens get well in my time. Things going all right now?"

"Fine! We've turned the corner and it looks good to me."

The old man smiled and remarked, "I got a dandy on Jake."

"What's that?"

"Remember that Kite Motors he bought?"

"Yes. It's gone down—away down."

"Of course. It was bound to go down. We're in for a depression soon, Charlie. Money's tightenin'. It wouldn't surprise me any day to see a panic."

"Gee, I hope not."

"Well, it's coming. So guess what I did."

"Sold short?"

"For the first time in all my life. I sold Kite Motors short. So whatever that namesake of mine loses, his daddy'll make. I figured we ought to keep it in the family. Don't you tell Jake now—not a word. I want to spring it on him."

"He's mighty worried. The bank wants its money."

"Certainly they do. I told 'em to clamp down on that boy and learn him a lesson."

Within a fortnight his forecast of business conditions was proved correct. The call rate suddenly shot up. The first distress signal in New York found almost instant repercussion throughout the country and the whole fabric of inflated values, wild credits and frozen loans came toppling down. Then arose weeping and wailing and groans of despair. Men jumped out of windows or drowned themselves in bathtubs. Emergency meetings of clearing-house committees and bank officials sat far into the night.

In his own town Mr. Raines was the central figure of these conferences. His step grew brisker, his manner almost cheery. Anybody could thrive in boom times but here was work for strong hands; here was a situation for which he had been preparing for years.

Their toughest problem was one of the largest stores in the state.

"It looks bad," he confided to Bassett, "But I think we can pull 'em through."

"How much do they owe?"

"About four million. But if they can raise a million right now, those New York fellows'll give 'em an extension and they'll be able to work out of it. This town can't afford to leave a firm like that go broke, Sid. It'd demoralize business."

"Sure. But why don't the banks——"

"They've already loaned 'em up to the limits their capital stock will allow. So I reckon some of us'll have to get under the load. Dabney!" he called to his secretary.

"Yes, sir."

"Get Louis Blum on the phone and tell Bill Sumner I want to see him."

Things hummed in his office during the next hour. Old Jake was flushed and happy. The responses he got were a tribute to his standing and judgment and he knew it.

"Half a million ain't so bad," he remarked. "And I haven't got around to more'n two-thirds of 'em yet. Dabney!"

"Yes, sir."

"Call the bank."

Over the telephone he said: "I can let those people have a million tomorrow morning, Preston. Huh? No, it ain't all subscribed yet, but if I don't raise any more I'll take half a million of the loan myself." And that was that.

Well, it was all very fine helping out other people, but how about his own troubles? Mrs. Griffith and her husband had filed suits against Jake 3d. The worst outfit of ambulance chasers in town was representing them and it looked as though the escapade might cost a hundred thousand dollars.

Mr. Raines resolutely ignored the affair until he had to step in. He had told his son it was none of his business and he washed his hands of it, but there came a day when Clay threw up the sponge and implored his father to see him through— just this once. If he didn't, Jake 3d would be ruined for life. They would have to settle, that was all there was to it, because if the case came to trial things might come out which would hurt the family far more than the loss of a few thousand dollars. And a jury—well, he knew what juries always did to rich people.

"A few thousand dollars?" retorted his father. "You talk like money grew on trees."

Nevertheless, he consented to attend a conference with the attorneys for the plaintiffs, although he hated even that much surrender. For lawyers of this type he entertained a fiery scorn and the meeting ended in an open rupture. The old man left the director's room where the conference had been held and headed up street toward his office. He was fairly champing his teeth with rage. So they thought they could tap him for a lot of money, did they, just to get a fool boy out of trouble? Well, he would show them. No shyster lawyers were going to get their paws on what he had slaved and schemed for during fifty years. No, sir! Let the kid go to jail. It would do him good. If he got him off this time, like as not he would go and do something worse. Let the whole story come out. People could think what they pleased—he didn't care. Nobody could blackmail him.

Sid Bassett was waiting for him.

"What puzzles me is, where do these kids get their meanness?" cried Mr. Raines, after unbosoming himself.

"Well, rich people nowadays——"

"It ain't that. Look at the Lukes. There never was a finer family. Money hasn't spoiled them. Of course, the Muma crowd now—well, nobody expects anything different from them. But my family is clean strain all through, Sid. So is mamma's. We've never had to get our men out of jail or hush up anything about our women. But here my grandson goes and ——'

"Oh, well, he's only a kid, you might say."

Mr. Raines was soothed by this attempt at comfort.

"That's so, too. But it ain't that either, Sid," he answered quietly. "I'll tell you what it is."

"What?"

"They've never been spanked. This third generation has never been made to mind. They've never been made to do anything except what suited them. Look at the way they treat their parents. I don't just mean the rich, but any of 'em who can afford to live high. Look how my own grandchildren treat me and mamma. I tell you, Sid, this unspanked third generation—Oh, well, what's the use?"

"Sure," Sid agreed. "Besides, it's bad for your blood pressure. How's the rheumatism, Mr. Raines?"

"Ain't had time to think about it," Old Jake grumbled, "But my shoulder hurts every time I move." He sat down at his desk and rummaged in a drawer. "I bet you don't know what this is," he remarked, extracting a document.

"Your will, ain't it?"

"Yes. How did you guess?"

"Well, you change it every time you get mad, Mr. Raines."

Old Jake grinned. "You talk too much, Sid," he said affectionately. Then he began to read the document as though Bassett were not in the room. Evidently it did not suit him. He frowned and made impatient movements.

"It takes a fool lawyer to hide what you're trying to say," he exclaimed. "Why can't they talk straight, instead of all this monkey business of words? Do you know what I think?"

"Uh-uh."

"I believe they fix things up so there's bound to be loopholes for trouble. That's what I think. It's good for their business, see?"

"Well, who gets it all this time?"

"I aim to leave it to charity."

Bassett threw back his head and roared with laughter.

"Say, I'd like to lay a little bet."

"What on?"

"That you ain't signed that—and never will."

Mr. Raines tossed the will away from him with a tragic gesture of helplessness.

"Correct again," he said glumly. "When it came right down to signing— well, I just couldn't do it."

"What's the use, anyhow? They'd bust it wide open."

"It'd make 'em sweat a while doing it though. There's one time they'd all have to work."

"Maybe so, but the lawyers'd get most of it. And I reckon you wouldn't specially care for that, would you, boss?" Jake made a wry face. "Best just leave it where it ought to go," the cowman said.

"Yes, but where's that?" cried the old man, flaring up again. "You mean my blood strain, don't you? Did you ever stop to think how far that goes? The third generation has only got one-eighth of my blood in 'em. And how do we know who they'll marry? They may tie up with the sorriest lot of rascals you could find in a day's ride. And they wouldn't hardly be kin to me. That's what hurts."

"All the same—"

"When I think of whole families that are strangers to me livin' at ease off what has taken me and mama fifty years to lay up, I can hardly stand it, Sid, and that's a fact."

"It's tough—mighty tough," Bassett conceded. "But you can't take it with you, Mr. Raines. Sometimes I wonder if the game is worth the candle, don't you?"

Jake got up from his chair and strode to the window. For a long while he stood staring out at the street and Sid did not interrupt his thoughts. At last he squared his shoulders.

"Worth the candle? You bet it is," he said. "Say, Sid, come here. See that kid across the street?"

A newsboy was running up and down the sidewalk, bawling his papers.

"We worry ourselves a heap about the third generation," Old Jake went on, "and wonder what the country's comin' to! And all the time we're thinking of our own families. The country ain't going to the dogs because our own stock peters out, Sid. There's others just as good who'll come up to take our places and do the work. Look at that rascal, will you? Say, there's a fine boy!"

"He sure is a rustler."

There was a wistful look on Mr. Raines' face as his eyes followed the flitting figure across the street.

"He's saved up forty dollars and eighty cents," he said. "Told me so yesterday. God, what wouldn't I give for that boy's chances! To be young and starting all over again!"

SURVIVAL
West Texas

Hi Garrett

Survival

HI GARRETT of the Bar P took a trip to Europe. Prices of cattle were right, the calf crop ran close to eighty percent, he had a fine set of grass and ample water. Everything looked lovely, so Hi took a trip to Europe and Mrs. Garrett and their grandson, Hi III, went along.

The climate and fogs of London so depressed the cowman that he went on a spree, and when Mrs. Garrett had sobered him up she insisted they should go to Paris where sunshine might revive his soured spirits. It did for a while, but he was always ill at ease among people whose language he could not understand, and soon grew lonely.

"Why don't you look in the American Express register and find out who's here?" his wife suggested. "Maybe we know somebody."

It was a goodly list: Mr. and Mrs. John B. Preston, Baltimore; Mr. and Mrs. Howard Pinckney, maid and valet, Boston; Mr. and Mrs. Charles Stacey, Miss Mildred Stacey and Master Charles Stacey, and Mr. William C. Buxton, Philadelphia; Mr. and Mrs. Alexander Greer, Miss Alice Greer and governess, New York; Mr. P. McGillicuddy, Cleveland; Mr. and Mrs. Oliver T. Drysdale, governess and maid and three children, Chicago; Mr. Hector McIntosh, Detroit, etc. etc.

"And ol' Phil Brent's here too" Hi told her jubilantly. "And Claiborne, the cattle buyer from Kansas City. Me and him're fixing to give a party, mama."

"You'd best leave me out" Mrs. Garrett said. "I know what sort of party that'll be."

However, the two gentlemen in question being also encumbered with wives, she joined the party and for years afterwards they talked about the high old time they had in Paris that week.

"Everything's fine" his range boss reported on their return, "Except your roan ropin' horse got cut up in the wire. And—oh, yes—there's a colony of furriners settled over on the West Fork. They done bought ten sections from ol' man Larrabie and a piece from Uncle Hans Wagner."

Hi said: "That may turn out a fine thing, Lafe."

"What? Well, I swan! I've seen you run hundreds of nesters off'n the school land inside your range, Mr. Garrett. What's come over you?"

"Well, Phil Brent and I got to talkin' on the boat. Phil claims this country's got to be settled up some day, Lafe, and I think he's right—too good farmin' land to stay pasture forever. It don't pay to run cattle on land you can get ten fifteen dollars an acre for."

Other cattlemen were being converted to the same view. The immensely increased value of land brought by a steady stream of immigrants from played-out southern and eastern farms—cheap feed these settlers would raise for the stock—a ready market for their acres whenever they felt inclined to turn them loose—these were the factors responsible for the change in attitude. Hi sold on small down-payments and long credit some smooth sections on the outskirts of his range to farmers from the Midwest and East. He picked these as the more efficient—and also because they were mostly of American stock.

With such increases in population several small communities sprang up and Doghole grew from a wide place in the road to a town of five thousand. Then they made it the county seat. Among those most active in promoting its campaign to become the county seat was Ben Strusky who blew into town one day from New Mexico and opened a general store.

Garrett was now the richest man in that country. Much of his land was quoted at twenty dollars an acre and the roughest of it would fetch two dollars—and he owned half a million acres. Also, he owned huge herds of white-faced Hereford cattle.

Nevertheless his income remained tragically disproportionate to his potential wealth—some years he had barely sufficient to buy feed for the cattle during the winter. Also, he spent a lot of money in various ways and a lot more simply leaked away. Young Hi III was at an eastern college and going all the gaits: as the only heir of a cattle king who counted his lands in square miles, Hi III cut a big dash and kept his doting grandfather scratching to find the money.

"By God, the cattle business is the sorriest business in the world" he told Ben Strusky.

"Sit donn ent cool yourself off, Mr. Garrett. Vot is by you to worry? You should oughta own it a store if you vant it a rotten bus'ness."

"Expenses just eat a cowman up, Ben."

"Ent you a foist-class cowman! Sure they do, the vay vot you run it, Mr. Garrett, ven you let everybody robbing you. Ent a leak here ent a leak there, they don't mean nothing to you a-tall."

Old Hi regarded him grimly.

"Son, I was runnin' my own bunch of cattle when you was gettin' your livin' out of a bottle. I reckon I know my own business."

"Sure you know by cattle, Mr. Garrett. Everybody they say it the same, there is no better judge by cattle in the country than vot you are. Me, I don't know nothin' about cattle, but I know bus'ness, Mr. Garrett, ent no matter vot line you're in, y'unnerstan', you got to play it close by your vest or it eats you opp."

Strusky's own affairs seemed to prosper. A Mrs. Strusky of ample girth appeared on the scene one day with two young sons and the family went to live in a shack Ben built back of the store. When not in school the boys helped their father and mother to wait on customers.

Selling largely on credit, Ben soon had most of the county in debt to him and it was not long before he was lending money on mortgages to farmers whose holdings lay close to Doghole. The prevailing rate in that country had always been ten percent and good traders like Ben had little difficulty in obtaining twelve on first-class security. Hi Garrett paid him twelve when he found himself in sudden need of ten thousand dollars to bail his grandson out of a chorus-girl scrape that meant either marriage or cash on the barrel-head. As the cowman did not want the loan to show among those at the bank where he transacted business, he paid Strusky his price.

A year of drought burned the Bar P range to a browned waste. Settler after settler gave up the struggle, abandoned his ruined crops and started for fresh fields westward as far as California. The families traveled in wagons with buckets banging from the tailboards and dogs trotting behind in the dust. Their milk cows stayed behind to apply on the debts they owed the store in Doghole, and as for their farms, Ben Strusky owned those.

Garrett lost fifteen hundred head by waiting too long before shipping to other pastures. Then bad reports scared one of the Middle West banks which held his paper. It declined to renew his note and, unable to make other arrangements on short notice, Garrett shipped five thousand head to market at ruinous prices. The necessity of the step made him bitter, but at least it maintained his credit. To get through a winter of no grass, he had to borrow more somewhere. Hitherto he had always been able to finance his needs by cattle mortgages, but prices were so low that this form of security became dubious and he was obliged to put a mortgage on the best portion of his range. Ben Strusky loaned him a hundred and ten thousand dollars.

He could buy his grandson out of a woman scrape, but money could not buy young Hi out of some scrapes with the college faculty and he came home. There he behaved as he had done at college—rode over everybody with a high hand and strutted his stuff in the face of cattlemen who had forgotten more than he ever would know in his life about the business.

Instead of curbing him, his grandfather was as clay in his hands. Young Hi had gained the notion that old-timers were back numbers and he proposed changes and schemes which Garrett would have hooted at from anybody else, yet he yielded to the boy almost every time and squared the losses without a whimper. An irrigation project based on some ideas Hi III had picked up at a convention of cattlemen proved so disastrous that the cowman was obliged to go to Strusky again.

Ben said "Too bad, too bad" and wagged his head and puffed out his lips. "You spoil that boy, Mr. Garrett. He is rotten spoiled. Just esk by anybody. Now, me, I learned my boys to vork ent save and look at them. Aindt they to me a credit?"

Hi assented, although he cordially disliked both of them. One had graduated from Harvard Law School, the other was at Boston Tech, and whenever they came home their fresh familiarity with old-timers like himself made Garrett grip his quirt.

Ben said: "Me ent you, Mr. Garrett, we had to rustle, ent it made us go ahead. So I says to my Rosie, I says 'Mama, our boys must vork, mama'. But ven a boy is born a silver spoon in the mouth, it is finished for him nine times out of ten, Mr. Garrett."

As he drove back to Bar P headquarters Hi was profoundly dejected. For the first time in his life he felt helpless, felt old. Life had become so complex—no longer the simple problem he had faced in the years of his strength when a man took, and protected what he took, with an iron hand—worked hard, drank hard, gambled, made big money or went broke with a noble crash. A man could not do business that way nowadays.

Why, once he had lost a check for ninety-seven thousand dollars a buyer from Amarillo had written out for him with a lead pencil while sitting on a loading platform, because he had stuck it carelessly in the hip pocket of his overalls and forgot all about it until the bank sent word two months later that he was overdrawn. Yes, nowadays a man must scrimp and save and make his family scrimp and save, too, or else—

"If he don't, they'll run him outa business!" he cried so savagely that the horses lunged. "They've bust most of us old-timers already."

By "they" he meant Ben Strusky and Barney Hadjianestis, the Greek who

270

owned the Kandy Kitchen, and Joe Patate, the dago who had started with a half-portion fruit store and now owned a wholesale and retail grocery that supplied the surrounding country for thirty miles. The best farmers in the country were Bohemians, Germans and Swiss, and a couple of Rooshians had even gone into the cattle business.

The outbreak of the war found Garrett in tight circumstances, and Europe's needs looked like the chance of a lifetime to him. He sold several hundred horses at high prices, but cattle prices did not soar as quickly as he had anticipated and drought took toll of his herds. However, conditions improved during the next two years and Hi was beginning to see daylight ahead when the United States went in with the Allies.

At first this meant little to Doghole, but presently the draft law set the county to buzzing like a hive. Hi III went off to an officers' training camp immediately; so did Strusky's two boys. One of these being an engineer, he was selected for duty in an ordnance factory; the other being a lawyer, managed to get into the judge-advocate-general's department after Ben had paid a visit to Washington. As young Hi didn't know a thing in the world except how to roll dice and drink liquor and ride and shoot, and die if necessary, he received a commission in the infantry and was in one of the early contingents to go overseas.

Strusky was a busy man these days. As buyer of hay and harness and mules and other war supplies for the Allied governments he cleaned up several hundred thousand dollars. Then the government at Washington awarded him a number of contracts. His activities had far outgrown Doghole. True, he accepted the chairmanship of the First State Bank there, but he was too much occupied with larger affairs to give any real attention to it although the bank occupied the lower floor of the new four-story brick building he had erected at the Main Street corner of the square.

In the tremendous boom of 1918 Garrett was able to scramble out of debt. Farmlands also shot upward to goofy prices and he determined to sell out half the ranch; but another dry spell hit the Bar P when he was all ready to put it on the market and land couldn't have been given away in those counties.

On his return from a trip to town one evening he did not answer the supper bell. Mrs. Garrett went out to the porch to summon him.

"Dad! Didn't you hear the supper bell? Supper's gettin' cold."

Hi did not answer. He was huddled down in a rocking chair.

She said "What's the matter?" and went to him. He lifted a haggard face and opened his mouth to speak, but the words would not come.

"What is it?" she cried, shaking him by the shoulder. "Tell me, do you hear? What's happened? Is it—Hi?" Her love for the boy imparted an animal ferocity to her and she shook her husband as though she would drag the truth out of him. "Don't sit there like a fool! Tell me!"

He mumbled "The boy—they got him" and held out a crumpled telegram. She stared at him in wild unbelief and then sank down beside his chair.

"Mama" said old Hi brokenly, placing his big freckled hand on her hair. She rested her forehead against his knee; he could feel her quivering, but she did not cry. It was late that night before tears came to her relief.

The loss of his grandson seemed to take the heart out of Garrett for a while. Then he plunged into business with redoubled energy as though he would bury his grief in it. Prices of cattle climbed sky-high. One could pay almost any figure for cattle and be sure of turning them over at a profit in a few weeks. Hitherto Garrett had been content to raise and sell them: now he began to speculate. When old age first realizes how brief a span remains, it is seized with a feverish activity. There is so much it wants to do before the end. Hi bought and sold, bought and sold. Several modest speculations having turned out well, he decided to go into it big and make a killing.

Then the banks unexpectedly gave him the fishy eye. They listened politely enough, but although Hi burned with eagerness and confidence, he could stimulate no responsive glow. They had seen storm signals he could not discern and the cowman finally strode out, sick of pleading with fellers who talked with finger-tips together in front of them.

When Uncle Hi finally laid his needs before Strusky, Ben said: "No. Not me, Mr. Garrett, ent that's flat, y'unnerstan. That's goin' awful strong ent me, I think the market's far too high."

"But I got to do something with my range, ain't I?" the cowman fumed. "It's way understocked. I could run ten thousand head more right now, Ben. You see, I sold out most everything I had in that last rise."

"Better is to have idle grass'n go broke, aindt it?"

"I tell you the market's bound to go up, Ben. It can't go down with Europe needin' beef to feed her starvin' people."

"Hunh! Can't it? How's Yurrup goin' to raise the money to pay opp by that beef, Mr. Garrett? Hey?"

However, he yielded in the end to Hi's greater experience and agreed to advance the amount he needed for the killing. In this venture Strusky undertook no risk whatsoever: the money he loaned was secured by a deed of trust to the entire Bar P ranch. Ben explained that he could not take a mortgage on the cattle under the existing uncertain conditions, and because the banks had told

272

Garrett the same thing, he raised no objection.

Old Hi went forth and bought ten thousand head to stock his range and thirty thousand as a speculation. These thirty thousand were to be grazed where they were.

Within sixty days after delivery he was bankrupt. The soaring prices stopped, wavered a while, began to recede. Then everything hit the toboggan at the same time and cattle tumbled farther than most. He soon stood to lose ten dollars a head and the bottom did not seem to have been reached. Hi hung on desperately, refusing to believe the market would not snap back although Strusky begged him to sell, arguing that worse and more of it was to come. He, Ben, had sold everything he owned except some city real estate, and was putting the money into U. S. Government tax exempt $3\frac{1}{2}$ percents, buying at every relapse in their quotation.

A day came when shortage of grass, a feed bill he could not pay and a host of other claims made selling obligatory. All over the country the banks were taking alarm and calling loans: distress cattle flowed to market in a flood and prices cascaded downwards. Hi closed out his speculation at a net loss of thirty-two dollars a head on forty thousand cattle. After everything was washed clean, he owed one million two hundred thousand dollars.

He told his wife, "Well, we're wiped out," trying to say it in the bluff hearty tones he had used in earlier years when misfortune overtook him.

"How much?"

The figures staggered Mrs. Garrett.

"That means we'll lose the ranch, don't it? Does that mean we'll lose the ranch?"

"I reckon so. It belongs to Ben Strusky now—if he wants it."

Her figure drooped in the chair. Poverty did not scare her and hard work was still her daily portion because, having toiled from dawn to sunset most of her life, Mrs. Garrett could never bear to be idle; but the prospect of leaving the ranch broke her spirit. Seeing her thus—suddenly crumpled, an old, old woman—blind rage boiled up in the cowman.

"It ain't right!" he cried, thumping the arm of his chair. "Goddam it, Annie, it ain't fair. It ain't fair. Here we've worked and sweated for fifty years to build up this ranch and along comes a pot-bellied buzzard who don't know the diff'rence between a dogie and a bitch pup and gets it away from me. He pinches and scrapes and watches and waits—yes he does, too—he gets the best of a bargain every time or he won't go into it. And it looks like the more bad luck other folks have, the more Ben Strusky makes. Look what them droughts brung him—all them farms. And now it's my turn. If it wasn't for you, I'd go get me my gun and settle with the bastard right now."

His wife roused and sat up very straight and said: "Don't talk foolish, Hi. Ben Strusky's been mighty good to you. You know he has. He's lent you money often when he didn't want to—you told me so yourself. You told me he advised you not to borrow it this last time."

"Huh! Lookit the security he made me put up—every acre we got."

"Well, what if he has made a lot of money? That just goes to show he's more clever'n the rest of 'em, don't it?"

"Cleverer hell! That ain't the point. What I got against Ben and fellers like him is this—you didn't see Ben round here when there was no pickin's except what you got by fightin', or sweatin' out on the bald prairie, did you? No, ma'am! Me, I come here and fit the Injuns and skinned buff'lo for a livin' when about all a man got out of it was sweat. You know what it took to win this country. You know it as well as me, or better. We made this country with the blood and bones of our bodies and then along comes fellers from Poland and Rooshia maybe—from every goddamned slum in Europe—and trades us out of it. Do you call that right? Do you call that fair?"

Mrs. Garrett heard him out patiently and said in her flat voice: "That's true, too, Hi. The people on top today aren't the pioneer stock. But that's history, ain't it? I mean—now—evolution, or whatever you call it. You know what I mean."

"The hell I do! How is it history, or ev'lution or what-d'you-call-it?"

"Well, we took it away from other people, you know. We done run the Injuns off first—"

"And why not? D'you mean to sit there and tell me we'd ought to of left this country to a lot of lazy scoundrels who never did anything with it?"

"Maybe Ben Strusky figures the same way—him and the others, Hi—maybe they figure they can do a lot more with it than what we've done."

"Go on" her husband said in a strangled voice.

"Well, how many nesters did you run off forty thirty years ago, Hi Garrett? —them poor nesters who dragged it out here to make a livin'? How many of them did you run off, you and your gunmen, Hi?"

"That's different. That's fightin' man to man, and none of this pinchin' and savin' and squeezin' a feller when he's down—"

"They were down, them nesters—way down" Mrs. Garrett said. "And if it was me, I'd druther lose my land in a trade than have it stole from me at the point of a gun. At least you got some chance that way—you can pinch and save, too."

Hi could only gape at her. Never in all the years of their married life had his wife spoken like this. About the worst he had ever suffered from her was a dead-pan silence and occasionally a mulish obstinacy he had found it hard to combat, yet now she was telling him the right and wrong of things—goddamn it, she was taking sides against him, his own wife was!

"Anything else?" he asked thickly.

"No-oo, I reckon not. Not just now, anyhow."

No more was said until after supper. Then Mrs. Garrett broached the subject which lay nearest her heart.

"When do we have to give up the ranch, Hi?"

"We don't have to give it up a-tall if we don't want to."

She gaped at him, and her voice was tremulous when she asked: "What you mean, Hi? What you mean? Why don't we have to give up the ranch?"

"Well, Ben says I can stay on here and run it for him if I like. Ben, he don't know no more about cattle than a baby and he says he'd sooner have a man he can trust than somebody else."

"How much?" she asked next.

"Six thousand a year until things get goin' right, and then ten thousand."

"And he'll put it in writing?"

"Hard and fast contract in black and white—for as long as I live, Ben says."

It was too much for Mrs. Garrett. She put her head on her arms and sobbed with relief. After a while she wiped her eyes and babbled happily: "Why, that's better'n if we still owned it our own selves."

"Ma'am? You mean workin' for somebody else is better'n workin' for yourself?"

"Don't you see, Hi? We'll always be sure of the money now. I'll know exactly where we stand and how much to spend. And there'll be no worry or frettin' about notes to pay, or feed bills, or taxes. Why didn't you tell me all this in the first place, Hi?"

Her husband stared at her.

"That's a woman for you, every time. Why is it wives'd always druther play safe, mama? Here we won't own a foot of land and I'll be workin' for a salary—wages—oh, hell, what's the use?"

"But don't you see, Hi? This is sure. It's sure."

Nothing he could say seemed to dim her satisfaction and after a while certain aspects of the situation began to appeal to old Hi.

"Well, anyhow" he chuckled, "There's one satisfaction—all the lazy hounds who've lived off'n me all these years'll have to go to work now. Ben can keep 'em if he wants to—but he won't. He done told me to cut down expenses and give some of the boys their time. I been too easy, Ben says. He aims to make this ranch pay."

"I bet he does, too."

"There's another thing" the cowman said slowly. "And it was right kind of Ben to think about it—mighty kind. He figured you and me might like to take a trip to France, mama—to see Hi's grave. Well, Ben'll give me time off and expenses. There won't be anything doing round the ranch for a coupla months, anyhow."

Six weeks later the old couple returned to Paris from a tour of the battle-fields. They were worn out, lonely and depressed. Mrs. Garrett took to her bed. The visit to her grandson's grave had upset her and all she wanted was to rest and think back.

For a couple of days the cowman divided his time between his wife's bedside and the hotel bar. Never a familiar face, not even a glance of interest cast his way. He grew desperately lonesome, longed for speech and contact with his own people, to hear again an unrestrained laugh and feel exuberant spirits bubbling up in reckless conversation.

Of course!—he was a fool not to have thought of it before! He bought a copy of the European edition of a Chicago newspaper and eagerly scanned the lists of visitors to see if perchance somebody of his acquaintance might be among them.

There was a column and a half of names: "Among recent American arrivals in Europe are Mr. S. Bogoljubov; Mr. and Mrs. I. Marogzy, Mr. and Mrs. Barney Doutelbaum, the Misses Florentine, Rosa and Yvonne Doutelbaum, and Masters Benjamin and Sidney Doutelbaum, all of New York; Mr. A. Kandachieff and Mr. Sol Laschober of Chicago; Mrs. Guiseppe Spanti Gattuso and her three daughters, of Boston; Mr. and Mrs. L. Stamoniskoff of Butte, Montana; Mrs. Charles Estensoro and Miss Mayme Estensoro of San Francisco; Mr. and Mrs. Max Oettinger, Master Max Oettinger and governess, of Buffalo; Mr. Joseph Gianotti of Worcester, Mass.; Mr. C. Papadopolous of Chicago; Mr. Eli Wertheim of Philadelphia; Mr. and Mrs. A. Visanska, Mr. and Miss V. Casmeze, Mr. Dmitri Petrosky, Mr. and Mrs. Astorbilt, Mr. and Mrs. Solinsky and Masters Lincoln and Roosevelt Solinsky, all of New York, etc. etc.

THE MORE ABUNDANT LIFE

West Texas

The More Abundant Life

WEST TEXAS

WHEN Sid Bassett stopped his car at the gate, Old Jake rose stiffly from an armchair on the verandah, held his back for a moment and then shouted into the hallway: "Mama! Mama! We're going now. I'll be back Friday."

"Lan's sake, there's no need to yell. I'm not deef" exclaimed Mrs. Raines, appearing in the doorway. "It's just ridiculous you going out to the ranch this way."

"I got to see those cattle shipped. Nine thousand head and no grass! Call that ridiculous?"

"But if you've got to go, why can't you go on the train? Eighty-three years old——"

"There you go, always trying to make me out older'n I am. I won't be eighty-three 'til November and you know it."

"Well, at least stop for the night at Amarillo so you won't be all tired out."

"Shucks, it's only three hundred and fifty miles. Well, goodbye. See you Friday."

He went down the walk and got into the car beside Sid. Neither said a word beyond "Good morning" until they were well out of the city.

"What's on your mind, boss?"

"Oh, everything. I declare I don't know what this country's coming to, Sid."

"What's the use of worrying? We'll work out of it somehow. We always have."

"Yeh, but things're different. In those days we worked. Nobody wants to work any more."

"Ain't it the truth? You know that nephew of mine, Sam's youngest boy? Guess what he up and told me yesterday—that the world owed him a livin'! Gawd-amighty!"

Mr. Raines grunted and presently said: "Say, Sid—remember how I carried all those farmers who bought them cotton and corn sections over on the South Fork? Carried 'em for seven years—yes, and kep' up taxes, too."

"Sure I do. They're good people, them Bohemians."

"They used to be—and so were their daddies. I never lost a nickel on a loan to their daddies. But listen to this: they've all been drawin' government money now for two years for leaving their land idle, and instead of payin' out they bought automobiles and radios and had a good time. I had to hire me a lawyer to get any money at all."

Sid agreed that it was a fright, but something had to be done for the farmers.

"Sure. Don't I know it? I wouldn't care about the money so much if— well, if it didn't ruin people the way it's ruining them. Why, those farmers used to be honest and decent men, Sid. They worked hard and raised crops and paid their debts—and now all they raise is Cain. Leastways their children do. A contract's no good any more. Neither is a lease."

"Well, the way I figure it, Mr. Raines, them damned crooks in Wall Street——"

"And the banks and most business everywhere else in the country—don't forget that."

"Sure. Remember the way we used to look up to all those guys and follow their lead like they were little gods? And look where they landed us! The gover'ment just had to step in."

"Do you know what government is, Sid?"

"Why, of course I do. It—now—it represents the people."

"Government's just a bunch of politicians, ain't it?"

"Yeh, I reckon so. I reckon it has to be."

"Well, you know what most politicians are. Did you ever hear of any situation being cured by driving out one swarm of rats just to put in a greedier swarm? . . . This country's being looted twice."

As a recipient of a governmental agency loan, Sid shook his head in denial but did not argue the point and the old man dropped the subject to give attention to the country through which they were flashing, to note the crops and condition of the cattle and any changes in the towns through which they passed. After their midday meal at a lunch counter he dozed a while. In late afternoon they dropped down from the caprock and entered the east pasture of his range.

"See that dugout?" he asked, pointing to a sod-roofed cabin sunk into a bank of earth, "That's where we lived when I started this ranch. One room. And

282

one window.   We thought it was fine."

"Say, that reminds me—Uncle Hi done told me you and him once fought forest fires over in New Mexico for seventy-two hours without a wink of sleep."

"Hi always did tell a good story.   We got some sleep ridin' along, or between change of horses—a few hours maybe."

"Mr. Raines" Sid asked abruptly, "How many times you been busted?"

"Couldn't count 'em" replied the cowman.   "We went busted after those fires that time—some ornery Mexicans set those fires. That's when we moved back to Texas.   And I been broke three times after drought.   Once we didn't get a drop of rain on our range for fourteen months.   The banks made me sell every horn and hoof for what I could get. Funny thing about that time, Sid—it rained clear up to our fences one day—a heavy rain, too—and quit right there."

"Well, I declare."

"Other times it was low prices that busted us.   Hell, we got used to it and just hung on. Why?"

"I was just wonderin'."

It was dusk when they arrived at headquarters. Mr. Raines took a stiff drink of whiskey and ate a hearty supper.

"Whose ol' auto was that down at the corrals, Clint?"   he inquired.

The ranch manager glanced at Bassett—it was like Old Jake not to miss anything, even in the dark.

"Belongs to a nester, Mr. Raines.   He blowed in here this evenin' and wanted a job but I didn't have none to give him.   I let 'em all have supper, though."

"See many of 'em now?"

"Not near so many go through as used to in your day, Mr. Raines.   The gover'ment looks after 'em, I reckon."

"This man got a family, you say?"

"Hell, yes.   A wife and five kids and a brindle dog.   And they ain't got a red cent, so he says."

"How come they travel in a car when they haven't got any money?"

"It looks like people figure nowadays every man was born with the right to an automobile, Mr. Raines."

The nester and his family were still there when Old Jake went down to the corrals early next morning.

"Good morning" he greeted them.

"Howdy. You gotta job for me, Mr. Raines?"

"Clint, there, is the boss."

"Yeh, but you're the owner, ain't you? I done heard you was."

"An owner nowadays has nothing to say about managing his property" growled Old Jake and walked off to join Bassett, who was to drive him out to see the herds.

The nester looked puzzled.

"What's eatin' on the old geezer, anyhow, Mr. Clint? He don't talk good sense."

"Maybe you don't hear good" said the boss. "You movin' on today?"

"Cain't you give me a job, Mr. Clint? I just gotta get hold of a piece of money. We ain't got any food and hardly enough gas to take us to town, and the gal's ailin'. We gotta buy some medicine, too, ain't we, Sally Jo?"

"I don't feel good, Mr. Jed, and that's a fact."

"I told you yesterday I didn't have any work for you here," the boss said.

"But with all his money he ain't going to miss a few dollars, Mr. Clint."

"All whose money?"

"Mr. Raines. Why, I done heard in town he's worth ten million dollars and maybe more."

"You can hear anything."

"How did he git holt of all this land and all those cattle we seen yesterday?"

"Work."

"I ben workin' hard all my life——"

"Sure—I know that kind of work. How come you left Oklahoma?"

"That's jest what I was fixing to tell you, Mr. Clint. I was doin' right well over there when this happened. Yessir. I owned a quarter section and drawed down from the gover'ment——"

"We was doin' fine ontil Dasher went and bit that gover'ment man, Mr. Clint," Sally Jo put in. "How could a li'l' ol' dog be expected to know he was a gover'ment man? It stands to reason he couldn't . . . I think they did you right mean, Mr. Jed."

"So they did, gal, so they did. Jest because I didn't have no influence, this sorry hound took me off the rolls, Mr. Clint, so I figured I'd pick up and go somewheres they wasn't so lowdown mean."

"Well, I can't take on all the people who drift through here every month——" the boss began and then the baby set up a wail.

"Wait a minute" he said resentfully and walked to where Old Jake and Bassett were waiting in the car.

"Lookit, Mr. Raines. Would it be all right if I found him a job that'd bring in a few dollars? He's a no-account, but they're desprit and I feel awful sorry for them kids."

"Sure. What kind of work can you use him on?"

"Well, we gotta build a new two-holer out behind for the boys and that'd mean fetchin' a man from town to do the job. There's a coupla days work in it, maybe more, what with diggin' and puttin' her up. I figured maybe ten dollars and his meals——"

"Make it twenty" said Jake. "Let's go, Sid."

Clint returned to where the nester waited and told him. The latter listened gravely and accepted the proposition. Soon afterwards he went to work with a pick and shovel.

A phone call from the station agent about the cattle cars took Clint to town, but he returned in mid-afternoon. To his surprise he found the nester sitting on the running-board of his flivver, smoking and whittling. A glance showed him that he had dug a hole scarcely a foot deep.

"What's the matter? Quit the job?"

"Yes, I have, Mr. Clint—onless we can come to terms."

"What d'you mean—'come to terms'? Ain't the pay satisfactory?"

"No, sir, it ain't. That's jest the trouble. I got to studyin' about it after you left and I figure—I figure, Mr. Clint, that I ought to charge Mr. Raines the same price for diggin' his backhouse as Mr. Raines would charge me for diggin' mine."

This is one of a privately printed edition designed by Allston & Depew, New York.